THE HAWK
AND THE
HANDMAIDEN

IN THE EYE OF THE HAWK

THE FIRST PONTIC CHRONICLE

THE HAWK
AND THE
HANDMAIDEN

IN THE EYE OF THE HAWK

DREW GALLAGHER

Paperback: 978-1-63767-794-0
eBook: 978-1-63767-795-7
Library of Congress Control Number: 2022904300

This is a work of fiction.

Ordering Information:

BookTrail Agency
8838 Sleepy Hollow Rd.
Kansas City, MO 64114

Printed in the United States of America

For Poppy, Bella, and Lola

A time and place where death is a constant companion.

The year is 493 BC. The insurrection in Ionia draws to a close with Persian victory assured. Sinister undercurrents threaten a fragile peace between the Scythian ducal states. The hand of treachery, and Persian destiny, is everywhere. In 'the lands between the seas', a fledgling alliance between historic rivals flourishes under the guiding hand of the illusive and baleful *Hawk*, chief regional spymaster of King Darius..

As Persia moves inexorably to war with Athens, the fate of the colonies in the Black Sea and the historic alliance with the Ur'gai become pawns in a dangerous ploy. Can the *Hawk* outwit the mysterious *Oracle*, jewel of the Hellenic espionage network? As the talons of enemies and traitors close fast, Queen Illir'ya despatches a loyal Handmaiden on a dangerous mission to unmask the designs of her regional rivals..

Stalked by the daemons of her past, the young Handmaiden is plunged in a web of intrigue, isolated by her enemies, as traitors close to the Queen plot her doom. In the plains south of Qu'ehra, she will face her childhood nemesis and thwart the designs of her adversaries. As a fugitive in Nymphaion she must rely upon her wits to evade her pursuers, protect the realm, and avenge her honour, *with the fury of an Amazon..*

PROLOGUE

Tyre, April 493 BC

An old man, garbed in a hemp robe and aged leather apron, enters the room carrying a bronze bucket of hot coals. He closes the door firmly behind him. The room is unusually warm and is dimly lit by a flicker of candles. A large stone hearth stands in far the left corner, adjacent to the door. It is constantly fed with coals from the hearth next door. The old man strolls to the dresser. Rows of shelves are filled with an array of various pots and jugs. He selects a small clay jug with a heavy base, thin rim, and a fluted lip for ease of pouring. This is laid on the table in the near centre of the room. The windows on the right side are draped with heavy black curtains, casting the room in perpetual darkness, save the light from the flicker of the candles. The old man pads across and draws the curtains, allowing rays from a morning sun to pierce the gloom in the rear of the room.

The old man paces to the far end of the room. This is flanked by cabinets, raised above the stone floor. Each cabinet has a heavy lid, drilled with numerous ventilation holes, opened via a sliding a hatch in the roof. The old man moves to the nearest cabinet on the left and slides back the hatch. Inside the cabinet lies a sleeping Indian spectacled cobra. The man smiles lovingly at the creature as it wakes from its slumber and their eyes lock briefly. He slips his hand inside and catches the snake firmly behind the ears. The cobra glowers at its master in petulant fury, yet it cannot bite him. The snake is carried to the table, its fangs exposed. The front of the mouth is placed over the rim of the jug, supported on the far side by the man's left hand. The cobra is milked. A small quantity of its highly toxic venom percolates into the bottom of the jug. The cobra is returned to its lair.

The old man pads across to a wooden table on the left side of the room, a safe distance from the cabinets. He selects a small brown mouse from a wooden cage. He pets the creature, tenderly stroking the fur of its head, as he conveys it to its fate. The mouse is dropped inside the cobra's cabinet, its last act of life a pitiful squeal of terror, as the snake strikes to silence the creature forever. The hatch is slid shut. The old man strolls back to the dresser and selects a small, delicate jug, with a long, fine flute. He fishes in a drawer and plucks a small ceramic vial. The clay is impregnated with *lapis lazuli* and is a beautiful pale blue in colour. The man opens another drawer and selects a bronze candle holder and a fresh candle. The candle is lit with coals from the hearth and mounted in the circular base of the holder. The old man decants the venom into the small jug, thence the pale blue vial. A cork stopper is inserted and is sealed with melted wax. A knock at the door interrupts his patient endeavours.

"Enter" the old man spoke curtly.

The door opens. The visitor enters and closes the door behind him. He is visibly uneasy. "I hope you locked that hooded bastard back in its box?"

The old man entreats his visitor to a mocking smile. "He is a fine specimen! He is also one of my most cherished. You are quite safe, Naelin, I assure you!"

"Do you have the venom? Time is of the essence and this place gives me the creeps!" Naelin shivered lightly.

"You get used to it, my friend. Do you have the payment?"

"You have, old friend, but I loathe those scaly bastards!

Three silver pieces, as you requested. I hope that is to your satisfaction?"

"That is most acceptable, and I am glad to be of service. The vial is sealed, just as you requested."

The old man passes the sealed vial to Naelin, who squirrels it away within his robes. "You do a considerable service to the cause, old friend. We will not forget it, I promise you!"

"I am honoured by your platitudes, my friend. However, considering what is about to happen, I would be a far happier man if you and your friends forgot I even existed!" the old man smiled tightly.

Naelin nods in acquiescence and turns to leave. The old man fishes out a small leather purse, loosens the drawstrings, and drops the three silver coins inside. As Naelin reaches the door, the old man turns back to him.

"No more the moon, old friend!"

"No more the moon!" Naelin replies. He leaves and closes the door firmly behind him.

~

A blonde girl, approaching the cusp of her teens, sits at a table to the left of the bed. She carefully removes the wax seal on a pale blue vial with the sharp edge of a dagger and teases the cork from its top. Holding the vial in her right hand, she inserts the razor-sharp point of a six-inch long iron hairpin into the end of the vial, ensuring the tip is well-tainted with venom. The child removes the hairpin and gently blows on the point. This is inserted into the hollow of a slender iron tube almost to the ornate, circular boss at the top. The cork stopper is teased back into the vial. She selects a lemon from the small bowl and cuts it in half. One half is squeezed into her cupped hands and rubbed over the palms and between her fingers. The exercise is repeated with the second. A fist hammers at the door. The girl blithely ignores it. The fist hammers again.

"Enter! I am quite decent, I assure you!" the girl quipped teasingly.

Naelin enters and closes the door behind him. "We must leave, my Lady. There is no time to waste. My spies report that Nischanesses has left his apartment and is heading towards the Wharf!"

"He will not make it! You may rest assured of that, friend!"

"You know where to go? You remember what you were told? We have no time to waste!" Naelin spoke impatiently.

The blonde girl eyes him steadily. She has piercing eyes of the purest blue and her gaze unnerves Naelin. "Just make sure that the ponies are coupled, do you understand? I will take care of everything, I promise."

"No more the moon, my Lady!"

"No more the moon, my friend!" said the girl.

Naelin leaves and closes the door. The blonde child stands and slips the vial into the pleated ringlets of her hair on the right side, just behind the ear. She plucks the iron hairpin in its metal sleeve and slides this into her belt on the right side. The dagger is slipped inside its scabbard on the left. There is a second, identical blade, beside it. She follows Naelin out of the room and closes the door.

⌐

Nischanesses instinctively knows he is being tailed. He increases his pace, weaving deftly through the throng of fellow shoppers in the Bazaar, in the vain hope of losing his pursuers. Quite how *they* had discovered his identity was a deeply troubling mystery, yet it was not as disastrous as it would surely be if he failed to deliver the urgent communique concealed within his robes. It must not be allowed to fall into *their* hands. He dived down a narrow alley between two garment stalls, turning left at the bottom, heading in the direction of *The Tower of Babel*, a notorious rough house on the Wharf Road. If his pursuers expected him to rendezvous with an agent there, they would be sorely disappointed. Neither he, nor his contact, would ever have been so guileless!

Naelin is hot on the fugitive's tail, accompanied by three retainers, all armed with staves and wickedly sharp blades. They have lost Nischanesses in the crowd but have since located him. Naelin turns to the first thug. "The two of you head south and cut him off!

Make sure that he sees you. We need to drive our quarry towards the Spice Merchant's District!"

The first man turns to the third. "Come with me!" The two men disappear into the crowd, heading east.

Naelin turns to the last thug. "Let's get going! We can't afford to lose this bastard!"

Nischanesses espies the first and third thugs as they morph out of an alley between two rug merchants, some twenty yards to his front. He knows they are his pursuers. He dives into the nearest alley, turns left at the end, and crosses the narrow lane, weaving through the throng of shoppers. He dived in to a second alley and heads south. Soon enough, he reaches the fruit and vegetable market. Nischanesses pauses at a stall and plucks an orange, smiling warmly at the seller. "These are fine looking oranges, my friend?"

"They hail from the citrus groves of Damascus. They are the best!"

Nischanesses fishes an aged copper coin from his robes and flips this to the fruit seller. "I will take it, my friend."

Glancing to his right, he espies Naelin and the second thug, idly loitering at a fruit stall on the opposite side of the lane. They are a dozen or so yards away. Nischanesses draws his dagger, smiling grimly, ensuring the second thug sees that he is armed. He saunters away, deftly peeling the orange with the razor-sharp tip of his dagger. He drops the peel in to a small basket at a fruit seller further along and turns right, moving swiftly down an alley. As he devours the fruit, he keeps a constant lookout for his pursuers. As he turns left at the end of the narrow lane, he espies them loitering at a fruit seller some twenty yards to the south. There is little time left, for he must shake off his pursuers before they reach the Wharf.

Nischanesses crosses the lane and slips down an alley, heading towards the Spice Merchants District. He no longer openly sports his dagger, which has been slipped into its scabbard at his right hip.

~

Nischanesses turns left at the end of the alley, weaving through the crowd, heading towards the far end of the Bazaar. He is sure that his pursuers are now far behind. He crosses the lane and makes his way towards a large alley. As he reaches the alley, a group of teenage girls are fast approaching. He steps back, to courteously wave them past, smiling at each girl in turn. He turns right into the alley and heads south. The alley is deserted, save for a blonde child, perusing the wares at one of the end stalls on the left side. Nischanesses strolls towards the girl, keeping to the right. The child is seemingly unaware of his approach, as she continues examining the jars on display. The Spice Merchant glowers icily at the girl. "Do you actually intend to buy something, child? I am a busy man and you have wasted enough of my time already!"

"You are unspeakably rude, old man! A pox on your poppy oil, I say!" the blonde girl spat indignantly.

Nischanesses is now directly behind the blonde girl. The Spice Merchant rubs his nose twice. The girl snakes her left-hand across to her right hip. She fishes out the six-inch long hairpin, its point lethally tainted with *kobran*, in a cautious movement unseen by her intended victim, ensuring the point is away from her body. Skipping lithely behind, her right- hand snaked around to clamp his unsuspecting mouth as the point of the hairpin is driven cleanly through the nape of his neck and deep into his brain. Nischanesses dies almost instantly, his legs buckling, as the girl eases his body to the ground. She sheaths the hairpin and retrieves the hollow silver ingot, sealed with wax at both ends, from the hidden pocket inside the trim of the dead man's robe on the right, precisely where she had been informed it would be. The spies had done their work thoroughly, as she had now done hers. The child slips the ingot inside a secret pocket under the left armpit of her own robe and darts out of the alley before diving into a throng of astonished shoppers. The first Spice Merchant raced to the stricken man, to be joined by the still dumbstruck merchant from the opposite stall and a handful of shoppers who bore witness to the barbaric slaying. There is little that can be done for Nischanesses, for he is dead!

"Stop her! Stop her! Murderer!" beseeched the first spice merchant.

"Murderer! Murderer! Call for the Militia!" implored the second.

"Stop her! In the name of the Gods!" bawled the first merchant. It was a futile plea, for the young murderess has vanished into the tangle of alleys between the stalls, heading southwest.

～

The blonde girl races south, turning right and diving into the last alley of the Spice Merchants on the right. When she reaches the end, she turns right, and weaves through the throng, heading north. She soon reaches the garment stall owned by Misu, a Nubian. Misu smiles warmly at the child and beckons her towards the alley at the right of the stall. The young murderess slips down the alley and dives through the open flap at the side, which is closed and fastened by Misu. The interior of the stall is draped with brightly coloured garments, hanging from wooden racks. A large, ebony luggage trunk, its lid ajar, stands in the centre of the dusty floor.

Misu urgently beckons the child to climb inside the trunk. "Climb inside, fair Lady! We have no time to waste!"

"Thank you, Misu! I will never forget this, I promise" the girl held out her right hand, which was warmly clasped by Misu.

"If I never see your face again, sweet child, it will be a rare blessing indeed! Now, get inside! The ponies are ready!"

The blonde girl climbs inside the luggage case. It is roomy and ventilated. Misu tosses her a spare key, which she places in a leather pouch attached to her left belt, together with the silver ingot. The lock mechanism can be opened from the inside of the trunk.

"May your Gods be with you, fair Corelya! No more the moon!"

"No more the moon, gracious Misu!" Corelya blushes.

The lid is closed and locked. Misu paces to the rear of the tent and opens the flap. He whistles to the first and third thug's, waiting patiently beside the cart. Naelin and the second thug are perched in the cabin. Both are armed with heavy pine staves. The two retainers enter the tent and ferry the luggage trunk to the cart and place this on the back. They climb aboard and Naelin whips the ponies to a trot. As they pass the Militia Station on the outskirts of the Warehouse District, a group of six Militiamen, mounted on thoroughbred stallions, amble past, heading west towards the Bazaar.

~

The Sycamore is berthed at the Wharf, readying to depart,

as the crew make their final preparations. The ship, its Captain, and its crew are Cretans. Naelin reins in the ponies next to the gangplank. Standing on deck, Captain Nekhamose smiles brightly at Naelin and raises a hand to the Chief Stevedore, who stands talking with two of his men on the Wharf. "I think we have a last consignment to board, old friend!"

The Chief Stevedore glances nervously at the surly thugs who sit in brooding silence in the back next to the luggage trunk. "Passengers, or freight, my good fellow?" the Chief Stevedore smiles amiably at Naelin.

Naelin fishes out a key and tosses this to the Chief Stevedore. "Take the case aboard and store it wherever the captain instructs you to. The key is to be entrusted to him, and none other, you understand?"

The two Stevedores collect the trunk and carry this up the gangway, under the watchful eye of Captain Nekhamose. "Take that to my suite, my good fellows. There will be a tip in it for you if you do!"

The Stevedores carry the trunk to the Captain's Quarters at the stern. The key is entrusted to Captain Nekhamose in return for a silver coin. "Have yourself a few well-earned beers with my compliments, my good man!" the captain beams at the Chief Stevedore.

"Thank-you, Captain, and a safe journey in the realms of Poseidon!" said the Chief Stevedore.

The gangplank is taken away. Shortly thereafter, *The Sycamore* unfurls it sails. The crew man their oars and the ship put to sea.

A few hours later, Corelya lies naked on the bed in a private cabin aboard *The Sycamore*, greedily slaking her thirst with a flagon of Scythian plum wodki. She smiles gleefully as she flips a single gold coin in the air to catch it as it falls.

Her passage for Rhodes has been paid for in advance with Persian gold, freshly minted in Susa, just like the coin in her possession. This gold was part of a consignment destined for King Darius' allies, never his sworn adversaries! The blonde girl is no friend to the Persian King, quite the contrary. Until that morning, Nischanesses had been King Darius' most trusted agent in all Phoenicia!

PART ONE

ONE

Susa, February 493 BC

"You will have some more wine, won't you?" the woman smiled sweetly at her visitor.

"Just a small drop, if only to please you, my sweetheart" the man replied. "It is getting late. I must be heading back."

"It is good to see you again. I have missed you. It has been too long."

"I have been hard at work with the new recruits. A soldier's life is not all drinking and whoring! You would know that?" the man teased.

The woman giggled. "It is for some! I assure you of that! The Royal Guard always seem to have a generous allotment of free time!"

"You surely mock me, sweet Ezar'ya" the man drained his goblet. "Ever since you were little! You were always so easy to tease!"

"I am glad you are keeping well. You are right, as always? It has been far too long since my last visit. I will endeavour to be more faithful!"

The woman eyed him warmly. "I think you say that to all the girls, don't you? You are welcome to come as often as you can, you know that? It is always good to see you."

"You are precious to me, my sweet. I cannot bear to think of what they would do to you" he whispered.

The woman raises a finger to his lips to silence him. "We both knew the risks, did we not? Not a single day passes

3

without shedding a tear for your fate if they discovered your treachery."

"Time is of the essence, my sweet. I would not have taken the risk otherwise" the man spoke softly.

"I will ensure this information reaches those who need it most urgently. I will not fail you. I swear it!"

"I must leave. Is the arrangement still as it was?"

"As it always shall be, my darling, nothing ever changes here!"

The man sighed sadly. "I fear that everything has now changed for the worse, my sweet."

The man embraced the woman, holding her tightly, biting back the tears. He kisses her forehead, then both cheeks, with genuine tenderness. "You are my world, darling sister, remember that."

"As you are mine, little brother, remember that."

Soon after the man had departed, a knock came at the door. "Enter" the woman commanded. The door opens, and a man, attired in an elegant blue robe with silver trim, enters and closes the door behind him. "I take it that our regular guest behaved with his usual courtesy" Semphiri smiled thinly.

"Indeed, he did, master. He is not your usual sort of visitor, is he?" Ezar'ya chided. "Nor has he been as regular, at least in the past year" the man replied.

Ezar'ya eyes him coldly. "You fear I am losing my touch, my master?"

Semphiri smiles brightly. "Not at all, my dear, I was simply stating a fact. Still, he was certainly as generous as ever with the King's purse, so you are assuredly not losing your touch.

"I shall take that as a compliment, in the spirit that I am sure it was intended" Ezar'ya smiled mockingly at the man she secretly detested.

Semphiri ignored the acerbity. "There is someone I would like you to meet. Unless you are too tired that is?"

"No. I am not at all tired, master" Ezar'ya replied simply. "Then follow me, my dear."

Ezar'ya follows Semphiri out of the room, closing the door firmly behind her. She knew her room would be searched in her absence and has taken necessary precautions to ensure the secrets so recently entrusted to her would not fall into the hands of her master. She entered her masters' Private Office and knew instinctively what fate he had decreed for her, for there was no other person present. The room is large, with a high, vaulted ceiling and elegant friezes on the walls. In each corner of the room, marble statuettes of the Old Gods; *Enki*, *Enlil*, *Marduk*, and *Ninurta*, gaze coldly upon a ny visitor. A large oak desk sits at the far end, facing the door. Directly behind it, mounted on a marble plinth, is a statuette of the Goddess Ishtar. The so-called *Whore of Babylon*! Semphiri held the door open for the woman and then closed it behind them, locking it with a key from within his robes.

Semphiri raps briefly on the door of the private bedchamber that adjoins the office on the near wall. "Come" a reply came from inside, clearly the voice of a girl. The man opens the door and ushers Ezar'ya inside. The girl, whom could have been no more than fourteen years, stands in front of a burnished bronze mirror, as naked as the day she had been born. She turns to face them, unashamed of her nakedness. She is a stunning visage, with long, beautiful red hair, a slim physique, long limbs, and pert breasts. Semphiri smiles sweetly at the girl and turns to Ezar'ya.

"This is Cordicca, my darling. She has only arrived in Susa this very day."

"Hello, Cordicca. My name is Ezar'ya. Are you well?" Ezar'ya addresses the girl in Hellenic.

"I am fine, Ezar'ya, and thank you for asking" the girl replied in Hellenic.

Ezar'ya suspected it is not her first language, nor the

5

only one she speaks with ease. A prick of fear tingles along her neck.

"I will leave you alone, I think. Perhaps you might like to get to know one another better?"

Cordicca frowned. Ezar'ya smiles sultrily at her master and slips out of her chiton, revealing her own nakedness. She saw a sparkle in Cordicca's eyes and knew she was certainly no blushing innocent! "Would you like to watch us?" Ezar'ya teased her master, enjoying the flash of anger in his eyes. Cordicca stifles a giggle. Without another word, Semphiri turns away and strides through the door, closing it behind him. Ezar'ya and Cordicca smile slyly at one another, revelling in their Masters' discomfort.

"I have never been with another woman before" Cordicca smiled sweetly, her eyes twinkling like stars.

"It is not so different from being with a man, my sweet! Yet, it is far more enjoyable and without the obvious complications. I can make that little treasure of yours weep like an infant. I promise you!"

"Then keep your promise, I beseech you" Cordicca chided, blushing lightly.

～

Dionysopolis, May 493 BC

The man smiles serenely at the pretty girl who dutifully replenishes his empty goblet. "I am in your gratitude, fair maiden" he sighs happily, raising the goblet to his lips. "This vintage is rather good, for a Rhodian, I will freely admit." The woman, sat directly opposite at the Banqueting Table, eyes him coldly. "I thought the food was rather bland. Not their usual fayre, is it?" he addressed the statement to the woman's husband, who simply shrugged in polite deference.

"I was not aware of your repute in matters of

gastronomy, my dear fellow" the woman said silkily.

The man's eyes sparkle with mischief. "But of course, my dear! I have a most discerning palate, after all."

"How are things in Chersonesus? Is business still booming, despite the current malaise?" the woman's husband tactfully steers the conversation to safer waters.

"It is indeed, despite the treachery of the Cypriots! You would surely agree that the conflict in the Ionian Sea has had little real impact on our business?" the man asked searchingly.

"I have spoken to friends who have interests in Chersonesus and elsewhere in the Crimea. They have expressed concerns about the current political malaise, particularly in light of recent events" the younger man sighed.

"My dear Aeschus, you and your friends have nothing to fear. Queen Illir'ya is universally admired in Chersonesus, and elsewhere, for that matter."

"Is that true of Nymphaion, my friend? There are some quite unflattering rumours emanating from Panticapaeum?" Aeschus sighed.

"You refer to the untimely death of King Tagar's nephew? Young Ach'ti, so tragically drowned at sea?" said the visitor.

"There are some in Panticapaeum, and perhaps even Nymphaion, who suspect that his death was not accidental?" Aeschus pressed.

"They have intimated foul play. How intriguing!" the man's eyes sparkle with delight. "The Orch'tai King is obviously crushed by the death of his beloved nephew, yet I have heard nothing in the way of a claim of anything sinister."

"Would you even tell us if you had?" the woman said airily.

Aeschus frowns at his wife's brusqueness, whereas the older man sat opposite smiled serenely. "Upon my honour, dear Lady, I would tell you had I learned of anything specific."

"The perhaps you would entreat us with your insights, Thassalor of Knossos?" Sybillya smiled thinly.

"It is true that there are certain aspects of the young man's death that are mysterious. Not least, the matter of how he even came to be on deck alone at such a late hour. There is the questionable conduct of the First Mate, who was supposed to be on deck on the very night!"

"Is it true that he was drunk? Some say otherwise?" Aeschus probed.

"You mean drugged? It is entirely possible, but you know sailors as well as I do!" Thassalor smiles wryly.

Sybillya eyes the man steadily. "We have always found them to be honest and trustworthy. Their integrity is admirable, quite unlike others I could mention."

Thassalor smiled brightly at the woman. "I suspect the man was drunk on duty. As for poor Ach'ti, it is most likely that he went to the deck for fresh air and simply lost his footing."

"In regard to fresh air, darling husband, perhaps I may be excused. I feel a little queasy myself, what with my condition and all."

"Of course, my love, there is nothing to apologise for. Our conversation must be tedious, even if you were not so heavily pregnant."

The woman climbs heavily out of the chair and plods across the Banqueting Hall to the lobby and the outside terrace. Thassalor watches her depart and then turns back to Aeschus. "Are you praying for another son, dear Aeschus?" the man teased lightly.

"Of course not, dear fellow. Another daughter would be a welcome addition to our happy brood."

"Your wife is well?"

"As well as can be expected, given her condition. She will give birth within a few moons, no more than that."

"Then I shall pray for a speedy deliverance and the good health of your family. Now, if I may be so discourteous, would you excuse me? I have an urgent matter to attend to" Thassalor shrugs ruefully.

"Of course, my dear fellow, it has been a pleasure, as always" Aeschus replied. As the man stood up and left the table, Aeschus begins chatting with another couple to his left.

Thassalor strolls through the double doors and heads out toward the terrace, clutching a goblet of red wine succoured from one of the young serving-girls. The woman stood alone, gazing out at the dying sun on the horizon. "You are troubled, my Lady?" He addresses the woman in Persian.

"Only by your presence, Thassalor of Knossos" the woman said icily, in the same alien tongue.

"Your husband seems preoccupied with the situation in the Crimea?"

"And why should we not be? Given events of the past few moons?" Sybillya countered. "There is nothing to fear in the Crimea! I would not trouble myself with such trivialities." There is much to fear, is there not? Things are moving rapidly, especially in the Phoenicia and Anatolia."

"Does your darling husband suspect anything?" Thassalor said silkily.

The woman glowers at him contemptuously. "No, he does not! He knows nothing of our endeavours. Do you have news from Rhodes?"

"As I have already told you, my darling, I have journeyed from Chersonesus?"

"Do not treat me like a child, Thassalor of Knossos!" Sybillya hissed. "I have heard the rumour. Persia has suffered a grave reversal in Phoenicia, has it not?"

"Yes, my dear, it has. Our friends have proven far more capable than I could ever have credited them" Thassalor seemed bemused by the Persians' misfortune.

"I have heard rumour the killer was a child. It is even whispered that it was a girl."

"Would that surprise you, in light of their strange attitude to the feminine sex?"

"Did this girl also kill Ach'ti?"

"I suspect so, although the Ur'gai would never admit to it, would they?" Thassalor sighed. "Do you have something for me?" Sybillya whispers.

Thassalor smiled thinly. "And why would you think that my dear?"

"You would not have sought me out here otherwise? You could have told me what little you have at the supper table?"

The merchant raised an eyebrow mockingly. "In front of your husband, is that what you would wish? Surely not, my Lady, for you are far too cautious! Your guileless husband has no knowledge of your secrets, benign or malignant!"

"Just hand it over and be on your way, Thassalor of Knossos, for I tire of your silly games!" the woman bristled.

Thassalor steps forward and gazes silently out across the sea. His hand slips inside his robe, retrieves something, then moves slowly to his right hip. Sybillya's fingers caress his clenched fist, which opens briefly, allowing a hollow silver tube to fall into her open palm. Her own elegant fingers clasp tightly as the shell of an oyster. The message-tube is slipped into a hidden pocket in her silk petticoat. "No more the moon, my sweet. I fear that things are fated to change for the worse."

"I will do all I can, I swear it!" the woman sighed softly. "You must, my darling, for everything depends upon it."

~

Tyre, May 493 BC

Andros the ship builder is visibly nervous, and with good reason! He sits at a table in his small office, surrounded by the paraphernalia of his trade. Sat across from him, is Mestarches of Susa, one of King Darius' most trusted counsellors.

"Your visit is quite unexpected, old friend! It might have been wiser if you had given some notice of your arrival" Andros sighed, with a rueful shrug of his shoulders.

"Do you think that wise in light of recent events? And besides, I have explicit instructions from King Darius himself!" the older man said coldly.

"King Darius no longer trusts us? Is that what you are intimating, old friend?" a pained expression fleeted across Andros' face.

"The King demands progress in this endeavour! Troubling rumours have reached Susa these past few moons. I have come here to ascertain the truth at King Darius' request.

"The new fleet will be ready on schedule, I assure you of that, Mestarches."

"King Darius is rightly worried, and will be even more so, when news of the death of Nischanesses reaches him?"

Andros was genuinely alarmed. "You surely do not suspect our involvement in this treachery?"

"I have said nothing" the older man replied softly. "Nonetheless, if there is truth to the rumours circulating in Susa, there is more than a whiff of treachery in this business! I am sure that you would concur, especially in light of our recent tragedy?"

"What else could we have done? We received no prior intelligence that Nischanesses was in grave danger!" Andros insisted.

"Neither did we, I must confess. It is quite a mystery how our enemies discovered his identity, much less the significance of his current assignment here in Tyre.

"We retain your confidence, old friend?" Andros smiled tightly. How many ships have been lost?"

Andros sighed heavily. *So, this was the real reason for*

Mestarches' sudden arrival in Tyre. It had been folly, to be sure, to labour under the pretence that the true significance of the situation had escaped the antennae of Nischanesses, King Darius' Spymaster in Phoenicia.

He drained his goblet of lemon water and reached across the desk for the jug to replenish it. With lightning speed, the left hand of the older man shot across to seize his wrist in a vice-like grip, the strength of which startled the younger man and caused the jug to skid across the table and smash heavily on the floor.

"I asked you a question, did I not?" the older man hissed.

Andros blanched. "We have lost seven vessels in the past six moons, my Lord. All were returning from the Crimea" he yelped.

"And since the previous spring?" the older man eyed him steadily.

"A total of fifteen vessels have mysteriously vanished. We believe they all fell prey to piracy. If that is so, my Lord, this is a matter for which we cannot be held accountable?"

"My dear fellow, we are all answerable to the King, I can assure you of that?" the older man spoke with a chilling politeness, yet his anger was unmistakable.

"I understand, my Lord!" Andros replied meekly.

"How many of these vessels had embarked from Panticapaeum or Nymphaion?"

"All of them, my Lord" Andros replied quickly, his voice barely above a whisper.

"It never occurred to you to inform us of this worrying situation?" the visitor hissed.

"We are bound by solemn oath to complete our obligations. You have my personal assurances on this!" Andros implored, with as little grace as he could muster.

"I would not be here if the King was placated by such platitudes!" the older man growled.

"You have my word, my Lord! The fleet will be ready

to sail within the next few moons, I swear it!" protested Andros.

"Minus the fifteen vessels that you have lost to pirates, of course!" the older man eyed him suspiciously. "Every one of those vessels was the property of His Royal Majesty, King Darius, first of his name!"

"We have despatched agents across the eastern Mediterranean and the Aegean"

Andros confessed. His terror was palpable. "Given the current discord, it is a near impossible task to discover either their whereabouts, or precise details of their disappearance. You must surely understand this, Mestarches of Susa?"

"Have you received word from Cyprus or Rhodes?" Mestarches probed.

"Not as yet, my Lord, I swear it!"

"What of Knossos? Have we despatched agents there?"

Andros was genuinely perplexed. "Why should we make enquiries in Knossos? We do not suspect the involvement of the Cretans. They have remained neutral throughout the recent malaise."

"This matter is no longer of your concern, you understand. We will make the necessary enquiries from now on. Perhaps our own resources, coupled with the unwavering dedication of our agents, might yield profitable results."

"We will endeavour to keep you abreast of any developments, I assure you of that!" Andros said quickly.

"That will not be necessary, for I shall not be returning to Susa. My advice to you, my young friend, is to concentrate your efforts on the completion of the fleet" Mestarches smiled thinly.

"I understand, my Lord."

"Everything depends upon its readiness by the fall. I will endeavour to discover the truth of this plague, its origins, and its beneficiaries, you understand?"

"Of course, my old friend, for you have my loyalty, as

always."

"On the contrary, my young friend, I have your life, and that of your pretty young wife and two children. Do not fail me again! Your entire future, and that of your family, is forfeit to the King if you do!" Mestarches said chillingly.

~

Saiga Plains, Crimea, July 493 BC

The girl kicked her heels in to the horse's flank as they approached the brow of the hill, urging it to increase its pace as they descended. Her long blonde hair, freshly washed and un-braided, almost shimmers in the rays of the glorious July sun as it trails behind as the horse spurs to a gallop and races almost effortlessly down the incline towards the promise of the rich pasture of the meadows and plains below. The rider was clearly enjoying herself, her normally serious expression transformed with unchaste effervescence. "And why not?" she mused, "Is this not what summer days were born for?" The child's face, youthful and unscarred by battle, is sharply chiselled, with highly angled cheekbones and a prominent, almost hawkish, nose. During the past month-and-a-half, her skin has tanned from a milky- pale to a rich, golden-brown. Whilst the girl was undeniably pretty, unusually tall for her years, there is a hardness that is unnerving, even to a casual observer. Her eyes, unblemished pools of azure, are strangely disconcerting: windows to a mind disturbingly precocious for its years.

The rider spurred the horse faster still as they reach the end of the slope and traversed the winding contour of the track at a breakneck pace. The breeze was light and the day, some six hours old, was already starting to feel hot, perhaps the hottest of the year thus far. She tugs firmly at her mare's mane and leans forwards to whisper in her ear.

The animal, as by command, gradually slows its pace. By the time they reached the river they were at a canter, a pace that should not alarm the piquet's into rash reaction, and they gently splash through the water and trot across the meadow. An entire army is camped on the Saiga Plains. Some twenty-thousand warriors from the Ur'gai Queen's Household Division, row- upon-row of tents, stretching almost as far as the eye could see.

"Halt!" the command came from the unseen sentry. The child steadied the horse to a still.

"Dismount!"

The girl leaps agilely from the saddle and steps forward to nuzzle her mare. "Rose petals!" the voice challenged.

"A summer's glory" the girl proffers the response. "Advance to be recognised!"

The child steps forward, leaving her mare to graze hungrily. "Closer!" the sentry commanded. "You are not wearing britches?"

"It is far too warm for britches" the girl replies unashamedly.

The girl toyed with the hem of her summer kurta with her right hand, teasing the material higher to expose more of her naked thigh. "I can see your fanny, Corelya!" The voice squealed.

Corelya giggled. "You certainly cannot, nor shall you ever. Not unless you intend to make an honest woman of me."

"If you let me see you closer?"

"If you carry on talking to me that way, Master Krit'ch, I shall never be your blushing bride" she sighed. "Now, may I pass?"

"Recognised, friend, and you may pass."

"Aren't you going to say 'Hello' properly, Master Krit'ch? Your shift must be finishing soon?" Corelya hazarded, studiously surveying the position of the sun in an almost cloudless sky. It certainly promised to be another beautiful day.

"Of course?" the voice replies, a little hesitantly. Krit'ch, a boy of barely fourteen- years, climbs out of his concealed foxhole and steps forward to greet her. He extends his left hand to shake her own yet, within an instant, the girl has pulled him violently toward her, stepping past and inside, with a flexed right leg. With the speed and ferocity of an asp, she twists lithely and smashes the boy viciously in the mouth with her right elbow. Krit'ch is pitched violently backwards and flipped off his feet by the girls flexed right knee, before slamming into the ground with an audible thud. Gasps and giggles peal from a line of hidden foxholes.

"Silence" Corelya hissed. During the brief struggle, the girl had plucked the crossbow deftly from the boy and now steps across his chest with her left leg, stooping to aim at his right eye. She does so, fully conscious of the fact that he now has a completely unobstructed vantage of her naked crotch. Corelya's azure pools twinkle mischievously.

"Enjoying the view, little runt?" She curls her index finger lovingly around the trigger, savouring the look of horror that fleets across the boy's face.

"No, Corelya!" the boy squealed. "I apologise, I was only joking! Please don't!"

Corelya steps back and lowers the crossbow. "On your feet, soldier!" she barked.

The boy stood immediately to attention, his eyes betraying anger and shame at this public humiliation. And yet, he rightly feared the girl's rage, for everyone knew of Corelya's temper. It had been gentle teasing, nothing more, and he had never expected her to react in such a manner. Now he was plainly terrified, for Corelya was a Superior Officer in Her Majesty's Army with the power to prescribe punishment to all inferior ranks. "I do not think it wise to publicly disrespect a superior officer, Master Krit'ch." There is no trace of amusement, merely a chilling authority.

"Understood, Commander" the boy replied softly. "I

can't hear you!" Corelya bawled.

"Understood, Commander!" the boy yelled.

"Attention!" Corelya roared. "About turn. Quick march! Left, right, left, right, left, right, left." The boy marches under his own pace, deliberately keeping his dressing, back toward camp. Whilst he is angry at his public humiliation at the hands of a girl, a year his junior and a slave to wit, no thoughts of revenge percolate within his mind. No small wonder, for the girl in question was not merely a superior officer, but Her Majesty's Royal Retainer; *Illir'ya's most skilled and trusted assassin*!

~

A few hours later, Corelya sprawled lazily on the bed, as naked as the day she was born, her mind preoccupied with the morning's scouting. Whilst she has not seen anything to arouse her suspicions, she nonetheless harboured grave doubts as to the wisdom of their current location. The opinion of the Ur'gai Royal Counsel was that the Argata did not have sufficient forces at their disposal north of the Caucasus to cross the narrow isthmus which links the Azovi with the Black Sea and effect an encirclement of the entire Household Division. The prospect of encirclement and annihilation continued to plague Corelya. The intelligence reports of Argata military dispositions in 'the lands between the seas' were woefully inadequate, that she would freely concede. Estimates of the true size of their army, especially cavalry contingents were, frankly, abysmal! An increase in Argata military force north of the Caucasus was specifically implied in the terms of the *Accord Scythiac*, for 'the lands between the seas' were now nominally under their control. It was almost as if the prescient threat of these accommodations had gone unrecognised by the Queen and her Counsellors!

The *Accord Scythiac* had been signed by the four

Scythian Ducal States almost a year earlier, at the behest of the Persians, in the immediate aftermath of the Ionian naval defeat at Lade. Corelya had attended the Ceremony, convened a few miles west of Hopa in the early summer of 494 BC, in the company of Her Majesty and the Royal Counsel. The Monarchs and respective Counsels of the four Scythian Ducal States, the Nur'gat, Ur'gai, Orch'tai, and Argata, had duly signed the *Accord*, albeit without much enthusiasm, at least from Corelya's recollection. The terms of thew *Accord Scythiac* were fully compliant with their existing obligations to Persia itself, agreed in the aftermath of Darius' successful incursion into Thrace and the Great Steppe, a decade before Corelya was born. It had been heralded as a triumph of Persian diplomacy, in Susa and elsewhere!

The *Accord Scythiac* was an ambitious entente that sought to guarantee harmony of trade from the Central Plains of Asia, via the Great Steppe, as far west as the delta of the Danube, the gateway to Celtic Europe. The significance of the Crimean Peninsula and 'the lands between the seas' could not be understated, for they were crucial to the success of the entire enterprise. At the time, Corelya had indulged herself a cynical smirk that the parties most responsible for ensuring the success of this idealized *harmony*; the Sauromatae to the east, and the Celts to the west, were not even invited to the signing ceremony! Perhaps Darius had assumed their acquiescence could be taken for granted! It was equally probable the Persian King had even less knowledge of these parties than he did the moral turpitude of his own trusted courtesans!

Ever since then, the Argata had aggressively expanded their influence across the Caucasus, into the forests of the foothills and the plains beyond, to virtually annex 'the lands between the seas'. This was Corelya's homeland! The lands her ancestors had migrated to and prospered in for more than a Century. It was neither right, nor proper, that *they* should have sealed such spoils! And yet, the settlement was entirely in accordance with the wishes of the "Great Pretender", a man of limited worth and birth, who now held the future of the world in his hands! *How could it be so willed by the Gods that a people undeserving of such power had even come in to being, and, in so a short space of time, with nothing but tyranny of arms?* Corelya smiled grimly. The Greeks may praise the virtues of their Gods and cast ballads and tragedies for all eternity, yet this world unto which she had been sired was now, assuredly, fucked! Proper fucked!

The Argata, a cruel and ruthless people of dubious ancestry, inhabited the lands south of the Caucasus and had their Royal City at Archaeopolis, on the fringes of the fertile Colchian Plain. From whence the Argata came, nobody really knew, for some say they are descended from the *Scythia*, others the *Cimmerians*, a barbaric tribe fabled for their complicity in the destruction of Nineveh at the twilight of the Great Assyrian Empire a Century-and-a- half before. The Argata were sworn enemies of the Sauromatae, and, ever since the signing of the *Accord*, they had systematically purged the remnant Sauromatae communities in the plains and forests of the foothills north of the Caucasus, forcing them into the refuge of the mountains. Corelya's community had sought refuge in the fertile valleys of the mountains two decades before she had been born, when the Argata had commenced their subjugation of the Armenians, unleashing a cascade of devastation upon the Sauromatae north and south of the Caucasus. For a while, a brief while, they had been at peace, and they had prospered. *Until they came!* No matter where the Argata ventured, death and destruction surely followed. They were a barbaric race, ruled with an iron fist by a woman whose very name could freeze the blood in the veins of the last of the Sauromatae in the plains and valleys of 'the lands between the seas'. To these long-suffering peoples, *Lezika*, the Argata Queen, was a name synonymous with death itself!

Corelya had journeyed far and wide since their arrival in the Crimea in the early summer, sometimes returning, sometimes not, for there was vital work to be done. The intelligence network she had strived tirelessly to flourish these three years past comprised a web of informants in Panticapaeum and Nymphaion in the east, Chersonesus in the west, and the surrounding hamlets of the southern coast. Further northwest, beyond the Crimea, was the Hellenic polis of Olbia, the wealthiest centre in the entire Pontic region. These centres were founded by Greek colonists who had ventured across the Aegean and through the Hellespont in search of their fortunes more than a Century before. *And what fortunes they had amassed?* Wealth beyond their wildest aspirations! They had established the most advanced pan-Continental trading network the world had yet known, where poppy oil and spices from the Central Plains of Kazakh'yi were sold for consumption in Athens, Corinth, Thebes, and Sparta, even further afield, in the colonies of North Africa, the Central and Southern Tyrrhenian, and the ancient cities of Egypt. Trade, of course, is always reciprocal.

It was true that the Greeks could not claim exclusive credit for establishing this market, to a greater degree it had evolved, due in no small part to the pioneering efforts of the Phocaeans in the Seventh Century and the Phoenicians in the Sixth Century to the present. Nevertheless, it had been the far-reaching socio-political reforms of the Athenians, further encouraged by the tyrannical Pisistratidae, who had fostered the peace and stability necessary for this market to flourish. The fruits of their endeavours were plain for all to see, for the Sixth Century had borne witness to an unprecedented expansion of wealth throughout the Aegean, Ionia, Thrace and the Pontic. And then, in the middle of the last Century, from the ashes of Assyria, Lydia, and Babylon, there emerged a power unparalleled in recent memory. *The Persians!*

The Greeks were notoriously distrustful of Persia, and rightly so, in Corelya's considered opinion! The Persians were a cruel and oppressive race who by force of arms, or threats of such, mandated absolute loyalty from their supplicants; *earth* and *water, the very necessities of life itself!* As for the network of Hellenic agents and informants scattered throughout the Persian dominions and beyond, most were loyal to their masters, to Athens, Thebes, Corinth, Megara, and Sparta. The Greeks were unashamedly distrustful of one another, which was part of the problem! In the latter half of the previous Century, through the auspices of the Peloponnesian League, Sparta had emerged as the unrivalled power in the Aegean. And yet, by the virtues of socio-political enlightenment, Athens had eclipsed Spartan influence in the wider world. An ever more intricate network of spies and informants had been established, orchestrated by a new Chief Agent in the region universally known as 'Oracle'. Corelya had no knowledge of the identity of the 'Oracle', nor where they were based, yet they were now the principal friendly intelligence source in the region. Only Persia had succeeded in establishing such an intricate web of intelligence agents and informants in the Pontic region, whose loyalty to their own Chief Agent, a shadowy spectre known as the 'Hawk', was equally unswerving!

Corelya uncorked the stopper on a flagon of wodki and drank greedily. Yari was forever imploring her to use a goblet, but the younger girl considered this an unnecessary encumbrance. If her conduct was not 'Ladylike', then so be it, for she was certainly no Lady! Corelya lay back on the bed and considered the conundrum bequeathed to her. During the past decade, the Hellenics had been prime architects of their own misfortunes, however unpalatable the confession, even in private! The malaise had festered in Naxos, a small island in the Cyclades, just off the south-east Peloponnese coast. A tyranny had been established on Naxos in the latter half of the last Century, encouraged by the Athenian tyrants, the Pisistratidae, yet this had been subsequently overthrown, and its dissidents expelled. These malcontents had fled to Miletus, the richest city in the Ionian Peninsula, where they had been received with cordiality by the tyrant's son-in-law, Aristagoras.

The true ruler of Miletus, Histiaeus, had long-since become a fixture at the court of King Darius in Susa. Corelya had met him as a young child and had been unimpressed by his oily charm, insincerity, and naked self-interest, which bordered on the pathological. During later years, she had privately counselled Queen Illir'ya to rebuff his overtures for a 'deeper and more meaningful' relationship between Miletus and the Ur'gai, for no good could ever come of it, except for Histiaeus! Following his treachery in a conspiracy that would galvanise the Ionian Revolt, Histiaeus had fled and was now being hunted by his former master!

According to the intelligence reports at the time, which Corelya had been privy to only quite recently, Aristagoras had offered military assistance to a group of exiled Naxian dissidents, presumably for considerable personal gain, and had then approached Artaphernes, King Darius' brother, then residing in Sardis. The Persians received the approval of Darius himself, and again it seemed likely that Histiaeus had promised his Master the moon and the stars, and a large fleet of several hundred triremes, under the command of Megabates, had sallied forth and eventually put to port on the Island of Chios, a little further north from Naxos to await favourable winds.

What transpired next literally beggared belief! Following a heated and public disagreement with Megabates, an indignant Aristagoras had reputedly jeopardised the entire endeavour by sending word to Naxos of an imminent attack. Whether such naked treachery on Aristagoras part was even credible, it mattered little, for Naxos duly withstood a siege for several months and the fleet retired to Ionia in ignominy! With his own position in Miletus now in jeopardy, not to mention that of his idiot son-in-law, Histiaeus embarked upon a fateful course that would make him a marked man, namely, encouraging his cloth-headed son-in-law to incite open revolt among the Ionian polities against the hated Persians.

Aristagoras is reported to have headed to Sparta for an audience with King Cleomenes to petition military assistance for the rebels, yet was soundly rebuffed, by none other than the Royal Princess Gorgo, aged only eight years, who had wisely counselled her father not to entertain the fool, or his extravagant promises. "Father, you must go away at once, or the stranger will be your ruin!" If the legend was true, and Corelya sincerely hoped it was so, it served only to reinforce her own opinion that a girl child, at any age, was clearly of superior matter to any *mere* man!

Astonishingly, the Athenians had been taken in by Aristagoras' silky platter and had involved themselves in the attack on Sardis, contrary to their obligations under an existing accord with Persia. Sardis had been raised to the ground by fire! One by one, from Cyprus in the south to Mytilene in the north, Hellenic colonies had taken up arms against their Persian oppressors and, one by one, had been ruthlessly subjugated! Wisely, the Scythian Ducals had proclaimed their neutrality. Only the Argata had furnished clandestine military assistance to Persia, a welcome distraction from slaughtering innocent Armenian villages! After the decisive naval victory at Lade almost fifteen moons ago, only Miletus remained in revolt, yet their days were surely numbered. Aristagoras had long since perished in an ill-fated military expedition to Thrace. The traitor Histiaeus remained at large, yet a reckoning was certain!

After the victory, King Darius had convened the *Accord Scythiac*, the terms of which were suspiciously favourable to feared Argata Queen, for she had gained oversight for the security of 'the lands between the seas'. The most perplexing riddle of the entire affair was the tacit acquiescence of the Orch'tai, the greatest military force among all Scythia, who had been at war with the Argata for much of the past thirty years! *Was there something she had overlooked, no matter how keenly she directed her mind?*

"Commander Corelya?" a voice clipped from just outside the door of the tent, unmistakably Gor'ya, the Queen's cousin and most trusted messenger and confidante.

"Yes" Corelya replied, swinging her legs to assume a sitting position at the edge of the bed.

"Her Majesty requests your presence at Counsel."

"I am at Her Majesty's grace and favour. Give me a minute."

A minute or so later, attired in the obligatory kurta, britches, and sword-belt, Corelya steps through the tent-flap. She greets Gor'ya with a smile of genuine warmth. "A fine morning" she declared, gazing up at an expanse of unblemished blue as far as her eyes could see.

"Did you enjoy your morning ride?" Gor'ya enquired. There was a faint trace of humour in her voice.

"Indeed, I did!" Corelya replied earnestly. "Have you heard something?"

"You really ought to wear britches, Corelya. It is unseemly riding bare."

"I think Master Krit'ch saw rather more of me than he had expected?" Corelya giggled.

"Everyone is talking about it, Corelya!" Gor'ya sighed. "You should not be such a tease. It is not becoming of you" she implored.

Corelya smiled sweetly. "He did deserve it, Gor'. He was being cheeky."

"So were you!" Gor'ya replied hotly then, fearing

24

Corelya's displeasure, she added hastily, "Or so I gather."

"I suppose I was a little 'arsey' with him!" Corelya snickered.

"He saw rather more of you than that, or so I heard."

"Quite" Corelya quipped.

"It is not Lady-like, Corelya, to allow everyone to see you so" Gor'ya admonished her.

"I was only being playful" Corelya protested. "I wouldn't be surprised if there wasn't anyone who hasn't seen me naked."

"We all used to run around naked when we were little, girls and boys, but you are not little anymore, are you?" reproved Gor'ya. Corelya, fast approaching the cusp of her thirteenth birthday was considerably taller than the petite Gor'ya, recently turned fifteen.

"No. I don't suppose I am anymore" Corelya sighed.

"Yet still you persist in taking your clothes off at every opportunity during the summer."

"I am a slave, remember? Nobody cares if I am 'Lady-like', because in their eyes I will never be an equal, will I?" Corelya's azure pools blazed.

"Don't say that Corelya!" Gor'ya retorted. "Whilst it may be true, nobody really treats you like a slave, do they?" she continued. "I never have, have I?"

Corelya smiled warmly at her companion. "No. You never have."

They continued the rest of their journey in silence. Normally, Corelya would have brushed aside any reproof from Gor'ya with a polished insouciance, yet now she was strangely unsettled. Gor'ya's intensity had surprised her. She really did *disapprove* of Corelya's conduct earlier that morning, yet the younger girl harboured an inkling that there was something left unsaid, perhaps deliberately so. They passed through the sentries at the palisade gate and strolled across an open central square that was flanked by a series of high- peaked tents on three sides. The Royal residence at the north side of the green comprised a series of interconnecting tents, including a central Audience Chamber, where Queen Illir'ya and her Counsel were huddled in discussion. Adhering to convention, Corelya refrained from approaching the guarded entrance and halted a few paces away as Gor'ya strolled past the Guards to disappear inside.

Gor'ya coughed lightly. "Your Majesty, Commander Corelya is here."

"Then show her in. Thank you Gor'ya, you are dismissed."

"Thank you, Your Majesty."

Gor'ya turned on her heels and strolled out into the sun. She smiled brightly at the younger girl as she approaches. "Do remember your manners, Corelya!" she whispered encouragingly.

Corelya simply nodded in acquiescence and strolled past the Guards. "Or else we might have to spank you!" Gor'ya mused silently, grinning wolfishly at the prospect, as she paced across the green in the light of a brilliant morning sun. If she were being truthful, and perhaps the truth was a necessity in this matter, Gor'ya had been thinking rather a lot about the younger girl during the past few moons. She had been genuinely alarmed, piqued even, by the revelation of Corelya's naughtiness earlier that morning. Then again, naughtiness might be rewarded, cherished rather than scolded, if confined to an appropriate setting, *like an empty tent with a warm fire*!

Corelya entered the Audience Chamber and coughed lightly. "Your Royal Majesty!"

"Commander Corelya!" the Queen smiled brightly. "You may state your report."

Corelya stated her report of the intelligence accrued during the past six weeks, including her scouting forays this week past. She had ventured far and wide, riding at least three or four hours equidistant from camp every morning, planning her forays in advance, stopping regularly to chat with local villagers, hunting and foraging parties, and travelling caravans visiting Panticapaeum and Nymphaion, with a view to gauging their opinions on the geopolitical climate, the favourability of the truce, and the general economic climate. A consensus, among locals and Hellenic traders alike, was that the boldness of the young Ur'gai Queen in exercising her rightful claim to a Protectorate in the peninsula was to be welcomed. This would surely foster stability in the region, encouraging trade, whilst discouraging the perennial plague of brigands in 'the lands between the seas'. The terms of the *Accord Scythiac* were laudable, in as much as a continued peace between the Scythian Ducals would increase prosperity for all, whether they be Scythia, Hellenics, the European trading centres of the Danube, even Orientals hailing from east of the Wol'yi. There had been encouraging signs that Persia was profiting from this "New Sun" and, if that were so, regional peace was assured.

There was little evidence that the *Accord* had been breached. No hostile incursions of Orch'tai cavalry beyond the margins of the 'demilitarised zone' along the north-west coast of the Azovi Sea had been reported. Rumours of reputed Argata aggression along the southeast coastline and eastern margin of the Straits, the narrow isthmus connecting the Azovi and Black Seas, were apparently baseless. Despite the obvious partisan allegiances of elements on the Councils of the City Fathers and Merchants Guild of Panticapaeum with an historic claim of Orch'tai dominion over the Azovi, the spectre of a determined military incursion along its northern coastline remained remote. Nevertheless, if the Orch'tai and Argata were no longer in enmity, then the greatest field army in the whole of Scythia could readily be deployed west against the Ur'gai, endangering the fragile peace and the security of entire Household Division.

"That is entirely consistent with our own intelligence, Commander Corelya" said Morch'ti, Her Majesty's *Kor'nai*, or Chief Counsellor.

"My skin is less milky than it was a week ago" Corelya smiled brightly.

Queen Illir'ya glanced away and grinned, whereas the rest of the assembly bristled at the impudence of the girl, a mere *slave* at that. Morch'ti reddened and his eyes burned angrily, yet he did not move to reprove the girl.

"I think you would do well to remember your manners, Commander!" hissed Zar'cha, the Commander of Her Majesty's Royal Bodyguard.

"Forgive me, Commander, I forget my place" Corelya replied humbly.

"Indeed, you do!" Zar'cha scolded.

"My explicit directive, Commander Zar'cha, if my memory serves, was to appraise the lay of the land, as opposed to the lay of my Handmaiden's brother" Corelya snorted.

Queen Illir'ya, now twenty years old, suppresses an urge to giggle. Her three young Handmaidens, including the six-year-old twins, exchange startled and excited glances!

Zar'cha blanched at the public revelation of her marital infidelity, her cheeks suffusing a scarlet hue as she exploded with rage. "How fucking dare, you speak to me like that, *slave!*" She almost roared the last word, the intensity of her fury cowing the little Handmaidens to an obedient silence. Her right hand moved swiftly to the sword-hilt at her left hip.

"Draw that blade, bitch, and I will slay you!" Corelya spoke evenly, a thin smile playing on her lips.

"Commander Corelya" the Queen interjected tactfully, "would you care to enlighten us further on your fears of a secret alliance between the Orch'tai and the Argata, if you please."

"If it pleases Your Highness" Corelya replied obediently, blithely ignoring the smouldering Zar'cha, whose hand had not wavered. "The Argata have suffered considerable disrepute by the assertion of our Protectorate in the Crimea. This is not simply a matter of wounded pride. The Argata are now, to a greater degree than they have ever been, little more than an informal satrapy of the Persian Empire."

Some of the Counsellors exchanged startled glances, for this was dangerous talk. It is Counsellor Alazar, and not the Kor'nai, who challenged the girl. "An intriguing perspective, Commander Corelya, yet one at odds with our own appraisal of the situation. Do continue, if you please?"

"During the past year, the Argata have expanded their influence along the southern coast of the Azovi Sea and effectively regulate all naval traffic, mercantile and martial, via control of its eastern shores and the Straits. They have inveigled sympathy among the Administrators of Panticapaeum and Nymphaion, who ultimately rely upon their grace-and- favour for their own security and prosperity. We have now demanded that these polities switch their allegiances to ourselves and, whilst that is perfectly logical, it has imposed unwelcome difficulties."

"What would you have done that we ourselves have seen fit to ignore, Commander Corelya?" Alazar, the youngest of Queen Illir'ya's Counsellors, toted as a potential future Kor'nai, spoke in a honeyed tone.

Corelya saw a twinkle of mischief in Zar'cha's eyes as she glanced quickly at Alazar, perhaps a little too longingly, to be replaced with an icy glare as she returned her gaze to the girl. *Sweet Tabiti! Is there anyone she isn't shagging, apart from her husband, that is*? Corelya mused.

"I would not have asserted a Protectorate over the Crimea. I think it a grave error of judgement on the part of Counsel" Corelya replied smoothly. The statement was met with gasps of astonishment from the assembled

Counsellors.

"We Scythians should be eternally grateful that your views, coloured by inexperience as they must be, are merely advisory, dear child" snorted Alazar.

"You are not worried by the recent reports of increased volumes of Orch'tai timber baulks passing through Nymphaion. These are not destined for Euboea, Attica, or the Peloponnese, at least not according to our sources" Corelya quipped.

"Our intelligence is consistent with their destination being Phoenicia" interjected Naz'mir, considered to be among the wisest of Queen Illir'ya's Counsellors.

"For myself, I am unsure of my faith in the value of these reports" Alazar countered. Corelya's azure pools sparkled with interest.

"Why is that Counsellor Alazar?" Queen Illir'ya enquired politely.

"They Phoenicians have no need for such trade with the Orch'tai. Not when they effectively control the trade in high-grade timber from Europe via Massalia, Your Majesty."

"So, their destination must be Sparta, if not Attica?" Morch'ti added his own opinion, not quite believing its certainty in fact.

"With all due respect, Honourable Kor'nai, I do not think so" chirped Corelya. All eyes turned towards the girl. "Sparta has no need for such timbers. They have no desire to challenge either Athens or Phoenicia in the realms of Poseidon."

"These timbers could be used to build wagons, could they not?" suggested Naz'mir. "These are military grade timber baulks, my Lord, of the kind used to build triremes. Even Phoenicia has no requirement for timbers such as these. For, as Counsellor Alazar rightly states, they can source directly from Massalia" Corelya countered.

"They must be for Athens then, surely? Our sources

could be mistaken?" ventured Naz'mir.

"They are destined for Persia, Your Majesty, of that I am certain" Corelya stated emphatically. "Darius has a mighty army, but to re-establish order in the Ionian Sea and extract revenge on the Athens for the insult of Sardis, Persia requires a navy of her own. That is what he is building."

"You seem quite certain of this, dear child" Alazar smiled thinly.

"If such a thing were true, why would Persia not secure such materials from Massalia?" interjected Naz'mir.

"If the Persians ever tried to source such timbers from Europe via the Phoenicians, Athenian spies would soon uncover the truth of it. The Hellenics, including the polities of the Peloponnesian League, would almost certainly declare war on Phoenicia. The Phoenicians have no desire to repeat the mistakes of Troy and incur the righteous fury of the Hellenics."

"The Orch'tai must surely be aware that such an overtly hostile trade would incur the fury of Athens? I cannot imagine for one moment that they would be so brazen. This would be a clear breach of the terms of the *Accord*" declared Morch'ti, to the approval of the rest of the Counsel, who nodded their concurrence.

Yet, the young Queen remained doubtful. "Is this perhaps the *real* reason behind the recent disputations between the Hellenics and the Orch'tai? There is talk of an ugly spat in Apollonia that turned violent. Several protagonists were badly hurt, or so I was informed."

"A mere quibble over the price of silk, Your Majesty. That, at least, is the considered opinion of our sources" Alazar said airily. "Tempers were frayed, or so I gather, tempered perhaps by the quantities of un-watered wine imbibed by the Orch'tai merchants."

"Other sources contradict that simplistic account" Corelya corrected him instantly. "Apparently, a brawl broke out at a tavern adjacent to the Merchant's Guild during which at least two Orch'tai merchants were stabbed and are lucky to be alive. The cause of the fight, at least according to witnesses, was a dispute over the recent price increases in hemp-rope used for rigging sails which is, as we know, a commodity over which the Orch'tai effectively have a monopoly. Athenian and Corinthian merchants were angry that the prices of hemp rope in the Hellenic ports are higher than elsewhere, especially ports on the southern margins of the Black Sea."

"Which could be seen as a hostile action, if taken with the tales of large consignments of timber shipped to Tyre?" Queen Illir'ya chose her words carefully.

"Perhaps it would wiser not to speculate too freely on such matters" ventured Alazar. "Yet, if we are to stay neutral." the Queen continued.

"That would be the most appropriate course of action in any event, Your Majesty" Morch'ti advised.

"Even if such a course of action were to compromise our relations with Athens? This would have a negative impact on trade and prosperity in the northern Black Sea" Naz'mir questioned.

"Whilst blithely ignoring our obligations under the terms of the current treaty with the Orch'tai" Alazar responded hotly.

"What if the Orch'tai had committed to a course that renders the terms of the Accord, the regional peace, and any pre-existing obligations between the Ducals, immaterial?" Corelya quipped.

"Such as, Commander, if you would be specific?" Alazar countered, his tone underscoring his irritation with the statement.

"An informal alliance with the Argata which, by implication, fosters closer ties with Persia. This would undermine a course of neutrality in our dealings with both parties, Persia and the Hellenics, alike" Corelya proposed.

"This is purely hypothetical, dear child" Alazar spoke

softly.

"I would concur with such a statement, Honourable Counsellor. And yet, it remains a feasible prospectus."

"I do not agree, dear child" Alazar countered. There were nods and murmurs from the rest of the Counsellors.

The Queen interjected. "Would you be so kind as to elaborate, Commander Corelya?"

"Such an alliance would undermine the current peace in numerous ways" Corelya proposed. "It could jeopardise our Protectorate in the Crimea, compromising the security and prosperity of the Hellenic polities here, and further a destructive war between ourselves, the Orch'tai, and Argata. In such an event, unlikely as it may seem, Persia would side with the Argata, whilst the Hellenics may feel obligated to support us."

"This is purely speculative, dear child. Whilst your imagination is valued, there is no evidence at all to support any immediate threat from the Orch'tai" said Alazar.

"This is quite true, my learned friend. Our sources inform us that the majority of Orch'tai cavalry units are engaged in action with barbaric tribes to the east of the Wol'yi" Naz'mir elaborated.

"What of the reports of a sizeable Orch'tai presence to the west of Astrach'yi?" Corelya interjected.

"They are merely support divisions, at least according to our intelligence sources. Is that not so?" ventured Morch'ti.

"According to the latest reports, at least three Ochta's are camped there. This equates to some nine hundred superbly trained and equipped cavalry. I may remind you, that these are among the finest warriors in the world" Corelya replied.

"A motley crew of inexperienced personnel who pose little threat to anyone, dear child! They are mere boys on ponies" Alazar simpered.

"Virile and quick-witted enough to mount an

impromptu offensive, should they be required to do so"
Corelya smiled sweetly.

"You surely cannot be serious?" a visibly startled
Morch'ti had at last realised the significance of the alleged
Orch'tai disposition.

"Astrach'yi is only a few days hard ride east of the
north-west coast of the Azovi. From there, they would be
within striking distance of the 'labyrinth'!" Corelya stated
the issue as succinctly as she could.

The 'labyrinth' was the interconnecting weave of
tidal land-strips and lakes that linked the peninsula with
the Great Steppe via a narrow isthmus. Whilst sited deep
within the Ur'gai domain, it lay a considerable distance
south of the fortified Royal centres of Trakhtemirov and
Rost'eya, where reinforcements were currently garrisoned.

"You think the Orch'tai are preparing an invasion!"
Alazar almost shrilled with ridicule at the suggestion.

"I think it would be wise to increase our patrols in the
'labyrinth', for we have sufficient forces at our disposal,
do we not? There is nothing to be gained from our
current disposition, is there? There is no direct threat to
Chersonesus from either the Argata or their sympathisers
elsewhere in the peninsula" Corelya stated pointedly.

"I am quite unconvinced by your logic, Commander"
Alazar countered pointedly.

"Nor am I, Your Majesty, though I must freely state
that there is virtue in the young Commander's assessment"
added Morch'ti. "The 'labyrinth' could be readily invested
by a sizeable and proximate contingent from the east. This
threat is acute given our commitment to desist patrols
along the north-west coast of the Azovi."

"If I may be so bold, I harbour some concerns as to
the accuracy of your sources, Commander Corelya. Is it
possible that your sources have some ulterior, perhaps even
sinister, motive?" interjected Sag'ra, the Queen's brother,
aged sixteen-and-a-half, who had held his silence thus far.

"Why *sinister*, dear brother?" said the Queen.

"Perhaps the Hellenics are not being entirely sincere in their dealings with us?

"Surely their greatest fear is not an alliance of the Orch'tai and Argata, but closer ties between Persia and us! Such fears may have been heightened since your bold assertion of Ur'gai supremacy in the Crimea?"

"I would be inclined to sympathise with that view, Your Majesty, in spite of the remonstrating of Commander Corelya" added Alazar.

"I have said nothing" Corelya spoke tonelessly.

"But your opinion *of*, perhaps distaste *for*, all things Persian is well known? Your keenly felt hostility is perfectly understandable in light of that embarrassing incident in Susa all those years ago" Sag'ra oozed his polished charm.

Corelya blushed hotly. Zar'cha's eyes twinkle with delight at the girl's evident discomfort. "On the contrary, my opinion of the Persians is rather more glowing than you would credit, Sag'ra. Yet they are of little relevance to the matter at hand" Corelya stated, quickly recovering her composure. "As for what happened in Susa, I scarcely think the sleazy designs of a trusted courtier toward me are of any relevance to the matters I report on here."

"I fear we may be diverging from the issues at hand, Your Majesty" said the Kor'nai. "Your report, and opinions, are noted, Commander Corelya. It is my duty to advise Her Majesty that such a threat cannot be vouchsafed by current intelligence. We do, of course, respect your assessment of the situation and will act as we see fit in the event of any change in the current circumstances."

"If that is all, then you are dismissed, my Honourable Counsel, and thank-you" Queen Illir'ya said.

As the meeting broke up, Corelya waited patiently until everyone had left. This was expected, given her status as both slave and Her Majesty's Royal Retainer. If any commands were to be forthcoming, these would pass solely between Her Majesty and her Retainer, for this might, in extremis, be an instruction to murder a soul who had recently departed the Queen's audience. Mercifully, Queen Illir'ya was not as inclined some of her predecessors to readily dispose of her Counsellors services and the Duchy had been at peace for almost a decade. Despite her lowly status, it was one of Corelya's solemn duties to give opinion, from time to time, requested or no, as to whether, in her opinion, the 'winds had changed'.

"Do you have anything specific to report, Corelya?"

"Nothing I did not report in Counsel, Your Majesty."

"You think our current geopolitical position invites potential disaster? You may speak candidly, for we are alone, my not-so-little Handmaiden" the Queen smiled brightly. "I have concerns, Your Highness, as I have already stated."

"They were noted" Queen Illir'ya sighed irritably.

"You think I am being melodramatic?" Corelya bristled.

"Of course not!" the Queen snapped. "If our intelligence, as imperfect as it is, that we have nothing to fear from our rear."

"If it is flawed, we are doomed" Corelya added gloomily.

"Any Orch'tai incursion in to north-west Azovi would constitute a violation of the *Accord*, would it not?" the young Queen appraised the child closely. "Our spies confirm that they have no intention of doing so. Your sources in Chersonesus have a different opinion of the current state of play, do they not? Are you certain they are entirely trustworthy?"

"I am, Your Highness. It appears that the Hellenics have a new chief intelligence agent in the region with unparalleled insights into the current dynamic. It was this source which pointed toward Persia as the recipient of the timber baulks" Corelya confessed.

"I see. Are you certain that this is genuine? Not a

Persian ruse? Or an Athenian bait? Counsel seems to think otherwise."

"Your brother certainly does if you will forgive my temerity! I do agree with Counsel that the Orch'tai would be taking a great risk in allying so openly with the Argata" Corelya respectfully concurred. "However, things have changed dramatically over the course of the past decade, especially in Persia. Darius has transformed the governance of his Empire, stifled hopes of independence in the Ionian Sea, and even now our spies report that significant reserves of gold, silver, timber, and food are being stockpiled in strategic locations."

"Please continue, Commander Corelya." Illir'ya smiled sweetly at the girl she had known, and trusted implicitly, for close to a decade.

"With all respect, your Royal Highness, King Darius has crafted his state, and is now fashioning an army perhaps greater than that of Cyrus. Then there is the matter of the timber baulks and hemp-rope, absolute necessities for the creation of a navy to match anything the Hellenics may muster! These the Persians cannot source from within their own dominions. The only rationale for such overt preparations is the pursuit of war! King Darius' opinion of the Hellenics, particularly Athens, is scarcely flattering, especially after the burning of Sardis" Corelya persisted.

"What a strange child you are, Corelya? Fretting about the Persians and the Athenians" the Queen smiled to soften the reproof.

"Our relationship with Athens is crucial to maintaining regional stability, Your Majesty? Perhaps even more so than our alliance with Persia, at least in wealth and prestige, and this ultimately legitimises our claim to a protectorate in the peninsula."

"You think our protectorate has ruffled feathers in Susa?" the Queen asked searchingly.

"We effectively control the Crimea, though the

arrangement is one of a consensual Protectorate. That remains the principal motive for favouring the status quo. Yet, if we were forced to choose sides in a war with Persia and Athens, this could forge new alliances, even between the Orch'tai and Argata, which could de-stabilize the current peace" Corelya postulated.

"As usual, your grasp of the finer points and the broader tapestry is exemplary" the Queen smiled sweetly at Corelya. "Do you have a proposal for me to consider?"

"I have, Your Majesty, and it is dangerous."

"How would likely die?" the Queen spoke softly.

"Just me!" the child quipped, grinning broadly.

"Perhaps you should enlighten me?"

Corelya talked for several minutes, without interruption. At the end, the Queen was left stunned by the girl's dedication to duty and her blithe insouciance to any personal danger. The mission was extremely dangerous yet remained the surest hope of resolving the riddle of the Orch'tai and Argata dispositions around the Azovi coast, 'the land between the seas', and, ultimately, their state of readiness. As the girl bade her leave, Her Majesty addressed a minor issue that had, up until now, been neglected.

"Good luck with your mission, Commander Corelya, may the Gods bless you and keep you. You will remember to take a spare set of britches, won't you?"

"Of course, Your Majesty! I wouldn't dream of doing otherwise" Corelya mumbled, her cheeks flushing hotly.

～

Dionysopolis, July 493 BC

"Your needlework is improving with every thread, Artemis. I think you may even be better than me, soon enough!" the woman smiled encouragingly at the child.

The girl smiled sweetly back. "I have my doubts,

mother. You began to learn when you were far younger than I, did you not? It is in your blood, is it not?"

"So is riding horses, little pearl, and that is something I cannot even contemplate right now!" the woman grinned.

"It won't be long now, will it?" the girl asked hopefully.

"Within the moon, my honeycomb, and no more than that, I would warrant."

"Does it hurt? I have heard tales that it hurts?"

"It is not pleasant, that is for sure! Most certainly not the first time?" the woman confessed. "Have you talked with your father about it?"

"No, it was just someone I met at Kassandra's birthday party. You remember?"

"That was just after I discovered I was pregnant, if I remember. I thought all of this was behind me, what with my age!" the woman sighed.

"But you are not all that old at all, are you?" the girl quipped.

"No, I am not!" the woman smiled wryly. "Yet, there are days when I think I have lived enough lifetimes for anyone."

"How old were you when you first gave birth?"

The woman studied the girl closely. "I was fifteen years old. That seems like almost an eternity ago. It was certainly a world away from here."

"Was it nice? Where you grew up?" the girl looked sheepish. "We don't have to talk about it, not if you don't want to?"

"I was born in 'the lands between the seas'. We settled in a valley in the Mountains. It was very pretty in the summer, with a burst of purple poppies carpeting the meadow. Yet, it was cruel in the winter. Many of us, including a great many infants and children, died in the winter" the woman sighed sadly.

"Do you think it will be a boy?" the girl asked shyly.

"Would you like another little brother?" the woman

raised an eyebrow mockingly. She had already guessed the answer.

"I would prefer a little sister, if that does not give offence."

The woman grinned at the child. "You do love your little brother, don't you?"

"Of course, I do!" the child chimed. "But I would prefer a little sister rather than a little brother. Kassandra has three brothers, older and younger, and they tease her incessantly for not being a boy!"

"I had an older brother, a long time ago, and he found it hard growing up with three sisters!"

"You are a twin, are you not? Those that look the same, rather than the other sort?"

"I was an identical twin. My sister died when you were very young, I doubt that you would even remember her?"

"I am afraid I don't. I am sorry" the girl looked sad.

"Death is never easy, my child. It leaves a hole that can never be filled."

"I feel like that some days, not as often as I used to, yet it still aches."

"I know how much it does, my little pearl. I have had more than enough pain for a thousand lifetimes" the woman sighed sadly.

"Father also feels sad, doesn't he? I know that he does, but we never talk about it?" the girl said meekly.

The woman studied the girl closely once more. Artemis was the imago of her true mother, or so her father always said, and there was little that slipped her notice. Of course, her father still missed her mother! Perhaps he still secretly loved her, as she still secretly loved her own childhood sweetheart, the boy to whom she had given everything: her heart, soul, and her virginity. *Though not on her wedding night!* "We can talk about it, Artemis, if you would like to? We can talk about your true mother anytime you want to, I promise. I think that your father would like it if we did?"

"I can't really remember all that much of her, for I was very little when the fever took her, wasn't I?"

"Yes, my little rose, you were" the woman said simply. "And yet, I am sure she would be so proud of the young Lady you are fast becoming. As are your father and I, of course."

"I often do wonder what she would think of who I am becoming?" sighed Artemis.

"You need not worry your sweet little head, darling child. I am certain that she would be ever so proud of your skills with a needle. Oh my!" the woman smiled and glanced at her swollen belly.

"Did he just kick you?" Artemis grinned. "I think that *she* just did so?"

"She? I thought you said the baby was a boy?" Artemis frowned.

"I am Sauromatae, my sweet child, and our girls kick harder than boys. It is our nature!"

"I have heard it said that you are a fierce people, is that not so? That you brought down the Assyrian Empire?" the girl watched the woman steadily.

"You should not believe such myths! That was a long time ago. You will be asking to see my secret horns and tail soon enough!" the pair chuckled together.

"Father once told me that you had boys and a girl? Did the girl kick harder when she was almost due? Is that how you know?"

The woman looked stricken, tears welling instantly in her eyes. "I am sorry, Artemis, I can't.I can't remember."

TWO

Tanais, June 493 BC

The visitor, fast approaching his sixth decade of life, reached the Hellenic polis of Tanais on the northeast shore of the Azovi shortly after dusk. He had taken the precaution of a brief respite at a local hostelry in the southern part of the city. The last leg of the journey was undertaken as the sun finally waned. Whilst Tanais lay firmly within the realms of the Ur'gai Royal Duchy, under the terms of the *Accord Scythiac*, Orch'tai military patrols were now commonplace on the outskirts of the city. In the interests of security, the visitor had refrained from visiting Tanais these past few moons, yet this journey was a matter of necessity. He had been astonished by the persistence of the Orch'tai cavalry on route and, whilst he had not been either accosted or molested, their casual manner had left him deeply perturbed. Under the explicit terms of the *Accord Scythiac*, "the lands between the seas" were effectively a Protectorate of the Argata, yet it was almost as if it were an Orch'tai dominion! *The Ur'gai must surely recognise the grave danger to their own interests in the Crimea, and that of the Hellenics, that now manifest itself so flagrantly in the immediate east?*

It was still yet light when the stranger arrived at a villa on the northwest outskirts of Tanais. His host had been surprised to see him. They were old friends, but if the younger man had been disconcerted by his impromptu visitor it had been carefully guarded. As his horse was stabled by a trusted servant, the visitor had been shepherded inside to a small study where he had graciously accepted a large measure of Scythian plum wodki served in an exquisite silver goblet. Zirca eyed his visitor with genuine warmth. They were friends, not merely comrades in arms. "This is a pleasant surprise, old friend. I trust I find you well, dear Zir'ca?" said the visitor.

"I am in good health and spirits, for sure, yet for how long?" Zir'ca grinned.

"You think I am an ominous harbinger, my dear fellow?"

"It would be strange for you to be here otherwise, would it not?"

Naemas smiled thinly. "I departed Qu'ehra as soon as I received correspondence from our mutual friend?"

"You have read it, I presume? How was the ride from Qu'ehra?" said Zir'ca airily.

"I have been cautious, naturally, if that is of concern to you? Qu'ehra is a hotbed of intrigue, buzzing with the locusts of Susa and their supplicants."

"Things are no different here, I assure you. King Tagar is beset with melancholy by the death of his nephew. And yet, there are sinister elements who may wish to capitalise on his misfortune."

"Is there anything to the rumour that Persia might be inclined to favour the King's replacement?" Naemas whispered.

"Treachery is everywhere! Not least of all here" Zir'ca spoke softly. "King Tagar is blessed with daughters, all of whom have sired daughters, not a son among their seed. None are suitable to take the throne if the King should die. That creates a dangerous vacuum. One that is ripe for exploitation, you would agree?"

"I cannot envision any great joy among the populace at the prospect of the ascension of the Royal Princess

Naemoria and her consort to the throne, could you?"

Naemas smiled thinly. "Her eldest daughter, the Princess Lal'ya is held in deep affection. So too is her younger sister, the Princess Katal'ya."

"They are little more than babes! The eldest of the King's granddaughters are the sires of his youngest daughter, the Princess Sychoria. The eldest girl is some years shy of marriageable age. What of the Royal Princess Miskal'ya, the next in line?" ventured Naemas.

"Her husband comes from a good family. There is no question of that. Yet, he is currently engaged in the defence of the realm against the hordes east of the Wol'yi, or so some would have us believe?" Zir'ca mocked.

"I read your latest despatch. Do you place any credence in these rumours of an increased threat from the Sauromatae?"

"I do not, my friend! Something is clearly going on in the east" Zir'ca confessed. "The traffic of caravans west has been notably thin thus far this summer. There is talk of a moratorium on mercenaries, unswerving in their loyalty to King, being denied an opportunity to ply their trade east of the river."

"You think these rumours are a ruse? Deliberately crafted to justify an increase in military dispositions south of the Signet?" Naemas probed.

"I have intimated as such. We have confirmation of a sizable, mounted contingent to the west of Astrach'yi. You have notified the Ur'gai Royal Court of this recent intelligence?" Zir'ca asked searchingly.

"They seem unconvinced, and unperturbed, to put it mildly" Naemas sighed. "Our esteemed friend appears to have received some quite disturbing recent revelations concerning this, and other, pertinent matters" The coded communique, hand delivered to his home in Qu'ehra a few days previously inside a sealed silver ingot, is now slid across the table to the younger man. The parchment is rolled tightly and is held fast by a small bronze ringlet, securing it at it's the centre.

Zir'ca reads the communique in silence. His brow furrows as he decodes and registers its importance. When he has finished, he gazes meaningfully at the older man. "I shall leave first thing tomorrow morning. This must be safely delivered to the Royal Palace at Rost'eya with haste! You agree?"

Naemas sighed despondently. "That is precisely why I came, my young friend. It is obvious that things are moving in a dangerous direction. We may already be too late to prevent the inevitable?"

"I disagree, my old friend. The Ur'gai can surely prevent a war, only they have the military might to face down the Orch'tai."

"What of the Argata? Are they of such little concern? I strongly advise you not to underestimate the guile of Queen Lezika in such intrigue. There are few who can rival her skills in endeavours such as this!" Naemas insisted.

"The real threat is surely from the east, and not the south? Whilst the Argata have considerable influence with the Phoenicians, they would never challenge the Hellenics in the Aegean?" Zir'ca protested.

"And what of the rumours of a new fleet, commissioned by King Darius himself. This fleet is under construction in the shipyards of Tyre, built with timbers sourced from the Orch'tai" Naemas pressed.

"If there is any truth in these rumours, and I know they are taken seriously by some with the ear of the Ur'gai Queen, it would be at least another summer before this fleet is ready to venture into the Aegean?"

"We must pray, my old friend, that your assessment of their capacity is true! The Phoenicians are adept shipbuilders, are they not? They have a large navy, and this fleet has been bolstered with additional vessels commissioned by Persia. We have the spectre of additional vessels flying the flag of those treacherous Cypriots! Whilst there is little in the way of reliable intelligence to confirm our worst fears, there are some who fear that a Persian fleet would be ready to venture by the autumn?" Naemas postulated.

"Whilst that is true, if those new ships had failed to materialise.?"

Naemas' eyes twinkle with mischief. "It would be a grave setback to Persian ambition, would it not? You have everything you need, and I have done my solemn duty. You must ensure this communique reaches our friends in Rost'eya. Everything depends upon it!"

"I will not fail, I swear it!" Zir'ca replied solemnly.

"No more the moon, old friend!" said Naemas.

"No more the moon!"

～

Saiga Plains, Crimea, July 493 BC

Yari shivers lightly in the chill of the early morning breeze as she pours boiling water on the fresh mint leaves and stirs the kettle vigorously. The day was a few hours old, and the temperature was still cool, yet the promise was of another beautiful summer's day. Yari loved the Crimea, for its climate was far more hospitable than the barren steppe, and the mornings thus far had been blissful. She had even enjoyed her training, for her horsemanship was improving with each passing year and her skill with a sword even more so, as it would need to, if she hoped to survive the crucible of her first combat. Yet, it was not the thought of mortal combat; the dread of killing, or being killed, even horribly disfigured like old Elin'ya, an ancient crone now in her fifth decade of life, which worried her this morning. The slave-girl sighs despondently and continues stirring the mint leaves in the boiling water.

"I would trade a honeycomb for your thoughts, little bear?"

A startled Yari looks up quickly to see Corelya standing at the side of the tent, smiling wryly. She had not even heard the other girl approach, not a good sign for a soldier! Corelya is dressed in her combat uniform, her sword at her right hip, twinned-daggers at her left, leaf-fanned armoured tunic, cradling a Corinthian helmet with its beautiful ornate red plume. "I didn't see you there!" Yari mumbled. "Would you like some tea?"

"That would be lovely, thank-you!" Corelya strode across to the small fire and knelt across, facing Yari. "You are angry with me, are you not?"

"No" Yari effected an astonished tone.

"You cannot lie for a honeycomb, Yar'? You never could!" Corelya smiled to soften the blow.

"Do you have to go?"

"You know I do" Corelya replied sternly. "Alone?"

"I can't take you with me, Yari. You know I can't" Corelya plucked a handful of twigs from the ground beside the fire and began to add them, one at a time.

"I could come part of the way. I could leave you at the west bank of the Donets?" Yari insisted.

"That is more than part of the way, Yari" Corelya giggled. "And besides, if we both go, they might think that we will escape once we cross the Donets. We are slaves, after all."

"They think we might head south. That we would run for the safety of the forests and the Mountains?" Yari groaned.

"They don't trust us, do they?" Corelya hissed softly.

"They don't even know the first thing about me, even after all these years! Some of these Scythians really are as dumb as dogshit! I don't wish to see the Mountains ever again!"

Corelya is stung by the outburst. "The mountains

are in our blood, Yari! More than that, they are in here!" Corelya admonished her, pointing at her chest where she thought her heart and soul lay sacred within its skeletal cage. "Our village was slaughtered by Argata, but we will always still Sauromatae! Nothing will ever change that. We will never be Ur'gai. They own us, we are slaves."

"Have some tea! As good as I have ever made!" Yari proffered a wooden goblet to her closest friend and confidant. "I do not think we should talk of such things?" she whispered.

"Not even in Sarmati?" Corelya ventured.

"Gor'ya speaks a little Sarmati? We taught her, remember?"

"You do not trust her?" Corelya whispered.

"Sirch'i is getting married in the autumn, isn't she? I think Gor'ya will be feeling lonely, sooner rather than later" Yari ventured airily.

"What of it?" Corelya responded in puzzlement. "Gor'ya is old enough to take a lover of her own, isn't she? There are a few girls coming of age soon enough."

"I suppose there are" Yari glances sideways and grins. Corelya's eyes widen and blaze.

"You *are* kidding, Yari?"

"You are old enough to be inducted in to the 'mysteries'" Yari snickered. "So are you! You are older, remember?" Corelya hissed, blushing furiously.

"Oh Corelya, sweet Corelya, please be my baby forever? At least until we can find a man dumb enough, ugly enough, and drunk enough, to be your husband" Yari was laughing hysterically.

"You are not in the least amusing, Yari? You think you are, but you're not!"

"Corelya and Gor'ya up a tree, Kay-eye, Kay-eye, Corelya and Gor'ya up a tree, K-I-S-S-I-N- G!" Yari was clearly enjoying herself. Only she could ever tease Corelya so without fear of immediate physical retribution. "You will make her tingle, from her head to her 'wingle'!"

"I shall make your nose tingle in a minute, Yari-Bear!" Corelya bridled.

"I can't remember the last time you called me that, Cory-Boo?" Yari smiled sweetly. She came round the fire and sat down next to Corelya on the grass.

"I miss home, Yari! I really do!" Corelya sighed.

"They will never let us leave, will they?"

"No! We will most likely be killed in a fight!" Corelya mused cynically.

"You can be quite the optimist, some mornings? Do you know that Cory-Boo?" Yari snakes her right arm around Corelya's neck. "Just promise me that you will take care of yourself. That you will come home safe and sound, as soon as you can. That you won't do anything rash.." Yari trailed off mid-sentence. "That is silly of me, isn't it? I am asking you to be someone else, am I not?"

"I cannot change who I am, Yari. Neither can you?" Corelya sighed.

"Not even the Gods could conjure such a miracle! I do love you for who you are, Corelya. Sometimes I wish I could be a little more like you."

"Sometimes I wish I could be a little more like you, Yari."

"I can always teach you how to make a decent brew of mint tea!" Yari snickered.

"I already know how to make tea! I just don't expect that it will ever taste as good as yours."

The rest of Corelya's day was spent on administrative tasks in preparation for the forthcoming mission deep in to Orch'tai territory. She would leave that evening, travelling alone, giving herself a few hours ride across open country to find a suitable camp for the night. Yari returned in the late afternoon from sword practice nursing a cut on her shoulder, apparently inflicted by Sorel'yi, a girl of similar age. Corelya treated the wound with ointment and dressed it. It should heal naturally in a few days. By all accounts, Yari's at least, honours had been even and Sorel'yi was nursing a broken nose. Corelya soon learned that Sorel'yi's misfortune was a source of bemusement to those blessed with sufficient wealth to wager as to whether the disfigurement would diminish her marital prospects to Milo'ch, a Prince from a neighbouring clan.

Corelya and Yari ate a light evening meal of bread, cheese, and wodki and, as her best friend settled down to slumber, Corelya mounted Sybillya, her trusty mare named in honour of a murdered mother and headed southwest toward Chersonesus. She soon arrived at the Causeway, the main track that skirts the woodland of the coastal fringe of the southern peninsula, linking the eastern port of Nymphaion with the western polis of Chersonesus, principal Hellenic city in the Crimea. If she were being followed, and this possibility could not be discounted, then she was simply conveying a message on behalf of her Majesty, benign or otherwise, and would not be hindered.

Corelya rode until nightfall and camped near a small stream, tethering Sybillya to a tree, lighting a fire and rolling out her sleeping blanket. She drank a further draught of wodki, tended the fire to ensure that it would burn for a further few hours and climbed a tree to keep sentry. This was the dangerous time. Brigands and assassins close quickly to the kill in thinly inhabited territory, and, despite the proximity of Queen Illir'ya's Household Division, the annals of past Royal Retainers had been written in blood. Nearly all were slaves, and few had died peacefully in their sleep. Yet, none were blessed with Corelya's alleged gift of 'second sight'. Despite the dangerous developments in the Ionian Sea which had culminated in war between Persia and the historic polities of the western Anatolia, the young Queen's dovish disposition, coupled with the enviable skill of her wise Counsellors, had nurtured a climate of rare harmony among the disparate Ur'gai clans. During Illir'ya's seven-year reign, including three years as Regent following her ascent to the throne at the tender age of twelve, nobody had ever tried to assassinate her. Among the Ur'gai, such popularity of a Monarch was unthinkable! *None of her predecessors had ruled this long without at least one attempt on their life by a disgruntled pledged allegiant.*

Corelya's victims numbered among them a few minor scions of noble Ur'gai clans' whose loyalty had wavered in the wrong direction, a Theban merchant who had greatly displeased Her Majesty by his brazen dishonesty and naked contempt for his clientele and, most recently, a plenipotentiary of the Orch'tai Royal Court to the Persian Royal Court at Susa. This last victim, despatched several months earlier, was a man of considerable talent yet, regrettably, an ability to swim was not among them. The poor soul had drowned, albeit in mysterious circumstances, on route by sea from Panticapaeum to the southwestern Black Sea port of Hopa. Corelya's main worry this night was the threat of brigands, as opposed to assassins. A few hours later, the girl climbed down from the tree and slept for a few hours.

⌒

"It was good of you to come, at such a late hour?" said the man.

"That annoying little bitch left camp a few hours ago, heading in the direction of Chersonesus, or so I am told?" the woman scowled.

"You would have me kill her?"

"Is that so strange for you to understand, after what she did?"

"No, it is not. Yet, we have little to gain by killing her, at least for the moment. In due time, you will have your vengeance. I have promised you such, have I not?"

"You have" the woman nodded eagerly. "I have heard

that she spoke privately with the Queen. Have you learned the matter which they discussed?"

"I have not? Have you?"

"I would not be asking if I had done so, would I?" the woman hissed. "Is this like the last time?"

"There was no last time! There is nothing to substantiate your wild fantasy that Corelya was involved in that unsavoury little incident in Tyre?" the man smiled thinly.

"What of the death of Ach'ti? Corelya was away from Rost'eya the whole time?" the woman pressed.

"Do you really believe this little slave bitch could accomplish such feats, surely not?"

"She is dangerous! You do not know her! Not like I do!" the woman remonstrated.

"I keep my dealings with her to the bare minimum. She is a trusted confidante of the Queen, is she not?"

"It is not natural! She is not even one of us!" the woman protested.

"And yet, if you are not alone in suspecting Corelya's involvement in such barbarism, one may wonder what our erstwhile friends would make of such revelations? I have a good idea where she has gone and, if I am correct in my presumption, there may yet be an opportunity to use this misplaced enthusiasm to our advantage."

"To besmirch her loyalty, and damn her, in the eyes of the Queen and Counsel?"

"What an excellent idea, my sweet. I think we may yet find a means to accomplish such a feat."

"Our agents in Nymphaion and in 'the lands between the seas'?" the woman ventured. "That would be my inclination, of course."

"When will you do this? Surely time is of the essence?"

"Is that all that is 'of the essence', my darling?" the man asked silkily.

"I have not the faintest idea of what you mean?" the

woman blushed hotly.

"I was thinking of a ride out in the morning, and a pleasant spot of fishing. It promises to be yet another beautiful day."

"Yes, I would like that. Perhaps we could go to the waterfall again?"

"Of course, my sweet, for your wish, is my command."

"You do know that I love you, don't you?" the woman beseeched.

"Of course, I do, my darling. But now, you must leave. You are, after all, another man's wife?"

It was still cool, as it had been for the past few mornings, as Corelya woke and packed her belongings for the days journey. She planned to ride for a few hours southwest before stopping for breakfast at a favoured spot that she and Yari knew well. The day was glorious, with not a cloud in the sky, as Corelya coaxed Sybillya to a gallop and they effortlessly cover mile after mile of some of the richest pasturelands in the entire Duchy. Strangely, despite the veritable bounty of the southern Crimea, it was, due to its recent acquisition and strategic significance, sparsely inhabited. Corelya dismounted at the spot, situated by a small stream a few hours ride from the outskirts of Chersonesus, lit a fire, and fished lazily for an hour or so. Having caught and gutted sufficient fish for this day and the morrow, she remounted Sybillya and headed northeast along the worn track linking Chersonesus with the northern Black Sea city of Olbia. Beyond Olbia, the track continued north to the capital at Trakhtemirov, a fortified settlement on the banks of the Borysthenes, the principal artery flowing into the hinterlands of the steppe. Corelya had travelled this journey many times before and knew full well that the bounty and security of the coastal woodland fringe would not last long beyond this night.

~

Nymphaion, July 493 BC

Naeschaxes frowned at the communique, delivered to his door by urgent messenger a few moments earlier, hailing from one of the known traitors within the Ur'gai Royal Camp. The message had been delivered in the early hours to a Spice Merchant in the Northern Quarter, a reliable source with unswerving loyalties to the Orch'tai Royal Court and, once its origins and significance had been verified, it had passed to a trusted intermediary in the Business District. The communicant was a soul of limited guile, for this was no true code. The message was drafted in Hellenic and read as follows:

Scythian rose has dispersed her seedlings to the Great Heartlands
Beware a Golden Handmaiden – Westerly winds of the Azovi
Treachery beware – The Queen of the Plains – A deathly ploy
The Young Retainer – A moon to fade – No guileless boy

Naeschaxes re-reads the communique and smiles thinly. He had grave doubts as to an allegation of a plot to kill 'The Queen of the Plains', an obvious reference to Queen Lezika of the Argata, yet such a rumour could have dangerous consequences if it were dispersed far and wide, reaching the ears of Argata agents in 'the lands between the seas'!

And so, the young Queen had sent a trusted messenger, a Handmaiden no less, perhaps travelling alone, to the Great Steppe to investigate the shores of the Azovi west of Astrach'yi. He had heard the whispers, of course, yet had paid them little heed. Was it not true that Queen Illir'ya's reputed Royal Retainer was a girl? And not just any girl! A child of foreign blood, no less! The communique would not require a re-draft, for there was little to add to its piquancy. Instead, it would be ferried across the straits that very day by his most trusted messenger. More to the point, there was little to be gained by clearing this with their Chief Agent in Nymphaion, was there? Not in such a trivial matter such as this? It would go to the 'Hawk' himself, and none other!

~

Qu'ehra, July 493 BC

Naeschaxes trusted messenger had caught the early morning ferry across the Straits from Nymphaion, disembarking at the North Quay. The man had stopped for a brief restorative draught of wodki at *The Lion of Judah*, on the outskirts of the Wharf, to banish the morning chill from his bones before spurring east. He arrived at Qu'ehra a few hours later and arranged for his mount to be stabled at the rear of the famed hostelry, *The Silk Road*, in the Central Square. Once inside, he ordered a jar of the famed rye beer, a large goblet of wodki, and made enquiries with the serving-girl as to the whereabouts of the home of Assikander the Goldsmith. His master desired an urgent commission as a keepsake for an esteemed friend. He was informed that Assikander lived just across the square at the corner house, yet it was unlikely that he would be home, given the eager throng of shoppers in the Bazaar, even at this early hour. The traveller, a seasoned hand named Saelaes, suspected that emissaries of the Goldsmith would likely attempt to contact him, as soon as they had learned of his arrival in Qu'ehra. He would simply bide his time for a few hours, leisurely sipping a few beers and wodki chasers, followed by a bite to eat, and then a pleasant ride back to the Wharf in time for the evening ferry. It was not a bad assignment at all, upon reflection. He was not to be disappointed.

Sometime later, a young teenager, garbed in the elegant attire befitting a retainer to a wealthy Merchant, sauntered into the bar and made a brief enquiry with the barmaid, whom he knew well. The barmaid nodded in the direction of the corner table where Saelaes sat alone, and the young man strolled across carrying a small tray of wodki goblets. "Forgive my intrusion, Honourable friend. I am Alsa'kir, servant of Assikander the Goldsmith, the man you seek. Alas, my master is at the Bazaar, and I do not expect his return for some time."

"I am Saelaes. I have an urgent commission for your master, young man. I have come at the behest of my own master, Naeschaxes of Nymphaion, and it is most urgent." Saelaes spoke softly.

"Perhaps if you had a design in mind, something on parchment, then I could convey this with haste to my master upon his return."

"Indeed, I do, young man. It is a highly intricate design, a work of considerable beauty, some might say. It is to be a gift for an esteemed friend."

"Assikander of Qu'ehra is a man without equal in such things. I am confident we could do justice to your master's designs, especially for such an esteemed friend?"

"There is none held higher in my master's affection than Nichassor of Pasargadae" Saelaes smiled thinly.

Alsa'kir nodded. "You have my trust and my confidences, dear friend, as does your master. I am certain that we can accommodate your request, especially for such an esteemed friend as Nichassor of Pasargadae."

Saelaes fished inside his robe and withdrew a small purse, together with a single freshly minted silver coin, and slipped them across the table, where they were quickly pocketed by the young Alsa'kir. "See that you do, young friend. My master is most insistent in this matter."

"It will be done, Sir. Upon my honour, I swear it!" Alsa'kir beseeched. He drained his goblet of wodki in a single gulp. "Now, if you will forgive me, dear friend. I have urgent matters to attend to."

"I understand, my young friend. You have my master's trust and confidence in this matter, as always" said Saelaes.

"Are you in Qu'ehra for the afternoon?" the boy asked slyly.

"I planned to take the evening ferry back to Nymphaion. What of it?" Saelaes said guilelessly.

"Perhaps you might wish to indulge yourself in the delights of Qu'ehra. There is a girl next door named Nili'cha, who comes highly recommended. I am certain she could give you a time to remember?"

"Perhaps she will, dear friend! Perhaps she will?"

～

By sundown, Corelya reached a stretch of woodland which promised security for the night, a bounty of kindling for a fire, and good fallow for Sybillya. Corelya checked her crossbows and donned her helmet. She rode tentatively into the woodland and scouted a perfect spot for the night, a large hazel tree close to a bend in a stream. Corelya lit a fire and drank greedily from the stream. It had been an incredibly hot day, perhaps the warmest of the year thus far and she and Sybillya were exhausted from the day's exertions. A brew of mint tea tasted almost as good as if Yari had made it and Corelya scoured fresh mint and wild basil from a nearby patch, more than enough to last the week. After a meal of poached fish, mint tea, and a draught of wodki, Corelya settled into nearby tree and kept sentry until the moon was high in the night sky. The night's sleep was blissful and uneventful. Corelya feared she would need it, for, on the morrow, she would enter the crucible of the steppe, an unforgiving landscape bereft of woodland and sparsely populated by prey, friends, or foes.

The morning was decidedly chilly. The sky is ominously overcast. Corelya sits by the stream sipping scalding mint tea as Sybillya drank and foraged nearby. She had filled two flagons with fresh water, ready to be tied to her saddle, and had breakfasted on poached fish cooked the previous night. Corelya galloped steadily north for the next few hours, by which time the woodland had long disappeared and the landscape was carpeted forebodingly as far as the eye could see only by shrub, gorse, and grass. This was the steppe, a vast expanse of nothingness which seemed to stretch forever. Corelya had often pondered quite how the Ur'gai had reached the pinnacle of regional supremacy given the abject poverty of the land they laid claim to! The present Scythian Ducal States, the Nur'gat, Ur'gai, Orch'tai, and Argata had been forged in the geopolitical crucible of the past half Century, sired by coalescence of disparate factions into frictional geographic confederacies in the turmoil after the demise of Lydia and the emergent threat of Persia. Ur'gai supremacy among the Scythian Ducals owed more to geography than anything else. Their heartland, the Great Steppe, was scarred by a series of great rivers, including the Bug to the west, upon which the principal Hellenic polis of Olbia was sited. In the east, they commanded much of the coastline of the Azovi Sea, demilitarized under the *Accord*, and in the middle, the northern Black Sea coast and the 'labyrinth', gateway to the peninsula itself.

⌒

In contrast with the Ur'gai heartlands of the Great Steppe, scarred by its network of rivers: the Bug, Borysthenes, Donets and Don from west to east, which supported dense gallery woodlands rich in wild fruits, nuts, fish, and game, the steppe of the north and central Crimea is largely uninhabited. *Uninhabitable*, or *plain bloody inhospitable*, would be more appropriate descriptor, Corelya mused cynically. This was 'home' only to transitory bands of nomadic caravans, replete with herds of horse and sheep, and rare bands of predatory brigands foolish enough to harass them. Few did, for the ferocity of these Scythian nomads in defence of their families and property was legendary. A few hours later, Corelya dismounted and allowed Sybillya to graze and drink from a proffered bowl of water as she scans the ground adjacent to the track for evidence of recent passage. On the strength of the evidence, or absence thereof, not a soul had passed this way during the past weeks. On the one hand, this was comforting, as an absence of caravans meant an absence of predatory marauders. It was well known that bands of brigands were invariably 'tipped off' about the passage of travelling convoys before they had even left Chersonesus. On the other, it was more than a little dispiriting, as she would be truly alone in this forsaken place.

A short while later, fortified by a draught of wodki, Corelya remounted and set off northwards across the open expanse of plain. By the mid-afternoon, judging by the locus of the sun in the sky, she surmised that they must now have reached the heart of the peninsula itself, and had yet to encounter a soul. She espied a suitable re-entrant on a series of low hills to her left which seemed oddly out of place in a landscape devoid of natural sculptures and decided to rest for a few hours. They would not camp here for the night, she decided, and instead would ride on until dusk. Now that the sky had cleared of clouds, the re-entrant would provide welcome shelter from the day's heat. Sybillya could rest for a time whilst she could make good strategic use of the high ground to scan the landscape for potential threats, especially from the south. The re-entrant transpired to be far broader than it appeared from a distance, large enough to house a few wagons for an evening's camp. Indeed, to her surprise, there *was* evidence of human presence in the form of a large hearth and a considerable quantity of ash. This told her two things: that a small group had camped here, perhaps for several nights and had done so very recently, yet the heat from the ash caused her to curse with surprise. *They must have left here just this morning on route northwards; else their paths would surely have crossed in the past few hours!*

Corelya quickly scrambles up the hill and began to survey the surrounding landscape with a soldier's eye. It was completely bereft of woodland or humanity. Suddenly, a glint of sunlight reflecting on metal catches her eye, far on the horizon to the south! Then, a second glint of reflection, and.. a third: riders! It was possible that a single rider was approaching, but this seemed unlikely. Corelya lay on the ground and quickly checked her weapons, removing her helmet and shrouding this with her cloak. It would be several hours before they caught up with her, but she would be able to precisely determine their strength with sufficient time to make her escape without discovery. If it were necessary, she could easily change tack and head for the safety of the ferry crossing with Olbia on the northwest coast. An eternity seemed to pass before she was able to accurately appraise their strength and quality of their steeds. The four riders, all clad in armour which dazzled in the reflection of the brilliant sun, were mounted on steeds as swift and as sure as Sybillya. The horsemen were at least an hour's ride away and must surely stop to rest in the next few hours, whereas Sybillya was now refreshed and could keep at a gallop for hours to come. *It was time to leave!*

Corelya spurred Sybillya to a gallop. They headed north, following the course of track. There was little point in glancing behind, it was better simply to keep scanning the horizon for signs of the travellers who camped in the re-entrant the previous night. Within hours, the temperature had chilled perceptibly and Corelya afforded herself the luxury of slowing Sybillya to a trot and halting briefly, turning to the rear to scan for any pursuers. The four riders were nowhere in sight. Satisfied that she must now be at least several hours ahead, she chided her steed to a gallop in the increasing cool of the early evening and cautiously appraised the landscape for any sign of human encampment. It was about an hour or so later that she espied, as clear as the setting of the sun in the sky to the west, a suite of campfires on the northeast horizon, presumably not far from the course of the track.

Corelya coaxes Sybillya to a stop, retrieves her Corinthian helmet from its sacking, and indulgently preens its ornate plume. She donned this and secured the chinstrap, before spurring on into the light of the setting sun. It would be nice to have some company for the evening, she thought, and, provided she were able to convince them that she was friendly, she could expect a warm welcome and wine in return. The hospitality of nomadic Scythian caravans was as legendary as their ferocity, yet only to those who offered hospitality and courtesy in return. Corelya carried spices, liniments, and a comparable fortune in gold and silver ingots, carefully hidden in her clothing, spare dress, and saddlecloth.

∼

Sounds and smells are heightened at night as the visual senses dim. Corelya's eyes had gradually adjusted to the dimming light as the sun faded to yield to the glory of a crescent moon. It was not surprising that the dogs heard, and likely even *smelt*, the girl and her mare as they approached, barking wildly in cacophony, long before she herself became cognisant of the unmistakable tang of burning wood, the enticing aroma of roasting flesh and the animated chatter of a large, familial, fireside gathering. The chatter died suddenly as she dismounted, adjacent to the track, a safe distance from their campsite, and led Sybillya toward the three fires.

"Have you come to die?" a voice challenged her in Scythian, coarse, cold, and unseen.

"I have come to eat, drink, and be merry!" Corelya chirruped. This was met with peals of mirth from a congregation of assembled children.

"We will decide your fate this night, missy!" another voice growled. The joyous peals of children's laughter were icily silenced.

"And Queen Illir'ya will decide yours!" Corelya bridled. "You will obey the Ur'gai Queen's command whilst you continue to enjoy Her Majesty's protection, or else suffer Her Majesty's displeasure" she hissed. "However, for the now, you may revel in Her Majesty's grace. If you have wine, then I have silver."

"You are with Queen Illir'ya's Household?" a female voice enquired.

"I am one of Her Majesty's Handmaidens. I am Corelya."

"Are you armed?" the first male asked. Any hostility had now quelled.

"Indeed, I am" Corelya replied. "So too are the four horsemen following the track behind me. I have no knowledge of whom they serve, yet I can assure you that they are not with me."

"They are mercenaries. They serve whoever pays them the most" the woman spat contemptuously.

"Where are they from?" Corelya enquired.

"They are Orch'tai. They hail from the lands of the Wol'yi and offer protection against the brigands, for a price, of course. At least that is what we have heard" a second male stepped forward to face her. He was not armed. "I am Sar'chai. I own one of these wagons and this is my family" he nodded to cluster of two adult females and a coterie of children, including a baby, settled around one of the smaller fires. The women nodded warily and the older children, a boy aged about five years-old and a very young girl, acknowledged her with a brief wave and silence. "This is my brother, Kir'gai, and his family" he pointed to the larger fire where Kir'gai nodded politely. He was older than Sar'chai and had two adult sons. "That is my eldest son, Nar'gai, and his family", Kir'gai jerked his thumb towards a smaller fire on the right where a young adult male and female sat with two small girls, presumably twins. "This is my younger son, Nir'gat." Corelya smiled warmly at an athletic young man aged about seventeen-years, she guessed, who greeted her warmly with a flash of teeth.

"You are Orch'tai?" Corelya enquired.

"We are not. We are Ur'gai, just like you!" a woman countered brusquely.

"I am Sauromatae, and yet I serve Queen Illir'ya of the Ur'gai" Corelya replied softly. "You are in Ur'gai territory, under your Queen's protection, yet these mercenaries levy fees for your security?"

"They have not levied fees against us, at least not yet. We have only been here for the past few days" replied Sar'chai. "We were heading to Chersonesus to sell poppy oil and spices from the Orient, in addition to some of our mares, but we were informed by a fellow trader we met that we could get a better price for our goods in Olbia."

Corelya believed him, yet she had grave suspicions as to the truth of what they had been told, for it simply defied logic. Chersonesus was the principal Hellenic trading port in the northern Black Sea. Whilst it admittedly paled in comparison with Olbia in size and opulence, it traded directly with Athens and Corinth, whereas Olbia received most of its exotic goods via Chersonesus. What seemed on cursory appraisal to be a preposterous arrangement constituted a phenomenally successful mercantile system that had evolved over the course of a Century. The merchants of Chersonesus assumed a proportion of the risk of loss of any shipment from Athens and, therefore,

Hellenic goods were priced slightly higher in Olbia to offset costs of the risks borne by the merchants in Chersonesus. In contrast, goods travelling across land from the Orient were shipped to Athens via both Olbia and Chersonesus on an equal footing and merchantmen assumed no burden of the cost for losses on route. If a particular commodity from the Orient became scarce, prices would rise in both Olbia and Chersonesus, and internal dynamics of supply and demand would effectively stabilise prices between the polities.

"Were you not surprised to learn that the merchants in Olbia would pay more for your goods?"

"Yes. We were" confirmed Kir'gai. "We were told that things had changed for the worse during the past few months. An increased threat from bands of brigands in the Crimean steppe has led to shortages of exotic goods in Olbia and Chersonesus, yet merchants in Olbia will pay considerably more for our goods, at least according to the caravan we encountered. Prices in Chersonesus have been further driven down by the costs of these mercenaries. Their wages are paid by the merchants in Chersonesus and are then levied on traveller caravans in reduced fees they will pay for our goods."

"There are twenty thousand warriors from Queen Illir'ya's Household Division just over a day's ride away!" Corelya saw the look of absolute astonishment register on the faces of the adults. "I think it might be best if I talked with these conscientious souls who have anointed themselves guardians of all those who pass through Ur'gai lands."

"What should we do?" Sar'chai and Kir'gai glanced apprehensively at one another.

"You could fetch me a cup of wine, if you please?" Corelya sighed tiredly. "Beyond that you shall do nothing" there was an edge to her request that was truly disconcerting in one so young. "By my reckoning, they should reach us in just over an hour unless they have made camp for the night already. The dogs will let us know when they have arrived. In the meantime, I could do with a seat. I have been in the saddle since this morning."

"Come and have a seat with us, Corelya, if that pleases you?" Nar'gai's wife pointed to a patch of earth next to the twins that offered a good view of the ground to the front, including the track, and was invitingly close to the fire. "Nar'gai! Where are your manners? Get the child some wine! She is our guest!" she clucked. Corelya turned away and grinned at the twins who grinned delightedly back at her. Corelya graciously accepted a proffered cup of wine, thanked her hosts for their hospitality, and flopped down tiredly on the ground next to the twins.

"Hiya" she said.

"Hiya" the twins chirped in cacophony.

"And what are your names?"

"Aisa" said the first girl. "Isha" said the second.

"They are beautiful names. They suit you" said Corelya, earning a look of heartfelt bliss from their mother. They were identical twins. Corelya thought they were truly lovely. Aisa and Isha were scarcely more than toddlers, approaching their second birthday, considerably younger than either she or Yari had been when sold into slavery all those years ago.

"I am Anyela" she smiled broadly.

Corelya gauged that she would be aged in her late teens. "It is a pleasure to meet you, Anyela. Your daughters are absolutely beautiful" Corelya cooed.

"Thank you" she gushed.

Corelya noted that Nar'gai seemed quietly contemplative. "Are you expecting trouble?" Corelya whispered.

"I think *you* are, Corelya?" Nar'gai sighed sadly.

"Experience has taught me to prepare for the worst, as opposed to the best" Corelya sighed. "Do you have weapons?"

"I have several bows, plenty of arrows, a sword and daggers."

"I do not intend to instigate trouble, if that puts your mind at rest. I doubt you have any desire to pay them a levy, if they demand it?"

"Not especially" Nar'gai grunted. "We have never had to pay anyone before. I don't see why we should have to pay them now?"

"I have been on the plains for the past two nights and have not encountered any trouble at all. I had not even met anyone until I came across your camp" Corelya confessed. "I presume it was you who camped in the shelter of the re-entrant a few hours to the south for the past few days?"

"We camped there for the past two nights" Anyela confirmed.

"You struck camp this morning?"

"We left there a few hours ago. The mares were grazing and had to be rounded up. We fed the fire just this morning. I presume it was still warm?" said Nar'gai.

"It was. That is how I knew you must have been close. I saw the riders from the high ground. They were only a few hours behind me" advised Corelya.

"We have never had to pay a levy before to guarantee security in our own territory. Is this Queen Illir'ya's doing?" Anyela enquired in a hurt tone.

"It is not" Corelya replied evenly. "Her Majesty would not permit excessive banditry in the Crimea. It would be an intolerable threat to our protectorate and would be stamped out. Neither the Queen or Counsel have heard anything of this malaise, either from the City Father's, the Mercantile Guild, or from our own interests."

"The Ur'gai has 'interests' in Chersonesus?" Kir'gai seemed dismissive.

"We have mercantile interests in Chersonesus and Olbia, and, to a lesser degree, in Nymphaion and Panticapaeum. One cannot have financial interests without concomitant political exposure. Political stability is fertile ground for mercantile endeavour and, with it, increased prosperity. Political instability would jeopardise future investment in the Crimea" Corelya declared.

"And your 'interests' have said nothing about supposed threats from bandits preying on caravans supplying Chersonesus with Oriental exotics?" Kir'gai probed.

"If they had, we would have aggressively patrolled the steppe and the hinterlands of the 'labyrinth' to deal with such threats. Our warriors would relish the opportunity to engage them, you have my word on that, if that means anything?" soothed Corelya.

"If your word is the command of Queen Illir'ya, then that would suffice. Should we continue on our course to Olbia?" Kir'gai continued.

"That is entirely up to you. If you decide to turn around and head to Chersonesus you will not be molested. I was travelling alone these past few nights and I was not molested.

Perhaps we should wait and see what happens when our friends arrive. If they do not appear tonight, they will certainly be with us early on the morrow."

"So, we wait?" This was more a statement of fact, rather than a question, by Nar'gai.

"And so, we wait" Corelya said firmly.

They did not have long to wait. Within an hour, the dogs began to bark and the pounding of hooves on the track heralded the arrival of the four horsemen a short distance from the camp. Corelya had taken up a concealed position next to Nar'gai's wagon with a loaded crossbow, ready to fire. A second weapon lay loaded on the ground next to her. The children and women were safely corralled in the wagons. The adult males, five in number, all now armed, sit around the middle campfire, and await the arrival of the horsemen. In accordance with accepted convention, if one wished to avoid an arrow in the chest or a blade in the belly, two of the horsemen remained with their mounts whilst their leader and a companion plod cautiously towards the fire. They were unarmed, naturally. "A fine day's ride, you would agree?" their leader declared. He spoke Scythian, albeit with a heavy Orch'tai accent.

"Indeed, I would, friend! We hope the weather holds for the next few days" replied Kir'gai.

"Are you heading to Chersonesus?"

"We are heading to Olbia?" Kir'gai confirmed.

"The Gods have favoured you! Olbia is our destination. We left Chersonesus at dawn and have ridden all day."

"Have you met any fellow travellers on the road?" Sar'chai asked pointedly.

"Not a soul. In either direction, more is the pity!" said the first rider.

"More is the pity?" Kir'gai raised an eyebrow quizzically.

"Forgive me, please. I am speaking in riddles. We had hoped to encounter the marauding scum who have been threatening, and even murdering, merchant caravans on the steppe these past few moons. If truth be told, we were surprised to see you camped out here in the open, so vulnerable to attack, with no obvious protection. We rode as fast as we could to offer our services" their leader declared.

"Why would we need your protection?" Sar'chai asked in a dismissive tone.

"It is not safe, Sir. As I have said, merchants have been *killed, entire families*" the Orch'tai mercenary emphasised the prescient threat posed by the marauders.

"We have not heard of such things?" Sar'chai affected what he hoped was an appropriately disconcerted tone. "We have learned that the merchants in Chersonesus have become greedy of late. They have significantly reduced the price they will offer us for our goods. And so, we will head to Olbia and sell our wares to the merchants there."

"The merchants in Chersonesus have been severely

affected by the recent malaise. They sent emissaries to the Orch'tai Royal Court and urgently requested our services. Hence, we have come. The merchants are willing to pay the appropriate prices for your goods, yet they must levy a tariff for our services on all caravans travelling through the Crimea. I can assure you, gentlemen, it is not safe to travel to Olbia, not without appropriate protection" the Orch'tai leader continued with his depressing prognosis of the current situation.

"But we are Ur'gai. We are in Ur'gai territory and are under the personal protection of Queen Illir'ya!" Nar'gai replied coolly.

"That fact was of meagre comfort to those 'unfortunate families' who were brutally slaughtered these past few months."

"And our thoughts would be with those 'unfortunate families', if they ever even existed, that is?" Corelya stepped forward, the loaded crossbow aimed at the ground.

"And who might you be, child?" the mercenary growled.

"I have spent the past two nights on the road, if you must know. I have travelled alone, have not been molested, and was never in need of your protection!" Corelya replied evenly.

"You have come from Chersonesus, child?"

"I have ridden from the Saiga Plains and joined the track just north of Chersonesus. Queen Illir'ya has twenty thousand warriors from her Household Division camped there?"

"And we should believe you, girl?" he sneered.

"The Crimean Peninsula is an Ur'gai Protectorate, regardless of how that may sit with the Orch'tai Royal Court, or with King Tagar himself" Corelya smiled warmly. "All merchant caravans, regardless of their ethnicity, enjoy the protection of Queen Illir'ya. As do you and your comrades, it happens?"

"We are here at the specific request of the Guild of Merchants of Chersonesus to provide security for their commercial interests. We do not need the permission or protection of the Ur'gai Queen!" the leader hissed.

"May I see your bronze disks?" Corelya enquired politely, suppressing an urge to giggle as expressions of genuine consternation fleet across the faces of the two mercenaries.

"Bronze disks?" the leader asked in puzzlement.

"The same bronze disks that the Polis Militia in Chersonesus are obliged to always carry on their person by the City Father's and Council of the Merchants Guild. The Polis Militia is Ur'gai, are they not? I am sure you are well acquainted with the despairing rectitude of Hellenics by now?" Corelya smiled sweetly at the dumfounded mercenaries. "To legally carry weapons and enforce the peace within the city walls of Chersonesus, the Polis Militia must have sanction from the City Guardians, hence the disks they are obliged to carry on their persons at all times. Moreover, they are obliged to present these for inspection upon request by any citizen of the city. If not, they would right properly be viewed as a hostile force."

"But we are not in Chersonesus, child! Your request is denied" the leader smiled tightly.

"You are in Ur'gai territory, carrying weapons and are dressed for combat, and have no legal authority from Her Majesty to even be here. I reserve the right to request confirmation of your status. You must comply with this request and present your disks to me. Now, if you please! You are obliged to carry those disks with you at all times, as I have already reminded you" Corelya stated icily.

"And, if we refuse?" the leader sneered.

"You will be detained! Forcibly, if necessary" Corelya replied firmly.

"And, if we resist?" the leader snorted contemptuously.

"You can kiss your arse goodbye, sunshine!" Corelya

snapped. She stepped back and aimed the crossbow at the leader's head. The five adults stood immediately, swords in hand and fanned to the sides.

"Wait!" the leader gasped. "There is no need for this! We came in peace!"

"Then drink!" Corelya commanded. "There is wodki and wine. You are welcome to join us, and we have much to discuss. Sit!"

The two mercenaries look anxiously at one another and shuffle their feet uneasily. Corelya knew that she had rattled them and that a potentially explosive situation had been successfully diffused. "What of our comrades, my Lady? Are they welcome too?"

"You are all welcome to join us. But leave your weapons where they are?"

"And you would trust us? To spend the night in such proximity to your families?" the leader gaped.

"You have a new assignment" Corelya quipped.

"What would that be?" the leader stared open-mouthed, and boggle eyed at the girl.

"You are looking for work, is that not so? The Merchants Guild having not gifted you the relevant authority."

"We would be interested in a new assignment. We have families back in Mamy'eva" the man sighed resignedly. "Our services were engaged by Orch'tai merchants in Chersonesus, who misled us with promises of steady work. Instead, they sought to use us to collect outstanding debts owed to them! Treacherous bastards! It doesn't even pay well, when it pays at all!"

It was an old story, oft repeated. "You have my sympathies" Corelya spoke in a conciliatory tone. "And so, you passed word to every traveller caravan you met that the region was no longer safe, the prices they could expect for their wares would be far lower in Chersonesus, and that they might consider Olbia instead, is that it? You must have caused considerable pain for certain people in

Chersonesus, I would wager? Yet, I have little sympathy with those who have wronged you."

"Is that what we did" the leader grinned. "In all honesty, I have no idea how any rumour of increased banditry in the Crimean steppe started. And yet, it would be dishonest of us to deny that this furnished a steady income stream these past few weeks, or that it has caused considerable damage to certain people in Chersonesus."

Corelya grinned back. "But all good things must end. It might not be the worst thing to put some distance between your little band and certain interests in Chersonesus, especially if there were prospects of steady work in Olbia?"

"A change of scenery might not be the worst thing in the world. There is little to keep us in Chersonesus and things might get very sticky, rather quickly, if certain people were to learn the truth as to why their revenues have dried up these past few moons. If there are good prospects of work in Olbia, then that would be fine by us. I suppose you might be able, even willing, to provide a reference of our good conduct and performance over the next few days for the relevant authorities in Olbia?" the leader conceded.

"I don't honestly see why that should be a problem" Corelya smiled happily. "The Ur'gai have no authority within the city walls of Olbia, above or beyond the Orch'tai, Argata or Nur'gat. Nonetheless, if you can get these families and their goods safely across the Borysthenes, then I would be perfectly happy to provide accreditation. So, do we have an agreement?"

"We have an agreement!" the leader sighed ruefully. His comrade glanced meaningfully at him, shrugged, and turned toward the two warriors who had been left at the side of the track. "Hey! You two! We are invited to sit and drink! Get your arses over here"

THREE

Central Steppe of the Crimea, July 493 BC

Corelya is rudely awoken by a poppy tickling the end of her nose. The twins squeal delightedly as Corelya sneezes. She opens her eyes and yawns tiredly. "Hey! Pack that in! It's naughty!" she remonstrated playfully.

"Time to get-uppy! Time to get-uppy!" they chime happily. They were an incredibly beautiful sight on what was already promising to be yet another stunning morning.

"It is too early!" Corelya grumbled sleepily. She had secretly hoped for a lazy 'lie-in', yet nomadic Scythian and Sauromatae families invariably rose early, with the sun itself, to check on their animals and possessions.

"Breakfast!" the twins yelled.

"Time to get-uppy, it is, then!" she hollered back, smiling serenely as they skipped away towards their mother. Anyela kneels by the campfire, in a huddle with the other two women. She scolds the children half-heartedly and, seeing Corelya is awake, waves in greeting. "I need some tea" Corelya sighed. She grabs her knapsack, replete with the small leather pouch containing the precious mint-leaves, and pads across the grass towards the fire that Anyela and the other two women were tending obsessively.

"We will need a much larger fire for the next few hours, what with the additional company"

Anyela greeted her.

"Have the men left already?"

73

"Kir'gai is still here. He has not long left on foot and is shepherding the horses towards a stream a short distance north from here. Sar'chai and Nar'gai left about an hour ago, heading north on horseback. They took the other two boys with them, Kul'cha and Nir'gat, and those *mercenaries!*" she wrinkled her nose with distaste at the mention of the four Orch'tai warriors.

Corelya glances away and grins. "You don't like them?"

"I don't like their 'kind'!" Anyela hissed. "Men!" she spat. "Why are they always looking for trouble? They are just like little boys, for they are always looking to prove themselves! I do not know why? Especially the Orch'tai, they are not like us!"

"I don't know" Corelya ventured evenly. "I would wager that they are far more like us than we give them credit. You have travelled far beyond the Wol'yi, have you not? The Orch'tai face a prescient threat of attack from marauders from east of the Wol'yi."

"That is where your people hail from, is it not?" Anyela sighed despondently.

Corelya is momentarily stung. "The threat to Scythia does not come from the Sauromatae, despite what the Argata would have you all believe" she countered bitterly. "The real threat is from the peoples further east along the Silk Road. They are not civilised!"

"I have offended you. I am sorry" Anyela soothed.

"There is no offence taken, I assure you" Corelya smiled wryly. "Perhaps the Orch'tai are the most warlike of all Scythians simply because they have to maintain such a large army for protection. Large armies require constant pre-occupation, or else they seek other avenues to amuse themselves. Look at the Hellenics. They have maintained standing armies ever since the rise of Persia, far longer in the case of Sparta, yet these are rarely used except in the furtherance of mischief amongst themselves" Corelya sighed despairingly. "I sometimes wonder if the Persians are secretly laughing at us! They do not need to conquer us to assert their dominance in this world. They merely need to keep all of us in a state of perpetual hostility and distrust of our neighbours. We hiss at one another like cats on heat, and they simply sit back and sneer at us. If the Orch'tai were ever vanquished we would all be in trouble."

"You have not been introduced to Sar'chai's daughters, have you?" Anyela nodded to the older woman "This is Nai'cha" and then, nodding towards the younger woman cradling her baby, "and this is Sun'chi.

"It is lovely to meet you both!" said Corelya.

Anyela eyed the girl shrewdly. "You are a long way from the Royal Camp? Are you on your way back to Trakhtemirov?"

"I am conveying an urgent message to the Royal City of Rost'eya. I cannot say too much, obviously, save that it concerns the Persians" Corelya lied smoothly.

You do not like the Persians?" It was a statement, rather than a question.

"I admire their society. Their laws, their culture, and their magnificent buildings, but I do not trust them. I am Sauromatae, after all! They loathe us. They blame us for the destruction of Nineveh and the fall of Assyria!"

"Your people have suffered, that is true" Anyela conceded.

"No more so than others who labour under their yoke. I admire their civilisation, yet I detest their Empire and its brazen sense of superiority. It is dangerous. It is almost as if they feel they are destined to rule the world and enslave all others" Corelya mused bitterly.

"You are wise beyond your years, child. Why would a girl be interested in such things?"

"I am curious, that is all. I want to know everything about the world. Why things are the way they are? Why things change? Why things stay the same? Why they so often do not change for the better, at least not for most people. It seems to be an itch I just cannot scratch."

"You have been to Persia?" Anyela asked interestedly.

"I have travelled twice with Queen Illyria to the Royal Court of King Darius at Susa." Corelya blushed at the admission. "I am a member of the Royal Household, Anyela, it is not like I had any choice in the matter. The first time I was very young. I was only five years old. The second time I went there I was eight. Susa is stunning. It must be seen to be believed. They are truly magnificent builders of wonders I could never have credited had I not seen them with my own eyes."

"If they wish to enslave this miserable place, then they are welcome to it!" Anyela grinned.

Corelya giggled. "They seem to like it?" She nodded in the direction of Aisa and Isha, who were playing with one of the dogs. The weather was now far warmer, and the twins had disregarded their clothing and were as naked and as innocent as the day they were born. Corelya smiled at the reminiscence of happier memories from an eternity ago. "Everywhere and everything is an adventure when you are that age, don't you think? I remember being blissfully happy just playing with a stick and a patch of mud when I was their age."

"Where are your people from?" Anyela probed.

"We lived in the mountains, in 'the lands between the seas', to the south of Qu'ehra. It is now in the territory of the Argata, yet it was once free. My people settled in the plains and the forests to the north of the Caucasus, before the Assyrians made war on the Armenians, or so I was told. It was absolutely beautiful in the late spring and the summer, but cruel in the winter."

"Where is not cruel in the winter, not in this world?"

"Persia is not too harsh in the winter. It is true that it is cold compared with the summer, but not like here. Should I make some tea?"

"That would be lovely Corelya, thank-you. We have

some bread, baked fresh only yesterday morning, and honey too" she pointed to the twins, who were playing with the older boy and his younger sister. "They love bread and honey for breakfast, perhaps too much, I think."

"I think everyone loves bread and honey for breakfast" Corelya sighed happily. "I would be deeply distrustful of anyone who did not!"

Sometime later, after a light repast of unleavened bread and fresh honey, Corelya and Anyela sit around the fire, sipping hot mint tea. "Kir'gai should be back soon. He must be getting hungry by now" Anyela said. "Then we will milk the mares before we break camp this afternoon and spend a few hours on the road northwards. We will make better progress towards Olbia tomorrow. We should be on the road the whole day."

The twins were playing with the dogs, throwing sticks as far as they could for the dogs to retrieve and return for a grateful pat. Suddenly, they begin to squeal with unchaste delight, dancing up and down with effervescent joy, as their beloved "Grada Kirgi" appears a mile or so away on the track plodding steadily back to camp with a herd of some twenty horses, all of them mares. Corelya strolls across to where the twins were still skipping excitedly and sits down on the grass. The dogs sniffed around her, and she ruffles their fur affectionately, squealing as a bitch licks her face lovingly with its tongue. The twins eventually quieten and sit obediently beside her, Aisa on her left, Isha on her right, and Corelya wraps an arm round them, grateful for a momentary blessing of a shared togetherness. Affection came instinctively to her. It was almost as natural as breathing, and the twins were all too easily adored. Revealing such human frailties, unnaturally considered *deficiencies* in the twin pursuits of survival and progression, was rarely advisable in a slave.

Corelya's nature had been hardened by brutal experience during the past eight years. *How she sometimes wished her life were different.*

"Good morning" she greeted Kir'gai as he approached his granddaughters.

"Good morning, Corelya! And what in the name of Hades have you done to be lumbered with these two furies!" he boomed at the twins, who grin back adoringly.

"I simply sat down next to them! I love the feel of them next to me" Corelya confessed blissfully.

"They will have you wrapped around their tiny fingers in next to no time."

"They already have" Corelya beamed. "Was the grazing good?"

"The mares are fed and watered. I left the stallions and colts a couple of miles up the track. They will be fine" He smiled wryly to placate a bewildered Corelya. "You have forgotten your roots, my Lady, for you are no *Amazon*, are you?"

"It is not like I have much of a choice, is it?" Corelya sighed. "And besides, you are no Sauromatae, that much is clear. I will forever be an *Amazon*. It is my birth right."

"It is not a bad life, sweet child" Kir'gai smiled wryly. "We are a simple people who take our joys where we can find them" he nodded at the twins. "I could go a draught of wodki?" he grinned at Corelya.

"That sounds like the best idea I have heard all day" Corelya grinned back, her eyes twinkling with delight.

Corelya spent the rest of the morning, huddled with Anyela and the other women, engaging in a pastime which had fascinated her ever since she was a toddler: *sewing and embroidery*. Anyela had fashioned a pair of stunning red kurtas and matching britches for the twins in heavy hemp weave for the forthcoming winter. These required fox fur to be sewn as a trim to the collars, wrists, and hemline. She had also made matching hoods that could be fixed to the collars with bone buttons and tied tight at the front with hemp-rope laces. These were to be trimmed with fox fur along their entire perimeter, providing protection against the frigid winds in the cruel months to come. Corelya started with the hoods, carefully pinning the fox fur trim at regular intervals with bone pins, before threading a bronze-needle with hemp tassel. This was then expertly sewn through the fur and cloth to bind the fur tightly. By the time she had finished the first hood, with a skill and agility that had surprised and impressed Anyela, she herself had trimmed the collar and wrists of the matching kurta, and Corelya commenced pinning its hood.

"You thread a needle almost as if you were born to it!" Anyela smiled sweetly at the girl.

Corelya blushed lightly. "I suppose I am, in a way. Both my mother and my aunt made garments to sell at the Bazaar in Qu'ehra. I used to watch them all the time when I was very small."

"They sell fine garments in Qu'ehra, or so we have heard?"

"They do! Not that I have been there since I was little" Corelya smiled brightly.

"Your people settled in the mountains? It seems a strange place to choose to live?"

"We settled the northern plains not long before the fall of Assyria, or so I was told. We only migrated to the mountains in the decades before I was born."

Corelya plunged the needle in to the underside of the hood until it pierced the trim of fur in the centre. "Am I doing this correctly? The trims are always sewn in the centre, not at the far side?"

"That is correct. It they were sewn at the far side, then they would be more likely to come away" Anyela smiled encouragingly.

"This is beautiful, coloured thread. Where did you get it?"

"It comes from east of the Wol'yi. We bought the thread and the materials from a Sauromatae caravan in the spring."

"Including the fox-furs?"

"Yes. They trade the furs of the white fox, which are not found anywhere south of the snow" Anyela confessed.

"Do they really trade tiger furs?" Corelya grinned slyly.

"They had two, but they were very expensive. We could never afford such luxuries for ourselves."

"I love the colour of this material. I think it would suit the little twins."

Anyela grinned. "So do I! That way I can always keep my eye on them in the snow!"

"This will be their first real winter, will it not?"

"They are not old enough to remember much of the last one, the Gods be thanked! I cannot imagine living in the mountains. Your people must be mad!"

Corelya giggled softly. "It is quite beautiful in the thaw, from what I remember. First came the rains, soon after the thaw, and then, within a moon or so, the entire valley was carpeted with purple poppies. It was stunning!"

"Your family made their living selling garments?" Anyela enquired.

"My mum and my aunt did, as did several other women in the village. We also made crafts, wooden bowls, spoons, and the like. My father made his living mending roofs, or so I recall" Corelya confided.

Anyela furrows her brow. "Your family is no longer alive?"

Corelya smiled sadly. "They died when I was a few years older than Isha and Aisa. I was sold as a slave at the Bazaar in Qu'ehra."

I am sorry, Corelya. I truly am."

"On mornings like this, which are rare, I might add, so am I!"

Embroidery is not merely art to the nomads. It is a sacred tradition. Its secrets are passed from mothers to daughters, and fathers to sons. Among the Scythia and

Sauromatae, especially the nomad's, there are few tasks from which either sex is excluded. The weave employed is sometimes silk, the most exquisite and expensive material sought by the highest bidders from the travelling Oriental traders. Even if it is not, the alternatives, usually wool and fine hemp yarns, are nearly always the most luxuriantly dyed of all materials employed in fashioning even simple, everyday garments. Once the second hood had been pinned and stitched, Corelya proceeded to fashion saffron-coloured woollen yarn in to tassels with a bone needle, carefully weaving the material into a series of ornate loops, which could be fastened to the hoods. Within a few hours, she had completed the hood to her satisfaction. This had four tassels for decoration which, when the hood was drawn closely, would dangle pendulously in front of the ears and down a little over the chest. Corelya had also attached the three bone ties that would allow the hood to be attached and detached from the winter kurtas as required: one at the rear and two either side of the hood just below the angle of the jaw. So engrossed in her labours was she, that she did not notice Kir'gai, who stood watching her intently a short distance to her right.

"Can you ride a wagon, Corelya?" Kir'gai interrupted her thoughts.

A surprised Corelya glances up and grins. "I can, though probably not as well as you or the other men" she replied.

"I will start preparing the wagons. Anyela can ride the other wagon. We will set off in the next hour if that is fine with you?"

"That is fine with me. I am looking forward to it, for it isn't often that I get to ride a wagon! It will be something to tell the Queen" Corelya grinned.

The three wagons set off a short while later with the children safely ensconced in their mother's wagon. They were excited to be on the move and Corelya, commanding the rearmost wagon, could hear their peals of wonder as they peeked through the ventilation slats in the sides at the sights around them. The day was now hot and the track firm, as the ponies plodded steadily north across the plain towards the grazing grounds that Kir'gai had identified a few hours earlier. Once they reached the horses, Kir'gai dismounted and clicked them to gather close. Only when the farthest grazing pair arrived, did Kir'gai remount and whip the ponies to a trot. The caravan trundled north, following the course taken earlier by the scouting party. The wagons were of a traditional design, crafted from heavy oak timbers and were never designed for speed. Corelya's prior experience of driving wagons had been admittedly limited, but she was pleasantly surprised by the ease of the progression and the doughtiness of the ponies. Over the next few hours, they covered a considerable distance across the featureless expanse of the central steppe, until Kir'gai called the caravan to a halt at a suitable stream where the horses could graze and water.

Corelya dismounted the cabin and stretched her legs. The ride, however brief, had been exhilarating, and she was looking forward to the afternoon's trek. She gazed around the barren expanse of grassland, attempting to fix any landmark that might rekindle a memory from the previous journey south, just after the last new moon. This would give some indication as to their locus and its distance from the 'labyrinth', yet there was nothing that pricked her memory.

Corelya took a slug of wodki and passed the flagon to Kir'gai. He takes a grateful slug and hands this to Anyela. "It certainly is a pleasant day for it. That is most agreeable."

"How far is it to the Borysthenes?" Corelya asked.

"Not that far at all. We should make good distance in the next few hours and camp for the night when we reach the others" Kir'gai declared.

"How far away are the others?"

"We should reach them within a few hours, no more

than that! We will reach the 'labyrinth' by tomorrow, no later than the early afternoon, I would wager. The plains of the Borysthenes would be a perfect place to camp for the night. Then another day to Olbia, I would say. You never know, we might even get some company on the road, this time of year."

"You have made this journey often?" Corelya asked interestedly.

"Every summer, ever since I was a child, as young as them" Kir'gai pointed to the gaggle of children who were picking wildflowers in the meadow.

"You never felt the urge to settle and reap the bounty of the forests?" enquired Corelya.

"We are traders, Corelya. The *caravan* is in my blood, as it is in yours."

"My people had long since given all that up and had settled in the mountains just south of Qu'ehra. We were farmers and merchants. We made clothing and jewellery."

"And we, my child, are the distributors of your goods. I have been to Qu'ehra quite often, although not for several years. The place has much changed, not for the better, if you ask me."

"The Argata are the nominal Governors of 'the lands between the seas', ever since last summer. It was once considered neutral territory, for everyone has interests there, Persia, Argata, Nur'gat, Ur'gai, Orch'tai and, of course, the Hellenics? But now, ever since the peace." Corelya trailed off and then blushed hotly. "My apologies, I am stating the bloody obvious, am I not?"

"You don't like the Argata?" Kir'gai looked bemused.

"No, I do not! They are Barbarians and murderers. They are not to be trusted" Corelya said emphatically.

"Their Queen is universally admired?" ventured Kir'gai.

"Queen Lezika is universally admired for her skilled manipulation of the mistrust between the Scythian Ducals in the negotiations leading to the conclusion of the *Accord*. As such, the Argata, and Lezika, received far more than they ever should, including the right to tax the merchants of Qu'ehra, in return for the 'protection' of their warriors" opined Corelya.

"The hand of Persia is everywhere" Kir'gai sighed heavily.

"That is true, old man. Yet it has been so ever since the reforms and expeditions of Cyrus the Great."

"Yet things are different now" Kir'gai brooded. "We have interests in the Orch'tai lands and beyond the Wol'yi. Things have changed, the Orch'tai are less accommodating than ever! There are rumours of discontent in the Orch'tai Royal Household and much distrust among the Commanders of their forces. We were certainly not welcomed by their Cavalry units when we encountered them on the northern fringes of the Azovi."

Corelya was greatly surprised by the revelation. She furrowed her brow. "You were molested?"

"We were hurried on, if that amounts to molestation. They did not wish us to spend longer than a few hours grazing our herd on the pasture that borders the northern shore and made that fact perfectly clear to us. They were quite insistent that we move on."

"When was this?" Corelya probed.

"About eight or nine days ago, certainly no more than that, I would say. If it were not for that, our paths would likely never have crossed. We had hoped to spend a few days grazing, as we have always done" Kir'gai grumbled.

Corelya felt the resentment in his voice keenly. "Fattening your herd for sale in Chersonesus? Did they give a valid reason for their conduct?" Corelya pressed.

"They claimed there had been increased brigandry in the region and that it was no longer safe."

Corelya snorted. "That seems to be a common story of late, wouldn't you agree?" Kir'gai smiled grimly.

"You think there might be something more to this?"

"I am honestly not sure. There are all shades of rumours circulating in Chersonesus, perhaps elsewhere at the present" Corelya sighed.

"It is the nature of folk to gossip, sweet child!"

"Things are definitely stirring, yet there is no consistent pattern, at least not that I can decipher. The Persians have completed their action against the rebellious polities of western Anatolia and even Miletus will soon be brought to heel. And so, we have peace, yet there are things happening that, if they were allowed to persist and fester, would surely jeopardise that peace" Corelya conjectured.

"So, the Orch'tai effectively now control the northern shores of the Azovi almost to the 'labyrinth'? This is peace?" Kir'gai seemed astounded.

"They are not supposed to extend their patrols west of the Donets. Those are the explicit terms of the peace. Yet, in the face of any perceived threat, say, from marauding brigands that jeopardise the security of pan-Continental trade, they would be allowed to engage within our territory" Corelya replied.

"They seemed to be more interested in protecting the border, from what I could see. It was strange, almost as if they were not actually scouting, but had arranged to meet someone?

Perhaps they were simply awaiting delivery of an urgent consignment on route from Olbia?" Kir'gai speculated.

This did make sense. Maybe it was something, maybe it was nothing. "How many riders were there?" Corelya enquired, trying desperately to sound disinterested.

"About fifty, perhaps a few more, I would guess. All were heavily armed and mounted on good steeds." This was of considerable interest to Corelya, although she kept her curiosity tempered.

"Did you meet anyone on route to the 'labyrinth'?"

"Not a soul! That is most unusual, given the time of

year. That was equally so on the plains here, at least until we encountered those mercenaries. So, they have been directing trade away from Chersonesus to Olbia?" Kir'gai grinned.

"It would appear so" Corelya grinned back. "Perhaps this has led to price issues in Olbia and the wagons are staying on longer than usual to get a better price from the Hellenics? Might that be the reason why you didn't encounter any traffic heading to the east?"

"That would be a fair assumption. No trader ever likes to ply their wares for the same price as what they paid for them, given costs incurred by transportation and provision. Even less a reduced one! We can only hope that the situation in Olbia has improved by the time we arrive. I was hoping for a few weeks rest on the Orch'tai frontier on route to the Wol'yi and the hinterlands further east" Kir'gai muttered bleakly.

The caravan set off in the mid-afternoon, planning to reach their destination by dusk. Kir'gai assured them that the advance party would secure a suitable spot to camp for the night, preferably in the vicinity of a stream where the horses, ponies, and sheep could graze and water. The afternoon sun was unbearably hot and Corelya had long-since abandoned her britches, allowing her bare legs to bask in its warmth. The train plodded north at a steady pace, the grazing animals following dutifully in obeyance of a series of clicks issued by Kir'gai. As ever, Corelya marvelled at the seemingly unbroken expanse of plain, stretching as far as the eye could see, devoid of any meaningful topographic features. The contrasts with the environs of the coastal fringe and the majestic topography of the 'labyrinth' could not be starker. Corelya always felt a thrill of anticipation whenever she traversed the 'labyrinth', yet only recently she had awoken to the true strategic significance of the narrow channels linking the peninsula with the mainland. Independent confirmation of Orch'tai incursions west of the Donets, deep into southern heartlands of the Ur'gai Duchy, would surely strengthen her case for a permanent garrison in the area. A detachment of two hundred light cavalry would surely be sufficient to deter the threat of hostile incursion from the "demilitarized zone" of the northern Azovi, quite despite the reservations of certain Honourable Counsellors.

The afternoon's journey was uneventful, and unencumbered. Corelya was becoming increasingly perturbed by the complete absence of traffic through the Central Plains. *Surely the mercenaries alone could not be responsible for a complete dearth of freight destined for Chersonesus?* Security of the summer caravans which rolled endlessly across the Great Steppe from the Hellenic polities in the west, to the lands beyond the Wol'yi in the east, was of supreme import. Any disruption would have serious political consequences! The Merchants Guild of Chersonesus had been unwavering supporters of the Ur'gai claim to a Protectorate in the peninsula, yet such support could easily evaporate if this were to have negatively impacted upon trade and their own prosperity. Queen Illir'ya was planning a Royal visit in the next few weeks, yet it was now early July and, if the situation had not improved, Corelya had grave fears that the visit might be an embarrassing failure. A shortfall in trade and revenue could inflame the displeasure of the city's merchants. *Corelya elected to broach the subject with the mercenaries this evening, tactfully, of course!*

When they eventually caught up with the advance party, a large central campfire was burning heartily, three smaller fire-pits were dug and ready to fire, and a large kettle of mint tea was almost at the boil. Kir'gai's youngest son, Nir'gat, only seventeen years-old, was vigorously stirring the leaves. At the sight of Corelya, he smiled and waved shyly. His father turns and grins at the girl, who blushed furiously. One of the mercenaries was stripped to the waist, methodically dismembering a large trunk with an axe, whilst his companion was splitting offcuts with a hatchet. Plenty of wood had been gathered, sufficient for the evening and the following morning, and it was obvious that the mercenaries had made a good impression on Sar'chai and his nephews. The mercenaries waved at Kir'gai and at Corelya as they arrived and went quietly back to their work. Corelya wondered where their companions, including the leader, had gone. Corelya said "Hello" to Sar'chai, Nar'gai and Nir'gat, her cheeks flushing lightly as she exchanged words with Kir'gai's youngest son. Kir'gai seemed to find her discomfiture amusing, yet the girl herself was quite disturbed. *What on earth was happening to her*? She graciously accepted a draught of wodki from Kir'gai and strolled across to the two mercenaries. "'Hello!" she greeted them.

"Hello!" they chimed back.

"I called Corelya. I am one of Queen Illir'ya's Handmaidens."

The taller man, chopping the trunk with an axe, turned towards her and grinned. "We know who you are, Miss. You are the *Amazon* who had Ar'gir pissing his britches last night!" His companion laughed heartily. "I am Sala'kir, and this is Masa'kor." Corelya considered herself to be a sound judge of character. She liked them.

"Where is Ar'gir? I haven't frightened him away, have I?" she raised an eyebrow mockingly. The men laughed. "He has gone scouting a further north with his brother, Isi'kor. They should be back shortly" Masa'kor replied.

"Not hoping to run in to any caravans, is he?"

The two men exchanged glances and grinned. Corelya grins back and proffers the goblet of wodki to Masa'kor who drains it in a single gulp. He sighed contentedly. "I needed that!"

"So, did I!" Corelya reproved him jocularly. If there was one thing, they were not short of, it was wodki. "I will fetch a flagon". She stepped away to the wagon and returned shortly with a flagon and two extra goblets. She poured three generous draughts and sat down on the grass with her knees drawn to her chest. She was, after all, bereft of britches, yet still prized her modesty. She sipped her wodki and yawned tiredly.

The men finished their tasks and pulled on their summer tunics. They sit down on the grass, facing the girl. "You must miss home?"' Corelya asked them.

"Not much work for soldiers at the moment, is there? Not with the peace?" replied Sala'kir.

"Is it not true that Orch'tai cavalry are currently engaged in military adventures east of the Wol'yi?"

"We have heard rumours of such things, of course. There is talk of a rising threat from a Sauromatae Confederacy" said Sala'kir.

Corelya giggled. "I always thought that soldiers engaged in action, not fantasies?"

"It has always been so, has it not? Ever since I was a child there was always talk of a Confederacy of the Sauromatae tribes and an imminent threat of invasion" Masa'kor mused.

"Did you come via the 'labyrinth', or did you cross via the ferry at Panticapaeum?"

"The miserly buggers wouldn't pay for the ferry crossing, would they? We were expected to make our own way here."

"Did you have any company when you crossed the steppe?" Corelya probed.

"Strangely enough, we didn't!" It was Sala'kir who answered. "We thought it was very strange. I thought trade was supposed to have bloomed since the *Accord*?"

"You would have surely heard of last year's bounty from the Merchants of Chersonesus? Then again, perhaps you did not. Not if they were trying to rip you off?"

"They never mentioned anything to us, obviously, the

miserly bastards!" Sala'kir spat.

"You must have made a pretty sum, screwing them over?" Corelya mentioned airily. The two men glanced nervously at one another. Corelya smiled sweetly back. "Look, I don't know what impression you have gotten of us. After what happened last night?" Sala'kir mumbled.

Corelya eyed them icily. She raised her goblet to her lips and drained the wodki in a single gulp. She plucked the flagon, poured a large refill, and raised the goblet with her left hand toward the startled men. *Drink or disrobe*! It was an old Sauromatae drinking challenge!

And from a child, at that! Sala'kir was visibly bewildered, but Masa'kor rose to the challenge and, grinningly, untied the drawstrings of his tunic, before downing the remnants of his goblet in a single gulp. He reached across and grabbed the flagon, pouring himself a large measure, which was raised to meet the challenge. Sala'kir grins inanely and drains his wodki, replenishing it instantly.

"Have you even got a pair of knockers worth flashing?" Masa'kor snickered.

"I would say so, sunbeam! Yet it still doesn't alter the fact that you haven't got a pot to piss in between you, do you?" Corelya giggled. "And besides, there is quite a bit more to me than my tits, is there not?" She pointed first at her mouth, and then at her crotch.

"We made sod all, if that's what you want to know?" Masa'kor confessed miserably. "You made nothing at all!" Corelya was aghast.

"We are well and truly on the bones of our arses, Miss! If that is what you wish to know?" Sala'kir sighed.

"How many wagons have you turned back?"

"Only a few, I swear it!" said Sala'kir.

"Are you serious?" Corelya was astounded. Her jaw sagged in bewilderment.

"*I know*? We couldn't believe it either!" Masa'kor spat

sourly. "We came here hoping to make some real money. Things have been tight at home. Normally there is a lot of work east of the Wol'yi after the thaw, with large caravans coming from the plains near Issit. Yet, this year we were told not to bother" he looked at Sala'kir meaningly. The gesture was not lost on Corelya.

"Is there anything wrong at home? We are supposed to be allies now, are we not?" Corelya ventured soothingly.

"That depends on what *you* may have heard?" Sala'kir said woodenly.

Corelya smiles and drains her wodki. She reaches across and plucks the flagon, refilling her goblet. "There is plenty more, help yourself?"

The two men looked at each other and nodded. They each drained their goblets in a single gulp and replenished them. It was Masa'kor who spoke. "I am not sure what you might have heard, but at home there is talk of increased deployments, especially cavalry units, east of the Wol'yi. We have heard nothing to substantiate an increased threat from the Sauromatae, either from the Central Plains near Issit, or the Ural'sk Mountains to the north. There is a strange malaise in Mamy'eva, but nobody really talks about it. Something must have reached the Ur'gai Royal Court, surely?"

"Our intelligence substantiates increased Orch'tai deployments west of Astrach'yi, but nothing of any substance concerning an emerging threat from the east" Corelya only revealed information sure to be common knowledge among all Orch'tai soldiers, serving and former.

"Then we are as much in the dark as you. We both have younger cousins serving their terms. A few have been deployed west of Astrach'yi, but a majority to the east of the Wol'yi. Something is afoot, but I am not buying the old wives' tale about a Sauromatae Confederacy. If such a threat did exist, I doubt the Royal Counsel would have let us leave. They would have recalled us, at least for territorial duties, would they not?" said Sala'kir.

Corelya smiled ruefully. "They would surely have notified the Ur'gai Royal Counsel of any such threats. Any large-scale deployment of Sauromatae cavalry would be a threat to all Scythia! Like you, I doubt that there is anything to fear from the Sauromatae. We are, after all, a peaceful people!"

"Except when you have drunk too much, or else you have completely run dry?" Masa'kor grinned as he raised the almost empty flagon of wodki.

"That's a bit rich coming from a bloody Scythian!" Corelya feigned offence. The two men laughed. Corelya liked them; there was certainly no vein of treachery in either man.

"I have told you; we have plenty of wodki and berry wine. I will ask Kir'gai to open a chit for you, that way there will not be any embarrassment, will there? Everything will be settled with them before I leave you and you will get a Royal silver ingot, I promise you."

"That is very generous of you, Miss, and would be greatly appreciated" said Sala'kir, grinning inanely. "I think we might need a few of these, and the berry wine. Also, we need more goblets!" He points to the southwest, indicating Ar'gir and Isi'kor's return.

"Oh my! That is a rare prize!" Corelya gasped with glee.

The brothers had not been merely scouting, they had been hunting! Their efforts had been rewarded with a rare prize; a stag downed cleanly by an arrow in a patch of gallery woodland a few miles further north. The carcass had been beheaded, gutted, and cleaved in two, and was now bequeathed to the travellers as a gift. The families were visibly astonished by such generosity of spirit, and flagons of wodki and berry wine were showered in return upon the Orch'tai mercenaries. Any misgivings from the previous night were banished forever. Corelya marvelled at how even strangers could seemingly overcome any social barrier imposed by worldly convention by courtesy, generosity, and reciprocity. Yesterday, the Orch'tai had been unwelcome guests, now they were adopted as family. Their rare gift had been matched with equal quantities of liquor and affection, and Corelya eagerly offered to assist in skinning and butchering the deer. Once that chore was done, two quartered portions were set to roast mouth-wateringly on spits, while the remainder hung to cool in the night air. Fresh bread had been baked, and the party grouped around the main fire to eat, drink, and be merry! *It was among the most memorable evenings in Corelya's young life.*

~

Northern Crimea, July 493 BC

Early the following morning, a few hours after sunrise, the group packed their belongings and readied for the day's journey towards the 'labyrinth' and the bridge across the Borysthenes. The 'labyrinth' lay at the far northwest corner of the Crimean Peninsula.

Nobody knew the genesis of its name, but Korta had reckoned its origins to be ancient, long before the ancestors of the present-day Scythia had migrated, presumably in waves of nomadic caravans, from east of the great Wol'yi or west of the Borysthenes. Corelya's first visit to the Crimea with the Royal Household had been during the summer of her seventh year of life, the summer following her first trip to Susa, a little more than a year after she and Yari had been sold to the Princess Regent, as the youthful Illir'ya had then been. Corelya shivered at the memory, not of her enslavement, but of the tragedy of that fateful summer. Following the thaw, it had first blossomed with uncharted promise, which at its bitter end had scarred her for all eternity, whilst the horror continued unabated into the early months of winter!

The 'labyrinth' is not a single *strip* of land that joins the peninsula with the Great Steppe, as vital as the umbilicus of a nurturing baby or stalk of an apple, but is instead a series of *strips*, some four in number, surrounded on either side by sea or freshwater lakes. It is these inland lakes, navigable by fishing boats and passenger vessels, which dominates the topography of the region to a far greater degree than the coastline of the sea. The most westerly of these *strips* lay to the immediate southwest of the bay and ferry port of Krasn'oya, serving the Hellenic polis of Olbia on the river Bug'sk. This narrows in the north to an isthmus bordered to the west by the sea and the east by Lake Sta're. A second is bordered to the west by the eastern margins of Lake Sta're and, in the east, by the western shores of the Great Lake Kras'ne. A further land-bridge is formed by the eastern margins of Lake Kras'ne, encircling in its entirety the margins of the 'dwarf-lake', Lake Kru'khe, and, to the southwest, the western shores of Lake Kyia'ske. The most eastern of these *strips*, and the one most suited to passage by the Royal Caravan and any invading army, comprised the southern margins of Lake Kyia'ske and the western margins of the great Lake Kyr'lusk, second in size only to Lake Kras'ne. It was easy for Corelya to banish the bitter aftertaste of that fateful summer with the enchanting notion that they were journeying in the shadows of ancestors long since vanished from the Great Steppe.

Corelya had ridden ahead with the scouting party, Sar'chai, Nar'gai, and the four mercenaries. Nir'gat had taken over the duty of driving the third wagon. A few hours after sunrise, the topography of the landscape changed dramatically. Small patches of fringe woodland, flanking inflowing streams, soon gave way to dense clusters in the hinterlands of the lakes. This was perfect ground for hunting, but also provided excellent security for cavalry! A sizeable body of armed men could obtain everything they needed: water, food, and fodder. There were no obvious signs of any recent caravans, the absence of which had begun to gnaw at Corelya. She believed the mercenaries and, if that were so, then something, or someone, must be actively discouraging the seasonal passage of merchants from the east. If the Orch'tai were behind this, it would surely constitute an egregious breach of the *Accord Scythiac*. As far as Corelya was concerned, a far more pressing concern was the procurement of sufficient supplies for her forthcoming trek across the Steppe. The girl sighed sadly at the prospect of her impending loneliness over the next week *Sybillya would enjoy the ride, but her spirits would require more than a few medicinal flagons of wodki*!

The group found a perfect spot to rest with good prospects for hunting and foraging. Corelya tethered Sybillya to a tree at the edge of the woodland, grabbed her long- bow and quiver of arrows, and headed into the gloom of the canopy. Within a few hours, she had managed to bag a brace of rabbits and a couple of pheasants to add to the evening meal. The men had hoped to down another deer, but the quarry had fled across a fast- moving stream to elude them. Rabbits were far more numerous, and each man had bagged at least one, in addition to a clutch of pheasants! It would promise to be another hearty meal and, sitting down to boil a kettle for a brew of mint tea, Corelya began to prepare the rabbits for the evening. First, she cut off the head, thence sliced open the skin in a clean cut from the neck to the genitals and anus, with a deeper cut in the centre of the belly, followed by side stokes along the contour of the rib cage to pierce the diaphragm. The intestines, the heart, and the lungs could now be removed in one stroke. The four paws were cleaved, and the skin carefully removed, before finally washing the carcasses in the stream. She would keep the furs. Anyela could use them to make gloves and booties for the twins against the cold of winter that must, within a mere matter of moons, be upon them.

The wagon train caught up within a few hours and, after a brief repast and obligatory flagon of wodki, they set off once more, the twins perched alongside Corelya in the cabin of the third wagon, gazing at the breath-taking scenery of the lakes that formed the heartlands of the 'labyrinth'. By the late afternoon, they had traversed the region without issue and had not encountered another soul when, suddenly, they espied the scouting party clustered on the horizon, an hour or so ahead of them, waving jubilantly.

"Something seems to have stirred them. It is obviously friendly faces" Kir'gai yelled to Corelya as she drew alongside his lead wagon.

Corelya felt a thrill of anticipation at the prospect of further company. "Is it a caravan? That would be a welcome sight after the past few days, would it not?"

"I would heartily agree, young Miss. The company, not to mention the news, would be most welcome" said Kir'gai.

⌁

Borysthenes, July 493 BC

The caravan comprised some ten wagons, heavily laden with exotic goods from the Central Plains of Asia, on route to market in Olbia. The travellers were extended families, comprising grandparents, parents, and children, who lived their daily lives in the back of their wagons. They were hardy people, these nomads, a heady intermingling of Sauromatae, Scythians and other, lesser-known kinfolk from the Central Plains. Corelya both admired and respected them. They were *good* souls, and she enjoyed a rare opportunity to converse animatedly with many, including the children, in her native tongue.

Corelya purchased a new set of leather saddlebags, beautifully crafted to withstand the elements, fresh and cured meats, herbs, spices, and flagons of blossom wine. Given the nature of her mission, it would be wise to carry exotics as potential gifts; for one never knew when you may have recourse to the kindness of strangers. The girl warmly embraced the twins, Aisa and Isha, for she had felt blessed by their company, and their parents. She received warm hugs from all of them. Finally, she approached the four Orch'tai mercenaries and paid them for their service with a single silver ingot. The ingot was marked with the symbol of the Ur'gai Queen and would serve as an introduction to the Merchants Guild of Olbia. Corelya presented the mercenaries, and Sar'chai, Kir'gai, Nar'gai and their families with gifts of wodki and blossom wine.

"It was good to meet you, Corelya. Please pass on our endearments to Queen Illir'ya" said Ar'gir. "I have high hopes for this peace of ours, after meeting you."

Corelya flashed them a winning smile. "We are all brothers and sisters, are we not?" she nodded in the direction of the traveller community.

"That we are. And long may it last" said Ar'gir.

"You will make sure that they reach Olbia safely?" she nodded in the direction of Kir'gai and his family. She had become exceptionally fond of them over the past few days and would miss them terribly.

"We will, I promise you."

Corelya embraced them individually, wished them good fortune, and bid the blessings of the gods for their future endeavours. As she made her final preparations to leave, including treating Sybillya to a handful of fresh rye and a quartered apple, Ar'gir turned to her and spoke. "We would be honoured to serve you again, Lady Corelya. Should the opportunity ever arise?"

Corelya blushed brightly, for she had never been called a 'Lady' before. She thanked them again and promised that, if the opportunity ever did arise, it would surely be a pleasure to renew their acquaintance. She could never have conceived of how the events of the next two moons and the whim of the fates would change the course of her destiny!

~

The Great Steppe, July 493 BC

The following morning, many miles from the great Borysthenes, Corelya rode east into the heartlands of the Great Steppe. She was exhilarated by the endeavours of the past few days yet beset by a crushing sadness at her rekindled loneliness. The heartlands of the Ur'gai Duchy are not entirely barren. Indeed, ever since she had joined the Royal Court as a child, she had marvelled at the eclectic topography of the Great Steppe. The contrast between the vast stretches of endless plain, devoid of trees and as unremarkable as Yari's *joi de vivre* on a mid-winter's sunrise, with the riches of the forests which flourished beside the artery-like network of rivers, was scarcely comprehensible. Following a mid-morning repast of bread, cheese, mint tea and wodki, the girl kicked her heels in to Sybillya's flank to urge her to a gallop. *On such a glorious morning and on such terrain, it was joy indeed to be alive!*

A few hours later, Corelya paused by the banks of a large stream and dismounted to allow Sybillya to drink from the cool water and graze of the lush pasture. She selected a comfortable patch of ground and made a small fire for a refreshing brew of mint tea. As she scans her surroundings, a glint of something promising on the ground, not far away, piques her interest. Corelya strolled across to the patch of grass and gasps in wonderment. *It was a gold coin!* "Wow!" the girl exclaimed, marvelling as she picked up the thick metal disk.

Enchanted by its weight, she proceeds to flip and spin the coin with childish delight to wonder at its dazzle in the sun's rays. It was Persian and superior in quality to anything the Hellenics minted. Corelya was holding a small fortune in the palm of her hand; riches greater than she had ever dreamed possible. *Who in Hades name had lost such treasure?*

Mere child-like curiosity dictates her next actions. Corelya went to the ground on hands and knees, oblivious to the fact that she was, as is customary on such days, bereft of britches, and began excitedly scouring for further treasure. Alas, except for a handful of pottery shards of dubious antiquity, there was nothing of any value and, sighing remorsefully at hopes unrequited, she padded back to tend to the fire. *If I fell into a river of gold, I would be blessed with a fistful of copper!* As she did so, a further glint of something metallic, equally as bright as before, catches her eye in a patch of grass a little to the north of the fire. Corelya squealed with unchaste delight and raced across. This time, there are two coins: both Persian and every bit as fine as the first. Her enthusiasm was at fever-pitch, for surely there may be more to be discovered? And yet, scanning the ground, none presented themselves. Still, with three gold coins now to her name, Corelya imagines herself among the richest girls in the world. *Imagine the things that could be attained with such untold riches?*

Corelya filled a wooden goblet with wodki and sipped it reflectively. Gazing at the sky, she espies a Hawk, or something akin to one, circling far above. "Happy hunting!" she muses gleefully and drains the wodki in a single gulp. She knelt and removed the pot from the fire and allowed the scalding liquid to cool. Sybillya was grazing hungrily and would be able to continue the journey uninterrupted until late afternoon when they would make camp for the night. Corelya wondered whether she might meet anyone in the next few days. After the blessing of companionship these few days past, the prospect of prolonged solitude was quite dispiriting. Corelya smiled at her mount ruefully; *how silly of her! She was not alone, was she?* It was only then that

she noted something which immediately captivates her!
It lay a little further north from the patch where she had
retrieved the last of her treasure and had gone unnoticed
until now. In contrast with the coins, whose glories had
been revealed by the glint of the sun, this was not bright
and shiny. Corelya refills her goblet with wodki and strolls
across to give closer examination to this new mystery.

It was only when she got closer to the patch of ground
that she realised that what had captivated her attention was
most unusual; *unnatural* even! There, upon the ground,
a collection of large pebbles, some eight in number, had
been deliberately fashioned into some form of structure,
three rows in height. The pebbles surely must derive
from the eastern shores of the Azovi Sea, two days ride
away? Someone had selected only large pebbles and had
subsequently laid them to create a central space, enclosed
on all sides by four, with three laid north-to-south across
to cover the crypt. A single large pebble was laid at an
angle on top of this second tier and it was this that now
intrigued her. For, whilst the others were greyish blue in
colour, this was honey coloured. It was a *cairn*, at least of
a fashion. Corelya glanced around, ensuring the coast was
clear, and then knelt to remove the top stone, placing this
carefully down in faithful adherence to its orientation. She
had every intention of refashioning the structure, yet only
after she had determined what lay within! Corelya removes
the central pebble from the next layer and peers inside.

Her initial hopes were confirmed and, to her supreme
delight, within the central chamber there lay a single gold
coin. Not surprisingly, it was Persian, just like the others.
Corelya plucked the treasure from its crypt and drops this
to the ground next to the structure. She carefully replaces
the stones to re-fashion the cairn. As she stands, the girl
shivered, despite the heat of the summer sun! *Was this some
kind of religious offering that she should not have disturbed?*
It was only when she had replaced the honey-coloured stone

at the top, ensuring its original orientation was faithful, that she realised its significance; *it was a directional marker that signalled something of purpose to anyone who viewed it from above.* Corelya stood directly behind the structure, facing north, then stepped to the side to orientate her body in direct line of sight of the pebble. She gazed searchingly toward the northwest horizon for anything of interest, anything *unnatural.* There was nothing. The girl steps deftly around the structure and repeats the exercise, now facing southeast. This time, there was something!

Almost at the edge of the horizon, visible and recognisable, perhaps a mere few hours ride away.

It was a *Kurgan.* In present times, such monuments were the mausoleums of Kings and Queens of the Ur'gai and Orch'tai, and of no other *Scythia* Yet, in hallowed antiquity they had not been so. Her own people, the Sauromatae, had built such enduring monoliths a Century before Corelya had been born, long before their cruel oppression by the Argata.

According to Korta, Sauromatae of the Central Plains, the *Saka,* and those to the east of the Altai, the *Ni'jan,* continued the tradition. Whilst it was true that males could be entombed either singly, or in multiple internments, no male could ever be entombed beside a female. Legend decreed that all Sauromatae daughters were *Amazons,* maternal descendants of the daughters of Tabiti, famed for their *fury* in mortal combat. Many moons ago, the Sauromatae had been masters of all the lands east of the Donets, the mythical realms beyond the Wol'yi, and the plains and mountains between the seas. And then, in the brief period before Corelya had been born, their world had been beset by the twin cruelties of Persia and the Argata, conquering *their* land, appropriating *their* legends, assuming *their* birth right.

According to legend, more ancient Kurgans existed, and these had been built in a distant world long before the existence of bronze or iron. They were claimed by some to be as ancient as the Pyramids of the Pharaoh's, yet there could never be any substantiation of this myth. Corelya had never been to Egypt, yet she knew of the existence of the Pyramids, of the Sphinx, and of the great Temples at Luxor and Abu Simbel, for she had read about them and of the history of their peoples in the Library at Susa during her first visit. It was there that she had fallen under the spell of Korta, then Chief Surgeon to Her Royal Majesty, Queen Illir'ya and, the tutor to whom she had been utterly devoted. *Was this some religious votive to the gods; to perhaps Tabiti herself?* If it were so, then Corelya, as wise for her years as she was, had never heard of such practices before and this presented an intriguing mystery; a riddle begging resolution. She stepped around the cairn to retrieve the single gold coin and her draught of wodki. *It was then that she noticed something most peculiar.*

There was something strange about a patch of ground, not far away, yet directly in the line of sight of the pebble. It was a patch of irregular grass, large enough to be obscure yet, strangely, at the same time so obviously distinct from its surroundings. Corelya strolled across and knelt. It was a *Cuca*. She could clearly denote the series of cuts which had been inflicted upon the ground to raise a section of earth, intact in linear sections, with the intent of concealing something underneath. The girl felt a thrill of anticipation and, drawing a dagger, she stabbed into the earth and hit something solid. *It was wood.* "Sweet Tabiti!" Corelya exclaimed. She began to excavate, cautiously slicing the soil with her dagger, removing entire sections intact, until she had exposed a large slab of wood with two crescent-moon shaped slots at the end. Corelya glances across to Sybillya and summons her with a series of tongue-clicks. She ran towards her beloved steed, nuzzled her affectionately, and drew her sword from its scabbard. Within a short time, the block is prized from the earth and what lay beneath is now revealed to the most unlikely of devotees.

The crypt contained two large saddlebags, well-made, and recently oiled to protect them from the elements, filled with Persian gold! Corelya had never seen such wealth in all her life and now imagined herself even richer than Croesus himself! Not even Queen Illir'ya could lay claim to such riches at her immediate disposal. She was positively dizzy, literally skipping on air, for this discovery had been so unexpected. The gold was obviously meant for someone else, yet now it was hers! And Yari's, of course, for she could never deny her childhood friend a share of such a bounty, could she? *It was half hers, and half Yari's!* And yet, it could never be so, could it? No child of her status could attain such riches so easily. There was something so blatantly wrong in all of this? This was Persian gold: *tainted and unholy*! This treasure was destined for souls as equally undeserving as Darius himself and, given its locus so deep in Ur'gai territory, such souls must be tainted with treachery! This was traitor's gold, and they must not be allowed to possess it! And, Tabiti had graced that it was within her power, hers and Sybillya's, to deny it to them. *But to whom could it be safely entrusted*?

FOUR

Upper Donets, July 493 BC

An old man, fast approaching his seventh decade of life, a grand age by any yardstick, finished his task of splitting the last remaining logs in to manageable halves. The pile of logs next to the chopping block should last the week and, by then, his son and two sons-in-law would have replenished the pile from the resources of the surrounding forest. The man lays down the axe, wipes his brow with his sleeve, gathers a large pile of chopped logs and carries them to the doorway of the cabin where they are laid in a pile near to the door. He returns to the chopping block to gather the remaining logs and carries them across to the cabin. As he stoops to lay them neatly on top of the pile, a quarrel hammers into the doorpost a comfortable distance above his head. The old man leapt back in startled surprise!

Whoever had fired the quarrel had obviously never intended to kill or even maim, and so, recovering his wits, he proceeded to examine the quarrel with a contemptible insouciance. A twine of long-golden locks is tied in a bow to the centre of the shaft. The man smiled at the ground, his broadening grin one of genuine delight. "I don't suppose you even bothered to bring gifts, Corelya?" he hollered, without deigning to turn.

"I can remember my manners, old man, when I chose to!" Corelya answered, stepping out of cover in a near patch of woodland, she strolled across the clearing to greet the old man she had always held in the deepest affection, even wonder.

"Since when?" the man raised his eyebrows mockingly.

"Ever since I was little, if your memory still serves you as it should?"

"My mind is fine, dear child, it is my muscles and bones which feel their age. It is good to see you again, Corelya! You have certainly grown these past few years."

"I have grown exactly as I should, Korta, I have grown tall and beautiful" Corelya smiled serenely at the old surgeon.

"You prize beauty above all else, dear child?" the old man smiled wryly.

"I do not, as well you know. I prize knowledge and fidelity unto others as the supreme virtues. Who instilled such nonsense in such an impressionable young mind, I cannot recall?" the child grinned at her erstwhile former tutor.

"Such virtues are to be lauded, not sneered at, Corelya! If I taught you anything it is to be true to yourself."

"You did, and I am!" Corelya replied instantly.

"Are you on an errand for your Queen?"

"My Queen is also 'Your Queen'. I should have no need to remind you of that?" Corelya admonished him lightly.

"I beseech myself, of course. How is Queen Illir'ya?"

"She is well, and in good spirits, especially since the spring."

"Is she with child?" Korta enquired interestedly.

"No, she is not. I am surprised that you would ask such a thing?"

"I would have thought the question entirely natural, given the circumstances?"

"I have not been sent by Her Majesty to kill you, if that is what you think?" Corelya countered.

"She has not forgiven me though! Has she?" Korta sighed sadly.

"You are retired now. Why should you trouble your mind over what happened?" Corelya chose her words carefully, for this was treacherous ground. "Nobody blames you. The Queen was angry and heartbroken. She had just lost her baby, her first child. It was a difficult confinement and it ended in tragedy. There was nothing else that you could have done. Queen Illir'ya does not wish you dead, I assure you of that."

"With all due respect, Corelya, what are your assurances worth?"

"With equal respect, dear Korta, if the Queen truly wished you dead then I would not have deliberately missed just now, would I?"

"Would you have aimed true?"

"I would not have wanted you to suffer, if that is of comfort to you?" Corelya replied evenly. "You would like some wodki?"

"Your own plum recipe, made with the lemon peel?" Corelya grinned.

Korta leads the girl inside the cabin where he lived alone. Corelya saw the shelves were stacked with carefully labelled jars of herbs, spices, and liniments. "Do you still practice?" she asked.

"I make and sell remedies to both the locals and passing travellers, mainly to supplement my meagre savings now that my services are no longer required at the Royal Court."

"You no longer teach?" the child asked sadly.

"Who would listen to a tired old man? Besides, there is no calling for it in such a remote place. Which brings me to the obvious question..?" He plucked a heavy-bottomed ceramic flagon from a side table and placed this and two wooden goblets on the main table in the centre of the room. "What in Hades name are you doing here, Corelya? All by yourself, in such a sparsely-populated part of the Duchy?"

"I could tell you, old man, but then I would have to kill you" Corelya snickered.

Korta laughed heartily and took a sip of wodki from a goblet proffered to him by Corelya. "Then perhaps you should keep your silence. Not that there is anyone to tell in these parts. We do get the occasional traveller caravans from the Orch'tai lands to the east. I have heard some troubling tales of late."

Corelya's ears pricked up. "Troubling?"

"There is wild talk of discordance in the matter of the succession. Perhaps King Tagar may not even last the next winter. He has left no sons and his daughters' hiss like feral cats" Korta confided.

"It has been ever thus, has it not?" mused Corelya.

"There is talk of a string of defeats against the Sauromatae tribes east of the Wol'yi. These loosely-related tribes have allegedly proclaimed a 'Confederacy' and are busy expanding their influence along the Silk Road to the west and east."

"Please do not tell me that you have fallen for that old chestnut?" Corelya rolls her eyes. "There has been idle chatter of a Sauromatae 'Confederacy' since the aftermath of Nineveh. My people are Scythia's illusory spectre! We stalk your dreams with our imaginary terror."

"You may scoff, dear child, and for obvious reasons. Have you not heard word of recent Orch'tai defeats?"

"Our spies in Mamy'eva have reported no such happenings. They would surely have sent word" Corelya confessed.

"Nothing from your agents ensconced within the Argata lands?"

"Nor from our agents in 'the lands between the seas', in Mesopotamia, or the Hellenic polities of the Black Sea" Corelya smiled sweetly and drained her wodki. "May I?" she indicated the flagon and the now-empty goblets.

"You may" Korta raised an eyebrow at the child.

"Another lecture on my drinking habits, darling tutor?"

"And how fares your Persian these days?"

"Exemplary, as well you know" Corelya smiled sweetly. "Do you have something for me?"

"Perhaps, I do. Firstly, you should tend to your mare. It is not as safe as it once was in these parts. We have had issues with brigands of late."

"Orch'tai?"

"Perhaps, but then again, possibly all is not what it seems." Korta let his words hang in the air.

Corelya drains her second draught. "I shall tend to my mare, and then perhaps you might enlighten me. I have meat killed and cooked only yesterday and blossom wine from a trader on route from Olbia."

"You came to get me drunk, Corelya? Perhaps you do intend to kill me?"

"I came to see you, dear tutor. I have no instructions to kill you. It would be nice to share a flagon of wine. The others I can leave as presents."

Sybillya was foraging close to the edge of the clearing. Corelya summoned her with a series of tongue-clicks. She retrieves the flagons of wine and the gifts of cooked meat from her newly purchased saddlebags and ties her mare next to a water trough. The presence of the water trough suggested that Korta, never comfortable in the saddle, received a regular stream of guests, perhaps more than he would readily confess. Whilst Corelya trusted her former tutor implicitly, the bitterness of his exile from the Royal Court still rankled and could easily have strained his loyalties. Then again, the region was an Ur'gai stronghold and, even now, she was within a half days ride of the Royal City and winter Palace at Rost'eya. No reports of increased banditry in the region had reached the Royal Counsel and she had not encountered any Ur'gai patrols, two issues of considerable import considering Korta's startling revelations. Something was clearly wrong! Corelya felt sure that her former tutor had knowledge of mischief of which the Royal Court ought to be aware. She strolled back towards the cabin.

"I have wine, saffron, some roasted meat and un-leaven loaves baked only yesterday morning. I also included this. A tribute to your services to the Royal Court and her Majesty the Queen" declared Corelya, upon re-entering the cabin. She addressed her erstwhile tutor in Persian and flipped a gold coin on to the table.

"You are rather generous with Queen Illir'ya's treasury, dear child" Korta said in mock reproof, speaking in the same alien tongue.

Corelya switched to Greek. "You are a good surgeon, Korta, and remain a faithful servant to Her Majesty. It pains me to see you cast aside in anger. And in any case, the coin does not belong to Queen Illir'ya, it belongs to me."

Korta was astounded. "And how did you acquire such riches, darling child?"

"I found several of them, about a day's ride west from here, just next to a large stream" Corelya confessed.

"Someone has been most unfortunate, and you have been blessed!" Korta smiled at the girl. The old surgeon pours two goblets of blossom wine and savours the taste. He sighed happily. "You always were a thoughtful child, Corelya. Your gifts are deeply appreciated" he addressed her in Greek.

"That isn't the half of it, old man! What do you make of this?" She replied in Greek and, leaving the old Surgeon furrowing his brow in consternation, she steps back outside and returns with the two saddlebags, heavy with gold. These are dropped on to the table.

"Sweet Hera!" Korta gasped. "Where in Hades name did you find this?"

"The same place as I found that" she nodded at the single gold coin on the table. "It was hidden in a *Cuca*. Someone had constructed a cairn to indicate its locus, but only to those who knew exactly where to look."

"This is Persian gold! Such a phenomenal tribute buried

deep within the Ur'gai heartlands is deeply disconcerting. There is more than a whiff of treachery here?"

"I have not bathed at all this week!" Corelya replied mischievously.

Korta grinned. "What would you like to do with this?" the two continued to converse in Greek.

"This gold cannot fall into the hands of those it was meant for, you would agree? I would concur with you that there is a whiff of treachery here. Perhaps, given time, this mystery will unravel itself and reveal the identities of the intended recipients. It is strange though, that I did not encounter any patrols from Rost'eya, especially in light of an increased lawlessness you were alluding to earlier" Corelya reverted to Scythian.

"Perhaps the issue to which I alluded is not something that certain 'interests' would prefer to acknowledge, least of all at the Royal Court?"

"Are we referring to brigands or, alternately, to illegal incursions by irregular Orch'tai cavalry detachments?" probed Corelya.

"An interesting line of thought, dear child, though from where the Orch'tai would hail is an obvious flaw in your reasoning. There are no garrisons to speak of within two days ride of here. They would be taking an awful risk."

"We have intelligence of Orch'tai detachments, possibly numbering over a thousand men, stationed to the west of Astrach'yi."

"That would be less than a day's ride from the Donets?" Korta conceded.

"A day's ride is a patrol, at least to a semi-accomplished 'saddle', wouldn't you say?" Corelya grinned mockingly.

"You never tire of reminding me of my shortcomings, dear child" Korta smiled wanly.

"I remember the time you fell off your horse into the river" Corelya snickered.

"So, could you venture how such Orch'tai warriors,

mounted on superb steeds, might be attired if, as you postulate, their intent would be to give pretence to banditry?" Korta brought the conversation back to the matter at-hand.

"I would postulate that they would be attired in non-issue uniforms, with a range of armour readily available from the Hellenics, yet their arms would be standardised, to a greater degree. They would certainly be armed with Orch'tai longbows and arrowheads. The parties would likely include some speakers of different dialects, perhaps Scythian and Sauromatae."

"Could they be Mercenaries? Hellenics perhaps, even hired hands from Central and Atlantic Europe?" Korta ventured.

Corelya was startled. "You mean Celts? Why would they interfere in our business?"

The old surgeon's eyes twinkled, as they had always done, as he outlined his synopsis to his once favourite pupil. "Have you ever considered that the world you seek to comprehend is merely a small fragment of a broader and richer tapestry encompassing interests: wealth, power, identity, and desires that may not be entirely compatible? Trade is wealth, dear child, and is the source of all power. Persia's regional ascendancy has created a turbulence whose tremors have been felt as far away as the Atlantic!" the old man sipped his wodki.

"So, you have lectured me many times!" Corelya smiled sweetly. "Please continue?"

"Consider this, if you will? That the Oriental Kings are far greater in wealth and influence than any the world has yet known. Yet, they are physically remote from us. They wish to increase their sphere of influence but cannot physically expand along the Silk Road or via the southern orient."

"If they are so powerful, why do they simply not conquer and enslave us?"

"They do not need to conquer, and instead seek opportunities to trade. The rise of Persia, coupled with its insatiable ambition and sense of destiny, however misplaced, is not an impediment to their desires. Rather, it presents an unprecedented opportunity. Europe, to a greater degree, remains a mystery to us. The Celts, despite the lowly opinions of the Athenians, have their own burning ambitions and these have been fanned by increased trade with the Hellenics and Phoenicia. We are in the middle, at least geographically, yet have sought to tie our hands, perhaps imprudently, to the destiny of the Hellenics."

"But the Hellenics are the true power in this region?" Corelya protested. "That was the entire basis of the proclamation of our Protectorate in the Crimea."

"And yet, you have misgivings about the entire endeavour, do you not?"

Corelya was astonished. "How do you know *that*?" she retorted, a little too harshly. "Please forgive me" she beseeched.

"I was your tutor, dear child, and I know your mind" Korta soothed. "And, if I did?" Corelya ventured hesitantly.

"You would not be alone. Of that, I can assure you. Nevertheless, you serve your Queen loyally. There are others who may have alternative agendas."

"You mean Traitors? Perhaps even in the Royal Court?"

"We are on dangerous ground, dear child, and must proceed with caution. And yet, you may well be right to question the loyalty of all those at Court. Perhaps the young Queen is more vulnerable than you would credit?"

"This is purely hypothetical. It does not address the issue to which you first alluded."

"You are Sauromatae? Look inside yourself for the answers you seek" Korta chided.

"I don't follow?" Corelya furrowed her brow.

"You are tired, dear child, and have ridden hard these

past few days. Perhaps you simply need time to consider all the relevant information. After all, you have access to intelligence that I do not. Is it true that there is a new intelligence source serving our allies in Chersonesus?"

"Perhaps we should have some more wine?" Corelya countered guardedly. "You are quite right, my learned tutor. I am sometimes overwhelmed by all that I seek to resolve."

"You have a rare mind, Corelya, the most impressive I have encountered in one so young. Now that you have blossomed, that rare mind of yours is struggling with a great mystery, perhaps the greatest posed in a Century. The fate of an entire people, our own people, and even the future of the Queen herself, may rest upon its resolution. But, for now, let us drink and think of other things."

Within a few hours, Corelya had drunk close to half a flagon of un-watered blossom wine, as was the tradition of the Scythians, and was feeling exhausted from her travels. She had journeyed from the southern coast of the Crimean Peninsula to the eastern fringes of the Ur'gai domains, encompassing the upper course of the Donets, all within six days. Korta had arranged a bed for her in the far corner of the cabin and the child laid her sleepy head down on a bundle of blankets for a pillow and was soon after ensconced in a deep and peaceful slumber. At last, for a brief time at least, and for the first in the past week, she felt entirely safe.

⤚

The sun had not long risen, when Korta roused the child from her blissful slumber. "Good morning, Corelya! I thought you might be starting early, so I prepared some mint tea and a platter of un-leaven bread, cheese and wodki for breakfast."

"Thank you, Korta. That sounds wonderful" Corelya

replied tiredly.

"You slept well?"

"I did and thank-you for asking."

"You snore, Corelya!" he chided her.

"So, do you, old man!" she snorted.

"Have some tea" said Korta, passing her a wooden goblet of scalding mint tea. He smiled slyly at the child and sipped his wodki. "I would like your opinion on something that has perplexed me, if I may trouble you. It may be important, perhaps extremely so, then again it may be nothing. I thought you might at least be intrigued, if only to demonstrate your knowledge of Persian." He slipped a small papyrus scroll, fastened in the centre with a small bronze ring, across the table. The papyrus was expensive, of the kind used by the wealthiest and most discerning of correspondents. The girl teases the scroll from the ring and unfurls it carefully. The communique read as follows:

Things are not all as they seem. The serpent in Susa is wary of discovery. The Great Pretender grows inpatient with each passing moon. Devoted saplings planted in every centre throughout the region. Treachery is everywhere. Extreme caution advised in all undertakings.

Scythian rose cannot bear the wilds of winter. Advise caution in the realm of the bear. The spice merchants enraptured by a new melody. Take care to avoid pig-meat destined for Panticapaeum – provenance questionable. Be wary of the Eagle of the mountains – Susa's Hawk, Each passing day brings ever closer danger to the fruits of labour. – O

"What do you make of it?" Korta enquired quizzically, when Corelya had finished her first reading.

"Where did you get this?" Corelya enquired coldly.

"It came off a corpse, if you would credit it?" He waived his hand to mollify her. "I did not kill him; I assure you of that. He was as already long dead when I found him. This was wrapped in a leather sleeve sewn to the inside of the trouser ends, if you would credit such a thing?"

"You found the corpse of a foreign agent this deep into the Steppe? When was this? How did he die?" the questions came breathlessly.

"He had taken an arrow in the chest. Likely as not from brigands, for his horse was missing, as was anything else of any value?" Korta confessed.

"When was this?"

"I found him yesterday morning, about a mile or so further east."

"Did he look Persian?" the child quipped. She wrinkled her nose as she grimaced. "What did you do with the body? You haven't taken a liking to human flesh these few years past, have you?" Corelya teased.

"No, I have not, young Lady! I am not Sauromatae, as you are!" Korta feigned outrage at the insult. "And, in answer to your final question, no he did not. If you were a spy deep in the steppe, would you be a Persian?"

"No, I would not!" Corelya declared. "I suspect that's why you stole his boots, isn't it? Might I read this again?"

"Indeed, you may, sweet child" the old man smiled slyly, for he had indeed taken the man's boots!

Corelya re-read the scrap of paper with a furrowed brow. It was obviously some form of code, yet deliberately crafted to appear, on the face of it, to be quite innocuous to an unlearned eye. Whilst it had been drafted in Persian, there was more than enough in the phraseology to venture that Persian was not the authors' mother tongue although, much like Korta and herself, the writer was almost fluent. "This is extremely troubling, you would agree?" The statement was uttered in almost a whisper.

"In what sense, apart from the obvious, that is?" Korta smiled wryly.

"The writer is clearly worried about recent

developments. In fact, the whole message is one of caution against multiple forebodings. '*The Serpent in Susa*' and the '*Great Pretender*', the latter a certain allusion to King Darius, and an entirely different person from the serpent, you would agree? So, we have the King growing impatient with each passing month and a serpent.dangerous, treacherous, not to be trusted., a Hellenic agent in Susa who is perhaps no longer entirely trustworthy? '*Devoted saplings planted in every centre*', an allusion to Persian agents ensconced in every regional polity? The Persians are engaged in something sinister at present and our own intelligence confirms a dramatic shift in their attitude toward the Hellenics, perhaps even ourselves. '*Treachery is everywhere*', none are to be trusted, including, perhaps even previously reliable sources?"

"There is an overbearing emphasis on treachery. With that I would concur?"

"Yet the engagement must continue as before?" Corelya chirruped.

"I think that is a perfectly reasonable assumption" said Korta.

"Then, we have an allusion to the situation in Scythia and the precariousness of the peace, '*the rose that cannot bear the wilds of winter*'. All signatories to the *Accord* in Hopa, the Nur'gat, Ur'gai, Orch'tai and Argata, exchanged a rose from the same flower, so that each was gifted four more-or-less identical flowers as a symbol of the peace. Is the writer perhaps suggesting that this delicate peace is not destined to last the forthcoming winter?

The phrases would certainly bear such an interpretation" Korta conceded.

"Our correspondent, whoever they are, and whomever they serve, has few reservations in tainting the Orch'tai with treachery! '*Advise caution in the realm of the bear*', a clear allusion to its natural territories, the forests to the north and east of the Wol'yi? The Hellenics are acutely aware of the greed of the Orch'tai timber merchants, and their apparent blindness to the true designs of Persia. The *'spice merchants'* is an obvious reference to the Phoenicians, and we are aware of their collusion with the Orch'tai, specifically in the matter of the timber trade in Panticapaeum. I will freely admit my bewilderment, for I know not what to make of the *'pig-meat of questionable provenance'*!"

"What are pigs?" Korta enquired, his tone lightly mocking.

Corelya was piqued by the question, for the old man had clearly missed teasing her. "They are animals, of course, you silly old goat! We keep them for food. They taste very nice, as a matter of fact. They are not much use for anything else, are they?"

Korta grinned wryly at the floor. "To see such innocence in one so worldly, it truly breaks the heart!"

"You always enjoyed teasing me, did you not?" Corelya eyed her former tutor coldly. "What else is a 'pig'?"

"You are! Along with the great majority of your sex, I might add!" Corelya replied brusquely. *"All* men are pigs?"

"Not *all* of you, just the great majority. You are beneath us, remember that!"

"And so, we have 'men' shipped to Panticapaeum? And, furthermore, these men are of 'questionable provenance'?"

"From where do these elusive men hail?" Corelya drained her tea. "I could do with a drink?" she sighed irritably.

"From a place famed for its pigs, perhaps?" Korta ventured. He refilled the empty goblets with wodki.

"Men from Massalia, for the hinterlands are famed for their pigs, are they not? Yet if these men came from Massalia, they would surely be Gauls?"

"Not necessarily, Corelya! You are thinking in simple colours" Korta chided her.

"They could have been assembled in Massalia from

anywhere, but their provenance *is known*, or at least determinable, for we could infer that they have likely come from Massalia? What *is* questionable is their *purpose*, their *mission*." Corelya mused. "Sweet Hera! Could it imply hired mercenaries from Massalia who have been shipped to Panticapaeum?" she gasped.

"The words may bear such an allusion, given that this is certainly some form of code."

"Our intelligence points to the Orch'tai detachments stationed to the southwest of here as being indigenous."

"And so, they likely are. But now we have a spectre of mercenaries in Panticapaeum. They would surely not be advertising their status or their mission?"

"That would be an act of war!" Corelya gaped.

"Not against the citizens of Panticapaeum, not if they were invited? Nor would it ever be so construed by the Orch'tai or the Argata, not if such elements were acknowledged as allies and not foes?"

"Nor by Persia, I would wager! Not if they are paymasters of the entire enterprise?" Corelya ventured.

"Which brings us rather timeously to the '*Eagle of the mountains*' or, as he, or perhaps she, is anointed, '*Susa's Hawk*'?"

"A Persian agent domiciled in the mountains? Or perhaps a Chief Agent with responsibility for overseeing intelligence gathered in the entire region?"

"That is quite possible?" Korta replied. "Such a soul would have an unparalleled grasp of the situation on the ground in both Panticapaeum and Nymphaion at the moment?"

"That would seem likely. The reference to the mountains could simply imply their regional significance. The mountains being the most notable feature of the region.?"

"They surely pale in contrast with the Steppe, sweet child?" Korta teased.

"A pox on your Steppe, I say!" Corelya sneered in jest. "Which only leaves the final sentence to resolve, but I am sure you have already deciphered that?"

"I admit to a certain degree of puzzlement" Korta sighed.

"The construction is entirely of a character with the rest of the letter with its emphasis on dread and melancholy. At least for what should, by now, be a happy time" Corelya smiled wryly, as the old man furrowed his brow.

"I am not sure that I follow, Corelya? I agree with the *tone*, but not the *sentiment*."

"The writer is female, and *she* is *pregnant*. Heavily so, I would wager, and likely due not long after the communique had reached its intended recipient."

"From what do you derive such certainty?" the old man gazed at the child in wonder.

"The sentence is framed in the past tense, you would agree? If this is code, the same simple sentence, innocuous to an unlearned eye, could mean several things. I agree that it is written to flow seamlessly with everything previously stated and there is little doubt that it conveys a sense of dread and importance simultaneously. The correspondents are engaged in mischief, presumably aimed at thwarting the very things that they refer to in the rest of the communique.

"Please continue, sweet child" Korta beseeched.

"Let us consider the likelihood that we have correctly deciphered the communique.

We have a Hellenic spy in Persia, an allusion to King Darius and his impatience with the unfolding of a grand scheme, which, the correspondent confirms, involves the treachery of the Orch'tai and the Phoenicians. We have the portent of a threat to the peace, involving a deliberate deployment of mercenaries to Panticapaeum, and a Persian spymaster in the region between the seas whose tentacles reach far and wide."

"I am in complete agreement with you, thus far. But

the last sentence.?"

'*Each passing day brings ever closer danger*', as clear an allusion as ever was to the importance of their shared endeavour. Yet, finally, we have '*the fruits of labour*' which, follows logically as a reference to their shared desires, but which could also construe that the correspondent herself is dawning near to her day of labour. All women have some dread of confinement, no matter how many times they have experienced it. *I think the meaning of the sentence is dual*. It is meant to be read as it should, yet it also conveys, as does everything else, a slightly different and *explicit* meaning."

"You think this communique hails from your new source? This alleged agent of the Hellenics in the region?"

"If this is genuine, rather than a Persian ruse, for the Orch'tai have not the intellect to concoct anything so elaborate, I would wager heavily that this hails from the pen of the mysterious '*Oracle*'" Corelya intimated.

"And this '*Oracle*' serves Athens, and not Sparta?" Korta pressed.

Corelya sipped her drink and gazed searchingly at her former tutor. "Are you privy to something that I am not, old man?"

"Not at all, dear child. And yet, if you still value my advice, then I shall give it freely. You would do well to remember that it is Sparta, and not Athens, who rival Persia in the dark arts of espionage, at least in my experience."

"If this is genuine, then the general threads of the communique are entirely consistent with our own intelligence sources, quite regardless of whom the new Hellenic source serves" Corelya replied. "We are in agreement, are we not?"

"Nonetheless, it is quite possible that your interpretation of the communique, as admirable as it is, is coloured by disparate threads from various sources that may pertain to entirely different matters?" Korta admonished her lightly.

"You think that I am being "Procrustean"? Fitting the

external facts, as disparate as they are, to constellate around the specifics of the communique?" the child spat.

"I am not inferring anything, Corelya" Korta sighed lengthily. "I specifically asked for your insights into the contents of the communique, which is clearly some form of code, because I value both your *intellect* and your *opinion*. I freely admit to being deeply troubled by the general tone, its emphasis on treachery and foreboding, specifically the reference to Scythia, yet I do not have the same grasp of the broader picture as you. I have no access to our own intelligence sources, and no-one values the opinion of a silly old man."

"You are not, and never have been, a 'silly old man', learned tutor. Quite the contrary, if you must know? We have missed you at Counsel these past years and things are not the same" Corelya was treading carefully, for this was dangerous ground.

"The Queen's brother?" Korta grimaced.

"I have said nothing" Corelya replied tonelessly.

"You don't need to, Corelya. You two have history, remember?" Korta smiled wryly.

"How could I forget? He hates me because of what happened to him at the wedding."

"And how is Gor'ya? Is she well?"

"Gor'ya is well" Corelya replied. "She has almost forgotten what happened at the wedding. We do not talk about it, nobody does. Sag'ra is an animal! He thinks that just because he is the Queen's brother, he can take whatever he desires, whenever he chooses, including his younger cousin's virtue. Gor'ya was only eleven when he tried to rape her. She didn't deserve that! To be treated so wickedly, he really hurt her."

"Not as badly as you hurt him, if my memory still serves me. There was a fair wager as to whether he had been 'permanently damaged', I seem to recall?"

"Mirel'ya is not yet 'with child', if that is what you

allude to?" Corelya raised an eyebrow mockingly.

"You did kick him rather viciously, Corelya?"

"He deserves never to use it again after what he did to poor Gor'! She was hysterical after he was dragged away and was bleeding badly. It was a good thing I heard her wails and was able to take down his two gormless mates stationed outside the door. Obviously, what happened was quietly hushed up. As far as everyone is concerned, Gor'ya is still a virgin."

"Would you like to keep the communique? After all, it is little use to me."

"No. I would like you to deliver this to Gor'ya in person. They are currently camped on the Saiga Plains. You will know how to reach them. If you have a horse, we can set off in the next few hours. Haste is imperative" Corelya said emphatically.

"I don't quite follow your reasoning, Corelya. *Haste is imperative*?" the old man was perplexed. "We have no clear idea when the communique was sent, do we? The fact that this was so carefully hidden and had not been destroyed suggests that it is prescient and was received recently. Very recently, in fact" Corelya replied.

"And so, we leave within the hour?" the old man smiled grimly.

"It will be good to appraise your horsemanship again, learned tutor" Corelya snickered. "I think I can remember how to ride, dear child!" Korta growled. "But first, I must show you the location of my secret *Cuca*, where we can deposit the gold. It is known only to my sons, and they would never look, even when I am not here." Korta slung the saddlebags over his shoulder. "Come child! We need to make sure that this is safe."

A few hours later, the pair had reached a small stream in a

patch of gallery woodland. Corelya suggested they take a
brief rest. She dismounts and busies herself making mint
tea, whilst her former tutor went for a stroll following the
path south, scouting for any evidence of recent human
activity. The two mounts drink greedily from the crystal
waters of the stream and then graze contentedly. The
temperature had risen considerably by this now and
any smoke emitted by the fire would be undetectable
from a distance, especially in the confines of the dense
canopy. Korta returns a short while later, the harbinger of
potentially worrying news!

"There is a spacious clearing a mile or so further south
along the track. There is nobody camped there now, yet
there was quite recently, judging by the evidence of copious
horse- dung." Korta revealed.

"Was it a caravan? Or perhaps something more sinister,
do you think?"

"No evidence of wheel ruts or patched grassland. I
would say a sizeable detachment of riders mounted on
thoroughbred steeds."

"They could be ours?" Corelya ventured.

"That is true, but then again.?" the question was left
to hang in the air.

"You have enough to trouble your mind simply staying
in the saddle!" Corelya chided. The pair sip their tea in
contemplative silence.

The next few hours took them cautiously south along
the path. Corelya led with her loaded crossbows ready to
hand. As was the habit of all Scythians, she also carried
a longbow and a large quiver of arrows with razor-sharp
iron heads and feathered fletching's.

Additionally, she carried an iron sword at her right hip
in its ornate scabbard, perfectly balanced for her height,
and twinned iron daggers at her left hip. Korta carried his
aged, yet razor-sharp sword, with its battered scabbard
and longbow with a quiver of arrows. In the event of any

prospective encounter, the lethal accuracy of the longbows would be a determining factor, yet these would be of little benefit should they fall prey to ambush by archers. Mercifully, the advantage of high ground was not an issue as their journey took them closer toward the featureless expanse of steppe between the Donets and the Dnieper.

In the late afternoon, the two riders stop for a brief rest. Their horses had not been unduly pressed by the day's ride thus far, though Korta grumbled incessantly about his weariness in the saddle. "If I had known in advance what a miserable chaperone you were, I would have left you back at the cabin!" Corelya mused teasingly. She busied herself lighting a small fire to make tea.

"Alive or dead?" retorted Korta.

"Nobody wants you dead! I have told you that several times. Apart from me, that is, on account of your incessant grumbling!"

"Strange that we have not encountered anyone thus far, don't you think?"

"Trakhtemirov is largely deserted this time of year, with the exception of the garrison, the merchants and a handful of pensioners, obviously!" Corelya raised an eyebrow mockingly. "The Royal Household, the Queen, her Counsellors, and their families are camped on the Saiga Plain. That will obviously change over the course of the next few months."

"I do wonder if I will encounter a single soul before I reach the Saiga Plains?"

"There are always caravans of traders from the Orch'tai lands to the east and Olbia. You may even have some company for the next day or so, at least until you reach the 'labyrinth'."

"Orch'tai? Sauromatae? Heaven's above!" Korta mused cynically.

"I *am* Sauromatae in case you have forgotten? I am sure you will be fine. I met a lovely family of traders heading across the northern plains of the Crimea to the labyrinth. We were together for about three days. It was special, at least for me" said Corelya.

"You dream of a different life, dear child?" Korta smiled ruefully at the girl.

"I am a slave. What other life could there be for me. I am pledged to serve my Queen, no more, no less."

"You have a strange view of life, Corelya, and of your own future. You are one of Her Majesty's loyal Handmaidens and, from what I have heard, among her most trusted advisers, reporting directly to the Counsel. It surely cannot have escaped you that it is within the Queen's grace to free you and Yari? You are no longer a child, Corelya, and are fast approaching the cusp of womanhood, even if you are a few years shy of marrying age?" Korta chuckles as Corelya grimaces at the prospect of marriage. "You do not wish to marry and raise a family of your own?"

"The family I met had a set of identical twins. They were beautiful, if not more than a little naughty! They were all too easily adored. I cannot imagine being married, not ever! It is not something I give much thought to, if I am being honest about it."

"Why on earth not? You have always had a generous disposition towards other people's children. Perhaps not as obvious as Yari, for it is all too clear that she desires nothing more than a loving husband and a gaggle of doting children."

"A perfect little housewife, don't you think?" Corelya could not keep the distaste from her voice.

"You are warriors, both of you! Among the most feared warriors in the known world. That is the nature of the training that you have undertaken thus far, the skills that you have developed, and will continue to hone over the next few years, quite respective of the status of the peace. That will never change. You are a warrior, Corelya, for that is what they have made of you, for better or worse" Korta sounded regretful, as if he wished things could be different.

"I am an *Amazon*! I very much doubt I require a lecture from a Scythian in the matter of my birth right!" Corelya snorted.

"And that is all you wish for in life? Is the sole kernel of your ambition to grow to be a mere agent of death and destruction?" Korta seemed genuinely pained.

"I should learn to mind my manners in respect of men, is that it?" Corelya mocked.

"Being a parent, a wife, a husband, is a natural desire shared by all adults. Sharing your life with another, having children together, becoming a parent with responsibilities for the welfare of those entirely dependent upon you for their very survival is a life-changing transformation. It both colours and re-casts your entire view of life. Nevertheless, it can never change what, or who, you truly are. Not unless Scythia itself changes..?"

"You would like meaningful change in Scythia?" Corelya eyed the old man closely.

"And since when was war a legitimate solution to any meaningful question, my dear child?"

"It is the nature of the world, since long before the rise of Persia" replied Corelya.

"Things have become ever more volatile in the decades since the campaigns of Cyrus! The world is a more dangerous place, perhaps more so now than at any time in the last three centuries?" Korta cautioned.

"I cannot reveal anything of the discussions of Counsel, or my personal conversations with the Queen, as well you know! I will not lie to you. The prospect of war is perhaps greater than ever before."

"You think Persia is moving towards an inevitable conflict with Athens and Sparta?"

"The author of that note certainly seems to think something sinister is afoot, you would agree?" Corelya sighed.

"I think we may have come close to unravelling the code. You also have the benefit of our own intelligence. Things are certainly worrying."

"Are you afraid?" Corelya quipped.

"Am I afraid for my own safety? I very much doubt that anyone would take much notice of an old man."

"It might be best to have a cover story, would it not?" Corelya mused.

"I am going to visit my Granddaughter, Gor'ya. She lives alone in Chersonesus and works in a Hostelry?"

"Which Hostelry would that be?" Corelya asked, grinning slyly.

"*The Star of Delphi*?"

Corelya roared with laughter. The '*Star*' was a notorious hostelry that served every taste. The thought of Gor'ya, sweet innocent Gor'ya, working in such a notorious dump, possibly as a prostitute, was simply outrageous. "I could imagine Gor'ya in a skimpy kurta!"

"Could you indeed?" Korta snickered.

Corelya blushed hotly. "Sweet Tabiti! I get enough of that from Yari!"

"The 'mysteries' are not to be feared, Corelya. I think Gor'ya would be a faithful and attentive lover" he grinned, enjoying the girl's obvious discomfiture.

"I do hate you some days, old man!" Corelya hissed.

They set off an hour or so later, following the course of the Donets towards the Azovi Sea. They were rightly wary, for, each footfall increased the risk of attack from brigands and marauders, and the distance from the safety of the Royal City of Rost'eya and its garrison. Corelya well knew the well-earned reputation for ferocity of the brigands who operated on the vast expanse of steppe between the Donets and the great Wol'yi. The great river flowed from the port of Astrach'yi on the north-west coast of the 'lesser of the two Seas', through the Royal City of Mamy'eva, some distance upstream, into the heart of the forests and the glacial wastes beyond. They would soon clear the gallery forest on either side of the river by the mid-afternoon. Given the increasing peril, the riders scan the landscape constantly and journey in silence, their weapons ready to hand.

By late afternoon, the lush covering of the woodland had given way to the vast, almost featureless, expanse of the Great Steppe. Corelya grimaced, drawing a chuckle from Korta who rode alongside her. "How can anything be so bare?" the child pondered. And yet, in truth, during the summer months, the Great Steppe was a rich expanse of wild grasslands that was perfect for grazing herds of animals. The banks of the rivers and streams were flanked with lush meadows and acres of pretty flowers, including clusters of wild poppies, with their arresting pink and purple petals.

Korta flashed the girl a winning smile. "I think it is quite stunning, especially on such a beautiful day. Just look at those flowers, aren't they beautiful?"

"And people think we Sauromatae are a strange breed! If you like the flowers so much, you should take some as a gift to Her Majesty?" Corelya ventured.

"I have several jars of prepared tinctures as a Royal gift" Korta declared.

"Everybody loves poppies, Korta! Queen Illir'ya, especially so" Corelya flashed him a smile.

"Of course, I quite forgot" the lie came smoothly. They stopped briefly whilst Korta dismounted and harvested a large bundle of beautiful poppies from the meadow.

Corelya scanned their surroundings for any sign of life, friendly or otherwise. "The Queen will command you to an audience as soon as you arrive, you do know that?" she cautioned.

"How will I deliver the communique to Gor'ya directly, without Her Majesty and Counsel knowing?"

"Ask for Gor'ya specifically at the piquet's. You won't

have the day's password, so they will scarcely let you through, even if they recognise you."

"And I should give this to Gor'ya straight away?"

"Once you are safely through the piquet's" Corelya cautioned. "Tell Gor'ya that you have spoken to me, that I am safe and well, and that I shall return shortly. Tell her that you have shown this to me and that we both think it is of supreme importance. Though we have no proof, it seems likely that this communique hails directly from the new Hellenic intelligence source in the region."

"Do you think that Gor'ya will believe me?" the old man ventured.

"She will when she reads it! Gor'ya may be able to confirm some of its allusions with our sources in Chersonesus, though I would advise caution given the likelihood that the place is crawling with Persian agents at the moment."

"Are things truly that bad in the peninsula? I had no idea that things had taken such a turn for the worse!"

"I am afraid that they have, ever since you left. Persian agents are everywhere, not just in Nymphaion and Panticapaeum, and they would pay a substantial sum in gold to obtain this information!" Corelya smiled tightly.

"I heartily concur with such a bleak prognosis, if what you say is true" Korta replied gloomily. "Well, well, well!" he exclaimed suddenly. "It seems that we might have some company for the night, after all!" he pointed in the distance towards the horizon.

In the east, at the edge of the horizon, a train of wagons snakes across the Steppe towards them. There were perhaps ten in all, accompanied by a drove of wild horses. "They do not look like they are military. You think they might be merchants?" Corelya ventured.

"They are heading towards the confluence of the rivers. Quite regardless of whether they are friendly or otherwise our paths should cross before dusk, wouldn't you say?"

Korta mused.

"I would concur with your assessment. We should have a clearer appraisal of their nature and strength within the hour."

"It would be nice to have some company for the evening?" Korta sighed happily.

"It will spare me the ordeal of your constant harping about the soreness of the days ride!" Corelya snorted.

"If I am being truthful, I could do with a good night's rest from this infernal saddle."

"A view entirely shared by your mare! I don't doubt?" Corelya sneered.

FIVE

Lower Donets, July 493 BC

They were traders, not brigands. It was the largest caravan Corelya had ever seen on the Steppe, excepting the Royal caravan which had journeyed south from the Palace at Trakhtemirov some two moons earlier. It numbered some thirty wagons, accompanied by a large drove of horses, more than fifty stallions, mares, and colts, which fanned out to graze on the lush pastures of the meadow and drink heartily at the river's edge. Corelya gaped in wonder! She and Korta had dismounted and now stood with their swords sheathed waving to the driver of the nearest wagon as it approached. This was the accepted protocol, if one wished to survive! To their relief, the driver of the wagon waved back in a friendly manner and hollered a greeting.

"Hello!" the waggoner boomed. "Hello!" Korta hollered back.

"Where have you come from?" the driver spoke Scythian.

"Further up the river, just south of Rost'eya. We left early this morning and were thinking of camping for the night hereabouts, if our company would be welcomed?"

"We were thinking of crossing the river and camping on the plain. Just over there, if that please you?" the driver pointed towards the wide expanse of plain bordering the meadow, which was accessible via the wooden bridge, which spanned the Donets at its narrowest point, a short distance to the south.

The bridge was constructed from a series of barges, fashioned from military-grade timber baulks, lashed together by heavy hemp rope. Heavy timber planks had then been hammered to form a wide platform spanning the banks of the Donets that was sufficiently sturdy to carry even Her Majesty's entourage! The bridge was new, completed only last summer as a joint venture between the Orch'tai and the Ur'gai with the express intent of increasing trade between the ducal centres and the Hellenic polities of the Crimean Peninsula and of Olbia, to the west. The structure was a monument to a renewed cordiality between former enemies, following a thawing of hostilities some three years before.

"That sounds ideal. It would be fine grazing pasture for the horses" Korta concurred.

"Where are you going to?" the man hollered.

Corelya shot Korta a warning look. "I am heading to Chersonesus see my youngest Granddaughter. My companion will be leaving early tomorrow morning on her own journey."

"We are heading to Olbia. You are welcome to join us for the rest of your journey until we reach the 'labyrinth'. Would you require any supplies this night?"

"You have berry wine?" Corelya asked.

"We have berry wine, plum wine, ris'ka and, of course, we have berry and plum wodki."

"What in Hades name is ris'ka?" Corelya whispered to Korta.

"It is from the Orient. It is very potent, far stronger than wodki. I would be wary if I were you" he replied.

"I don't suppose you have shoki?" he hollered to the driver.

"We also have shokas, many shokas. Indeed, we have everything, including poppy oil and tinctures!" the driver spread his hands expansively.

"Conveyed within so many wagons?" Corelya was incredulous.

"We have come from the lands of the Saka. We have clothing, crafts, and a selection of weapons" Corelya's antennae twitched at the mention of weapons.

"Do you have kindling for sale?" Korta enquired, steering the conversation to safer ground.

"We do. I have some in the back of my wagon. You may have some for free if our wine and meat is to your taste."

It certainly was. Corelya had never seen such quantities of smoked and salted meats, cheeses and curds, wheat flour and even rice, which she had never tried. The array of spices was simply bewildering, an aromatic siege of the senses. Corelya saw a look of unchaste joy on Korta's face as he perused the jars and chatted animatedly with the waggoners as to their origin. Corelya purchased two coarse ceramic jars of berry wine, a brace of freshly killed rabbits, wrapping cloths, oil and spices for the evening meal and walked a short distance away from the gaggle of wagons to site their campfire for the evening. Soon enough, a fire was roaring, and she had headed down to the bank of the river to wash her hands and fill a pot with water to make tea. She had chatted animatedly with a Sauromatae family and had managed to scavenge some cooking stones to be placed among the charcoals at the edges and the base of the fire. The rabbit carcasses, hunted earlier that day, were expertly skinned and rubbed with oil before being sprinkled with spices. These are wrapped tightly to form a parcel and left to season prior to cooking. It would be at least another hour before the coals were ready, and Corelya added further fuel to the flames.

Korta soon returned with several bags of spices and two bottles of ris'ka. He had also acquired a shoka and a bag of shoki, the dried leaves and flower buds of the hemp plant, *Sativa*, which could be smoked. Corelya was naturally curious about the *shoka* and wondered how it worked. She had never tried shoki, few people she knew had, and had been greatly surprised by her former tutor's enthusiasm in his pursuit of the herb. Corelya used a dagger to slice the beeswax seal on the wooden stopper of a jar of wine and passed a filled goblet to the old man who smiled at her appreciatively. "This is a rare treat for me, dear child. A little adventure is good for the soul at any age" he sighed, drinking heartily from the wide- brimmed wooden cup.

"I will have to leave tomorrow. My mission is most pressing. Are you sure you will be fine?" Corelya asked softly.

"I will be in good company. They are fine people who hail from the southern fringes of the Ural'sk Mountains and traverse the Silk Road twice a year, to and from Olbia. They set off in the early thaw and have only just returned."

"You will be glad of the company, I don't doubt?" Corelya smiled sweetly.

"I am not quite the unloved loner that you would credit, Corelya!" Korta admonished lightly.

"Do you see your children and Grandchildren often?"

"I do. More often than perhaps I should, given my disgrace" Korta sighed.

"The food should be ready to cook in the next hour, possibly less. The fire is coming along nicely" Corelya deftly changed the subject. "You have other visitors though, for you said as much?"

"Indeed, I do. Yet I rarely travel, if ever. It is good to see you again, darling child, after all this time. Will I see you again this summer?"

"I hope to return to Court within a week or so. No longer than that. You never know, the Queen may look favourably on your return."

"I have no intention of spending any time in Her Majesty's detention, Corelya" Korta said gloomily.

Corelya laughed. "Detained in what exactly, Zar'cha's bed?"

Korta guffawed. "And what do you know of such things?"

"A lot less than Zar'cha, that's for sure!" Corelya snickered.

A short while later, the rabbit carcasses were roasting on the oiled cooking stones.

They are turned regularly and seasoned with the remaining salt and spices. The first jar of berry wine was nearly finished, and the conversation had been easy and amiable. Corelya enjoyed her former tutors' company and had missed him terribly these past two years. She watched with particular interest as Korta prepared the Shoka for smoking after the meal. Corelya was naturally inquisitive and wondered why anyone would ever bother with anything more complicated than an open jar and a waiting goblet? They drained the first jar of berry wine and toasted the day's peace and their rekindled friendship with a modest ration of Corelya's wodki. She would purchase a few flagons from the traders before she set off early the next morning.

The meal was excellent! The roasted flesh is crisp on the outside, yet tender on the inside as to almost melt in the mouth. In appreciation of its near perfection, it was eaten in silence. Only afterwards, their goblets replenished, did their conversation resume. After their goblets had been drained and refilled, Korta busied himself with the final preparations for lighting the shoka. Corelya watched with interest as her former tutor inhaled deeply and began to cough uncontrollably. His cheeks were suffused ruddy by the time he had finished coughing.

"I don't know why you would even bother! Not if that's how it makes you feel!" Corelya said snidely.

"I will be fine in a minute, trust me. It has been quite some time since I have smoked a shoka."

The shoka was laid to heat on a pile of embers at the edge of fire and, the moment smoke began to rise through the perforations at the conical lid of the shoka,

Korta carefully picked it up by the neck and closed his lips around the reedpipe inserted through the draw-hole. He inhaled deeply, paused briefly, and exhaled a thin stream of smoke from his mouth. "Ahh!" he sighed. The shoka was replaced on the embers.

"More wine?" Corelya asked.

"Please. That flagon should almost be finished?"

"I have a flagon from the traders I met a few days ago."

Korta retrieved the shoka from the embers and inhaled deeply once more. He accepted the proffered cup of berry wine from Corelya with a knowing twinkle in his eyes. Up until that point, she had noticed no obvious change in his behaviour, yet now his eyes were strangely glazed. "Thank you, Corelya. You have always been an extremely generous child. Always thinking of others first, rather than of yourself, Yari especially."

"I have always been protective of her. Ever since.what happened? Some days she is more like my little sister than my best friend."

"She is well?" Korta asked earnestly.

"Yari never talks about what happened. She refuses to even mention it. I suppose it is just her way of coping with things. Her horsemanship and her skill with a sword are improving considerably, as it may need to. She certainly smiles at lot more nowadays than she used to and she still has her cheeky sense of humour."

"That is good to hear. I was always incredibly fond of her, as you know. If I am being truly honest, I miss neither the intrigue, nor the enmity, of Court life. Yet I do miss my practice, obviously, and both of your company" Korta confessed.

"You were like a surrogate father to us, Yari and I. It was you, more than anyone else, saving the Queen, who made us feel like we were real people, not mere slaves. It is more than some others do, even now."

Korta sighed and busied himself refilling the shoka

with shoki. He was keenly aware of the child's burning resentment at her enslavement, quite regardless of freedoms she had always enjoyed compared with other slaves. "It is not a fair world, Corelya! You know that full well. You have travelled with the Royal Court to exotic places and have gazed upon wonders others could only dream of. Despite your assertions, your existence *is* privileged. Yet, you have also known cruelty and terror, ever since you were young. Because of that, you are fully conscious that a great injustice, wickedness even, thrives in our world. As such, you are not happy with life and dream of something different. A world encumbered with less inequality, more charity, and a greater cognisance of the needs and desires of others. You always have."

"You think I am a hopeless dreamer?" Corelya sighed softly.

"If I have taught you anything, it is that the fabric of this world cannot be sustained by cruelty and repression of the basic desires of others. There are simply too many conflicting desires and far too little natural provision to satiate them." Korta ventured.

"You think it is natural for us to aspire to Empire?"

"I think the pursuit of Empire stems from the purest shade of greed! It is fuelled by nothing noble, and, despite its proclaimed glories, is nought but naked self-enrichment at the expense of others! It is founded on the delusional premise that your own desires are morally superior to those of other nations. Empires are always achieved by war, repression and, ultimately, by a liberalisation of wickedness! Are these truly the virtues to which we should logically aspire?" ventured Korta.

"They are not! What of the Hellenics? They seek to expand their influence and glory through dissemination of their culture and philosophy. They do not seek to conquer, but rather seek to colonise" Corelya asserted.

Korta stoked the fire with a stick and collected fresh,

glowing coals to the edge.

The shoka was placed on top of these coals and, in no time at all, smoke was literally billowing out of the perforations at the top. Korta inhaled deeply and subsequently blew a wispy stream of smoke. "Would you like to try?"

"I think I might?" Corelya even surprised herself by her eagerness. She inhales deeply and nearly chokes on the harsh fumes. Smoke exhales from her nostrils. "Hades aflame!" she cursed loudly.

"It is always this way the first time. Have a drink of wine and then try again. I will let the shoka heat again."

He passed the shoka back to Corelya and she inhaled deeply, again she coughed.

She inhaled again and began to feel decidedly lightheaded. The shoki was harsh and her mouth felt dry. She drained the goblet of berry wine in one gulp. Korta replenished both goblets with the last of the wine. "How do you feel?"

"I feel light-headed, and my mouth is very dry. This is different to poppy oil."

"You might wish to lie down for a while, if it's your first time?"

"I will be fine, honestly. I just need a drink, and that is all." Corelya took a large gulp of the berry wine. "That feels better! Oh fuck.. I need to be sick!" Corelya turned away from the fire and vomited violently. "Urghhhh!" she moaned piteously. "I feel terrible! I feel really fucking terrible!" She vomited again and almost fainted. Korta snaked his arms around her shoulders and helped her to her feet, but she stumbled heavily and nearly fell.

The girl is drowsy and has gone a deathly pale. Her forehead sweats freely as she shivers in the cool night air.

"Let us help you to bed. Come child, you can sleep on the other side of the fire."

Korta swept Corelya off her feet and carried her around

the fire to the opposite side. He laid her gently down on the lush grass and strolls across to Sybillya to retrieve her sleeping blanket. He plucks a small blanket from his own horse and folds this to fashion a headrest. When Korta returned, Corelya had passed out in a drug-induced stupor and he quickly covers her body with the blanket, tucking the edges under her torso and hips to warn against the increasing chill of the night. He quickly checks her pulse. The rhythm was slower than normal, yet not worryingly so, and a lowered pulse rate was a direct side effect of the alcohol and shoki. He gently lifts Corelya's head, stroking her crown affectionately, and laid this tenderly down on the headrest. Korta walks back to the other side of the fire and pours himself a goblet of berry wine.

Corelya awoke early the next morning, flushed with embarrassment at her previous night's conduct. Korta had been awake for an hour or so and had prepared a small cauldron of mint tea. There was bread, honey, mint tea, and a small goblet of wodki for breakfast.

Corelya grimaced at the mention of wodki, causing her erstwhile former tutor to smile wryly. "Good morning, Corelya! It is good to see you back in the land of the living! I trust you slept well?" Korta asked breezily.

"I am truly sorry about last night. I made a rare spectacle of myself, did I not?" Corelya sighed miserably.

"We have fresh bread, baked in the past hour, and honey, mint tea, and some plum wodki!" Korta smiles reassuringly at the girl.

"That sounds heavenly. I still ought to apologise, though."

"Not at all, dear child. Perhaps I ought to have told you that dizziness and nausea are a common reaction the first time you smoke shoki. It rarely happens again, not unless you use it excessively."

"I shall never use it again!" Corelya spat.

"Smoking shoki is far more common among the

Sauromatae than it is among the Scythia" chided Korta.

"My kinfolk can bloody well keep it!" Corelya growled.

"It does have proven medicinal qualities and some quite interesting psycho-somatic effects" Korta opined.

"It is used by King Darius' Immortals, is it not?" Corelya sipped the proffered tea gratefully and devours a piece of bread that had been smeared liberally with fresh honey. It tasted divine.

"Indeed, it is! You remember them from the Royal Palace in Susa?"

Corelya drizzles honey on an unleavened loaf and gnaws hungrily. She smiles brightly and sips her tea. "They are very impressive! Although I do not think appearances alone can win a fight!"

"Their valour is legendary, Corelya. And their devotion to their King is unswerving" mused Korta.

"Is it really true that they have never been defeated?" Corelya enquired interestedly.

"That is true, dear child" Korta confirmed.

"Yet they have never taken to the field against the Spartans?"

"That is equally true. It is a prospect that they would relish, no doubt."

"They should be careful what they wish for. The Athenians rate the Spartans as the best warriors in the known world, at least according to our sources."

"The 'Immortals' smoke shoki before they fight a battle. It induces a state of euphoria, a shared belief that their souls are prepared for the journey to the next life. They thus have no fear of death and are, or at least have been, undefeated on the field of battle."

"Perhaps they simply need a harsh lesson in reality" Corelya mused cynically.

Within an hour, the caravan was ready to continue its journey westward across the Steppe toward the 'labyrinth' and Olbia. Corelya reckoned it would take two days to reach the gateway to the Crimea and harboured no fears for Korta's safety or the security of the vital document concealed within his robe. Instead, she felt a brief pang of jealousy that the next few days of his journey would be filled with companionship, perhaps even memories. Her own mission demanded solitude and, above all, a constant vigilance. She bids her former tutor a fond farewell, embracing him warmly, and repeated her assurances that the mission should take no more than a few days. Hopefully, they would be re-united once more, however briefly, in a weeks' time. Corelya beseeched the old man to pass news of her well- being to Her Majesty, Gor'ya and, of course, to Yari. Corelya mounts her trusty steed and watches the caravan snake into the distance. Then, her natural vitality fortified by a generous slug of wodki, she gallops across the bridge, heading east.

Once across the eastern banks of the Donets, Corelya rides south-west towards the frontier of the 'disputed territories', rather than the Orch'tai frontier to the north-west.

Given recent intelligence, there was a strong possibility she would encounter Orch'tai cavalry detachments in the region. Whilst they would be armed, Corelya did not fear them, not whilst the two Ducals laboured under the peace of the *Accord*. Nor, for that matter, did she fear the Argata, despite their deserved repute for casual brutality. During the past decade, Sauromatae communities of the plains and forests to the south of Qu'ehra had been ruthlessly purged. According to Ur'gai sources, remnant Sauromatae communities persisted in the hinterlands of the Caucasus, in the valleys of the mountains themselves, even in the plain and gallery forests north of Qu'ehra, in defiance of the brutality of Argata Royal Army and their sponsored marauders.

By the late morning, she had ventured deep in the so-called 'disputed territories', the gateway to 'lands between the seas', the region her ancestors had settled more than a Century earlier. The Ur'gai and the Orch'tai had waged war for more than seventy years over the jurisdiction of the hinterlands of the lower Donets and Dnieper, the eastern and southern shores of the Azovi, and the northwest margins of the Kas'pa. Shortly after midday, Corelya and Sybillya traversed a narrow stream in a patch of gallery woodland, which demarcated the southern border of the Orch'tai realms, and plunged into lands now designated as an Argata Protectorate. Despite the historic enmity between the Ur'gai and Argata, they had been at peace since the signing of the *Accord Scythiac* the previous summer.

As fate would have it, she had not encountered a soul thus far, and it was unlikely she would meet any Orch'tai patrols, not so deep within Argata territory. If she did so, then it would be tantalising support for her theory that a new cordiality had blossomed between the two rivals over the course of the past year. Corelya found a perfect spot for a short respite, nestled in the shade at the edge of a patch of gallery woodland. It was then that she espied a small caravan on the horizon, heading north towards her. *Their paths would almost certainly cross within the next hour or so.*

Corelya felt in far finer fettle than she had earlier. She brewed a cauldron of mint- tea and imbibed a further draught of wodki from her last flagon. Hopefully, the approaching caravan would have flagons for sale, and she hoped to barter with the hemp-rope acquired from the merchants the previous night. The caravan, numbering two wagons, and several horses belonging to a single family, crossed her path in the early afternoon, and confirmed that they had encountered no-one else on the plain that day. They had no need for the rope but, much to Corelya's relief, were perfectly happy to exchange a flagon of wodki for one of berry wine. They parted company amicably, and Corelya kicked her heels in to Sybillya's flanks to urge her to a gallop. There was nobody else around, at least according to the travellers, and it would be wise to reach the safety of the river and woodland on the horizon before the early evening. Both she and Sybillya would enjoy the exercise.

～

Nymphaion, July 493 BC

A merchant vessel, *The Maiden of Samos*, proudly flying the insignia of the peacock feather, symbol of the Hellenic Goddess Hera, docked at the South Wharf in Nymphaion and began unloading its cargo. This included a bewildering array of fine ceramics of the deep-ochre clay prized by the most discerning patrons, together with woollen rugs, woven winter tunics, and copious quantities of the famed red wine that are the principal exports of the island of Samos. In recent times, the Island and its populace had been sworn enemies of King Darius and were in open revolt, yet they had been pacified and had now pledged solemn allegiance, *earth, and water*, to their rightful King in Susa.

Except for the Captain, an amiable old sea-hand named Mithras, and his crew, all Samians born and bred, the vessel had embarked from Rhodes a week earlier with a single passenger on board, a wealthy merchant of some notoriety, who was a frequent visitor to the ports of the Black Sea and the Crimea. The man made no efforts to disguise his identity, for there was surely nothing to fear in this dreary little backwater. The visitor, above average height and slim build openly sported a heavy iron sword and dagger, both sheathed within ornately embossed scabbards at his hip, and a heavy pine staff. The traveller was Thassalor of Knossos and was no friend to King

Darius, the Persians, or any of their allies, including his Phoenician brethren. His arrival piqued the interest of certain agents who clandestinely monitored the arrival of all overseas vessels in the port. These men were loyal to the Persian King, their loyalty vouchsafed by a princely sum in silver, or, in the case of two watchful souls on the Wharf this day, a handful of battered and aged bronze disks!

"Are you sure it is him?" said Chisos, a native of the city who had sworn his allegiance to the Persian King for a regular payment in freshly minted bronze.

"I am positive of the fact! And I will swear to it! He is a regular visitor to *The Delphine* and a good tipper" replied the burly man standing next to him. The man is Iscaertes, a native of Nymphaion, employed as security at the famed hostelry in the Eastern Quarter of the city, not far from the Wharf.

"I will tail him to his residence. It cannot be all that far away, surely? This flash bastard doesn't seem overly bothered about hiring a livery!" hissed Chisos.

"I will go to *The Mount Olympus* and inform Saelaes about our friend's arrival. He will know what is to be done about him, that's for sure."

"You can get the first round in then? I shouldn't be all that long, should I?"

"Just make sure you don't lose him, understand?" Iscaertes cautioned.

Stalking this clown to his address will be a piece of piss! Just like taking a honeycomb from a baby, the gullible twat!" sneered Chisos.

Chisos was assuredly not the first man to misjudge the guile of Thassalor of Knossos; famed womaniser, gastronome, sommelier to the noblest families in the civilised world, and ardent seducer of more than a few of their prettiest daughters. Thassalor was no stranger to Nymphaion and knew far more of its virtues and vices than he did the virtues and vices of *The Delphine's* most ardent and sought-after companions. Sensing intuitively that he was being tailed by a brute of commonly low intellect, he lost subsequently his pursuer in the warren of the residential district of the Eastern Quarter, before quenching his thirst for a time at a little Vintner's shop he knew well. Happily, this was a mere stone's throw away from his preferred place of residence. He would, of course, take the elementary precaution of booking a room for an extended period at *The Merchant's Chalice* in the northeast of the city. This was a scandalous indulgence, given it would serve only as a venue to bed his whores! Whilst Thassalor was no friend to the Persian King, he had little aversion to spending the man's money! By curious twist of fate, the gold he would use to pay for his rooms in Nymphaion originated from the same consignment of stolen lucre that had covered the expenses of a golden-haired maiden on her recent sojourn to Tyre! *Now who could have credited that?*

⁓

Perhaps it was inevitable that the blessing of peace, so welcome during the past week, could not last forever. Something dark and turbulent stalked Corelya, step-by-step, hand-in-hand, ever since she was a child, a restlessness of soul and spirit that invited, even welcomed, danger. Perhaps Yari had been right! To expect anything less would have been an exercise in folly, though not, it might be recorded for posterity, as great a folly as Corelya herself could commit, on rare occasions.

It was mid-afternoon, judging by the locus of the sun, when Corelya first became aware of the riders. This was likely a small group, numbering less than ten horsemen, mounted on good, heavy steeds, galloping at an angle to her current course on the opposite side of a steep ridge which bordered the plain to the east. *They could surely not have been aware of her presence, or else they would be closing*? A large stream, its meandering path flanked by gallery woodland which clothed the ridge, meandered west toward the centre of the plain on the horizon, a few hours ride away. Almost at the centre of the horizon, where the ridge levelled with the plain, their paths must surely converge? Corelya glances to her rear and then veers left, kicking her heels and spurring Sybillya to a gallop towards the gallery forest and the ridge. She instinctively knew her conduct was reckless! The threat to her front encompassed a stretch of ground several miles wide! She had no clear idea of the exact course of the riders, or whether they were friends or foe! In the event of the latter, any engagement would be delayed until the last few seconds with an almost certain predictability of outcome - death! *As Her Majesty's Royal Retainer, death was a constant companion, and even a friend*!

Corelya slows Sybillya to a canter as they reach the edge of the wood and, inhaling deeply, she plunges into its depths. This *was* the moment, when a spike of exhilaration immersed her soul as the adrenaline coursed through her arteries to conquer any animalistic dread. She was the *predator*, not the *prey*! Corelya's heartbeat raced with a rhythmic patter to the drumbeat of Sybillya's measured footfalls on the ground beneath their feet. Further and further, deeper, and deeper, they plunged into the forest until they met the stream and crossed, to pause at the opposite side. This would be as good a place as any to stop for a break, she decided. Corelya dismounts to allow Sybillya to drink heartily from the stream and eat greedily of the oats and rye mixture kept in her knapsack. A cursory scour of the terrain yielded a bounty of berries to accompany the fish cooked the previous night. The tranquillity is cruelly shattered by a series of ear-piercing screams, audible even from a distance within the dense canopy. Corelya reacts instinctively, grabbing her weapons, and darted into the forest, weaving effortlessly through the undergrowth, her feet barely kissing the dirt.

The acrid tang of burning wood was thick in the air before she saw the smoke. A once proud home of a humble family was now aflame. Corelya sprinted uphill, skirting unseen around the edge of the clearing to a vantage point on the high ground, blessed with both defensive and offensive merits. The screams continue, a monotonous, blood-curdling howl of despair, certainly that of a girl. Corelya dived to the ground and scurries forward on her belly through the undergrowth to survey the unfolding drama in the clearing below. The entire family, excepting the eldest child, aged a few years older than she, had been murdered, their bodies set ablaze with flaming oil. The survivor, a young teenager had been stripped naked. Her breasts, though not full, were pendulous, and she had a rich covering of hairs where a few years prior she had been bare. Whilst she was of marriageable age, she was still very much a virgin. That virtue was to be stolen, in the cruellest manner imaginable, at the behest of captors who were clearly enthralled by her hapless terror. The girl sobbed piteously as she was thrown to the dirt and pinioned tightly, her legs parted to reveal a treasure that was surely the right of a future husband, never these vermin! *Corelya felt her soul burn with hatred and murder, with the fury of an Amazon*

"You shall all meet your maker this day, you evil bastards!"

She drew two quarrels from her quiver and laid them on the ground next to the loaded weapons. The offensive would be quick and brutal, she decided. It would be a massacre, for nothing less would assuage her *fury* in the face of such brazen outrage! Corelya elected to afford the eager rapist the meagre courtesy of dropping his britches and prepping his cock to lustful readiness, before she shot him through the throat. The second weapon was discharged into the chest of a gruff-looking man standing to his immediate right. Both weapons were swiftly re-loaded and discharged with chilling insouciance. In a mere matter of heartbeats, Corelya had stilled the rhythm of four of the vilest creatures she had ever had the misfortune to meet, now despatched to the tender mercies of their maker! The surviving marauders had scattered like startled rabbits into the woodland and must now be hunted down and killed. This was no small feat, yet the Sauromatae girl had long since flowered into an accomplished predator. Corelya rolled as two arrows thudded into the tree to her right and crawled quickly away from the edge of the ridge, before darting downhill through the tangle of the undergrowth. She quickly located suitable cover next to the track and dived in to the undergrowth, her body concealed from view.

She suddenly stilled, breathing softly, the blood pounding in her ears, as a lone figure darted out of cover one hundred yards to her left. He was obviously a decoy, yet her thoughts were disturbed by the thud of an arrow into a sapling two paces to the front and right of her position. The angle of the arrow confirmed that a single bowman, or possibly two such assailants, for there was surely more than one pair of footfalls edging closer on her right! Corelya slid her hand to her left hip and checked her daggers. They were secure and ready to hand in the event she should need use of them at close quarters. She was certain that they had not seen her, they were merely trying to draw her out and confirm this was a single hunter with whom they were now locked in mortal tryst. The first figure darted again from a crouched position between the trees some thirty yards to her left. A second figure dived behind a large tree to her immediate front and right about twenty yards away.

Corelya scanned the forest to her right and, as a third figure broke cover, she discharged one of the quarrels through his stomach, dropping him instantly. The man to her front left broke cover and charged forward with an axe, screaming his battle-cry which rattled hollow as Corelya shot him through the throat at close range. She broke cover and sprinted right, only the sword at her right and daggers at her left, when the heavy hiss of an axe caused her to dive and roll instinctively across the ground, twisting the scabbard with her left hand to clear the soil. The axe bit heavily into a nearby trunk, showering the vicinity in an explosion of splinters. Leaping to her feet, Corelya charged the single figure some ten yards away, her right hand reaching across her hip to the daggers at her left side. The gesture succeeded in duping the marauder in to mistaking her for a 'normal' person, a right-handed attacker. The challenger screamed with rage as he drew his sword from its scabbard and readied for the girl to close.

Corelya knew instinctively what he would do, for she was close enough to smell the fear oozing from every pore as death closed upon them. She saw a flicker of indecision, albeit briefly, as the man recognised the sword at her right, her hand now poised in the region of her upper left hip, for there was something not right but, too late, he stepped deftly to the right and swung the blade viciously at her neck. The arc of the razor-sharp blade should have killed her. Had she been right-handed, perhaps it might have done so, yet the girl side-stepped to the left and danced under the arc of the blade, drawing a dagger, which she plunged mercilessly into his right groin. The man screamed as the blade was pulled free, Corelya's heavy leather tunic drenching instantly with an arterial spray that signalled certain death and, dropping his sword and falling to one knee, this was driven cleanly through his right eye with her left hand. "*Bastard!*" Corelya screamed, her fear evaporating in the exhilaration of deliverance. "*Now you fucking die!*"

A peal of sardonic laughter stilled her *fury!* "I know you, don't I? Murderous little cunt!" the voice mocked.

"Then show yourself!" Corelya chided. "Come and face

me!" She slipped wiped the dagger clean on the jerkin of the corpse and let the man's body fall to the ground.

The raider snickered. "You are a feisty little cunt, aren't you? I have a use for that mouth of yours!" he taunted.

"You call yourself a man?" Corelya sneered. "Then come and face me! If you have the balls, that is?"

The challenger loomed in to view, some twenty yards to her front. He was built like a colossus, with a barrel chest, thighs like trunks of an oak, and forearms akin to timber- baulks. "You are a feisty one, aren't you, bitch? You are a ripe little plum for the plucking, if ever I saw! I shall savour the sweetness of your honey even more than that other fresh little whore!"

Corelya drew her sword defiantly. "Then come and taste my honey, filth-ball!"

The man laughed harshly. Corelya felt a boiling and merciless rage that cooled within an instant as an unseen hand closed around her mouth. She had failed, and now she would die! He was both clever and skilled, for she had not even heard a whisper of footsteps as he had stalked and then closed behind her. Her head was pulled violently to the rear and the left, her blade falling silently to the ground in submission to the fates, the wicked gleam of a knife perhaps her last vision, as her body relaxed and waited for the cut that would sever her throat and dim the light forever. *Astonishingly, it never came!* A hiss of arrows took the burly man cleanly in the chest and she was pitched violently forwards as her assailant grunted his death-rattle and slumped forwards. Corelya writhes free as they land heavily in the dirt, and, grabbing her sword, she turns to face the new threat. Two arrows thud into the ground next to her feet. She steps back from a posse of riders that close around her on all sides.

The lead rider, a cruel and surly brute, at least judging by appearances, dismounts and strides toward her. "Drop the blade and kneel, bitch!" he snarled. Corelya dropped her sword and remained standing, eyes blazing defiantly, fists balled in impotent rage! "I said kneel!" he roared as he cuffed Corelya hard across the left cheek with his right hand, tears springing instantly to her eyes.

"Go fuck your mother!" Corelya snorted.

"You little slut!" the man raged and struck again, this time the force of the blow dazed the girl and knocked her off her feet. Yet, unbelievably, within an instant she was on her feet and facing him, her face a mask of fury, even as the tears streamed freely down her cheeks.

"I said fuck your mother!" Corelya roared, spitting blood into his face.

"Fuck yours, you little Scythian cunt!" the brute growls as he drew his sword, a gleam of pure malevolence twinkling in his cold, brown eyes.

A voice, softy spoken, yet cultured and strangely alien, cuts through the tension like a Surgeon's knife. "Touch her again, Siladar, and you will die!" A tall stranger stepped away from a mount some twenty paces to the rear and sauntered breezily towards them. He wore a heavy black cloak with its hood drawn close around his face and a soft black hat, shielding his eyes from the sun. Corelya felt the faintest prickle of recognition and, with it, a sickening terror! "She will not kneel, my friend! Not this child. She has too much Sauromatae pride in the blood of her veins."

"Those veins are easily drained!" Siladar spat sullenly.

"You may well prove that point in due course, Siladar!" the stranger mocked. The stranger removes his hat. He smiles wryly at the girl, his grey eyes twinkling with irony.

"It is good to see you, Corelya! The fates have decreed our paths should cross once more!"

"Treacherous cunt!" Corelya seethed. "I swore I would kill you if they ever did!"

"As true as that may be, sweet child, I think it even beyond your reserves in light of the present circumstances" the stranger teased, drawing back his hood. It was a face that had once haunted Corelya's dreams, and, as much as she tried, she could not erase it from her memory. *He* was a Persian and, with the born arrogance of a Prince whose every desire could be satiated by simple command, he stalked 'the land between the seas' as the lion is master of his pride. "You truly have begun to blossom in to a rare Sauromatae rose, have you not?" he smiled at the girl with a genuine affection.

"*I hate you!*" Corelya sobbed. The shock of seeing him again, so overwhelming after all these years, disrobed all defiance to reveal the helpless child Nichassor had saved from certain death all those years before. "*I fucking hate you!*" she screamed, before she collapsed, weeping hysterically, into his outstretched arms!

⌒

Saiga Plains, Crimea, July 493 BC

The man pours two generous measures of wodki into a pair of polished bronze goblets and passes one to his guest. He eyes the woman courteously, as hers twinkle with mischief.

"Where is your husband, my Lady?" asked the man

"Whoring, I would wager?" the woman smiled sweetly. "Do you truly believe I am that nai:ve?"

"I would never presume anything, my sweet. I am deeply saddened by your husband's serial infidelity."

"Spare me your condolences, for I knew full well the nature of the man I married. Does your darling wife know that you are here? I think not?" she mocked.

"We are merely talking, my Lady, nothing more" the man replied.

"You really do believe that don't you? Is that how you sleep soundly at night? By pretending that our little trysts are of such little consequence. Is that how you embrace your darling children in the morning, with such endearing piety?"

The man eyed the woman hungrily. "You are a tease, my sweet! You have bewitched me, for there is not a single moment in a day that I do not yearn for you. We are both living a lie, are we not? And yet, I long for you, my sweet, as the rose longs for the bee that will truly make her whole."

The woman giggled. "Save such platitudes for your darling daughters. For it is they, and not I, who believe such honey-drizzled nonsense!" the woman mocked. "As for myself, I have only one motive for accepting your invitation to meet this night. There is talk of a Royal Banquet to be held in Chersonesus within the moon. Furthermore, I hear pray tell that the Queen has entrusted you with the solemn duty of arranging this little soiree, isn't that so? I would obviously require new attire for such a gala, would I not?"

"It is true, my love, that Her Royal Majesty has entrusted me with this honour. I am to begin correspondence with the City Father's and Council of the Merchant's Guild within the next few days. Does that please you?" the man replied silkily.

"It would, my sweet. Yet I simply cannot countenance my attendance at such an event in the garb of a beggar, you would surely agree? I require something a little more exquisite, would I not?"

"It would delight me, obviously. It would be remiss of my, my sweet, to presume that your darling husband would pay for such a fine garment?" the man smiled slyly.

"Do not taunt me!" the woman hissed. "I hear pray tell, if such rumours are to be credited, that your darling wife is thinking of enrolling your eldest daughter, Naria, at school in Corinth? Now who would pay for such an indulgence? Isn't that a worthy subject for uncouth campfire tittle-tattle?"

The man's eyes blaze in anger. "That is none of your concern, my sweet. I have family money, more than enough to cover the expense of our daughter's education" the man spoke icily.

The woman smiles serenely. "Do not mock me, my

honeycomb, for you have more than met your match with me. As for myself, I care little where you school your whelpling! Nor, for that matter, would I be inclined to indulge in such base malice, certainly not against a mere child? I cannot speak for others, of course!"

"You desire a new dress for the Banquet? If that is so, then I am sure our mutual friends can be relied upon to entreat your heart's desire!"

The woman's eyes twinkle in triumph. "I knew you would understand, my sweet. That is your forte, is it not, grappling with the subtler nuances? That is my price, nothing more, nothing less."

"Is there anything else?" the man said evenly.

"Perhaps we could meet at our favourite place tomorrow? Say, just after midday, would that suit you? For I yearn for you, my love, as a spider courts the fly."

~

Nymphaion, July 493 BC

It was dusk when the last merchant charter of the day dropped anchor at the North Quay in the city of Nymphaion. This vessel, named *The Enchantress*, flew the insignia of the ankh, the key to life itself, proud symbol of the renegade Cypriots who had pledged allegiance to the Achaemenid King in Susa. The ship had embarked ten days earlier from Morphou Bay on the north-west coast of Cyprus, laden with wine, spices, and olive oil. In addition to the crew, commanded by Captain Nerkhuri, they had conveyed a group of passengers, some twenty-one men, all sworn servants of King Darius. The men had been hand-picked for the mission more than two months earlier in Susa and had initially journeyed from Tyre. The crew were wary of them, and of their master, for these men were obviously soldiers, despite their fine civilian attire. *What in Hades name would a contingent of Persian mercenaries, travelling with the blessing of their King, possibly want in such a backwater like Nymphaion?*

The twenty retainers stroll nonchalantly down the gangplank to wait beside a pair of waiting passenger carts, as their luggage is loaded as a matter of priority by the Stevedores on to a third cart. Their master, a man of obvious wealth and status, travelled alone in a bespoke covered carriage at the front, having issued instructions to the drivers of the carts to closely follow the carriage north. As the moon shines brightly in a clear night sky, the train of vehicles trot north along the Avenue, turning left into the West Road. When the convoy reaches the junction with the North Road it turns right, heading north into the heart of the Upmarket District, home to the wealthiest and most influential families in all Nymphaion.

PART TWO

SIX

Northern Plains of the Caucasus, July 493 BC

"King Darius has no plans to wage war on the Hellenics, Corelya. My sources are quite clear on this" said Nichassor. He and Corelya are sat by a stream, eating wild plums picked from trees which grace a small stretch of the bank further to the west. The afternoon's ride had been arduous in the blazing sun, yet the evening was cool, and a faint breeze ripples through the trees.

"Is that what your spies tell you?" Corelya chided. She dangled her feet in the stream, and wriggled her toes in childish delight, enjoying the blissful cool of the water.

Nichassor glances at the girl and raises an eyebrow in mock severity. "You doubt my integrity in this matter?"

"Both Cyrus the Great and King Darius gave repeated assurances of their noble intentions toward the Scythia and Sauromatae. Yet, if my memory still serves, they engaged in hostile actions without any provocation."

"A minor misunderstanding between neighbouring powers, nothing more" soothed Nichassor.

"Really?"

"Persia desires only peace with the Hellenics, especially with Athens. However, we must deal with the threat from our dissidents and traitors. Surely Scythia would understand the necessity of our ongoing campaign?"

"You do not fear Sparta?" Corelya enquired mischievously. "I would fear Sparta."

"Sparta is undeniably a regional power; in that respect you are correct. But Sparta has not the *energy*, or *ambition*, of Athens."

"You are still an accomplished liar, Nichassor, even after all these years" Corelya sighed.

"That is harsh, child" Nichassor adopted a pained expression. "King Darius is no Cyrus, and he has not the ambition to be. His position is far weaker than either Scythia, or the Hellenics, would credit. King Darius is perceived by regional Governors to have only a limited legitimacy. He rules by transient consensus, as you have witnessed during the insurrection of the past few years. There is neither support for, nor any necessity to, engage in wider hostilities with the Hellenics" he opined.

"Yari always said you were full of shit!" Corelya smiled serenely.

"How is the delightful Yari?" Nichassor asked interestedly.

"Like you even care?" Corelya sneered.

"I often thought of you, both of you, in the months after we parted. I had such high hopes for you both" said Nichassor.

"You received a high price for us, is that what you mean?" Corelya spat indignantly.

"Your security was everything. That was all that concerned me. You could not have stayed with us. Nicharassa would have let you die if your memory serves you still."

"Nicharassa was a prick!" Corelya cursed feelingly. "Is he dead? He deserves to be!"

"You have certainly grown in the intervening years. You look healthy and well- nourished. I think you have fared far better among the Ur'gai than I could ever have imagined" Nichassor diplomatically changed the subject, for Nicharassa was his younger brother.

Corelya turns away and grins. "Was it painful? It would please me if it were?"

"Such bitterness in one so young is scarcely a virtue, sweet child? Perhaps the 'mysteries' will cure you of such ills?" Nichassor grins as Corelya's cheeks flush hotly.

"I often dream of killing you, Nichassor! It is slow, it is cruel, and it pleases me!"

"If you dream of such things, Corelya, then perhaps it is time to take a lover?" Nichassor chided.

"Perhaps I shall dream of killing you tonight!" Corelya said nastily.

Nichassor laughs heartily. "You are surely not afraid of such things, Corelya?" He grinned again as the girl looked steadily at her toes wriggling in the water. She was truly embarrassed by, and perhaps even terrified of, the prospect of physical intimacy. "I am surprised no-one has 'courted' you yet?" If it were possible, Corelya's cheeks burned even more fiercely. Nichassor was clearly relishing the rare pleasure of teasing her.

"What will you do with Nirch'ii?" Corelya tried to steer the conversation towards safer ground.

The girl was sleeping soundly on a reed mat, shrouded with a wool blanket, next to a small fire a short distance away. She had been drugged with poppy oil and would not wake until the morning. Corelya had approved drugging the girl, for it would help keep the daemons at bay, at least for the next few nights.

"What would you like to do with Nirch'ii?" Nichassor mocked.

"You really are a shit!" Corelya reprimanded him icily. "Is that what you and your little band of like-minded pigs would like? Would it please you to see us embrace?"

"It would not please me, Corelya" Nichassor soothed. He smiled sardonically, signalling with his hands towards the rest of the group further to their left. "Though I cannot speak for the rest of my 'little band of pigs', as you so quaintly term us."

"Promise me, Nichassor! Promise me no harm will

come to her!" Corelya beseeched.

"Are my promises worth anything at all to you, after all this time?" Nichassor asked softly.

"Your promises aren't worth dogshit! Your life is worth even less to me!"

"You truly hate me, don't you?"

"No" Corelya responded instantly. The admission was sincere and Nichassor studied afresh the child that he had not seen in more than eight years. "I still can't forgive you, I never will."

"I saved your life, Corelya. Without me you would be dead. Not even Tabiti would have spared you."

"I was worth money to you, you said so. That was the only reason you saved my life."

"I sold you to Queen Illir'ya. She needed Handmaidens and your safety was assured."

"My safety was assured!" Corelya blazed. "By the Gods! I was wrong about you, Nichassor! I thought you wise, yet it seems you nought but a fool!"

Nichassor guffawed. "That is a little rich coming from someone who almost lost their life this day on account of her own supreme foolishness?" he chided her. "Would you and Yari have been safer among the Hellenics, the Orch'tai, or the Argata?"

"I was a person, Nichassor! Yari was a person! Then you and your filthy brethren traded us for money, and we became slaves. That is all I am now, and all I ever shall be, just a slave!"

"A mere slave would not have been allowed to travel so far from the Queen's household alone, Corelya?" Nichassor ventured dangerously.

"I was carrying a message. I am going to present Queen Illir'ya's terms to the Argata" Corelya replied softly.

"A single rider, a mere child no less, with no accompanying escort?'" Nichassor chided. "Do you think the Argata will be awed by Illir'ya's 'Pomp and

Circumstance'?"

"I became separated from my escort during an attack by a band of brigands only yesterday. The two riders who came with me died from their wounds" Corelya lied smoothly. "Regrettably, I did not have time to bury them. They will likely be fodder for the carrion now" she sighed. Corelya affected a demeanour of suitable discomfiture, as if she were truly ashamed of her conduct and breach of honour. She glanced down at the water, her gaze fixated on her toes, wriggling in the cool water.

"Do you believe the Argata will accept Queen Illir'ya's terms?" Nichassor enquired searchingly.

"Why would they not do so? The terms are extremely favourable to the Argata. We are allies, after all, are we not?" replied Corelya evenly.

"And Queen Illir'ya is prepared to risk the goodwill she has nurtured with the Orch'tai these past few years, since before she signed the *Accord Scythiac*, in favour of a closer regional ties with the Argata?" Nichassor probed.

"You may rest assured, Nichassor, that the Ur'gai have no intention of pursing anything other than closer ties with all of our neighbours, including Persia" Corelya declared. "Really?" mocked Nichassor.

"A few years ago, we were in a state of perpetual hostility with the Argata, were we not? Surely you would concede that we have many more bridges to build with them than with the Orch'tai, who are currently plagued by innumerable internal problems of their own? Chief among these is the issue of succession, which is far from certain, especially considering the recent tragedy. And, if that were not enough, they have fallen foul of Athens, both by their amity with Phoenicia, and their recent posturing."

"What if the Orch'tai were inclined to seek a closer alliance with the Argata themselves? Forgive me, for I am simply a curious man, but I am interested to know how this might be received at the Ur'gai Royal Court?" Nichassor quipped.

"Why would such a thing pose a problem?" Corelya sighed. "Scythia would be at peace, would it not? The enmity of the Orch'tai and the Argata runs far deeper than with either we or the Nur'gat? If such a thing were possible, then I can assure you that a closer alliance between the Orch'tai and the Argata would be favourably received at the Ur'gai Royal Court. We would maintain our trading alliances with both Persia and the Hellenics. That would be favourable to all, would it not?"

"Peace and prosperity for all!" Nichassor chided cynically. "As a man with considerable investments in the Pontic region, I freely admit that I would be pleased by a prospect of ever closer relations between the Scythian Ducals."

"Your *investments* are not in peril Nichassor, I assure you of that!" Corelya smiled slyly. "In deference to your cynicism, which has scarcely mellowed with the advancing years, I would venture the following. *What is the alternative?* A bloody, destructive war that leaves all parties worse off, combatants and neutral polities alike, including Persia. Persia is not the sole power in Asia, despite their claims to the contrary. Peace is always preferable to death. If you do not believe me, then just ask Nirch'ii?" she gestured towards the sleeping girl.

"And a new accommodation between the Ur'gai and the Argata will deliver such glories?"

"You may sneer, Nichassor! But any new accommodations between the Ur'gai and Argata would not be to the detriment of the Orch'tai, quite the contrary!" Corelya quipped.

"You fear the Orch'tai?" Nichassor smiled thinly.

"The Orch'tai can mobilise a powerful army, the greatest in the region. They remain potent threat to both the Argata and the Ur'gai. However, their current internal instabilities render this threat less potent than it once was."

"Would they attack Olbia?" Nichassor seemed

intrigued by the prospect.

"You have *investments* in Olbia, is that it? Such a course of conduct would mean certain war with Athens. Much of the Orch'tai's wealth derives from their timber trade, does it not?

Athens could impoverish them" Corelya stated the fact bluntly.

"But Athens requires these timbers for their ambitious naval programme?" Nichassor ventured.

"And run the risk of a disastrous war with Persia? Forgive me, Nichassor, but if the Athenians harbour ambitions for an enlarged navy, it is merely to counter the growing threat from Persia and its allies in the realms of Poseidon."

"Surely, the Ur'gai must fear the rude health of the Orch'tai treasury? They have prospered greatly during these past few years?" Nichassor smiled slyly.

"The Orch'tai have grown rich and powerful from the enmity of Persia and Athens, especially during the revolt in Ionia" Corelya conceded.

"And so, we have peace" sighed Nichassor.

"For the moment, at least, we do. Who can truly predict the future?"

"The barbarians have their soothsayers, the Greeks their sages, and the Trojans their Kassandra? I prefer to place my faith in the virtues of diplomacy. Without diplomacy, we are no better than dogs!"

"If that is so, we must keep talking, must we not?" Corelya stated emphatically.

～

The band struck camp early the next morning, while the air was still cool, trotting south across the plains to the east of Qu'ehra. Corelya had exchanged brief pleasantries with Nirch'ii over a breakfast of fried fish and fresh plums. The girl was pale and withdrawn, only to be expected given the horrors of the day before, yet Corelya had taken note of the fact that she still appeared to be lightly drugged, surely not the effects of the dosage administered the previous night. Corelya decided that she would speak to Nichassor, for it was unwise to drug the girl constantly, however light the dosage! Nirch'ii desperately needed to grieve, as she and Yari once had, in the days following their discovery by Nichassor and his band all those years ago. A few hours later, with the sun rising fast and the air warming perceptibly, the group reached a large stream. Nichassor reined in next to Siladar and spoke briefly with him, loud enough for everyone else, including Corelya, to hear.

"This is as good a place as any to rest, wouldn't you agree?"

The brute merely grunted his assent. The group crossed over to the opposite bank and fanned out. Corelya dismounted and immediately sought out Nirch'ii, who stood deep in conversation with Nichassor. The younger girl scowled at Siladar, who shot her a glare of pure hatred. He had evidently not forgiven his public reprimand at the hands of Nichassor the day before. Corelya stuck her tongue out at the skulking thug, much to the amusement of two brothers, Korbazaithe and Izibilan. Siladar growled at the pair!

Corelya led Nirch'ii away from the rest of the band. "We can make a fire here if you would like? I have plenty of kindling and wood" she addressed the older girl in Sarmati, the language of their ancestors. Nirch'ii simply nodded her ascent and began scraping a section of ground to site the fire.

"How are you feeling?" Corelya smiled reassuringly at the girl "Tired and sore" the girl answered.

"You ride well enough?" Corelya

"I am Sauromatae, and it is in my blood!" Nirch'ii said emphatically. "At least that is what my father always told me."

Corelya saw the raw pain in the girl's eyes as she blinked back the tears and moved quickly to embrace her.

"It is not unwomanly for Sauromatae to cry, Nirch'ii."

"I thought we were supposed to be a fierce people. I was always told that we are a proud people?" Nirch'ii mumbled sadly.

"Even Persian's cry, Nirch'ii, and they are the most arrogant bastards in all creation!" Corelya stated this as fact, for it was fact, at least as far as she could see. She enjoyed the smile that played at the corners of Nirch'ii's mouth. "Sauromatae cry when we hurt because sometimes it is a blessing to hurt. The pain makes us stronger, more resilient" Corelya ventured. "I hurt when my entire family was slaughtered. Our entire village was killed by marauders and I lost everything, except for Yari. I felt pain like I had never felt before in all my life. Yari felt the same."

"Who is Yari?" Nirch'ii asked interestedly.

"Yari is my best friend in the whole world" Corelya said proudly.

"You must miss her?" Nirch'ii frowned.

"Of course, I do" Corelya smiled warmly at the older girl. "I will be seeing her again soon enough. I am on an errand for my Queen."

"I don't even have a 'best friend'. We only really met small groups of passing strangers, though nearly all of them were friendly. The paid us for bread, cheeses, game from the forest, fruit wine, and wodki. I never really knew any other children, apart from my siblings."

"Well, you do now!" said Corelya emphatically. "You can be my newest 'best friend'!"

"What about Yari?' Nirch'ii asked quizzically.

Corelya grinned. "Trust me, Nirch'ii. A girl can never have enough 'best friends!"

⌒

The previous night had been uneventful, with Corelya and Nirch'ii falling in to a deep, liquor induced sleep, having consumed the last of the younger girl's wodki. Predictably, Corelya awoke irritably and immediately sought out Nichassor to confirm their destination. She was to be sorely disappointed, for Nichassor had left shortly after sunrise, travelling alone to Qu'ehra. "Did he say how long he would be gone for?"' she asked a scowling Siladar, who knelt next to the fire, sharpening a hunting knife.

"No" came the caustic response. He seemed genuinely irritated by the interruption. Corelya turned away and strolled back across the grass to where Nirch'ii sat stirring mint leaves in a kettle of bubbling water.

"Miserable prick!" she swore feelingly.

Nirch'ii snickered. "Has Nichassor left?"

"He left for Qu'ehra early this morning, all by himself, at least according that that sullen bastard! I have not the faintest idea when he shall return." Corelya sighed. "If he does not re-appear by tomorrow morning, I swear I will shoot that prick!" she spat and jerked her thumb in Siladar's direction.

"Will we be safe?"' Nirch'ii whimpered. Corelya saw the terror in the girl's eyes.

"Of course, we will be! They wouldn't dare go against Nichassor!" Corelya asserted confidently, whilst neglecting to inform Nirch'ii that she did not trust any of these heathen bastards, *especially* Nichassor. *This was, after all, a matter of diplomacy, was it not?*

"What will we do?" asked the girl interestedly.

"I suppose we will stay here for the day. It would be nice to have a break. We could forage for some fresh mint leaves and fruits? I know my mare would like a day's rest! She can graze contentedly for the next few hours" Corelya proclaimed. She turned and pointed at the gallery forest in the distance, perhaps an hour's ride to the east. "It would be nice to take a short ride downstream to the gallery forest. I could do with a bathe."

"Me too" chimed Nirch'ii.

"When we get to Qu'ehra we could have a look at some nice kurtas, if you would like to?"

"I don't have any money" Nirch'ii blushed. "I don't have anything?"

"I do! And don't worry, it is Queen Illir'ya's money" Corelya snickered.

"That would be lovely" beamed the girl. "I honestly don't know how to thank you."

"We are best friends, remember?"

They drank their tea in silence and enjoyed a few hours lazy relaxation on another glorious summer's day. Later, when the sun was at its zenith, the two girls climbed into their saddles and clicked their mounts to face east. "I am really looking forward to this!" Nirch'ii beamed happily.

"Me too.Oh fuck!

Nirch'ii turned to face Corelya, her face ashen. "What shall we do?"

"Ignore him! I will deal with this prick! Let's go!"

The girls click their mares to a trot. A scowling Siladar stomps across the grass to intercept them, waving his drawn sword to emphasise the threat! Corelya scowled and her hand moved instinctively to the twinned daggers at her right side. Siladar issued his challenge "Where are you going?" he growled.

"Over there" Corelya pointed to the canopy in the distance, smiling sweetly at a man she openly despised.

"No!" Siladar spat truculently.

Corelya shook her head defiantly and addressed the brute in Persian. "We were going to forage for fruits, nuts and mint leaves. We also planned to spend a few hours fishing and hunting. We will bring food back for everyone, as good girls ought to."

"No!" Siladar snorted.

"It isn't far. Nor is it dangerous. We have left most of our belongings by our fire" Corelya pointed to their fire.

"I said no!"

"And besides, both of us could do with a bathe. So, could you, judging by the smell!" The rest of the band laughed raucously.

Siladar burned with anger. "You have a tongue on you, Missy! You had better watch yourself! That tongue of yours will get you in to trouble one day. Much sooner than you think!" he hissed.

"You really are quite the tease, Siladar!" Corelya simpered. "What we all would dearly love to know is, do you go 'all the way'?" The other men howled with laughter! Siladar blushed hotly and glanced sullenly down at the floor. He knew when he was beaten. *This sneering bitch would get her just comeuppance, he would see to it personally.*

The two girls trot east. Only when they were safely out of earshot of the reast of the band did Nirch'ii broach the altercation with Siladar. "You shouldn't taunt him, Corelya! Siladar is a dangerous man! He scares me!" Nirch'ii cautioned. She was plainly terrified of the toad-witted thug.

"Siladar is an arsehole, nothing more than that!" Corelya snarled. "He is a typical male specimen, never forget that! He is brainless, charmless, and likely dick-less!"

Nirch'ii giggled "You *do* have a low opinion of men, do you not?"

"Most of them *are* low-lives!" Corelya spat. "We females have a duty to stand up to them and put them in their place. They are beneath us, not above, and we should never forget that!"

"Spoken like a true Scythian!" Nirch'ii teased. Corelya grinned inanely at the girl.

"I am Sauromatae, but my ways are Scythian. They don't go in for all that 'equality of the sexes' bollocks that we seem to cherish. In Scythia, men are inferior to women, it is a given. They are nothing without us. Most of them think with their dicks anyway, once they are old enough and their balls have dropped!"

Nirch'ii turned in her saddle and smiled slyly. "Fancy

a race to the edge of the woods? I reckon it should be just under a mile by now?"

"That sounds like an excellent idea. It would be good to work up a sweat before a cooling bathe! Ready when you are?"

"Go!"

The girls kicked their heels and thundered east across the deserted plain.

⌒

The pair chide their steeds to a canter, then a gentle trot, as they approach the fringe of the woodland. They enter the canopy and soon reach a well-worn track, heading east. Corelya suddenly clicks her mare to a halt and raises a hand.

"What is it?" Nirch'ii whispered frantically.

"Listen! You can hear the trickling of the stream?"

"Yes"

"That means that the current is fair, and the water is fresh. Great for everything, drinking, fishing, and bathing" Corelya proclaimed. "I can't wait to get in!"

"Nor me" said Nirch'ii.

The girls soon reached the stream and Corelya leapt from the saddle and strolled down the bank, cupping her hands in the cool water. She takes a sip, found it delicious, then splashed her face eagerly. After that, she slakes her thirst. The stream was sufficiently wide and deep enough for bathing. Corelya undresses and wades into the middle. She tested the bottom of the stream for anything that might do her a mischief, and sits down, beaming happily as she splashes water over her shoulders, breasts, and tummy. A naked Nirch'ii wades in and sits directly opposite the younger girl, gleefully splashing water over her own shoulders and naked breasts.

"How old are you? I never asked, I apologise" Corelya

asked suddenly.

"I turned fourteen just after the last Solstice. It seems like an eternity ago!"

"That would explain why your boobs are so big!"

Nirch'ii giggled. "They are not all that big! They seem to have been growing for ever! We are all different, Corelya! We all grow slightly differently. Some girls grow quicker than others."

"You don't need to tell me about it! Yari is only a few months older than me, yet her boobs are much bigger. Then again, she does eat a lot more honey than I do!"

Nirch'ii convulses in hysterics. "I don't think eating honey has anything to do with it! How old are you?" Nirch'ii quipped.

Corelya smiled serenely. "How old do you think I am?"

Nirch'ii glances quickly at Corelya's crotch, with its light wisps of golden pubic hair, and giggled. "You are certainly not a baby anymore, are you?"

Corelya grinned. "No, I don't suppose I am. That still doesn't answer my question, does it?"

"I would say you were at least twelve, for you have already sprouted hairs down there. Yet, you have none in your armpits. It will be a couple of years before you start to bleed regularly!"

"I am actually dreading it, if I am truthful."

"It is nothing to be afraid of, or ashamed of. It happens to all of us, we cannot escape it. It is called being a woman!"

"It won't happen to me if I bloody well die soon!"

Nirch'ii giggles and smiles shyly at the younger girl sat opposite her. "Have you spoken to anyone about this? I don't mean a man, obviously! I mean an older girl, or a woman, who has been through it all?" Nirch'ii asked.

"It didn't seem appropriate to ask the Queen!" Corelya snickered.

Nirch'ii eyed the girl closely. "Well, I can assure you, you have already started your journey! There can be no going back now." She points at Corelya's chest. "You start to swell here first. They are not boobs, not like a woman's, you just start to swell. Your nipples change and you start to swell more. They continue to grow, just like mine, and will do so for a few years yet, or so mum said. That is nothing to how you change down there!" Nirch'ii pointed to Corelya's crotch. "You have likely started to swell already?"

"I swell there?" Corelya gasped incredulously, pointing at her crotch.

Nirch'ii burst into hysterics. "I am sorry, forgive me! I did not mean to alarm you. You don't swell like a bee-sting, but things get bigger and.less neat. I cannot explain it. My mum told me that every girl is different, even though we all start the same."

"Is that before or after you get hairs?"

"When I was nearly thirteen, I started to develop hairs at the front down there, then a few months later in my armpits. Then things start to change down there and, well, the hairs seem to grow around you as you change. Before you know it, you are now completely covered by hair, and you have changed forever. During this time, you start to bleed, every month. Only a little at first, but then a lot! I was terrified at first, but you simply learn to live with it. It does affect your mood though. You get very angry, especially when it really hurts. It feels like you are being stabbed in the lower tummy. Mum told me to drink warm milk with lots of honey and a little poppy oil. It really works wonders when it gets bad."

"It sounds bloody awful!" Corelya grimaced.

"It isn't pleasant, but you do get used to it. It isn't like you have much of a choice in the matter! happens every four weeks, just like the cycles of the moon."

"Why does it take so long? It sounds excruciating!" Corelya scowled.

Nirch'ii giggled. "I suppose it takes so long because it is quite scary, at least at first! It would be terrifying if it happened overnight, within the space of a summer!" The older girl grinned slyly. "There are some blessings, if you can believe that?"

"Like what?" Corelya remonstrated. "If there are, then I can't see any! It sounds like the worse kind of torture!"

"Mum told me that it takes so long because we are allowed to have a little fun before we become women! That's why all the interesting changes happen first, long before your start to bleed. Not that I would know anything about it, I have never done anything with a boy!"

"In the name of the Gods! I can't believe I am hearing this! I have to endure all of this, just to please men!"

Nirch'ii giggled. "You don't like men at all, do you?"

"No, I don't!"

"That will change, trust me! You can't stop it from happening, Corelya?"

"Why does everything have to be about them? I have seen the way some of the older boys behave. All they seem to talk about is girls!"

Nirch'ii burst into hysterics. "And what do you think girls talk about? Not that I would know" she said quickly.

"I could beat them up all the time when I was little, for I towered over most of them!"

"Life would be pretty boring if everything stayed the same, Corelya. My life was boring! Most days were no different from the previous or the next, even though I was looking forward to being married in a year or so. I doubt that will ever happen now. I have no idea what I will do anymore." Corelya snakes her arms around Nirch'ii's naked shoulders and hugs her tightly.

"Did you have a suitor?" Corelya asked interestedly.

"No" Nirch'ii confessed sadly. "My father was going to tie a rope around my neck and sell me at the market in Qu'ehra. He thought he could display me along with our cheeses, cured meats and homemade wines."

Corelya's eyes boggled. She could scarcely credit what

she was hearing. "You *are* serious?"

Nirch'ii convulses in hysterics, her lungs heaving and shoulders rocking in Corelya's arms. Then she broke down, sobbing relentlessly, the bitter tears coursing over Corelya's naked shoulders as she hugged the older girl for dear life. Corelya let the girl weep, stroking her damp hair, soothing her with comforting kisses to the head.

"You *were* joking about the market?" Corelya persisted.

"Of course, I was" Nirch'ii snickered. "I was to be betrothed to a young man in a village south of Qu'ehra. We would have lived with my parents in the forest and raised our children there. I don't have anything he would be interested in anymore."

"I think you might, Nirch'ii" Corelya grinned slyly.

"Well, there *is* obviously *that*!" Nirch'ii blushed. "There must be prettier girls in his village who are coming of age."

"I can't believe that Nirch'ii, you are beautiful" Corelya smiled warmly at the older girl.

"I am not, Corelya" Nirch'ii sighed. "My mum always said I was a pretty girl and that I have a good heart. I may even have to be a good wife, in every way." she giggled. "You, on the other hand, are destined to be beautiful, Corelya. You remind me of the stories I was told as child, about how Tabiti is supposed to look. I would wager there are lot's boys have a secret crush on you."

"You think I look like Tabiti?" Corelya was surprised. Her physical features, and how others perceived her, had never been all that important to her. She was, after all, a *mere* slave!

"Tabiti is Persian, and they have dark hair like Nichassor and I. I think you look like one of those Greek goddesses I have heard tales of. Say, Athena, or Aphrodite?"

"I have never thought about it, to be honest. I suppose it will become more real over the next year or so. I will soon be old enough to be 'inducted'" Corelya sighed wistfully. "You are talking about the 'mysteries'? I have heard of them, but I do not pretend to understand it. Are you frightened?"

"I am really not sure. Should I be?" Corelya blushed hotly.

"I wouldn't think so, Corelya. It is not supposed to hurt, at least not after the first time, and it would surely be less terrifying with another girl. Especially and older girl who has some experience. According to mum, that is the whole point of changing down there" she nodded at her crotch.

"You talked with your mum about this?" Corelya gasped incredulously.

"Everyone talks to their mum about things like this, Corelya! It is perfectly natural. Although as a Sauromatae, I was not especially concerned about the prospect of a female lover. You Scythians really are quite strange?"

"I think it comes from the Hellenics. Spartan males are encouraged to take male lovers before marriage, and they are acknowledged to be the finest warriors in the world. Then there are the Priestesses of Lesbos, who take only female lovers. I think it comes from there, though only Ur'gai daughters are inducted in to the 'mysteries'. My mum died when I was little. I can't discuss this with anyone?" Corelya gazed at her toes.

Nirch'ii cupped Corelya's cheeks in both hands and, leaning across, she kissed the younger child on the forehead. "I can be your 'big sister' if you would like me to be?"

"Yes" Corelya squealed excitedly.

The girls spent the next few hours foraging. The gallery forest furnished a bounty of wild plums and apples, plucked from the trees, and the hazel and chestnut trees were carefully preened for their edible nuts. Corelya taught Nirch'ii the art of stalking, and their efforts were rewarded with a rare prize; a stag cleanly taken down by quarrels to its throat. This was hung, gutted, and then skilfully cleaned and portioned by Nirch'ii, while the younger girl fashioned branches with a dagger into rods for fishing.

Further downstream from where the two girls had bathed lay a bend in the stream, and here the water was deeper, and the fish plentiful. The girls sat on the bank and fished leisurely, bagging four common Bream, with honours even. These were expertly gutted by Corelya. The catch and the portioned stag were wrapped in parcels of maple leaves and then were tied with twine. These fish were stored in saddlebags, whereas the deer was slung over the front of the saddle cloths and attached with hemp-rope to its loops.

As the heat of the mid-afternoon sun began to wane, the two riders headed back to the camp laden with a bounty of food, enough for the next few days. As they reached camp, they espied Nichassor, who had returned from his day's excursion. He strolled across the grass to greet them. "I trust you had a pleasant few hours' sojourn, ladies?" he greeted them with a smile.

"We brought food! More than enough for everyone, including that snake Siladar!" Corelya quipped. She eyed Nichassor steadily. "I would wager that you are definitely up to something, Nichassor? I would wager a King's ransom it is mischief!"

"There was nothing sinister in my early morning departure, Corelya! I didn't wish to wake you this morning, for you were both sleeping soundly. Still, I do have some news that might interest you."

Corelya's eyes narrowed with suspicion. "What would that be?"

"We should eat first, should we not? I have some fine red wine from Qu'ehra, if that would please you?"

"Indeed, it would, Nichassor!" Corelya smiled thinly.

"We have enough fuel for the night. I have arranged a small pile for your own fire. The coals should be ready within the hour" Nichassor smiled brightly.

Later that evening, Corelya and Nichassor sit on the bank of the stream a short distance from the remainder of the group and share a flagon of wine. Nirch'ii was sleeping blissfully, and Nichassor had been at pains to allay Corelya's fears over the matter of drugging the girl with poppy oil, at least for the next few days. Only then, after an orange had been peeled and halved between them, did Nichassor reveal the true reason for his impromptu excursion to Qu'ehra. "Do you remember much about your family, Corelya? Do you have any memories of your early life, and of your community?"

"A little, but only a little, for it was all such a long time ago and I was very small. I remember the important things, of course I do" Corelya sighed sadly, for even now, the memories were coloured by unimaginable grief.

"You must surely have fond memories of your parents?" Nichassor asked softly. "I do, of both of them."

"What were they like?" he smiled encouragingly at the child.

"My father was a Thatcher, or at least that is what I remember him doing. He was clean- shaven, much like you, which was rare. Most of the men had beards" Corelya replied.

"What about your mother?"

"My mother was tall and very beautiful. I look a lot like her, apparently. At least that is what everyone used to say to me when I was very small. My mother was an identical twin, born in the early spring. My aunt Azulya and her family lived next door. We were a simple people, a peaceful people. We farmed, made cheese, wine, and crafts to sell at the market. We were not poor. I had two older brothers. Then *they* came.."

"Do you know who 'they' were?" Nichassor asked softly.

"No. Neither Yari nor I saw them. We heard them, of course, for we hid from them. We could hear the attack, the screams of the people and the animals as they killed them. We saw the smoke from the fires and knew they had destroyed everything. We stayed in the woods until they had left" the girl was on the verge of tears.

"So, you have no real idea who they were?" Nichassor stated this as fact.

"I suspect that they were Argata. I hate the Argata, I loathe them" Corelya hissed.

"They were not Argata, Corelya" Nichassor corrected her. "They were Armenian renegades, descended from the fugitives of the last war with the Lydians. During the past decade they have raped, murdered, plundered, and terrorized many communities like your own, for they loathe the Sauromatae. It is true that they are, or rather once were, in the paid service of the Argata. It is also equally true that their indiscretions, however deplorable, were tolerated and even encouraged, at least until recently. Yet still they terrorize with impunity, when everyone else desires peace."

"Do you know where they can be found?" Corelya asked softly.

"I have found them. If that is something of interest you?" Nichassor sighed.

"Of course, it would interest me! I want vengeance for what they did to us! To all of us, not just our community, mine and Yari's, but for everyone else" Corelya hissed. "This filth will pay with blood for the insults they have visited upon my people."

"I met with certain people in Qu'ehra and then headed further south. I gave notice to the leaders of the band of renegades that I will meet them in four days' time at a location of their choosing in the forest. There will only be three of them."

"Why should I trust you?" Corelya ventured. "This could easily be a trap?"

"These renegades are no longer welcome in 'the lands between the seas', if they truly ever were. Whoever kills them will earn the lasting gratitude of the Argata" Nichassor said firmly.

"That means gold, does is not?" the child eyed the Persian with distaste. "How much have the Argata offered you for their heads? A princely sum by any reckoning, I would wager! You will be a wealthy man, Nichassor, though not as rich as Croesus?"

"You really do have a low opinion of me, don't you Corelya?" Nichassor sighed sadly.

"I don't fucking trust you, if that's what you mean? Nor do I trust that feral brute Siladar, whom I fully intended to kill, if you had failed to return by the morning."

"You seem preoccupied with death for one so young, particularly a girl, despite the curious Scythian attitude to men. I have often wondered whether you simply keep your men alive to sire more Scythian women" Nichassor teased.

"You are Persian, Nichassor. I have seen the servility of your women. It is not to my taste."

"Then perhaps this last morsel may be to your taste, Corelya?" Nichassor smiled slyly. "I heard a strange tale from a man I met today. I have received countless pieces of information from him in the past and have always found him a most reliable source. He has heard word that Queen Illir'ya has despatched her most skilled assassin to kill Queen Lezika. He has also heard word that this assassin is a child, though it cannot be certain whether this child is a girl or a boy."

Corelya felt the blood freeze in her veins. "That just doesn't make any sense. What would the Ur'gai expect to accomplish by assassinating Queen Lezika?"

Her mind was now racing and had deduced that any such information could only have filtered from a source within the Ur'gai Royal Court: a traitor! *Only Yari had known of her mission in advance and could be absolutely trusted to keep her silence.* With the sole exception of Yari, only Queen Illir'ya herself had any knowledge of the details of her mission. Even now, nobody could know of her true plans, as these had been altered radically by events of the past few days. The rumour was a patent falsehood and had been deliberately crafted to cause mischief. Her status had been cleverly revealed, presumably by those who had noted her absence from the Royal Camp, and then drawn inevitable conclusions in light of her last discussion with the Royal Counsel! *And yet, the sole beneficiary of this deception could be none other than a latent alliance between the Orch'tai and the Argata*! This was treason! The aim was not the destabilization of the Argata, but the furtherance of an alliance between them and the Orch'tai, followed by a bloody war with the Ur'gai. Considering the size of the Orch'tai Royal Army, and the tacit acquiescence of Persia, such a conflict must surely end in a crushing defeat for the Ur'gai and the end of Illir'ya's reign!

"Destabilizing the Argata would be in interests of the Ur'gai, given their recent stance in the Crimea, would it not?" Nichassor chided the clearly rattled child.

Corelya smiled ruefully. "It would certainly be in the interests of the Orch'tai, don't you think?" Corelya countered. "They would be the sole beneficiary of subsequent political instability in Archaeopolis."

"Do you intend to murder Queen Lezika?" Nichassor smiled tightly.

"That is cute, Nichassor, very cute! I have no plans to murder anyone, nor would I ever have been privy to such discussions, had they taken place! I was instructed by my Queen to convey the essence of a revised treaty to the Argata, and that is all" Corelya protested.

"You are a war-like people, Corelya? Surely the Ur'gai hope to make considerable gains from stifling any further expansion of Argata influence in 'the lands between the seas'?" Nichassor mused. "Your declaration of a protectorate in the Crimea is consistent with such naked ambition, is it not?"

"You have not changed at all have you, despite the

passage of time?" Corelya eyed the older man steadily.

"In what sense have I not changed, dear child? I have certainly grown wearier!"

"One eye is always fixed upon the future, whilst the other jealously guards your *investments*! The Ur'gai would never welcome war with the Argata or the Orch'tai. Either now, or in the immediate future, despite the devilry of traitors at the Royal Court who may wish to further such aims!"

"You are Her Majesty's Royal Retainer, are you not?" Nichassor persisted.

Wow! Corelya thought. The source of the leaked information had been specific and may even have disclosed her name. "I assure you that I am not, Nichassor! Nor do I have any knowledge of who is. I am a humble Handmaiden and a slave" Corelya lied smoothly.

"My source seemed certain of the matter! There is much distress among the populace of Qu'ehra over this perceived outrage" Nichassor sighed sadly.

Corelya suppressed an urge to giggle, for this was pure bullshit! "Did your source reveal any further details? Such as whether the Argata are aware of these alleged threat to their beloved Queen?"

"And if the Argata were in possession of such information?" Nichassor smiled slyly.

"It would be dangerous for me to even be here, would it not? I am a servant of Her Majesty, deep in Argata territory, am I not? I suspect that they would not be receptive to any overtures of peace at the present, however generous!"

"So, your journey has been wasted?" Nichassor seemed pained.

"It would appear so, would it not?" Corelya sighed despondently. "And yet, I may at least have now uncovered evidence of a traitor with ties to the Ur'gai Royal Court."

"Why would you think that?" Nichassor mused cynically.

"I scarcely think that the cook's apprentice would gain from circulating such a clever ruse, do you Nichassor?" Corelya chided. "But a Counsellor.?"

"Perhaps this is little more than an unsubstantiated rumour?" Nichassor said airily.

"That may be so" Corelya sighed, "nonetheless, it is all too clear that someone is trying to instigate mischief between the regional powers! That is a grave matter of concern, and one which has obvious implications for my immediate safety!"

SEVEN

Qu'ehra, July 493 BC

The market at Qu'ehra was a sea of humanity. The transitory settlement in the plains north of the Caucasus Mountains was home, such as it was, to the largest density of populace in 'the lands between the seas' and thronged with souls from all regions of the known world. There was a myriad of locals, including Sauromatae, Armenians, and Scythians; swathes of Hellenic, Egyptian and Persian merchants; swarms of Phoenician gang- masters; and, most surprising of all, a smattering of Orientals from the east whose facial features were strikingly distinct from all others. You could purchase anything in Qu'ehra: weapons, spices, clothing, furniture, arts, and crafts and, of course, people. Qu'ehra was the largest slave market in the western world, save perhaps Massalia, and the trade in people greatly exceeded even opium! Qu'ehra was a vineyard of vice, boasting parades of plaint whores of all races, ages, and tastes. There were legions of petty thieves, common swindlers, and murderers for hire at the corners of every thoroughfare. *Corelya was rightly wary, for dying was a way of life in Qu'ehra*

Corelya and Nirch'ii had only just arrived, having spent the past two nights staying with a family in a local village a few miles to the east. Corelya had been greatly surprised to learn that the villagers held the venerable Nichassor in some affection and were, quite naturally,

indebted to his band. Nichassor and his men had ridden
ahead the previous day for a clandestine meeting with the
Armenian renegades at a remote location to the south of
Qu'ehra. The girls were freshly bathed, attired in simple
peasant kurtas of pale blue, with their hair pleated in
ringlets, the current fashion of the region. Neither wore
jewellery and, despite protestations, Corelya openly sported
her sword at her right hip and twinned daggers at the left.
The sun was shining brightly in a brilliant blue sky and
both girls were enchanted by the smells, sights, and sounds
of the emporium. Despite the geographic proximity of her
homestead, Nirch'ii had seldom visited Qu'ehra since she
was little and could furnish little practical information
about the place or its dangers. Corelya had not visited since
she had been sold into slavery at the Bazaar! In childish
delight, the pair had gleefully accepted white roses which
were now fixed in their hair, just behind each ear. If they
had not been noted before, they most assuredly were now!
Corelya knew instinctively that they had been monitored
ever since their arrival and had identified a potential pair of
stalkers who seemed to shadow their every move, with no
obvious inclination to strike. She did not inform Nirch'ii
of this sinister ploy, but, in the interests of security, the
younger girl had acquired a heavy pine staff that could be
resolutely employed against any would-be harasser!

⁓

Nymphaion, July 493 BC

Chisos and Iscaertes would surely have concurred that
this day had gotten off to an ominous start. Chisos had
been enjoying the virtues of the latest in a string of casual
girlfriends, for he was not the settling-down sort, when
the door to his tenement near the Wharf had been rudely
kicked open in the early hours by a coterie of well-dressed

strangers. Chisos' girlfriend, a sweet little teenager named Naealla, had suffered the twin indignities of being forced to watch her lover being subjected to a merciless beating by the intruders, conducted with commendable vigour, before she herself had been horse-whipped naked out of the house and into the street! Iscaertes had scarcely fared any better, for he had been beaten insensible with heavy staves on the front porch of *The Delphine* several hours earlier by a group of equally well-attired assailants, who alighted a bespoke carriage and thence departed, leaving him bloodied and unconscious on the paved floor. Neither was in any doubt as to the identity of the architect of their misfortune, nor its justification. And so, eager to avoid further misadventure, they duly presented themselves as requested at a warehouse in the Eastern Quarter the following morning.

To their astonishment, they had been given a generous measure of wodki and their injuries had been tended by a hired surgeon, at no small expense. Despite such courtesy, both men were plainly terrified, for there was a price to be paid for the old surgeon's services! Saelaes suddenly morphed in the open doorway of the small office and gazed pityingly at the bruised and battered specimens arraigned before him, as the Surgeon, Adramos, finished suturing a small wound on Chisos' upper left arm. Once he had finished, the old Surgeon cleaned his hands in a small bowl of water, and then sterilised his cleaned equipment with vinegar and lemon. He turned expectantly to Saelaes, who flipped a silver coin across the table. "Will that suffice old man?"

Adramos sighed contemptuously at Naeschaxes most trusted retainer. "Do you not wish to inquire as to the long-term health of the pair?"

"I honestly couldn't give a fuck! I am sure that they have learned their lesson!"

The old Surgeon drains his goblet of wodki and lays this down on the table, next to the flagon. "An expensive lesson, I would wager?"

"They won't be requiring your services the next time, old man!"

"Then I trust, for their sake's at least, that there will be no next time!" Adramos smiled tightly.

"We would hope so, old man."

Adramos smiles thinly at the pair, then at Saelaes, and leaves the room. Neither Chisos, nor Iscaertes, utter a word. Saelaes fills three wooden goblets with wodki and passes one to each man. He takes a vacant chair directly across from the pair and eyes them coldly. "You fucked up royally, didn't you?"

"It was my fault, honestly. It won't happen again!" Chisos mumbled through bloodied and puffy lips.

"The Boss paid for the Surgeon. I doubt you would have gotten anything from that other fucker!"

Chisos and Iscaertes exchange bewildered glances. "I am not sure that I follow?" Iscaertes spoke in a hushed tone.

"Finish your drinks and follow me! I think it is high time you two dickheads met the man who really pays your wages!" Saelaes grinned.

The ignominious hirelings were escorted to the corner office to face Naeschaxes, who sat in conference with a stranger. Naeschaxes eyed the battered and bruised men with considerable fascination, for he was quite unused to the methods of his esteemed visitor, perched lazily on an ornate chair in the corner of the room.

"I gave you pair an assignment of considerable importance, did I not?" Naeschaxes addressed the pair icily. The men nodded sullenly. "And you have failed me, have you not?"

"It was my fault, Boss!" Chisos muttered bleakly. "I tailed the man, as requested, into the residential district of the Eastern Quarter, where I lost him. I'm sorry, Boss, I underestimated him. It won't happen again, I promise you."

"See that it does not, my good fellow. The man in

question is of supreme interest to us at the present time and we are eager to discover his current whereabouts."

"He has not been anywhere near *The Delphine*, Boss! I can assure you of that" mumbled a chastened Iscaertes.

"He is a frequent visitor to Nymphaion and of your esteemed establishment, is he not?" Naeschaxes asked eagerly.

"He is a regular visitor, Boss, that is true. I have seen him several times during the past few years."

"Even during the winter months?" the stranger interjected. His accent was foreign and cultured.

"Not in the depths of winter, but late enough in the year, and early enough in the following year, my Lord!" Iscaertes confessed eagerly. He was a man all too eager to please at this moment.

"So, it is likely that he will be frequenting your establishment at some point in the next few days, isn't that so?" Naeschaxes probed.

"It would be strange if he did not do so, Boss. That would be most untypical of him."

"As is your recent failure, I might add. Now, and I cannot stress this enough, my colleague and I urgently seek this Gentleman and will pay handsomely for any information leading to the discovery of his current whereabouts. Do we understand one another?" Naeschaxes gazed at the men coldly.

"Yes, Boss" the men chimed.

"Then be on your way, and happy hunting!"

After the pair had been escorted off the premises by Saelaes and his henchmen, Naeschaxes and his visitor were alone, savouring a restorative goblet of fine Hellenic red. "I think they got the message, don't you, Honourable Mestarches?" Naeschaxes smiled thinly.

"I want Thassalor of Knossos found! Do we understand one another? May I remind you, my dear fellow, that King Darius is notoriously intolerant of failure! So am I, as it happens!"

⌐

Corelya paused with Nirch'ii for several minutes as they excitedly perused the kurtas on display at one of the more expensive merchants in the bazaar. They were stunning creations, fashioned from fine material, dyed beautiful, vivid colours, and exquisitely embroidered by the mountain communities of the south. She espied one of their stalkers loitering at a nearby stall, where he engaged the merchant in awkward conversation. Corelya glanced around, searching for the whereabouts of his companion, and instead saw Nichassor, alone and unarmed, weaving through the crowd towards them. "Is that snake one of yours?" Corelya snarled gutturally by way of a greeting, jerking her thumb towards the shifty character at the nearby stall. The man shuffles his feet uneasily and glanced away furtively as Corelya glowers at him menacingly.

"Yes" Nichassor replied simply. "You have been closely watched ever since your arrival. This is for your own protection, naturally. There is nothing sinister in my conduct. I assure you of that" Nichassor continued. "What are you doing?"

"Shopping" Corelya beamed.

"It is unwise to draw attention to yourself, Corelya? Especially so, considering the disturbing rumours circulating around the town, you would agree?"

"Nobody knows who I am, do they?" Corelya chided. "And besides, we are two attractive young females! We would naturally draw attention, would we not?"

"You are armed, Corelya?" Nichassor sighed irritably. He was not in the mood for Corelya's acerbic wit, given the gravity of the situation.

"So, are you?'" Corelya chirped cheekily, nodding to the dagger at his hip.

"And yet, it would be unusual for a female, a child at that, to be so heavily armed? Perhaps it might be wiser to let me have your sword."

"Where would you like me to stab you with it?" Corelya quipped.

"Your sense of humour is invariably coarse Corelya, particularly for one so delightful to the eye."

"You really are an old smoothie at heart, aren't you, Nichassor?" Corelya gushed. "Do you have any news?"

"I do, but I do not think it wise that we discuss such matters here. It is, after all, a little public, you agree?"

"I agree, but first we need to... Nichassor!" Corelya screamed in terror.

Nichassor twisted instinctively and, miraculously, took the point of a dagger aimed to plunge into his lower back in the left forearm, the tip grating agonisingly against the bone. Nichassor screamed in agony, and then roared incoherently with rage, as he pivoted on the balls of his feet and unleashed a piledriver of a right, his fist connecting satisfyingly with the assailant's left eye. Quickly drawing his own dagger, he plunged it mercilessly in to the right eye of the would-be assassin. Corelya reacted instantly and smashed a second attacker hard in the face with the end of the pine staff. The force of the impact shattered the man's nose and blood spurted out to pour down his face. The girl kicked him mercilessly in the balls and the man dropped, hissing in agony. "Go, Nirch'ii! Run!" she screamed as she moved fast to the right to attack a third assailant.

"Plucky Sauromatae cunt!" the man sneered. "It is time for you to die, little whore!"

"Then come and kill me, dickhead!" Corelya hissed.

The attacker thrust at Corelya, the point of his sword aimed at her groin, yet the girl parries the blade with the staff, causing an explosion of shavings as the edge of the blade scored the staff. Corelya batted the man viciously across the face with her right hand, yet astonishingly, he managed to partially duck the sweeping arc of the staff as Corelya warmed to her task. The tip of the staff glanced off his head, causing him to stagger back. He roared with rage, slashing wildly at the girl's midriff before, feinting left, he delivered a killing thrust aiming to skewer Corelya through the right groin. She deftly sidesteps the slash and twists, pivoting lithely on the balls of her feet, to allow the blade to pass by. The pine staff: comparably light in weight relative to its strength, is agilely manipulated in her hands and is brought down sharply on the attacker's wrist, fatally loosening his grip on the sword, which fell to the dirt.

Before the man could recover his wits, the ends of the staff are cruelly smashed into his face in quick succession, a lightening right-left combination that draws gasps and cheers from the ecstatic crowd. Corelya dropped the staff, drew her sword, and skewered the assailant in the right groin. Corelya turns to face a fourth assailant who turned and sprinted into the safety of the throng. Corelya turns back to Nichassor, who stands with his dripping dagger over the prone form of the second assailant, the man whose nose had been badly broken. His throat has been slashed, liberally showering Nichassor with warm, arterial blood.

"How are you feeling? Are you going to be alright?" Corelya asked. The concern in her voice was genuine.

"Thanks to you, I am. You saved my life, Corelya" Nichassor sighed heavily. He was visibly shaking and had gone a deathly pale, possibly due to the adrenaline coursing through his veins.

Corelya turns and scans the crowd, searching anxiously for Nirch'ii. The girl makes her way through the crowd, now sporting an iron sword, borrowed from a merchant in the metal-workers district. "Nirch'ii!" she yelled. Within an instant, the older girl was at her side. Corelya nodded to Nichassor "He needs a Surgeon. Do you know of one in town?"

"Yes, I have heard tale of one. He is the finest in the region" Nirch'ii replied eagerly. "I shall go and fetch him immediately." She turned on her feet and sprints back into crowd, still clutching her drawn blade.

"I will be fine, Corelya" Nichassor winced. "It is merely a flesh wound, dear child, nothing more than that."

"It is in a bad place Nichassor!" Corelya corrected him. She eyed the wound with an expert eye, for her former tutor had taught her well. "The point has been driven in deep. It is a dangerous site for infection and there will likely be a lot of pus to be drained."

"I had no idea you were so knowledgeable" Nichassor raised an eyebrow in surprise. "You really do care if I die, don't you?" He smiled wanly at the girl.

"Of course, I do" Corelya reproved him sternly. "I may not trust you Nichassor, but I don't hate you. I have told you this before."

Nirch'ii returned presently, her cheeks flushed pink as she pants from her exertions. She informed them that a treatment room was available at a Surgery in the Central Square, adjacent to a renowned local hostelry, *The Silk Road*. The Surgeon was named Mosh'ii, and his skills were held in high repute throughout the region. Much to Corelya's surprise, Nichassor consented without protest and was meekly led away by Nirch'ii, with Corelya following a safe distance behind them, her sword drawn in readiness.

"Move your arse, you shifty prick!" she snarled at the shifty character. The man bows his head and follows Nirch'ii and Nichassor, a few paces to their rear.

As they weave through the narrow lanes between the Merchant's tents, the crowd parts to allow them through. Corelya scans around for any signs of danger, left and right, fore-and-rear. She suddenly caught sight of a familiar face, a person from recent memory. Her cheeks flush hotly and she averts her gaze and picks up her pace. *Surely, it could not be him*? Had he not recently been promoted to the rank of Supreme Commander? *What in Hades name would a Supreme Commander of an Orch'tai Ochta, a division of six cavalry detachments, numbering three hundred superbly trained and heavily armoured mounted warriors, be doing skulking incognito in the market of Qu'ehra?*

The group eventually cleared the vast expanse of stalls and strode blinkingly across the paved central square toward *The Silk Road*. There were few permanent structures in Qu'ehra, save the Temple of Tabiti, the adjacent Temple of Aphrodite, *The Silk Road* inn, and *The Pharaohs Crown*, an established 'house of ill-repute', famed throughout the region.

The surgeon Mosh'ii greeted them at his premises, adjacent to *The Pharaohs Crown*, with a grudging enthusiasm. This was understandable, given that no contract of service existed between the parties and, as such, no genuine concern for the patient's welfare. Corelya presented the elderly Surgeon with two silver discs, entrusted to her by Nichassor, and watched with interest as his entire demeanour transformed within the blink of an eye. The patient, *his dear Nichassor*, was now the *sole person of interest in the world. His* health and welfare were *paramount*, and nothing was too good for *this* patient. Corelya, a consummate cynic since early childhood, resisted a momentary urge to knife the old bastard. *He would probably stiff her for two coffins!*

◡

Dionysopolis, July 493 BC

The Bosporus is the name given since ancient times to a narrow channel that cleaves Anatolia from Thrace and is the gateway to the Black Sea, the Crimea, and the untold riches of the Pontic Steppe. Its strategic importance could never be understated, yet it now fell within the territory of the Persian Empire. Despite such geopolitical realities, its entire mercantile foundation remains *Hellenic*. For more than a Century, prior to the meteoric rise of Persia under

Cyrus the Great, the Hellenics had founded a constellation of settlements, wired trading networks amongst these, and forged interdependent networks with regional non-Hellenic centres, including the Scythia and even the Sauromatae. This is the land of Jason and his Argonauts, the realms of the mythical Golden Fleece, a source of untold riches. It remained a prism of influence for the Greek polities, especially Athens and Corinth, and a weeping sore of perpetual jealousy for both Sparta and Persia.

If we follow the coastline of the Black Sea northwards into Thrace towards the mouth of the great Danube, lifeline of Europe and the site of ancient Varna and its gloried riches, we locate the Hellenic polis of Dionysopolis, situated twenty miles northeast of the delta of the Danube. On its southwest outskirts lies a palatial villa, replete with a large farmstead, vineyard, olive and citrus groves, and a luxurious family garden. Its residents are a wealthy Greek family, with considerable influence in the mercantile and political establishment of the polis. On this morning, three children are engaged in a game of 'hide and seek' among the ornate sandstone statues and immaculately pruned rose garden. Their game is interrupted by the unmistakable groan of the heavy wooden gates being opened and closed. The younger children, including the 'baby' of the family, a healthy three-year-old girl, skip excitedly out of their hiding places and squeal with delight as they race to stand beside their elder sister. The eldest girl, fast approaching her eleventh birthday, wears a worried expression as she leads her siblings to meet the wagon as it approaches along the driveway. The driver of the wagon, the perpetually cheery Atticus, aged in his middling twenties, is well known to the family.

Atticus hails the elder girl as he reins the ponies to a halt. "Good morning, Artemis!"

"Good morning, Atticus!"

"Is your mother well?"

"She is confined. Apart from that she is well. It is father you ought to be worried about!"

"It is the nature of men to be nervous about these things, Artemis" Atticus declared.

"Are you the Nurse?" Artemis politely directed her question to the older woman sat beside Atticus, rather than her companion seated in the back.

"I am, young Miss. My name is Nichelle" the older woman confirmed. She turns and nods to the girl seated in the back of the cart. "And this is my apprentice, Nae'veh." The girl, aged fourteen years, nods politely at the children as they meet her gaze. She knows little Greek and converses with her mistress in Scythiac.

"My father is expecting you" Artemis confirmed.

"Then we should not keep you father waiting, sweet child" the Nurse declared.

As the wagon trundles on towards the villa, the two younger children begin to squeal excitedly in an alien tongue spoken by all three children, yet by few others in Dionysopolis, including Atticus and the Nurse. The young apprentice, Nae'veh, gapes at the little boy and girl is bewilderment, for she has understood every word and is astonished to hear the language of her ancestors spoken so fluently by the children of a wealthy Greek family. Young Nae'veh is Sauromatae, and the little boy and girl had been conversing in *Sarmati.*

Corelya left the accommodation quarters at the rear of the Surgery alone and strolled leisurely towards the Central Square, turning left at the corner She is accosted outside *The Pharaohs Crown* by a leering drunk who mistakenly presumed she was 'available for business' and, if it were so, how much such a 'sweet little plum' charged for her time. Corelya smiled angelically and disclosed that she would charge nothing for her time, casually moving on a few seconds later, as the man writhed upon the floor, grasping frantically for air and bruised testicles! She elbowed her way rudely past a throng of drunks congregating at the entrance to *The Silk Road* tavern and strolled inside. The girl approaches the bar and orders a large draught of rye beer, a local favourite, and a goblet of plum wodki.

Corelya drank steadily for the reminder of the afternoon, replenishing her beaker twice, as she absorbed the local gossip furnished by a group of regular's only too eager hold forth on all manner of subjects, provided their drinking vessels were regularly refilled. Of the rumoured threat to the life of Queen Lezika of the Argata, there was simply nothing to credit it! No-one had any earthly idea how such a rumour could have started, yet there were always malcontents, were there not? Perhaps the Armenians were the source of this malicious tale, for they were no friend to the Argata Queen! The consensus among the regulars in *The Silk Road* was that the prospects for a lasting peace in the region were more favourable than they ever been. Was it not true that the Ur'gai and Argata were exploring avenues for even deeper relations than prescribed in the provisions of the *Accord Scythiac*?

Such an initiative would surely persuade even the most irascible among the Orch'tai of the merits of the *Accord* and the furtherance of regional peace?

"Somebody is talking shite!" Corelya muttered darkly, as she weaved her way through the tangle at the front door, pausing briefly to inflict the promise of a pearl of a shiner upon a misguided pervert whose hand snaked up her kurta to fondle her naked bum as she passed by. "Cheeky Bastard!" she spat indignantly, as she stomped off, heading in the direction of the bazaar, which closed for the day's trading. It was now early evening and, whilst the sun still shone brightly in the sky, the air had cooled perceptibly. Two men, well- known in the criminal fraternity in

Qu'ehra, left *The Silk Road* immediately after Corelya.

They now followed the child south towards the Bazaar, maintaining a safe distance behind. Earlier that afternoon, they received specific instruction from their paymaster to dispose of the 'meddlesome little bitch'! The men were vouchsafed a tidy sum in silver upon completion of the task.

It would surely be the easiest redemption in the disreputable annals of contractual murder!

⸺

The *code* of the assassin is that the mission is *pure*. Neither motive, nor the act of killing itself, is material. Satisfaction lies entirely in the *deliverance*. The method, the wilful act of killing another soul, is merely a deliverance of the *code*. The girl sensed intuitively that she had been marked for death. She had carefully chosen her ground, for the tangle of the Bazaar surely offered her best hopes for survival this night. She was no longer certain of anything, apart from the *true* target of the attack in the Bazaar that morning. It was time to send a message to her enemies! I am not the *prey*; I am the *predator*. Her heart races as she savours the thrill of the hunt to come!

Corelya saunters breezily down a main thoroughfare in the maze of tents. Without warning, she veers left and darts down a narrow lane, diving into a random tent on the left side. She drops to one knee and scans the inside of the lair. Satisfied with its suitability, she draws the iron hairpin, a six inch long killing spike with a razor-sharp point and an ornate boss that fits perfectly into her palm from the left side of her hair. A small vial concealed within the ringlets on the right of her head contains *kobran*, one of the deadliest known poisons milked from the Oriental cobra. The point of the hairpin is quickly tainted, the vial buried in her hair. Corelya slipped under the bench against the outer wall of the tent and quickly covers her form with an old blanket, the tainted hairpin held tightly in her left hand and away from her body. The first assassin tiptoed past, close to the outer wall of the tent in the lane outside, and then halted, a mere foot away from her still form, almost as if to *smell* her. He continues north, heading further along the lane away from her. Corelya almost sighed with relief as she heard his footfalls fade into the distance. Suddenly, she freezes, her breath stilling in her throat, eyes widening in terror, as footsteps pad lithely towards her!

From inside the tent!

The second assassin enters through the rear flap. The man moves stealthily towards the front of the tent, yet he seems unaware of the presence of the girl, much less, precisely where she was hidden. Corelya readies her body to strike, the tainted tip of the iron spike poised to deliver its deathly fate when, unexpectedly, the assassin's head inadvertently clashes with an arcade of metal ladles hanging from a hook in the ceiling. The clash is heralded by a series of jangles, momentarily startling the stalker, distracting him from the threat of immediate danger. "Shit!" the man curses softly. He scurries past the bench, unaware of the deathly spectre cloaked beneath, and tiptoes towards the entrance to join his comrade in the lane outside. And yet, as his lead foot touches the ground a mere few feet from where Corelya's head had been just moments earlier, a delicate hand clamps firmly across his mouth, as the hairpin is driven through the nape of his neck to plunge deep into his brain. Corelya held his body tightly as he folded instantly to his knees and quivered violently, then cradled him gently to the ground. The hairpin was crudely cleaned by driving the point into both open eyes, for the fluid within was well known for its cleansing properties. A lemon or a lime could be obtained later. This assassin had died silently and without unnecessary suffering. His companion would be condemned to a very different fate!

Corelya draws a dagger from its sheath attached to the belt tied around her naked waist and drops to one knee, listening intently. She is careful to ensure that her entire body is cloaked by the drapes of the tent and that first assassin would not see her if they stooped and scanned along the ground. Stilling her breathing, the girl can discern the sound of movement further along the lane and then, inexplicably, there is silence. Shortly thereafter, she hears the scuffing of sand and stones, slightly further along, as if the first assailant were searching for her in the merchant's tents on the right side of the lane. Corelya rose and tip- toed to the entrance of the tent. She drew the entrance flap carefully aside and peeked sneakily outside, espying her would-be killer slipping through the entrance to a stall some twenty yards further along the lane on the right. There is a sharp clanging of metal, followed swiftly by an audible curse, as the man's head connects inadvertently with an array of objects dangling from the roof. Corelya grinned and fastened the tent flap so that it was now partially open. She takes a deep breath, then darts diagonally across the lane and dives into the cover of the stall next along on the right, easing through the partially closed entrance. Once inside, she drops to one knee, ensuring that her entire form is concealed.

She scanned around and saw that this was a metal-workers supplier and contained, among other implements, several hammer-and-tong sets for working red-hot metal. Corelya plucks a hammer and tests it, finding the weight suitable as her fingers curled lovingly around the handle. She laid the implement gently down on the ground, a mere few feet away, and reached for a set of tongs. She paused, breathing softly, listening intently for any sound that could alert her to the danger of her pursuer. The girl grins as the man displaces several objects hanging just inside the entrance of the tent as he leaves. The sound of their impact on the dirt is strangely comforting, for this fool has more than met his match this night! Peering cautiously outside, Corelya watched him stalk to the entrance of the next stall along on the same side. He paused, ready to strike, then swiftly drew back the entrance flap and ducked inside, leading with the knife clasped firmly in his right hand.

Corelya plucks the hammer from the dirt and glances across at the open flap of the tent diagonally across from her. She stands, takes a deep breath, and threw the tongs across the alley and through the open flap of the tent, praying they would hit something, *anything*, with an audible clang. The girl smiled grimly as the peal of chimes from within the tent across the lane was followed by a muttered curse and a shuffling of feet further along. She lowered the open corner of the tent flap, dances a few feet further back, and readies herself to strike, her right leg leading, left leg flexed. This was assuredly not her preferred combat stance, for she held the dagger tightly in her right hand, rather than her left. Corelya retrieved the looped cord from the belt-pouch on her right side and slipped this between clenched teeth. Suddenly, she froze, her heart beating frantically and blood pounding in her ears as her would-be killer skulked silently past outside the entrance flap.

Corelya could hear him breathing as she stilled her own to silence. Suddenly, the assailant roared with rage and, tearing back the tent flap, he lunges murderously at the girl's midriff with his dagger. Corelya reacts instinctively, terror electrifying every sinew, as she danced outside the blade and drove her own between his ribs on the outer left side. The wound was not mortal, nor was it intended to be, as she had targeted the lung as opposed to the upper left quadrant of the abdomen where the strike would have been fatal. The man screams with pain as Corelya twists the knife between his ribs. She drew the blade from his body and punched him hard in the face. The wounded man staggered backwards, wheezing as his punctured lung began to fill with blood. Corelya steps deftly around him to plunge the blade in to the lower right quadrant of his back, aiming for the kidney. At the same time, she drove her right knee hard in to the back of his. The assassin's legs folded and, as he collapsed to the dirt, Corelya plucked the cord from her mouth, unravelling it expertly, before throwing it daintily around his throat and yanking violently to a throttle.

She held the throttle with all her might as her victim scrabbles helplessly at the cord with his fingers. Soon enough, Corelya felt him beginning to sag as death fastens its talons upon him. She cruelly releases her throttle on the cord and the man falls forward to the dirt, gasping for breath, his mouth gaping breathlessly as a floundered fish. Corelya plucks a hammer from a hook on the rack and, smiling tightly, proceeds to bludgeon her victim mercilessly, striking him seven times about the head, grimacing as her face is showered with blood and gore! At the end, the girl is left panting and shivering with exertion and adrenaline. She drops the hammer next to the bloodied corpse, steadies herself for a few moments, as the adrenaline courses relentlessly through her veins. Finally, her *fury* satiated, she strolled out into the lane without a trace of remorse.

The bodies would be soon discovered; their fate heralded to their paymaster!

⌇

Corelya cleaned her hands and swilled her face with water from the well in the stable yard of *The Silk Road*, removing most of the gore, yet there was little that could be done about the state of her clothing! She decided she had earned another drink this night.

Arriving at the bar in *The Silk Road*, the gore-smattered murderess gaped in astonishment as a clearly inebriated Nirch'ii morphed next to her and grinned inanely. "Hello

Corelya! I wondered where in the name Hades you had vanished to!"

"I went for a walk, Nirch'ii. I needed some air. What made you look here?" Corelya probed the girl. Given the prescient danger, it was safer not to trust anyone.

"Nichassor suggested I come here. I didn't want to spend a moment in Siladar's company."

"That prick has finally turned up?" Corelya grimaced.

"He arrived not long after you had left" Nirch'ii confirmed. "Nichassor gave me some coins and advised me to come here and wait for you. He said you would turn up here, sooner or later."

That's if I didn't turn up dead, sooner or later? Corelya mused silently. Siladar's arrival was not unexpected, for he had been in Qu'ehra since yesterday, his sudden re-appearance so soon after her own departure was highly suspicious, especially in light of her recent travails. Corelya's brooding silence was interrupted by a clearly troubled Nirch'ii tugging eagerly at her wrist. "Is that blood?" Nirch'ii gasped, pointing to her gore-smeared kurta.

"Yes" Corelya confirmed. "Don't worry, it isn't mine. More is the pity, at least as far as some might be concerned."

"I don't follow, Corelya? What do you mean?" Nirch'ii whispered frantically.

A young barmaid morphed in front of them and smiled sweetly. "There is a free table in the corner. Sit yourself down and I will bring you over a tray of drinks?"

"Thanks" said Corelya.

Corelya led a visibly bewildered Nirch'ii across to a vacant table next to the far wall. "Somebody wanted me dead, Nirch'ii. They hired assassins, two of them. Neither is alive anymore. I have no doubts they were hired in Qu'ehra, presumably in the past few days, perhaps even the past few hours" Corelya confessed.

"Is this connected with what happened earlier in the

market? Those armed men who tried to kill Nichassor?" Nirch'ii ventured.

"It might be" Corelya conceded. "Yet, in light of what has just happened, I would be inclined to be more than a little suspicious of what happened to Nichassor."

"I am confused, Corelya" Nirch'ii frowned. "Are you saying that the attack on Nichassor wasn't opportunistic? I thought they were robbers."

"I am pretty sure they were hired killers, Nirch'ii, not robbers" Corelya sighed. "I just can't be certain anymore that Nichassor was the intended target."

"Why would you think that?" Nirch'ii persisted.

"Both Nichassor and I were armed, Nirch'ii. Neither of us had anything worth stealing, apart from our weapons. They can be easily obtained in Qu'ehra. A group of robbers prepared to risk everything for next to nothing when there were far easier and richer pickings on offer. It just doesn't make any sense, does it?"

"There are a great many poor people here in Qu'ehra, Corelya? They are desperate people, with families to feed! They will do anything, just to survive!"

"I agree" Corelya replied "And desperate people are compelled to desperate action by necessity of circumstance. Yet our attackers were not beggars, for they were quite well-dressed, well-nourished, and clean-shaven. They had also bathed very recently, likely as recently as we have, if not in the past day or so."

"How do you know they had bathed that recently?" Nirch'ii furrowed her brow.

"When you are in a fight, you sweat. You stink especially in the heat. It's animal-like. But your senses, including smell, are heightened in a fight. The two I took on didn't smell that bad at all. I probably stank worse than they did" Corelya explained patiently.

"You probably do now!" Nirch'ii snickered. "You should change your kurta Corelya. It is revolting!" the older girl wrinkled her nose in distaste.

"I am alive, Nirch'ii, which is more than can be said for certain other people. Trust me, they will stink a lot worse than I do in the morning" said Corelya brutally.

"They surely couldn't smell any worse than you do now!" Nirch'ii grimaced.

"You are right though; I do need to change. I am not sure where I would get a kurta at this hour?" Corelya smiled ruefully.

"I do. I will be back in a moment" Nirch'ii grinned slyly.

Corelya was too astonished to utter a reply as Nirch'ii got up from her stool and twirled away, vanishing into a throng of newcomers who made their way towards the bar. She suddenly re-appeared, a brief while later, carrying a stunning purple kurta that was elegantly embroidered with saffron thread. Corelya appraised the material. It felt expensive. "It is simply beautiful, isn't it? Do you like it?" Nirch'ii cooed.

"Where in Hades name did you get this?" Corelya gasped. "Or, more specifically, who in Hades' name did you get this from?"

"From him" Nirch'ii nodded eagerly past Corelya at an approaching figure.

The older girl's behaviour had been more than a little disconcerting since Corelya had arrived at the tavern, possibly because of the liquor she had imbibed, or perhaps because of some other strange elixir. Yet now, Corelya saw an unmistakable look of absolute adoration in the older girl's eyes and immediately snapped her head to follow her gaze. "Sweet Tabiti!" Corelya sighed, her own eyes twinkling like stars in the night at a vision which loomed ever closer to their table.

He was, quite simply and without compare, the most beautiful person she had ever seen in all her life. He was tall, above six-foot in height, long-limbed and muscular, with an unruly mane of long-blonde hair, unusual for a male. His face was simply gifted by the Gods. How could any mortal be so *perfect*, so *beautiful,* and so *alluring*? Corelya began to tingle all over, and despite her tender years, she felt light-headed. She guessed he was at least six years older than herself, certainly within Nirch'ii's range for a prospective suitor. No wonder the older girl was so smitten, the lucky bitch! "Oh my!" Corelya sighed in wistful adoration. "Pinch me, please? I must be dreaming?" she implored Nirch'ii.

"You must be Corelya?" he spoke in passable Sarmati. "Yes" Corelya replied, her cheeks flushing brightly.

"Do you like the kurta? I have others, if this is not to your taste?"

"What is your name?" Corelya asked eagerly.

"Minas" he replied simply.

"And you stalk the hostelries in 'the lands between the seas' giving away beautiful kurtas?" the girl chirped.

"So, you do think it is beautiful?" Minas pressed.

"I think it is beautiful" Nirch'ii cooed.

"It is stunning" Corelya concurred. "It must be expensive?"

"You would be surprised at the price. They are quite reasonable, all things considered. Exceptional quality at affordable prices" Minas smiled broadly.

"Where are you from?" Corelya quipped.

"Olbia" Minas smiled warmly. "You know Olbia?'"

"I heard of it, of course, but I have never been there" Corelya lied smoothly.

"I have never been anywhere" Nirch'ii flushed with embarrassment.

"Olbia is beautiful. Almost as beautiful as that kurta you are holding in your hand, Corelya" Minas proclaimed. "Yet, not as lovely to the eye as the two of you are, for you are surely the most beautiful girls in Qu'ehra! We have only items that enhance your natural beauty, Nirch'ii. We are not in the business of selling items that would ever detract from it" he smiled angelically at Nirch'ii, who almost melted.

"You are a long way from Olbia?" Corelya continued her interview, unembarrassed by her brusqueness. She was, quite simply, enjoying every moment.

"We are here on business, my older brothers and me. We are traders and come to Qu'ehra twice during the summer months. We buy and sell both clothing and jewellery. We trade with Athens, Thebes and Corinth."

"Would you like to drink something?" Nirch'ii beamed at Minas.

"Please, allow me to buy the drinks. It would be a privilege to buy two delightful young ladies a drink."

"I am sure it would. A rye beer and a plum wodki chaser for both of us" Corelya chirruped.

"Then that is what you shall have." Minas beamed at her. "Would you mind if I joined you?"

"Of course, you may" Nirch'ii chimed, before Corelya could utter something far less diplomatic in reply. "It would please both of us if you would, would it not, Corelya?"

"Yes" Corelya smiled winsomely. "It would be lovely if you would join us."

As Minas moved away from the table and headed across to the bar, Nirch'ii took the opportunity to politely redress Corelya on her behaviour. "Sweet Tabiti, girl!" she hissed. "You should never be so *direct* with men. Be a little more *oblique*! Give them the impression that *they* are in control of the conversation. They like that. It makes them feel powerful. They are the *hunter,* you, their *quarry*."

The younger girl was visibly crestfallen. "I was only trying to be friendly" she mumbled in a chastened tone.

"I know you were, but you have to let them do most of the talking. You must steer the conversation in the direction you would like it to go yet let them feel they are steering you to where they wish things to go" Nirch'ii advised.

"It isn't like I fancy him or anything?"

"Really?" Nirch'ii cooed mockingly.

"He is dreamy, but I am a little young, am I not?" Corelya sighed. "Minas is more your preferred age rather than mine?"

Nirch'ii giggled. "I don't think you should be overly worried about finding a man to 'settle down' with, Corelya, at least for a few years" she soothed. "I do think Minas is eager to see how you would look in that kurta, and not just because he is keen to close the sale."

"Are you serious?"

"I think he genuinely wants to see how it looks on you. Why don't you head back to Mosh'ii's, have a quick wash, and change your kurta? I will let Minas know that you will be back in a short while, that way he won't think that you have absconded" she suggested.

"Are you sure? You don't think he won't mind?" Corelya asked.

"Go! He will be fine, honestly."

Minas returned a few minutes later and was startled to learn that Corelya had left, taking the kurta with her. "Corelya will be back shortly, I promise" Nirch'ii told him. "We thought you might like to see what it looks like on her, you being so wise about how we should best enhance our natural gifts."

"You don't believe me, do you?" Minas feigned sorrow at the girl's evident lack of faith, in both his judgement and sincerity. It was all an act, obviously.

"I am not sure of anything. Why don't you convince me?" Nirch'ii batted her eyelids.

"Both your hair and eyes are dark, Nirch'ii, and that is a blessing. It means that you can wear almost any colour without fear of a clash with your eyes."

"I don't follow?" Nirch'ii smiled shyly.

"In the summer months, during the day or the evening, you might wish to consider brighter colours as opposed to dark ones" Minas warmed to his calling. "I am not saying that the purple kurta wouldn't suit you, Nirch'ii, but you could carry off shades many other girls could not. I think you would look beautiful in saffron, lemon, perhaps even lavender."

"You don't think I suit the colour I am wearing at the moment?"

"Of course, I do. Your hair and eyes are dark, Nirch'ii, so they contrast with lighter shades. Believe it or not, in the light of these torches I would venture you look even more beautiful than in the glory of the midday sun."

Nirch'ii flushed crimson. "You think I don't see through you? I think you say these things to most of the females you meet, women and girls."

"But, of course," Minas grinned "It is all part of the act and is the surest means of closing a sale!" He saw a fleeting hurt in the girl's eyes. "Yet, in your case, I am not trying to sell you anything, am I?"

"You may later?" Nirch'ii ventured.

"The future is a world of unrivalled possibilities, and we must seize all that is presented to us" Minas grinned.

"How long will you be staying in Qu'ehra?" Nirch'ii asked.

"A few more days, I think. We are awaiting an order from a trader coming from the east. Then we must." Minas suddenly trails off, his eyes widening and jaw sagging in wonder. "Sweet Hera!" he gasped.

Nirch'ii immediately turned and followed his gaze. "Oh my!" she sighed.

The raucous chatter of the public bar, a constant background thrum to any conversation, however private, suddenly ceases as all eyes turn their gaze upon a newcomer, who breezes through the entrance. Corelya blinks in the torchlight and her cheeks flush a momentary angry hue as she stands, framed in the doorway, basking unwittingly in universal adulation. She looked stunning! There was no other way to describe her. The kurta, made from rich silk fibres, dyed a vivid lilac, and embroidered with saffron-coloured thread, seems almost to shimmer in the glare of the torches, and perfectly complimented her golden locks.

"I see what you mean?" Nirch'ii whispered across the table. "I could never carry that off the way that Corelya does. It suits her blonde hair better."

"Sometimes even I can be wrong" Minas sighed, almost in disbelief.

"I don't follow?" Nirch'ii pressed.

"I had thought the kurta would complement her natural beauty, despite her age. Now I cannot envision anyone in it. It is almost as if it were crafted for Corelya, and only her."

Corelya scowls as she approaches the table. "I wish everyone would stop staring at me!" She swallowed the wodki in one gulp, her cheeks flushing an even deeper shade of rouge. "Thanks!" she smiled gratefully at Minas. "'I really needed that!"

"You look beautiful, Corelya" Nirch'ii cooed.

"People think I look like a *whore!*" Corelya bridled. "About half-a-dozen sleazebags propositioned me before I even made it through the door."

"You did walk past *The Pharaoh's Crown*, Corelya? Perhaps it was just a simple misunderstanding?" Minas grinned inanely.

"Oh really!" Corelya scowled, her blue eyes blazing. "How would you like it if someone put their hand down your pants and tried to fondle your 'bits', Minas?" she let the question hang in the air for a moment. "No need to answer Minas, I bet you would love it!"

Nirch'ii and Minas giggled hysterically, drawing startled glances from a group of drinkers at a neighbouring table. "It really does suit you, Corelya" Minas purred. "Everyone else seems to think so."

"Are you propositioning me as well?" Corelya chirped.

Nirch'ii giggled. Minas' eyes twinkled.

"So, you would like to keep it? We do have many more that might interest both of you, including several stunning creations from the Orient. They are called Sari's."

"Will you be around town tomorrow morning?" Corelya asked politely.

"I could meet you in the Square tomorrow morning, if you would like to see our current range. Far away from *The Pharaoh's Crown*, if that would suit you Corelya?"

Corelya snorted. "You really are a confident bastard, aren't you, Minas?"

"Yes. I suppose I am" Minas proffered the girls a winning smile.

Both Nirch'ii and Corelya were so taken aback by his honesty that they laughed heartily and promptly ordered another round of drinks, paid for by the last of Nichassor's funds. Several hours later, with the moon high in the night sky, the two girls kissed the delightful Minas goodnight, weaved their way through the tangle at the front door, and strolled uneventfully back to their lodgings at the rear of Mosh'ii's Surgery. The two arrived at their room, quickly undressed, and snuggled naked on the bed under a light blanket. Soon they were fast asleep.

~

The sun was still low in the sky when Corelya took Nichassor a cup of mint tea early the next morning. If Nichassor was genuinely surprised to see Corelya alive, his expression did not betray the fact. "How are you feeling?" asked Corelya. The concern for his welfare was genuine.

"Sore" Nichassor replied simply. "You were drunk last night."

"I was. Not that it is any of your concern" Corelya smiled sweetly.

"Are you prepared for the day's outing?" Nichassor

smiled tightly.

"That question might be more properly addressed to the vision in the mirror, Nichassor?" Corelya chided.

"I can still ride a horse, Corelya. And so, there is no reason not to proceed with the meeting as planned this afternoon."

"Are you sure?" Corelya asked earnestly.

"Absolutely" Nichassor assured her. "I have already despatched Siladar to the south in search of them. He should be back within the next few hours. All things being well, we shall meet with them as arranged this afternoon or possibly tomorrow, at the latest?"

"Either is fine by me" Corelya insisted.

"You are certain about this, Corelya?" Nichassor probed.

"I have never been more certain of anything in my life!" Corelya confirmed. "They must be stopped, once and for all, and I must have my vengeance!"

"Then it is done?" Nichassor said simply.

"It will be, Nichassor! It will be!" Corelya said coldly.

⌇

An hour or so later, Siladar and three other members of Nichassor's band enter a small clearing in a stretch of woodland located a few hours south of Qu'ehra. The group was immediately surrounded by thirty armed brigands, the kind of men who murder simply for fun! They were the scourge of the surviving Sauromatae communities in the region, and unrepentant slaughterers of their long-departed kinfolk. They were, of a fashion, erstwhile allies of Persia in the paid service of the hated Argata Queen. Three men, two of whom are aged in their early forties, the other in his early twenties, stroll out of the doorway of a log cabin to the right of the clearing and approach their visitors.

"You are Siladar?" asked the leader of the brigands, a

gruff character with unruly hair and a weather-beaten face.

"I am Siladar?" the brute grunted.

"I am Seart'i" the man confirmed. "I am sorry to hear of Nichassor's misfortunes."

"Nichassor lives. Your sympathies should lie with the families of his would-be killers! They are the unfortunate ones" Siladar spoke evenly.

"Is it true that his life was saved by a girl?" Seart'i raised an eyebrow mockingly. A ripple of raucous laughter convulses the assembled brigands. A well of anger stirs in Siladar.

"That is surely of no concern of yours, Seart'i?" spoke softly. Inwardly, he was seething.

"Our current arrangements are more than satisfactory, Siladar, you may rest assured of that. We await delivery of our tribute this very afternoon."

"Here? It will be just the three of you, is that it?" Siladar seemed surprised.

"Of course," Seart'i confirmed. "We have nothing to fear from you, or anyone else for that matter!" Seart'i grinned and spread his arms theatrically. "Why in Hades name should we fear a man who owes a life debt to a child, and a girl, at that?" His chide was met with a cacophony of sneers and laughter.

"There is one last thing, Seart'i. It is a small favour, requested personally by Nichassor" Siladar spoke evenly, mustering his last reserves of grace.

"If his request is within my power to grant, then I shall grant it!" Seart'i was clearly enjoying his moment in the sun.

"Would you have any reservations about murdering a child?"

"This feral Sauromatae whore-bitch, I presume?"

"She is all that and more!" Siladar spoke softly, yet his hatred of the child was keen.

"Deliver this vermin to us and I can promise you she

will be dealt with."

"There are two of them, Seart'i. Both are Sauromatae scum! The rest of the party is not to be touched! Do we understand one another?" Siladar insisted. "We have an agreement, yes?"

"As per our arrangement, Siladar" Seart'i sighed. "And now, you may fuck off back to where you came from, shitbucket!" Seart'i moved dangerously close to Siladar's steed yet spoke loud enough for everyone to hear. "The next time, I will speak with his Lordship personally! Not his fucking privy!" he growled.

Siladar smiled thinly and nodded respectfully. "Come on!" he barked at his comrades, turning his horse, and trotting away along the path towards the woodland edge. Despite the threats and the insults, it promised to be a most gratifying day. Siladar may have detested Corelya with a singular passion yet, after events of the previous morning in the Bazaar, he could at least find solace in the belief that Nichassor's faith was not misplaced

Corelya would murder this lice-riddled Armenian cunt, his prick of a brother, possibly even the lanky bastard too! If she failed, it mattered not. Either way, she was fated to die this day, for Nichassor had sworn it so. *All eventualities had been duly accounted for!*

Alas, there was one eventuality that had not been given the consideration it ought to have! It was lore almost as ancient as the mountains themselves. *There is no honour among thieves!* Regrettably, it was not the only eventuality that Siladar, as brutish, short-sighted, and dishonourable as he was, had failed to apply his mind to.

That other eventuality was Corelya; a peril unto herself and a maelstrom to all around her!

EIGHT

Qu'ehra, July 493 BC

"How are you feeling this morning?" Corelya asked Nirch'ii when she returned from her visit to Nichassor.

"My head feels a little fuggy!" Nirch'ii sighed miserably.

"Let's have a cup of mint tea. It will make you feel better!" Corelya insisted.

A short while later, the two girls sit perched on the end of the bed sipping scalding mint tea. Nirch'ii had added a little poppy oil to her own tea, and this was beginning to take effect. "What do you think of him?", she asked suddenly.

"Minas?" Corelya guessed.

"Of course, I meant Minas!" she snickered. "I wasn't referring to Siladar, was I?"

Corelya grimaced at the mention of Siladar's name. "I think he is lovely! He is obviously very pretty, but he is also quite a genuine person?" Corelya surmised.

"That is what I thought. I talked with him at length whilst you were away from the table. I am honestly not sure what I expected, him being a trader and everything, but he is both honest and genuine. I am not certain if that is a blessing for a trader?"

"We will soon find out, won't we?" Corelya sighed. Her mind was elsewhere.

"Is everything fine with you, Corelya? You seem a little distant?" Nirch'ii asked.

"My mind is elsewhere. I was miles away, literally" confessed Corelya.

"Can you talk about it? If you, would you like to, of course?"

"As a matter of fact, it does concern you, Nirch'ii. You have nothing to fear, I promise. We must go on an errand this afternoon. It might be dangerous, but not for you."

"Then why do we have to go? Is this not something that Nichassor could handle himself?" Nirch'ii pined.

"It isn't that simple, Nirch'ii" Corelya explained. "There is a band of Armenian renegades who are currently corralled a few hours ride south of here. They are in the pay of the Argata and have systematically targeted our people for more than a decade. This is the slime who slaughtered my family, Nirch'ii, and Yari's family, too! They exterminated our entire community and took everything we had!"

"This is about vengeance? You believe that by killing them that you will make things, right?" Nirch'ii gasped incredulously.

"No, it is not, Nirch'ii!" Corelya bridled. "I believe that by killing three of them, the leaders of the band, I can secure a better future for all Sauromatae communities in 'the lands between the seas'. This is *our* home Nirch'ii, not theirs. Nor does it belong to the Argata, whatever the Persians may think!"

"Everybody has to be from somewhere, Corelya?" Nirch'ii protested.

"The Argata are migrants too, just like our ancestors were, yet we have lived here for centuries. Things have been desperately bad for years. The Armenians have suffered too, that much is true, especially at the hands of Persia and the Argata. Now everyone desires peace, even the Argata, yet this filth keep on slaughtering! They won't ever stop, Nirch'ii, not until the last of the Sauromatae in 'the lands between the seas' are gone forever. I must do this! I don't have a choice. This isn't just about vengeance; this is about justice!" Corelya remonstrated passionately.

"Do you need my help? What would you like me to do?" Nirch'ii smiled sweetly at the younger girl.

"I have an idea, Nirch'ii. I will be the only one directly exposed to any danger. You have my solemn vow on this. I do need your assistance. You can help choose a nice kurta for me and help with my hair. I need to look my prettiest, and not for Minas!"

"Of course, I can. It would be a pleasure" Nirch'ii replied.

~

Mistral, July 493 BC

Some twenty miles south-west of Qu'ehra, stands a fortress constructed to house a large detachment of Argata heavy cavalry, up to one hundred strong. On this morning, soon after sunrise, it was a hive of unusually frenetic activity. Horses had been fed and watered since first light and were now saddled, ready to move at a moment's notice. The air thrummed with the whir of circular sandstones as swords were sharpened by experienced armourers. Individual soldiers honed their daggers and arrow-points to a state of lethal readiness. *This was an elite detachment preparing for action*! If news of such happenings had ever reached the ears of the populace of Qu'ehra, it would have precipitated mass panic! For there, it was assumed that the security of the fragile peace between the four regional powers, Persia, the Argata, the Orch'tai, and the Ur'gai, was assured under the terms of the *Accord Scythiac*. The panic would have reached epic proportions if it became widely known that the current detachment were Orch'tai regulars, stationed sixty miles south of the Argata-Orch'tai frontier! These were superb warriors, amongst the finest equestrians in the known world, well trained, equipped, and battle-hardened in the campaigns against the Sauromatae tribes east of the Wol'yi.

A few hours later, a single rider, passed through the West Gate and trotted into the parade square. The man dismounted, removed his helmet, and grinned at a fellow comrade to whom he entrusted his steed. The young officer strolled cross the parade square to a small building situated in the far south-east corner. This was the Commandant's Quarters and Administration Bureau, sited far away from the stables and its unpleasant stench. The soldier approached the door, knocked twice, and entered the room without formality. All eyes turned to face him. A small group of Orch'tai officers were briefing for the day's action. The soldier saluted crisply, closed the door behind him, and approached the Commanding Officer. This was Tar'gai, newly appointed Supreme Commander of an Orch'tai *Ochta*, a division numbering three hundred cavalry, not this small and irregular force. Except for their weapons, the uniforms were non-issue and the men had been encouraged to buy their own footwear in order to avoid suspicion that they constituted a regular military force. It was not unusual for bands of brigands and marauders to enforce some general consistency in dress to aid recognition and avoid unnecessary fatalities during combat actions!

"State your report, soldier!" Tar'gai rapped. He eyed the newcomer steadily.

"The ground is firm, Sir!" the soldier replied.

The pithy riposte is met by an outburst of laughter. "Spoken like a true cavalryman, Gosh'kar!" Tar'gai smiled wryly. "Nichassor's men are on route back to Qu'ehra?"

"Yes Sir. They should be in Qu'ehra within the next hour. Nothing has changed, Sir. All we have to do is move into position?"

"Their main force is as we expected?" Tar'gai smiled grimly.

"You can smell the rank bastards a mile off! Not to mention the smoke from their campfires, and these should burn for a few hours more! That is all the time we need, is it not? I checked out the ford, Sir. It is suitable, undefended, and we can easily slip most of our contingent in behind their lair without fear of discovery" Gosh'kar stated his report.

"You would stake your life on that, soldier?" Tar'gai clipped.

"I already have, Sir!" the reply was infused with a whiff of impertinence.

Tar'gai's eye's twinkled at the indiscretion. "What about their forming up point and method of attack? Is it as we predicted?" he enquired.

Gosh'kar smiled slyly. "It is elementary and poses little risk. However, it would be relatively easy to spring, for they appear to have neglected the prospect of an attack from the rear. These are brigands, not soldiers!" his contempt was visceral. "They will use the main track to the plain and mass their horses in the woodland, probably fifty paces to the rear."

"Our proposed pincer positions remain available?" Tar'gai probed.

"These are currently unguarded, Sir" Gosh'kar let his word's hang in the air. His fellow officers shared knowing smiles.

Tar'gai smiled at the soldier. "The flaw is as we expected?"

"There is an escape, Sir, depending on the skill of the horsemen."

"With the exception of this rabble, the two we are targeting are children, and girls at that!" There was a ripple of laughter. Tar'gai had elected not to inform his brother officers of the tale of the previous nights' misadventures. The barbarity with which one of his assassins had been despatched to the other side of the Styx left him decidedly queasy! *Perhaps, the blonde child had not killed them, after all*?

"Then we should be fine, Sir!" Gosh'kar said emphatically.

Tar'gai turned away from the soldier and addressed the rest of the assembled officers. "Now to your steeds, my fellow braves, and the joy of the chase to you all!"

⌒

Nichassor received Siladar in his bedroom, soon after his return to Qu'ehra, with a smile of genuine warmth. "You look much improved, Nichassor" Siladar commented, his relief genuine.

"I am on the mend, my dear friend! The God's be thanked. The wound is painful, but the damage is far less than I first feared."

"Zoroaster be praised, my Lord" Siladar sighed.

"Let us hope that Zoroaster smiles on our endeavours this day, my most trusted friend."

"Do you really think she is up to it?" Siladar smiled grimly, yet it mattered not, in any case.

"I believe that Corelya is up to the task we have set her! I have every confidence in her abilities, especially if yesterday evening's performance is any indicator" Nichassor smiled ruefully.

"The Orch'tai lost their bet! They are not very happy about it!" Despite his feelings towards the whore, Siladar seemed bemused by the misfortune that had befallen the assassins, and by the chagrin of their paymasters.

"Their happiness is no concern of ours, my friend. Their assistance at the present time is welcome and necessary" Nichassor breezed. "Life is a gamble, is it not? They gambled on two occasions yesterday! Their losses will serve our purposes."

"They hope to redeem themselves this day. It is a

matter of pride" Siladar smiled thinly.

"I sincerely hope so!" Nichassor spoke icily. "Corelya's survival should play to our advantage this afternoon. All I care is that she delivers on her promise. Once she has done so, the Orch'tai may feed her body to the wolves."

"It would please me!" Siladar mused nastily. "She has offended your dignity, old friend?"

"I will smile when she is dead."

"I will not, Siladar" Nichassor sighed sadly. "Corelya's death is a regrettable necessity, not something that I particularly welcome. Nevertheless, she cannot be allowed to survive beyond this day. There is too much at stake. All these years of patience will finally begin to bear fruit."

"I am weary of being poor!" Siladar sighed despondently. "I often dream of my villa in the plains and my retinue of concubines."

"There is more to life than property, women and drink, my friend" Nichassor rebuked the brute. "Our endeavours will deliver the promise of a Persian triumph over those treacherous Hellenics."

"And what will be the fate of these allies, the Argata and the Orch'tai, once our victory is assured?"

"They are useful brutes, no more than that!" Nichassor burned with the passion of the zealot. "We have succeeded in curtailing the perennial threat from the Sauromatae, that heathen slime who wrought a close to the glories of Assyria. Persia is the true successor to Assyria yet, until now, our destiny was by no means certain. King Darius will prove a worthy successor to Cyrus and, once we have tamed the Hellenics and the Ur'gai, once we have subjugated their ambition, we will deal with these so-called allies, the Argata and Orch'tai!"

"Do you think Corelya suspects anything untoward?" Siladar frowned.

"No, I do not. I fear that she is pre-occupied, obsessively so, by the prospect of an alliance between the Argata and

Orch'tai. She has yet to make the leap that Persia welcomes such an alliance, for it is consistent with our own ambitions. As for the Ur'gai and their nai:ve young Queen, they are our true enemies, for as long as they remain allied with Athens! If Corelya is to be believed, the Ur'gai labour under the misguided premise that Persia remains committed to the current regional consensus and the continuity of the peace."

"And so, this bitch must die!" Siladar's eyes twinkled with delight.

"And so, this bitch *will* die" Nichassor stated brutally.

~

Northern Plains of the Caucasus, July 493 BC

Two Orch'tai cavalry troops, numbering some fifty warriors and Officers, reached the ford as the midday sun was at its zenith in a clear blue sky. The journey had taken a mere two hours and the men were in excellent spirits. Once the last man had crossed the river a cohort of thirteen riders detach themselves from the main body and head towards a stretch of woodland on the horizon. Once they reach the edge of the woodland, they head north, following a well-worn track and the course of the stream until they near the plain. There they would remain, skulking in the screen where they could monitor the traffic from the north, until required. The main force of eighty-seven men continues south across the plain for a few miles further until the southern edge of the woodland becomes clearly demarcated in the distance to the east. They head east, angling toward the southern edge of the woodland and skirt its perimeter, continuing east, until they reach a stream. Once across, the men dismount and allow their horses to graze and water for half-an-hour as the officers held a brief meeting. Some men brew mint tea in their kettles and scalding cups of the beverage are passed among comrades. The soldiers remount and assemble in to five files of fifteen men, some five files deep. A sixth cohort, comprising some thirteen men under the command of Dor'kir, forms up at the rear of the main force and awaits the order to advance. Tar'gai rides silently forward on the west side of the formation and draws his sword, raising this high in the air in his right hand. His arm falls. The first file advances silently into the woodland at a trot. The rest of the force follows.

The stream lay immediately to their left as they entered the woodland. It then veers off, disappearing from view until, unexpectedly, it reappeared immediately to their front. The men troop silently across the stream. A short distance beyond its course, the first five files dismount. The sixth cohort trots east, following the course of the stream until it flowed almost at right angles to its previous course, towards the edge of the woodland. The men dismount and go to ground in the undergrowth with a clear view of the plain to their front. If everything has gone to plan, this force should now be almost directly opposite their thirteen comrades, hidden in the screen of trees a few miles away on the far west of the plain. The Commander of that force, none other than Gosh'kar himself, grimaces as the midday sun glints off metal on the horizon. Word is passed along the file. A party of riders is approaching across the plain from the north. Soon enough, the travellers amble past their concealed positions, quite unaware of their presence. The party comprises a dozen or so heavily armed men and a single rider in a black cloak. Two teenage girls ride beside him. The elder of the two is raven haired and slender, on the cusp of marriageable age. The younger girl was considerably taller and golden-haired. Gosh'kar scowls as an electric whisper passes on the line of hidden men. *This was the mythical 'gold witch'!*

⌐⌐

Earlier that morning, while Siladar and Nichassor sat in conference, Nirch'ii and Corelya had met Minas in the Central Square and strolled leisurely through the Bazaar to his brothers' stall on the northwest outskirts. The kurtas *were* stunning, and several creations even paled the *lilac* kurta, for Minas had insisted that it was not 'purple', that Corelya had already consented to buy. Stepping into the fitting room at the rear of the tent, Corelya's attention was drawn to a beautiful red-and-white creation hanging forlornly in the far corner which rekindled strong childhood memories of those fashioned by her own community, all those moons ago. She strolled across to examine the garment closely "Is this new?" she asked interestedly.

Minas blushed. "I am afraid not, Corelya. It is quite old, yet I assure you that it has never been worn. In that respect, it is new, or at least it would be on you."

"Where did you get it?" Corelya asked earnestly.

"We purchased it from a trader in Olbia. They are expensive and only the very wealthy can afford them, at least in Olbia, for the prices are greatly inflated compared with here in Qu'ehra. In this case, I think it may originate from the Sauromatae in the south." Minas confessed.

"It *is* Sauromatae, I am certain of it" Corelya asserted. "Might I have a closer look at the embroidery around the neck?"

"Of course, you may" Minas handled the garment respectfully, and passed it to the child.

"By the grace of sweet Tabiti! I can't believe what I am seeing!!" Corelya gasped, blinking back the tears that sprang instantly.

"*What is it*? *What's wrong*?" Nirch'ii frowned in puzzlement. Minas could only gape at the distressed child in silent bewilderment.

"It *is* one of ours, I know it is! Can you see the

embroidered star on the left side at the neck- line?" both Nirch'ii and Minas nodded. "There isn't one on the right side, is there?" There was not. "If the star had been on the right, not the left, this was crafted by my aunt Azulya."

"Oh Corelya!" Nirch'ii gasped and moved quickly to embrace the ashen girl.

It was a still uncomprehending Minas who asked the obvious question. "And if the star was on the left side, as it is on this garment?"

"My mother made this! This is her creation!" Corelya said simply. Tears were flowing freely now, a torrent coursing down both cheeks.

"Hush baby" Nirch'ii desperately tried to sooth her.

Minas is dumbstruck. "Then you must have it, Corelya. I cannot sell this to anyone else. It is yours by right."

Minas nodded silently to the older girl and turned away, stepping outside the tent to speak with his brothers. He returned soon afterwards with a flagon of wodki and three goblets. "I have spoken with my brothers, Corelya, and we are at one on this. We would like you to have the kurta, yet we cannot charge for it. First, we must toast your family. Forgive me, please. I do not wish to intrude, but you are obviously very distressed by the sight of the kurta. Something truly terrible happened, didn't it?"

"I was born into a Sauromatae community in the mountains, a few days ride from here. It was peaceful, until they cane! My entire village was murdered! Only Yari and I survived!"

"I am deeply sorry for your loss, Corelya. And now, we must toast your family and your community" Minas insisted.

Corelya gazed deeply into his blue eyes. To her surprise, she saw a *purity* she could not have imagined existed. Her heart skipped a beat. Minas was certainly good marriage material. The three chimed their goblets and swallowed the liquor in a single gulp. Minas' elder brother, Daenys, loomed in the doorway with a bundle of brightly coloured kurtas from the display at the front. The first garment was a striking saffron creation that was guaranteed to turn heads, then came a gorgeous lavender slip that was the cinch of *understated*, and, finally, a captivating turquoise confection that simply screamed *allure*! All crafted from the finest weave and elegantly embroidered. To everyone's astonishment, Corelya plucked the wodki flagon, drank greedily, and announced that she would purchase all three items for Nirch'ii, in addition to the other two for herself, with silver ingots. Daenys was flabbergasted that a mere child could afford such luxury, yet a quick glance from Minas was sufficient to still any remark. Corelya suggested that she and Minas vacate the fitting room to allow Nirch'ii to try on her new garments, well away from prying eyes! Minas pointed to a draped cubicle in the near corner, and the girl skipped happily away, clutching the three garments.

Corelya led Minas outside, and the pair strolled away from the stall towards the covered wagon a short distance away. "I need a favour, Minas?" she whispered conspiratorially. *There was a definite edge to her voice.*

"What is it, Corelya?" Minas smiled warmly at the girl.

"Have you heard of a band of brigands, led by a slime-ball called Seart'i, who have been operating in the region for the past decade or so?"

Minas was astonished by the question. "Who has not heard of them? They have a deserved reputation for unbridled cruelty and are a scourge of all foreign traders."

"Have you ever paid them tribute?" Corelya asked softly.

"I am sorry to say that we have" he shrugged ruefully. "Most of the foreign traders must pay them, at least from time to time."

"Would you have any idea where they can be found?" Corelya probed.

"They are based a few hours ride to the south. They

make no effort to conceal where they live. Instead, they are happy for everyone to know where their tribute should be paid."

"*They make you go to them to pay*?" Corelya was astonished.

"Most of the time you simply pay one of their brethren here in Qu'ehra" Minas advised. "They are not stupid, Corelya! They have spies everywhere. Every wagon is closely monitored, they know *everything*! When you are leaving, which route you will take, and what you are carrying? They even have an accurate gauge of how much each consignment is worth?"

"Precise?" the child was intrigued.

"It would appear so. There is obviously endemic corruption in the administration, as there sadly is in many trading centres, yet I have never heard the like of it." Minas shrugged ruefully. "What can you do?"

"Money and morals are not the most amorous of bedfellows, are they?" Corelya quipped.

Minas laughed. "And what would you know about such things?"

"I am an ardent learner, if you are a patient teacher?" Corelya teased.

"You are a little young for my tastes, Corelya" Minas laughed heartily.

Corelya smiled warmly and slugged from the wodki flagon. "These vermin have touts in Qu'ehra? These are worthless people who would betray their mothers for an old copper coin!"

"I agree with you. Such people have no honour. But we merchants must make a living! If we do not pay them, they take or destroy our property, perhaps even kill us" Minas shrugged apologetically.

"Does this apply to everyone? What of the Oriental traders coming from Orch'tai territories?

Are their wagons threatened with attack?"

"The tariffs only apply to Hellenic merchants, never to the Oriental traders from the Orch'tai lands! Nor are traders from the Persian territories levied. It is only those with obvious ties to the Greeks. There are a few other unfortunates, mostly Celts, who are plagued by their tyranny" Minas spat feelingly.

"Are you implying that this is aimed exclusively at Hellenic interests?" Corelya spoke softly.

"It is difficult to say. Nobody here talks openly about it. It is generally accepted that you pay if, and when, you must. I have spoken with fellow-traders in Olbia and at other centres in the Crimea. From what we have learned, all have some experience of being levied, particularly during the past year! Before that, there was a different pattern to the levies and the threats."

"There was a definite pattern?" Corelya pressed.

"Once, if you transported poppy oil or weapons, you were particularly vulnerable to attack and, by extension, levies. Yet, this summer, they have levied fees on virtually all traders from the Hellenic colonies and Europe, regardless of the consignment or its relative worth."

"Since the Ur'gai declared their Protectorate of the Crimea and its Hellenic polities?" Corelya ventured.

"It might appear so, might it not? Then again, it might have something to do with the Argata, for they have an equivalent authority in 'the lands between the seas", have they not?"

"There must be rumours, surely?" Corelya pressed.

"There is talk, perhaps little more than unfounded rumour, that the Persians are not happy with the Ur'gai's Protectorate of the Crimea. That you assumed too much."

"Yet Athens, Thebes and Corinth were, and remain, in accord on this issue?"

"Their influence scarcely extends to this region. Persia is the dominant regional power. Even the Scythia, whether they are Ur'gai, Orch'tai, Argata or Nur'gat, cannot challenge Persia's power?" Minas sighed resignedly.

"I think Persia's power, at least militarily, may be greatly overstated. They have never faced Sparta on the battlefield. I am not sure they would win."

"But Persia can field an army of unparalleled size!" Minas remonstrated.

"Not much use if they can't, or won't, fight. Even less use, once they are dead!"

"You said you needed our help. We surely cannot be of assistance in such great matters of politic?" Minas quipped.

"We are heading south in a few hours to meet with this slime at their lair. I need you to follow us in a goods wagon. If things get bad, we may need somewhere to stow away?"

"Both of you are going?" Minas gasped. Corelya took note of the keen concern in his voice. She knew in her heart that it was not for her!

"Nirch'ii will be coming too. She won't be in any danger, not at the beginning, I assure you" she soothed. "I am not sure I trust the men we are with anymore. Anything could happen after we meet with the brigands."

"You have to pass through a central plain, only a few miles wide. It is flanked by dense woodland and would be a good place for an ambush. You would have no escape, except one, and even that could be cut-off from the rear."

"Could you draw a map for me?" Corelya implored. "Of course, it would be a pleasure" Minas said instantly.

Nirch'ii suddenly re-appears, strolling toward the wagon with a small bowl of fruit. The bowl contained oranges, limes, and bunches of red and white grapes. "Are you feeling better, Corelya? Please, have some fruit?" Minas smiles shyly at the girl and walks back towards the stall.

Corelya plucked an orange and a lime. "Thank you, Nirch'ii, that is really sweet of you."

"What time are we due to leave?" Nirch'ii asked.

"Probably within an hour, I would venture. Nichassor hopes to be there by the early afternoon, just after midday.

He seems insistent on the schedule."

"Are you worried?" Nirch'ii spoke softly, yet the fear in her voice was naked.

"I am a little concerned, I will freely admit, and perhaps with good reason!" Corelya sighed. "I presume Nichassor, and that scumbag Siladar know the 'lie of the land' well enough, but I have no idea what we are walking in to. I don't trust these brigands, nor do I trust Nichassor. I have a bad feeling about all of this!"

"Is that why you were talking to Minas?" Nirch'ii probed.

"He knows the area quite well and has agreed to draw a map. It seems that these sleazebags aren't overly concerned about advertising their location" Corelya confessed. "They don't expect to be attacked, which may suggest that they may have a formidable force at their disposal. Given the increase in rainfall and seasonal ebb of the rivers, there are a lot more trees south of Qu'ehra, more than I am used to on the Great Steppe or the plains of the Crimea."

"You think we might be in danger?" Nirch'ii was biting her top lip and her hands were trembling.

"Can you use a sword, or a bow, preferably the latter?"

Nirch'ii raised an eyebrow mockingly. "I am Sauromatae, Corelya? My father taught me to hunt with a bow. There was always a problem with wild boars, especially during the rutting season when the females are on heat. They are extremely dangerous, especially to young children and domesticated pigs" the girl said proudly.

"Could you shoot a man?"

"Minas? I would much rather kiss him?" Nirch'ii blushed, as her eyes sparkled like gemstones.

Corelya shrieked with laughter. "You certainly have a way with words, Nirch'ii! Not Minas, one of these animals! Perhaps even Nichassor?"

"If it comes to it, then I could. If our lives are in danger, I would not hesitate, I swear it. I will deal with Siladar, if it comes to it. You can kill Nichassor."

"No way, young Lady" Corelya protested. "Siladar is mine! I promised that scruffy bastard to myself!"

"I think I like being called 'young Lady'! It seems appropriate, all of a sudden" Nirch'ii gushed and performed a little twirl in her new lavender slip.

"Won't you tell me more about kissing Minas?" Corelya teased.

"Why don't you let me do your hair now?" said Nirch'ii, deftly sidestepping the subject.

～

Corelya strode through the door of the cabin with two baskets containing wild fruits, salted meat, and fresh cheeses. She places the first basket, covered with muslin cloth, down on the floor and closes the door firmly behind her. The girl picks up the basket and strolls across to the small table on the other side of the room. The three leaders of the brigands are sat at a large table in the centre of the room, sharing a flagon of berry wine.

Corelya fishes a flagon of berry wine from the first basket and turns to face the three men. She smiles shyly as the men gaze hungrily at her.

"I should leave these here, for you. They are a gift from Nichassor, with his blessings?" She addresses the men in Sarmati, knowing they will despise her for it!

None of the brutes answer. Corelya smiles sweetly and saunters across to the table, placing the flagon down in front of them. She turns and twirls away, back towards the smaller table with the baskets, and then turns back to face them. Seart'i is sat facing her across the table, whereas his brother, Sorghar, has his back to her. He would be the easiest kill, Corelya decided quickly. It was the youngest man, aged a decade or so older than herself, upon whom she now lavishes her attention. He was tall, muscular, and had the air of a man who could handle himself in either the saddle or a fight. He would be the first to die! Seart'i would die last, but only once Corelya had revealed her identity. *How she yearned to reveal to him that his fate had been sealed many moons before*!

The younger man eyed the girl steadily, then turned and grinned at his companions. "You can leave your kurta there too, you sweet little plum!" he quipped. The other two brutes laughed raucously.

Corelya frowned. "I am not sure that I understand?"

"Was it a good harvest?" enquired Seart'i mildly. He didn't even look at the girl.

"Of sorts" Corelya replied. "The Gods were satisfied."

"And the men?" asked Sorghar, smiling wryly.

"I don't understand what you mean?" Corelya frowned.

"Where are you from, girl?" asked the third man.

"There is village to the west. It is only a couple of hours ride away. I was instructed by my father to pay homage and present these gifts from Nichassor, as I have already said."

"Does your father often let you off the leash? A pretty girl like you?" the third man persisted.

"I am not yet of marrying age, nor will be for a year or so. I don't suppose that he minded, for Nichassor told us that you were noble and honourable men, to be absolutely trusted. My father believed him" Corelya lied smoothly.

"Is your father the village fool?" the third man sneered. His companions laughed heartily.

"No!" Corelya scowled. "My father is renowned in the village for his wisdom!"

The youngest man pushed his chair back and eyed Corelya hungrily. Corelya blushed faintly and smiled nervously back. "I should leave now, my Lord?"

The man returned her smile and then turned and grinned conspiratorially at his companions. "Now, my friends, what should we do with this juicy little bitch?"

"Don't call me that!" Corelya hissed. "It is not

respectful. You are supposed to be nice men."

The men were stunned by the girl's outrage. "There is fire under that kurta, isn't there, my honeycomb?" the third brute sneered. Corelya suspected he was already hard for her.

"I don't understand?" Corelya affected a puzzled expression. She was beginning to enjoy herself.

Sorghar turned in his chair to appraise the girl more closely. "That is a nice kurta, Missy. Is it your best?" he enquired.

"Oh yes!" Corelya confessed, her face brightening. "Do you like it? It is certainly my favourite!"

"Your father wished you to make a good impression?" the third man asked eagerly.

"Of course, my Lord" Corelya replied quickly. "I am here to pay our tribute. Nichassor said that we should give tribute to you, for you are noble men, and our protectors."

The third man climbed out of his chair and steps towards her, stopping a short distance away. To Corelya's astonishment, he bowed ceremoniously, a mocking gleam in his eye. "Your father has our compliments, darling child. My name is Kilagar, this is Sorghar, and this is Seart'i" he made the introductions. "What is your name, sweet honeycomb?"

"Nae'meh" Corelya replied. It was the name of Nirch'ii's murdered mother.

"It is a lovely name, for truly lovely girl" Kilagar sighed. "The kurta suits you, Missy, for it compliments your hair. I wish to see what lies underneath."

"I don't know.. you can't mean *that*?" Corelya whimpered.

The knife blade was drawn quickly from its sheath to hover only inches from her left cheek "But I do little plum!" Kilagar hissed. "Now, my little peach, let us have a closer look at you?"

The point of the blade now hovered close to the

drawstrings of the kurta, just below Corelya's throat. She moved her right hand to the drawstrings, whilst her left hand moves cautiously towards the blade, her fingers caressing it lightly. She gazes solemnly into the man's eyes and smiles sweetly. "You do not need this! This is what you need" she purred. She steps back, quickly unties the drawstrings, and slips the garment over her shoulders. It drops to the floor, revealing her nakedness for all to see. Corelya would have happily wagered every coin in Korta's *Cuca* this scumbag's cock was gorged for action!

Kilagar stepped to one side, allowing Corelya's naked body to be lewdly appraised by the others, before he sheathed his blade and stepped closer still. "You are a little young, to be such an eager flirt, even if you do have hairs around your honey-pot?" *Corelya was already savouring his death! It would be all too easy!*

"I thought you just wanted to see me?" Corelya simpered, smiling shyly.

"Then let us all have a closer look at you, you naughty little bitch?"

Kilagar steps in close to put his hands to Corelya's naked hips. He picks her up and lifts her on the table. Corelya keeps her eyes locked with his own as his hands move quickly from her hips to the inside of her thighs, to prize her legs apart. The man dropped to one knee directly in front of her and forces her knees even further apart, gazing wolfishly at her naked crotch, with its wispy smattering of pubic hair. Corelya smiled slyly at the man, her eyes twinkling with mischief.

"Do you like what you see?" she purred.

His response took her completely by surprise. "Ahhh!" she gasped sharply, the breath exploding from her lungs as a single finger was inserted, first roughly, then more deftly, expertly even, inside her. The pain she had first experienced soon gave way to a pleasure she could never have imagined, increasing steadily, as she quickly moistened. She arched her back, resting on her elbows, her legs spread wider still as he teased her to an almost insatiable hunger. Despite her revulsion, she was moaning softly, her cheeks flushed angrily, nipples stiffened and prominent as never before. She hadn't meant for this to happen, and, despite her disgust, she felt an exhilaration, liberation even, she had never thought possible. Her hands reached for the pleated bun at the back of her head, and this was prized apart as mercilessly as her legs had been with an explosion of golden locks.

Corelya's left hand curled lovingly around the ornate boss of the iron hairpin, which she cupped in her palm. Her eyes remained fixated on her naked crotch and the rhythmic strokes of a finger that was a source of hitherto unimagined bliss. *She would enjoy killing him! Yet, for now, she would simply enjoy the moment!*

Kilagar removed his finger and grinned at the trembling girl. Corelya smiled serenely, a sultry twinkle in her eyes. Her cheeks have flushed a radiant pink. "Did you enjoy that, bitch?"

"Oh yes!" Corelya sighed. She was telling the truth, no matter how he repulsed her!

"Would you like to try something else?"

"Kiss me, please?" Corelya whispered hungrily.

"I will do anything you ask, you naughty little bitch!" Kilagar sneered

"Make me whole again, you murderous cunt!" Corelya purred. Her left forearm flicked forward, the iron spike protruding from between her middle fingers, to be driven home with a lethal speed in to Kilagar's right eye. Kilagar died, just as his murderess had intended, a look of guileless incomprehension on his face, his last sound a blood-curdling scream that stilled almost as quickly as his heartbeat! A stunned silence submerges the room.

"You evil little whore!" Sorghar roared, as he rose swiftly from the chair with murder in his heart. Yet, Corelya was nimbler, and before he could draw his blade, her left hand had swept away the muslin cloth covering the nearest basket. The basket contained two loaded crossbows and, within an instant, a first had been aimed and discharged in to Sorghar's throat at almost point-blank range. His death had been satisfying, despite its effortlessness. Now came the moment Corelya had dreamt of for years, never believing that it would ever come true. The second weapon was now in her grasp, and she leapt lithely off the table, striding swiftly across the dusty floor to face her lifelong tormentor, the man who had murdered her family! She assumed her preferred killing stance, directly facing Seart'I across the table at an angle, her long legs flexed as springs, completely unashamed of her nakedness.

"I have waited so long for this, Seart'i. I could scarcely credit that you were to be delivered unto me after all this time. What's wrong, slag-pile? Lynx got your tongue?" she hissed.

"Who are you?" Seart'i spoke hoarsely. His fear was palpable, from the bead of sweat trickling down his left cheek, to the hesitancy in his voice. A man who had revelled in inflicting unimaginable horror on the young and the old, the defenceless and the weak, now cowed with terror himself. For the better part of two decades, Seart'i and his brethren had mercilessly preyed upon the lands of the Sauromatae, raping, murdering, and pillaging, without fear of either justice or reprisal. And now, deliverance had finally come in a most terrifying guise. *This naked fury of an Amazon*!

"Would you like to know why I shall enjoy killing you, Seart'i?" Corelya spoke chillingly.

"Yes" the simplicity of the answer was unexpected.

"I was a child, Seart'i! Just a little girl when your band of murderers paid us a visit. I suppose it would be hard for you to remember, wouldn't it? We were just another village, weren't we? We were a community, Seart'i, just another group of simple, peaceful people.

Like so many others you raped, pillaged, and slaughtered!"

"Then how would I remember? And why should I even care?" Seart'i sighed. "So, you survived, you precious little cunt! And now you think I should remember you, is that it?" he sneered.

Corelya blinks back the tears. "I grew up in the mountains, Seart'i. A few days ride from here. We settled on a plain next to a large stream in a valley, where we grew poppies! Beautiful purple poppies which clothed the entire valley in the spring, and which were prized even by the Persians. We grew rye, emmer, spelt, and barley, and grazed cattle and goats, to sell and to eat."

"Just like all the other scum! Just filth! Sauromatae slime!" he sneered.

"You liked the kurta, didn't you?" Corelya inquired icily. "Didn't you recognise it? That was one of ours. We made beautiful kurta's, Seart'i, and we made a small fortune selling them to the wealthiest traders. They were dyed vivid colours and elegantly embroidered. We were famous for them and anyone who could afford them bought them from us. It made us rich, almost as rich as the sale of the poppy oil. We had silver, Seart'i, lots of it! You and your filthy slime took everything we had, including all our silver!"

Seart'i' was ashen. All arrogance and defiance seeped away as the memory returned in vivid colour, almost as vivid as the red and white kurta that lay on the floor a short distance from the child. That had sealed their fate! Not the kurtas or the poppy oil *per se*, but the price the traders had been willing to pay at the Bazaar in Qu'ehra. Such silver he had never seen before and, such beautiful women, especially the tall, leggy blondes! They were sisters, physically indistinct to a casual observer, sharing a single birthday. One had worn a red and white kurta, much like the one the child had been wearing, whereas the other had been dressed in a blue and yellow creation. Neither had worn britches! His riders had tailed the party of traders, men, and women, back to their village in a valley in the mountains. He stared afresh at the girl stood in front of him. She was everything a man could desire! Tall, blonde, leggy, and beautiful, enough to make any man as randy as a billy-goat, even now!

"Your mother was a twin? They were virtually identical, were they not?" Seart'i sighed disbelievingly.

"My mother was an identical twin. I look like her, or so I was always told. Do you remember now?"

"She had a birthmark on her forearm. She wore a red-and-white kurta at the Bazaar in Qu'ehra, just like the one you wore. The other was identical, but slightly taller."

"My mother was tall, just like I am!" Corelya corrected him. "Azulya had the birthmark. She was my aunt. My mother was named Sybillya."

"They lived next door to each other. They both had sons. I don't remember a daughter?"

"They were my brothers and my cousins!" Corelya hissed. "I wasn't there, was I? I would have been slaughtered, just like you slaughtered them!"

"They were spared. They were the only two we kept alive?"

Corelya gapes at the man in astonishment. "I don't understand?" she stammered.

"They were not killed. We killed everyone else, but not those two beauties! They were far too valuable to us alive!" Seart'i sneered.

"You are lying to me?" Corelya spat.

"Have you not heard of the 'golden whores of Olbia', sweet child?" he chided. "They are renowned among the most discerning of patrons, especially the Hellenics."

Tears course down Corelya's cheeks. She stares wide eyed at her tormentor. "Liar!" she screamed.

"I have heard it whispered that they put on quite a performance, those hot Sauromatae bitches! Their tongues are like honey, and they moan with ecstasy just like you, you little heathen slut!"

Corelya fired. The quarrel took Seart'i clean through the mouth. A gout of blood exploded from the back of his throat as his head rocketed backwards with the impact of the projectile as it punches through tissue; soft, then hard, to sear into his brain. He fell heavily to the floor and bled copiously.

Corelya plucked the open flagon of berry wine from the table and took a grateful slug. It tasted good, almost as good as the wine in the unopened flagon she had brought with her and would now take away. A little celebration would be in order this evening. The girl dressed quickly, re-loaded the crossbows, and grabbed the two baskets. She steps out into the clearing and closes the door behind her. The baskets are tied to Sybillya's saddle at the rear. Corelya vaults agilely into the saddle and trots away, heading north along the woodland path to where Nirch'ii and the others await at the entrance to the plain.

As she did so, she had no idea that she was being watched!

~

Saiga Plains, Crimea, July 493 BC

"It is good of you to spare me the time, Commander Zar'cha" Alazar stood to greet the Commander of Her Majesty's Royal Guard, as she was ushered into his private chambers by his secretary. He nodded to a vacant chair. "Please, sit down, Commander. Would you care for a small draught of wodki?"

"Of course, Honourable Counsellor, I came as soon as I could" Zar'cha replied. "I take it you wish to discuss the security arrangements for the forthcoming Royal Banquet in Chersonesus?"

"Indeed, I do. I received a communication from Commander Vu'kir, Head of the Polis Militia in Chersonesus, requesting an update on our security provisions just this morning.

Am I to take it that we would require all available accommodation at *The Athenian* for the Royal Guard?"

"That would be the most appropriate venue for the Guards, don't you think? It is happily close to both the Central Square and the Merchant's Guild. I have been led to believe that the Merchant's Guild consider their own Banqueting Room far more suited to the Banquet than the Council Chamber of the City Father's?" Zar'cha probed.

"It was my intent to reply to Commander Vu'kir and inform him of my plans to visit Chersonesus early next week to press the issue of the Queen's security" Alazar smiled brightly.

"I had not been informed of your plans, Honourable Counsellor" Zar'cha was startled by the revelation.

"I thought it might be wise if we travelled together, Commander? Your insights would be invaluable. After all, you will have ultimate responsibility for Her Majesty's security throughout the visit?"

"I think that a most excellent idea, Honourable Counsellor. It would afford a welcome opportunity to survey the lay of the land, so to speak" Zar'cha concurred. "I take it you have particular concerns as regards the political situation in Chersonesus?"

Alazar frowned. "Her Royal Majesty is universally admired in Chersonesus, is she not?"

"Not by her enemies, Honourable Counsellor" Zar'cha smiled thinly. "Is there any truth to the rumour that certain elements plan to disrupt the festivities with a protest?"

"Commander Vu'kir alludes to this in his communication. Any such protest would surely be peaceful, would it not?" Alazar said airily.

"May I remind you, Honourable Counsellor, that many a peaceful protest has turned suddenly violent, often without warning! The passion of the mob is fickle, is it not? There is also the spectre of more sinister elements, who may attempt to capitalise on any public display of enmity?" Zar'cha ventured.

"You mean *assassins*? Such a thing would be unthinkable!" Alazar frowned.

"It has happened before, Honourable Counsellor. In my humble opinion, it could all too easily happen again, especially in the present climate of distrust."

"I would obviously defer to your considerable experience in such grave matters, Commander" the Honourable Counsellor smiled grimly.

"Naturally, Honourable Counsellor, for I may be privy to intelligence that you are not?" Zar'cha's eyes twinkled with mischief.

"Do we have firm grounds for suspicion that Her Majesty's life would be imperilled by these treacherous elements in Chersonesus?" Alazar enquired brightly.

"I suspect it far more likely that such personnel would be recruited outside Chersonesus. It would be easy to recruit suitable people in Panticapaeum, perhaps even Nymphaion?" Zar'cha smiled slyly.

"I see" the Honourable Counsellor sipped his wodki. "Such individuals would command a high price, would they not? The sums involved in such an adventure would surely be beyond the means of a gaggle of disaffected merchants with loyalties to the Argata or Orch'tai? We are, after all, talking about professional killers, are we not?" surmised Alazar.

"At least the impromptu nature of the visit does not lend itself readily to the recruitment of accomplices from more distant polities, you would agree?" Zar'cha replied evenly.

"There is that, obviously. In the unlikely event that such treacherous agencies did wish to engage professional killers to assassinate Her Royal Majesty, they would make enquiries in Panticapaeum or Nymphaion?" Alazar pressed.

"I would favour Nymphaion, Honourable Counsellor. There is talk of a shadowy group of dissidents with ties to sinister elements in the City Administration. They may consider themselves qualified for such a mission" Zar'cha said airily.

"Then we have much to fear, Commander Zar'cha, do we not?" Alazar sighed sadly.

"It would be strongly advisable to gather as much information on these individuals as we can over the next few weeks. We might even engage surveillance of their movements?"

"I would concur with your assessment, Commander. Is there anyone in Nymphaion we could make initial contact with? This individual would obviously be a loyal servant of the Crown, of course?"

"There is such a person. Moreover, this individual would not compromise any of our other intelligence sources in Nymphaion?" Zar'cha replied evenly.

"Splendid! I don't suppose you would be willing to reveal our contact's name. In the pursuit of the security of the realm, of course! I would never deign to ask otherwise?"

"His name is Solthazar. He is an Apothecary with premises in the Market Square within the city walls. He is a man of unswerving loyalty to Her Majesty, and I can vouch for him personally in this regard."

"That is most gracious of you, Commander Zar'cha. I shall contact the man with haste!"

"In the interests of security, Honourable Counsellor, perhaps it might be wiser to engage the services of an agent with no obvious ties to the Royal Counsel. We must surely have knowledge of a loyal servant of Her Majesty, with no obvious ties to the Royal Court itself, now resident in Nymphaion, or else Panticapaeum?" Zar'cha smiled sweetly.

Alazar smiled thinly. "I know of such a man! His loyalty is unquestionable."

"It might be wiser to engage our humble servant in any direct contact with Solthazar. After all, Honourable Counsellor, these are dangerous times, as you have stated more than once!"

"I thank you for your wisdom, and your discretion, of course. I shall detain you no more from your solemn duties, Commander Zar'cha. I will be in touch, just as soon as I hear anything with respect to this most pressing and delicate matter."

"I serve Her Majesty and Counsel with equal devotion, Honourable Counsellor" Zar'cha smiled sweetly.

As the Commander drained her goblet and rose to leave, the Honourable Counsellor remembers something that piqued his curiosity earlier in the conversation. "Forgive me, Commander, but as a simple exercise in curiosity, how little would someone be prepared to accept to kill our beloved Queen?"

"To be paid in Persian gold, naturally? Perhaps as little as seven pieces, even as few as six" Zar'cha replied evenly. "All life has a price, Honourable Counsellor. As I am sure you will soon discover, the price of life in Nymphaion is a trivial sum indeed!"

NINE

Nymphaion, July 493 BC

Thassalor of Knossos was not a man given to carelessness or flights of fancy, except where pretty girls were concerned. He knew that he had been pressing his luck for the better part of a year! *Surely, his enemies must by now have acquired an inkling of the treachery that had befallen them in the pursuit of their endeavours* Thassalor had avoided the delights of *The Delphine* and its companions for the past week, for the place was regrettably now an obvious security risk. This was not to say that he had been bored, for he had devoted himself to meetings with valued clientele, often over sumptuous suppers at their luxurious private residences, lasting until the late hours of the night. He had taken the precaution of hiring a covered carriage from a bespoke operator in the business district, through the auspices of an acquaintance whose loyalty and discretion could be trusted implicitly. In doing so, he had thwarted the dogged endeavours of Saelaes and his band of eager hirelings, including the penitent Chisos and Iscaertes, to discern his present whereabouts. On this sunny afternoon, Thassalor strode out of his modest lodgings in the residential district of the Eastern Quarter and climbed aboard the covered carriage, closing the door, and drawing the drapes to avoid recognition. *This was the dangerous time, yet time was of the essence, was it not?*

His carriage cantered west along the Poseidon Way

towards the junction with Grove Street, the imposing artifice of the southern city wall and South Gate to his right, and stopped at Euboea Square, where he alighted. He threaded through the busy throng of late shoppers and headed south towards the Butcher's Market, via the warren of apartment buildings on the eastern side of the Southern Quarter, until he reached the home of Androcletis, former officer in the Athenian Army, who had retired to Nymphaion to be close to his youngest daughter. Over the course of the intervening decade, Androcletis had established a thriving business providing security personnel to the Merchant vessels on their passage across the Black Sea to various ports in the Ionian Islands. Androcletis was no friend to Persia and had provided invaluable assistance to the Ionians these past few years. Thassalor glanced slyly left and right, rapped a brief tattoo on the door, and waited patiently for a response. The door was opened by a disarmingly pretty girl in her early teens. Thassalor smiled warmly at the child. "Hello Callia! I do hope that the grumpy old goat is up to seeing visitors?"

Callia smiled shyly. "We have been expecting you for some days past, Thassalor of Knossos" the girl waved the visitor inside.

"It pains me, to have disappointed you so, my Lady" Thassalor took the girls hand and kissed it lightly.

"I do hope you remembered your manners, Thassalor of Knossos!" a voice growled from the doorway to the far right of the Reception Room.

Thassalor glanced quickly up and smiled warmly at the old man. "I make a mental note to never leave home without them, General Androcletis. Were you pleased with the gift I sent to you?"

"A fine Bordeaux, my old friend, and a most welcome addition to my cellar" the General smiled warmly. "You may leave us, sweet child, for we have business to discuss. I fear that it may bore you beyond the Styx!"

When the girl had left, Thassalor was ushered through a doorway to the left of the Reception Room and thence to the General's private study, where Androcletis quickly brought matters to hand. "I hope you were careful, old friend. Your enemies in this city grow legion by the hour, or so it seems."

"I have been careful, as always, I assure you of that, General Androcletis" Thassalor smiled tightly. "What is it that you know that I presumably do not, if you would be gracious to extend me that meagre courtesy?"

"We have a visitor, my friend. I could scarcely credit the news when it reached me only yesterday, but the source is unimpeachable."

"Mestarches of Susa, I presume?" Thassalor smiled mockingly, enjoying the flash of surprise in the old soldier's eyes.

"He is not alone, Thassalor, I can assure you of that!" the General said icily.

Thassalor raised a hand to soothe the General. "Two thugs, one of whom is known to me, were badly beaten a few nights ago by a gang of well-attired assailants" Thassalor spoke softly. "One such deplorable incident occurred outside a well-known establishment, in full view of several witnesses, including a coterie of terrified young ladies, if you would credit such a thing? Then again, subtlety never ranked highly among Mestarches' virtues, such as they are! I doubt the incident will cause too much of a stir among the current contingent of Civis Militia?"

"Surely you must have concerns. Mestarches of Susa could only be here with the blessing of King Darius himself, could he not? And, if that is true, there can be only one reason why he was despatched here, is there not?" the General stated pointedly.

"It was only a matter of time, surely?" Thassalor replied softly. "I trust that you have taken the necessary precautions?"

"My precautions were impeccable, as well you know!" the General replied testily. "I never met with any of the mercenary detachments hired for these passages, nor do the names of any these men appear on my ledgers. However.?"

"I think you might at least offer me a goblet of wine, old friend, especially if you intend to be a harbinger of bad omens" Thassalor smiled tightly.

"Of course, please forgive my unforgivable lack of civility."

The General poured two goblets of Hellenic red from an ornate ceramic flagon which sat on a corner table. He handed one to his visitor, who first savoured the nose, before taking a small sip and rolling it lovingly over his tongue. "One of Throstocles' better wares, is it not?" Thassalor sighed happily. "And you are right readily forgiven, old friend. Continue, if you please?"

The General eyed the younger man shrewdly. "If the Persians have gotten wind of something sinister, the evidence could point to the involvement of one, and only one, contractor."

"I would be safe in presuming this contractor has no obvious legal ties to your own operations?" Thassalor spoke softly.

"Absolutely not!" the General replied emphatically. "To all intents and purposes, we are entirely independent and competing operations. Great care has been taken to ensure that, at least to our enemies and their network of informants her in Nymphaion, that we are barely on speaking terms. I steadfastly refused to send a gift in honour of his eldest daughter's wedding!"

"I did, naturally. Acting upon your behalf, of course" Thassalor grinned.

"Diastios is, and always will be, a brother to me Thassalor. I was his Commander in Athens for many years, and he was one of my best men. You know this?" the General spoke in barely a whisper.

"I have said nothing" Thassalor replied simply.

"You do not need to! I know your train of thought!" the General sighed resignedly.

"So too, perhaps, does Mestarches of Susa? Have you tried to contact Diastios?"

"I wished to speak with you first, of course?" replied the General.

"Of course, you did, my old friend" Thassalor smiled thinly. "Could Diastios be persuaded to take an extended holiday to Attica? Expenses should not be an issue. I can guarantee that?"

"Such a sudden departure would arouse suspicion, would it not?" the General smiled ruefully.

"Mestarches may have been impulsive in his treatment of the two retainers, but he is scarcely advertising his presence in Nymphaion. Even I do not know his current whereabouts. If I remember correctly, Diastios has a sister who now lives in Corinth, is that so?"

The General nodded. "That is true?"

"I have acquaintances in the city who could contrive a letter heralding a grave family emergency. They really are first rate; you may rest assured of that. Even a learned eye would fail to spot a difference in the marque?"

"How soon can this be accomplished? Time is of the essence, now that our enemies are close, you would agree?" Androcletis ventured.

"The letter will be in our dear friends' hands within the next two days. You have my word on that?"

"Truly, my old friend?" the General implored his guest.

"This really is an exceptional vintage, is it not?" Thassalor raised the goblet to his nostrils and inhaled. "May the Gods be with us, my old friend, now and forever?"

"No more the moon, old friend!" said Androcletis.

"No more the moon!"

Southern Plains, July 493 BC

The remainder of Seart'i's tribe of brigands were blissfully ignorant of their leader's fate. A majority were corralled deep in the forest, awaiting news of the day's 'hunt'. Their leader, a grizzled warrior named Vikt'a, grimaced with distaste at the spectacle unfolding before him. Two of his subordinates, aged in their late teens, were enjoying the virtues of a young girl, no more than thirteen years of age, right in front of everyone! Most of the men looked away, for this was as insulting as it was demeaning, not that anyone cared a fig for the girl's reputation, for she was nothing more than a local village slut. Once upon a time, they had been proud warriors, yet now they had been reduced to this. *Skulking in the forest, awaiting delivery of their prey, like a faithful dog beside the supper table awaiting the gift of a bone!*

The girl was clearly enjoying herself and, for the record, why ever should she not.

At this moment, she had the complete attention of two erect penises. Her mouth was open, completely enveloping the swollen glans of one of her succours, whilst the other rhythmically probed her blood-gorged vagina. So ensconced in the moment was she, so immersed in a swirl of sexual nirvana, she could never have felt the arrow that pierced her heart and ended her brief life. Aloya, for that was her name, was at least spared the insult of her lover's end. They fell, within an instant of her passing. *Death had fastened his talons upon those who regaled in the mortality of others!*

The cleave of a sword took Vikt'a's head cleanly from its sinewed pillar as those around him fell without mercy; for there was none within the grace of sweet Tabiti on this day! The Orch'tai advance was professional: engage and destroy; the solemn business of all those who undertake the calling of a soldier. The brigands fell in their scores and, as the panicked screams of those at the front acknowledged the hitherto unimagined threat from the rear, the blood-curdling wail of the death march was drowned by a herald of trumpets. *The Orch'tai had come for deliverance*!

~

"I trust that everything is in order?" Nichassor greeted Corelya with a wry smile as she loomed in to view at the edge of the woodland.

"They are dead, if that is what you wish to know?" Corelya replied evenly.

Nichassor smiled brightly. "You did well, Corelya. Your efforts have secured peace and prosperity for many of the rural communities in this region."

"There was nothing to it, Nichassor! I even brought back the berry wine! They were slime, nothing more!"

"We shall toast your success as soon as we return to Qu'ehra" Nichassor gushed. "Now, we must leave, before their deaths are discovered."

Corelya trotted Sybillya towards Nirch'ii and embraced the girl warmly. As they parted, the girl gave Corelya a knowing look. "Would you like to talk about it?" she whispered in Sarmati.

"No. I am fine, honestly. It is done! They are dead, and that is all there is to it! But thank you, anyway" Corelya sighed.

"I am worried" the girl whispered. There was fear in her voice.

"What's wrong?" Corelya whispered back.

"Do you speak Persian?"

"Yes. I can also read Persian. Why?"

"I can't read. Not even Sarmati, my own language" Nirch'ii confessed, without blushing. "I know a fair bit of conversational Persian, more than some would give me credit for" she glanced towards Nichassor and Siladar. "We used to get a lot of Persian traders passing through our settlement, travelling to-and-from the Orch'tai lands. We became something of a fixture to them, for they knew they could always obtain any necessities from us, and they became a reliable source of income during the summer months."

Corelya grinned slyly at the girl. "So, you might be able to follow the conversation of Nichassor's band. Particularly if they thought that you couldn't understand a word of what they were saying? They would have no reason not to talk openly in front of you?"

"Nichassor did ask if I spoke any Persian. I lied" Nirch'ii blushed hotly. Corelya smiled.

Nirch'ii truly was a sweet, if not guilelessly innocent, girl. "And?" Corelya probed.

"What is an '*Ochta*'? I know it is something to do with the Orch'tai, because they were talking about it, but I have no idea what it is?"

Corelya nearly fell from the saddle in astonishment. "An Ochta is a cavalry division of the Orch'tai army, numbering some three-hundred strong. The effective fighting unit, a *korg*, has fifty men. Six *korgs* make an Ochta, usually with additional senior Officers. *They were talking about the Orch'tai and an Ochta?*"

"Nichassor was talking to Siladar about it. It was soon after he returned from escorting you to the meeting with the brigands. They all seem on edge, like they are expecting trouble."

Corelya gaped. "Sweet Tabiti" she hissed. "Why in Hades name would an Orch'tai Ochta be stationed this deep inside Argata territory? *Not unless they were invited here!*" her mind was racing.

Now it all made sense. The man she had espied in the market in Qu'ehra! *Had he not seemed as embarrassed as she when their gaze had met*? She knew she had met him before and had been equally certain that he was an ambitious and well-connected young Orch'tai cavalry officer! *A soldier of such repute that it would be fitting he be given command of an Orch'tai detachment stationed deep inside Argata territory*! If such a detachment did exist, and she must now face the realisation that it did, it could never have been quartered here without the tacit acquiescence of the Argata Queen! *If this were so, then she had succeeded in verifying the existence of a secret military entente between the Argata and Orch'tai, the very thing she had set out to discover*! Her mission was accomplished, and now she must return to the Crimea, as swiftly as surely. A sense of foreboding knotted her stomach. *Corelya now knew she was truly alone, surrounded by sworn enemies, and in mortal peril from each and all*!

"Corelya!" Nirch'ii was tugging at her arm, whispering softly. "You look pale. Are you sure you are well?"

"I am fine, honestly. But I agree with you. Something isn't right here! We shouldn't have come."

"What should we do?" Nirch'ii was trembling.

"Stay close to me. We will move to the outside of the group and keep a few paces to the rear. If anything happens, then shadow me, you understand?"

"You think we are in danger?" Nirch'ii bit her lip.

"I have a horrible feeling that we might be" Corelya mused gloomily.

Suddenly, there was a glint of metal and movement at the edge of the woodland to their right. The younger girl's eyes widened with terror. "Shit!" she hissed. "Those are brigands! This is a trap!"

The brigands, sensing their moment of triumph, charge on horseback and foot from their concealed position at the edge of the woodland screen to the north-east where they had lain in wait for hours.

Nichassor's small band and their two fellow-travellers were assuredly doomed!

From his vantage in a dense screen of shrubbery to the far northwest of the plain, some two miles away, Gosh'kar had seen exactly what Corelya had espied; the ill-advised glint of metal as the leader rose to signal the attack with his drawn sword. He observed the advance and charge of the brigands with dismay. They were nothing more than a feral mass of flotsam! An ill-disciplined horde, foaming wildly at the mouth as they scream their battle- cries and close with their enemy! *Fucking amateurs! Nothing but scum!* Gosh'kar hissed his men to silence. Concealed within the veil of the woodland's edge on the eastern flank of the plain, a mile or so to the east, Dor'kir and his detachment watched with equal interest as the enemy raced to the slaughter, and Nichassor's panicked warriors hurried their dressing to meet the onslaught. The two girls were farthest away from the brigands, hugging the right wing of the small band. Gosh'kar grimaced as the first of the mounted brigands met with Nichassor's warriors, the air ringing with the peal of clashing swords! No matter their courage, nor skill with a sword, such a small band of defenders faced almost certain apocalypse!

Then again, if Tabiti willed it so, perhaps they would not do so?

Minas swilled his face in the cool water of the stream. He had come alone, riding a wagon filled with a consignment of poppy oil, hemp-cloth and plum wodki. The wagon had been borrowed from a fellow Hellenic merchant from Olbia who owed Minas and his brothers a favour. This wagon had been specifically requested for an obvious reason: the hidden compartments which lay beneath the interior floor on either side of its centre. These were disguised as reinforcing beams, presumably fitted to a vehicle destined to carry an unusually heavy load. Each chamber was sufficiently capacious to entomb a consignment of precious metals, weapons, and even an adult fugitive. *It would easily hide two teenagers fleeing for their lives!* The compartments lay open, and the heavy rolls of hemp-cloth were neatly stacked at each side of the rear doors ready to be laid on top of the panels once the two girls were safely ensconced inside. It was a glorious day, for the sun was shining brightly in a clear blue sky and the world was at peace.

Without warning, the tranquillity is cruelly shorn by a clarion of trumpets, heralding death!

～

"Nirch'ii! With me!" Corelya commanded. Within an instant, the older girl was at her side. Corelya passed her a loaded crossbow and quiver of quarrels. "Whatever happens, stay with me. I'll do my best to keep you alive!"

Nirch'ii had gone a deathly pale. Corelya thought she might faint and fall from her saddle at any moment. She plucked the longbow from its fixture on the left side of Sybillya's saddlecloth and adjusted the quiver she now wore at her left hip. She threaded the notch in the arrows end into the bowstring and, steadying Sybillya at an angle to the advancing attackers, the bowstring was drawn taut as she took aim at a horseman. The bowstring was released and slapped viciously into the leather gauntlet around her right wrist. The arrow took the horseman in the belly with a sickening scream, before he pitched from the saddle to fall heavily to the ground. Corelya plucked an arrow from the quiver and notched it effortlessly, drawing it taut, and taking aim at another target.

Nirch'ii had already dropped one attacker on foot with the crossbow and was aiming the re-loaded weapon when, suddenly, she screamed in terror as her mare reared in agony, an arrow protruding bloodily from its flank. Nirch'ii fell from the saddle and hit the grass with a sickening thump, the crossbow dropping harmlessly to the floor beside her, the quiver a short distance away. Corelya glanced quickly at the girls' motionless form and concentrated on the band of attackers to her front. This was not the time for regrets or remorse! That could come later, provided she survived this day. She fired and took a mounted attacker in the chest. They were now closing fast and, as she re-loaded the bow, she saw one of Nichassor's men fall from his horse with an arrow in his chest. *The brigands had their own archers*! "Shit!" Corelya swore viciously. Whilst their bows may lack the distance of professional Scythian weapons, this was of little import now that they were within killing range. Another of Nichassor's men fell, a shaft protruding grotesquely from his mouth, as blood gouts in torrents from his throat. An arrow hissed past her left hip. Scanning her front for danger, she located a kneeling archer and fired, aiming for the man's chest, grimacing in triumph as he instantly fell, his bow dropping harmlessly beside him. Corelya glanced toward Nichassor and saw his rage as he engages a mounted attacker with his sword. Nichassor parried cleanly and stabbed the man in the stomach. The man screamed and fell from his saddle, writhing in his death throes beneath the feet of Nichassor's horse as its rider twists in the saddle to peal his sword with another marauder.

A clarion of trumpets heralded the arrival of the Orch'tai! Death wears a myriad of guises on this day!

Gosh'kar heard the clarion call of the trumpet and roared at his men to rise and mount their steeds. "Move, you idle bastards!" he roared.

His detachment of thirteen warriors race towards heir steeds, secured to trees some thirty yards to the rear of their position. They leap into their saddles and click their stallions to face the front. Gosh'kar is at the centre of the line, six of his brothers on either side.

"Prepare to advance! Advance at the trot! By the centre!" Gosh'kar bellows.

Without warning, the thirteen horsemen morph in single file from the edge of the woodland and troop on to the plain, some two miles north of Nichassor's beleaguered band. They continue their advance for a mere few footfalls until Gosh'kar gives the command.

"Wheel right!" yelled Gosh'kar.

The thirteen mounted warriors turn their steeds crisply to the right, facing south, in a breath-taking display of professional dressage. On the opposite side of the plain, a mile or so away, Dor'kir and his detachment are eager not to be outshined!

"Arrowhead formation! Advance at the trot!" Gosh'kar bawled.

The Commanders in the centre advance several footfalls, as their comrades on either side remain stationary. One. Two.Three...move! The pair of horsemen on either flank kick their heels to goad their stallions to the trot, advancing behind their Commander. Soon enough, the two detachments on either side of the plain are on the march, trotting south in arrowhead formation, a staggered chevron, with their Commander at the apex of the "V". The two Commanders turn in their saddles to nod in silent greeting and then yell their order simultaneously "Advance at the canter!" A mile-and-a-half away, the remnants of the brigands fleeing the slaughter in the woods have now reached the safety of their comrades. They race in terror towards them as the mounted Orch'tai warriors suddenly morph at the woodland edge and rain arrows down upon the unsuspecting survivors on the plain. The attention of these survivors is now focussed on the threat from the woods, rather than Nichassor's band. Corelya leapt from the saddle and raced across to where Nirch'ii lay, still motionless, grabbing the loaded crossbow and quiver of quarrels from the ground.

"Treacherous fucking snakes!" Corelya hissed to no-one, as she saw that the obvious escape route to the north was blocked by the advancing Orch'tai cavalry. As Corelya reached the stricken girl, Nirch'ii miraculously came to, literally shaking with rage. Her reaction was instinctive! *For a Sauromatae, that is*!

"Give me that fucking crossbow!" she snarled.

Corelya gaped at the girl. Throwing the weapon towards her, to Corelya's astonishment, Nirch'ii caught it effortlessly and, pivoting lithely on the balls of her feet, she engages a target, a boy of similar age to herself, and dropped him cruelly with a quarrel in the back. "Fuck you!" Nirch'ii screamed. Corelya takes aim at a target with the second crossbow and felled him with equal ruthlessness.

"Give me those bastard quarrels!" Nirch'ii hissed.

A visibly astounded Corelya handed over the quiver without remonstration. She reloaded her own weapon and grinned at the ground. "*Might as well reason with a hazel tree as try to quell an Amazon when her blood was spitting*" she mused. Nirch'ii was a Sauromatae, an *Amazon*! *Death was her birth right*! *Hades itself hath no fury like an Amazon*!

"Nirch'ii! Let's go!" Corelya hissed.

The two cover one another, targeting the surviving mounted brigands, as they edge across the grass towards Sybillya. The survivors of Seart'i's band were being mercilessly thinned by the murderous accuracy of the Orch'tai bowmen. Corelya leapt on to Sybillya's back and glanced north to face the advancing Orch'tai cavalry on the plain. She reached down and grabbed Nirch'ii by the hand, as the elder girl vaulted on to Sybillya's back.

Looking up, Corelya espied Nichassor turn briefly in

the saddle and wave in greeting to the Orch'tai advancing cavalry. She could credit it! Of course, she could, the prick!

"You treacherous Persian cunt!" she hissed. "Let's get the fuck out of here! It's a trap!"

Corelya turns Sybillya to face the woodland to the south and sights the pinnacle of the mountain on the far horizon to the southwest between her ears. Their escape route lies just under a hundred yards away.

"I hope to Hades that Minas has kept his promise to us!" she yelled to Nirch'ii. She kicked her heels in to Sybillya's flank.

They flee, as fast as Sybillya cam carry them, heading southeast towards the woodland and the waiting Minas on the opposite side of the stream. As the distance from the melee in the centre of the plain widened, Nirch'ii cautions that the Orch'tai detachment on the west flank was now pursuing them with vigour. To her eternal bewilderment, Corelya coaxes Sybillya to a halt and dismounts.

"Take the reins!" she commanded. "And keep low! I need space to fire!"

As Nirch'ii moved forward in the saddle, almost to Sybillya's neck, Corelya slips the quiver of arrows over her right shoulder, adjusts its position at her left hip, and then vaults agilely on to Sybillya's back. She notches an arrow and pulls back the bowstring, steadying her breathing, to take aim at their pursuers.

"*Go!*" she screamed. "Ride like the wind!"

⌒

"Faster! You glorious bastards!" Gosh'kar screamed.

The drum of the hoofbeats is deafening! Gosh'kar kicks his heels to the flanks of his stallion to urge the beast to a gallop. The cavalrymen maintain their V-formation as they race past the remnants of Nichassor's band, pursuing the two fugitives as they flee south.

The remnants of Seart'i's brigands, what few remained, would be dealt with by Dor'kir's detachment. Their steeds were rested, watered, and superbly conditioned. Despite their light size, the mare the girl's rode ferried the weight of two riders and the distance between them was narrowing by the second. Then, everything changed. The golden-haired girl twisted lithely in the saddle, took careful aim with her bow, and fired. Gosh'kar's world exploded instantaneously in a kaleidoscope of colour as Corelya's arrow punched through his right eye and seared into his brain. As his head rocketed back, a jet of blood spurted high from his ruined eye-socket, terrifying the horses to his left and right, who were immediately soothed by their riders. The cavalrymen following him thundered on, even as his body slipped gracelessly from its saddle to fall heavily to the ground! This was no time to pay homage to the passing of a much-respected brother and Commander.

The chase, the mission, was everything!

$\sim$

"Armenian slime!" Nichassor roared his challenge as his sword clashed with a mounted brigand. The challenger swung his sword viciously, aiming for Nichassor's neck when, to his astonishment, his opponent bobbed under the arc of the blade, caught his wrist. Nichassor twisted the man's sword wrist and yanked this forward, stunning the man momentarily with a vicious headbutt to the face. The sword fell to the ground and Nichassor skewered his opponent mercilessly through the throat.

"Armenian filth!" Nichassor raged triumphantly as the man slid from the saddle and hit the grass with a heavy thump. The current situation was anything but triumphant and, despite the arrival of the Orch'tai cavalry, his own band remained in mortal peril. Half of his men were dead, mostly felled by the Armenian archers. He seethed inwardly! They had promised him, the bastards! They had sworn that only the two whores would die! To his right, the doughty Siladar was still alive and fighting like a daemon, gorging on the blood of his enemies. Nichassor glanced towards the approaching Orch'tai cavalry and enjoyed a brief smirk of satisfaction as he surveyed the final slaughter of the remaining brigands on horse and foot. He twisted in his saddle to witness the desperate escape of the two girls, now far to the south-west, gaping with horror as the Commander of the pursuing detachment is felled by an expertly aimed strike from Corelya's longbow. His jaw sagged in bewilderment as, moments later, yet another pursuer fell heavily on the left-side of the chevron, downed with a breath-taking sangfroid by the golden-haired she-devil!

"I should have let you fucking die all those years ago!" Nichassor hissed malevolently.

The Orch'tai were superb horsemen and were closing fast. They would surely be in range of their spear-points soon enough? Nirch'ii and Corelya were doomed, for there was little hope of making their escape. Despite the treachery of these bastard brigands, all was not lost.

The Great God, Zoroaster himself, still smiled on their endeavours and the glory of King Darius!

⤳

"On, you glorious bastards! On!" Isi'mar roared. He had witnessed both Gosh'kar, and their immediate subaltern, Nabas'kor, felled at the hands of the 'gold-witch', yet the ground still thundered under their charge and deliverance was surely theirs. The golden-haired girl turned once more and took aim with the longbow, yet surely distance would now count? The two fugitives would soon be within range of their spears, before they even reached the woodland edge. He reaches for the spear at the right of his saddle, smiling grimly as his fingers curl around the shaft as he draws it from its fastening.

"Death is ours, you Sauromatae cunts!" Isi'mar roared.

His left hand clasped firmly on the reins as he raised his right arm, taking aim at the blonde girl. *That stinking bastard of a Sauromatae whore! Now, is the time!*

It was a massacre! The men died, as they had lived and breathed, *as one.* The pursuing Orch'tai cavalry crumpled amid a hail of arrows unleashed with murderous intent by an unseen enemy. The fifteen archers, all expert hunters since childhood, morph as daemons from concealed positions in the undergrowth to the west, to rain death upon this most recent transgressor of their ancestral lands and birth right!

"Sweet Tabiti!" Corelya gasped breathlessly as she surveyed the destruction of their pursuers.

She instinctively raised a hand in greeting to the men who now formed a straight line, deftly notching their arrows. The nearest archer grinned and waved back, then turned his attention back to the melee in the centre of the plain. A further volley was unleashed in the direction of Nichassor's group and the newly arrived Orch'tai. Corelya bore witness to their slaughter, as men screamed, and bled, to topple from their saddles as the arrows struck true! The archers, who were equipped with distinctive Sauromatae bows, aim a final hail of arrows at Nichassor's band and the Orch'tai detachment under Dor'kir's command, who turned their steeds to charge at the new threat from the south-west. Corelya whooped triumphantly as Nichassor fell heavily from his steed. Miraculously, the treacherous prick was on his feet in an instant, seemingly unscathed.

"Fucking charmer!" Corelya scowled.

The bowmen now raced from the edge of the woodland to the safety of their steeds. It was time for them, and the two girls whose fates they had so surely blessed, to flee this butcher's yard. "Keep up the pace Nirch'ii! We need to get out of here!"

Nirch'ii kicked her heels in to Sybillya's flanks, urging her to quicken her pace, as they race into the cover of the woodland towards the safety of the stream.

~

Dionysopolis, July 493 BC

In the ornate atrium of the villa on the outskirts of Dionysopolis, Aeschus paces anxiously as he awaits news of his wife's confinement and its terminus. The younger children were being supervised by their sister and had already eaten a late afternoon repast of bread and cheese. It would soon be time for their early evening nap before supper. Their father, plagued by a melancholy which now bordered on mortal terror, strolls continuously around the pillared passages of the atrium, selfishly absorbed in his own tyranny of gloom.

"Father?" Artemis addressed him from the doorway. She carried a small tray with a goblet of watered wine, some bread and cheese. "Please sit and eat. You need to keep up your strength." She placed the tray in the centre of a small table with two accompanying chairs and sat down, beckoning her father to join her.

"You are a sweet child, Artemis" he smiled at his eldest child warmly. "And you are fast growing up to be every bit as beautiful as your mother."

"Everything will be fine, father! Has the nurse spoken to you?"

"An hour or so ago, but not since then. She seemed certain things were progressing as they should."

"Then you must eat. I will take care of Hermes and Hera. They are currently having a nap. We will have fish for supper and then I will bathe them and put them to bed" the girl implored.

"You will make someone a good wife one day, darling child."

Artemis blushed. "I do not think of such things, Father. Not yet at least."

A light cough interrupts them. Artemis and Aeschus turn to face the young Handmaiden, Nae'veh, who stands in the centre of the open portico. "My Mistress urgently needs more boiling water and linen. It has started. Everything is well and the child should be born within the hour."

"I have water on the boil" Artemis beamed proudly. "We have linen in the closet. I will show you where it is." Artemis leaned forward and kissed her father lightly on the cheek. "I told you that everything would be fine, Father, didn't I?"

~

Nirch'ii and Corelya cleared the stream and followed the track towards the far edge of the woodland and the southern expanse of the plains. There was neither sight nor sound of any pursuers. As they reached the edge of the treeline, Nirch'ii let out a whoop of effervescent joy as she espied Minas, a short distance away sitting in the back of the wagon. He glanced up quickly, smiling brightly, then jumped to his feet and immediately started preparing the horses to move.

"Thank the Gods that you are safe! Have you been hurt?" he asked His concern was genuine.

"We are both fine, Minas. Thank you!" Nirch'ii insisted.

"Who in Hades name were those bloody archers?" Corelya demanded breathlessly.

"I only met them a few hours ago. They are Sauromatae from the southern plains out on a hunting expedition. They advised me of the threat of the brigands, and I told them I was waiting for you. They seemed only too happy to lend a hand, should that be required.

Apparently, they have no love for Seart'i or his ilk. Am I to understand that they did help you?" Minas confessed.

"They saved our lives, Minas! It was a trap. Nichassor double-crossed us, just as I suspected he might. The Orch'tai are here! Scores of them, none attired in regular uniforms, deep in Argata territory! At least one hundred of them, I would wager. They were busy slaughtering the last of the brigands as we fled."

"We have no time to lose! Please, climb in the back and hide in the compartments. I will take care of your mare" Minas insisted.

The two girls climb tiredly into the back of waggon and snuggled down in the hidden compartments. The covering planks were replaced, and a tattered rug was laid across the floor to cover them. Minas inserted two hollow reeds through punched holes in the foremost edges of the tattered rug into the planks below to allow air to flow in. In the event of necessity, these hollow reeds could directly assist breathing for the stowaways. Once the rolls of hemp cloth had been stowed, Minas closed the doors and bolted them. Sybillya was tethered to the side of the wagon and the horses were clicked to a gentle trot. With any luck, they should arrive safely at a pre-arranged site on the outskirts of Qu'ehra before dusk.

⌐

The slaughter of the brigands was finished, and the mission adjudged an emphatic victory, as the Orch'tai Commander had always expected it would be. No losses had been incurred by the Orch'tai contingent as they had swept mercilessly through the woodland to the plain, slaughtering all they encountered. Sadly, the engagement on the plain had been an entirely different affair. Some eighteen men, including Gosh'kar and his sub-altern Nabas'kor, had perished along with all their brothers. Dor'kir lay on a table in a far corner of the cabin, beyond any hope of recovery. Soon, perhaps mercifully so, he would join the four slain brothers of his detachment. Tar'gai paced the cabin with the fury of a caged tiger, as Nichassor and Siladar, both wounded in the fray, sipped medicinal goblets of wodki.

"This is a fucking disaster!" Tar'gai growled menacingly at Nichassor. "What the fuck do you think the King will make of this?"

"Your performance was exemplary, my dear fellow! We were betrayed" Nichassor soothed.

"Treachery is a constant companion of you fucking Persians, isn't it?" Tar'gai seethed.

"Mind your fucking tongue, twat!" Siladar spat, wincing at the pain of a flesh wound in his upper arm. The injury had been inflicted by an arrow strike.

Nichassor raised his hand to silence the offended Siladar. "We were betrayed by Seart'i and his treacherous swine! Had it been not so, Corelya and her companion would have been delivered to you, as you requested."

"May I remind you, Nichassor, that it was you who wanted them dead, not us!" Tar'gai sneered contemptuously. "For all I know, you betrayed the little bitch to Seart'i and his filth, who then failed to do you the necessary service!" Their bodies had been removed and dumped in the nearby woodland for the carrion to feast upon. "I care nothing for those bitches."

"But you should, Tar'gai, you should" Nichassor spoke icily. "Corelya has the ear of Queen Illir'ya herself. She is one of her most trusted Handmaidens, perhaps her most invaluable."

"I do not follow you, Nichassor? You speak in riddles" Tar'gai raised an eyebrow.

"Surely Orch'tai intelligence sources are aware that Queen Illir'ya's current 'Royal Retainer' is a child?"

"You think this child, this 'gold-witch', as my men have

named her, is Queen Illir'ya's principal assassin! I fear you have taken leave of your senses, Nichassor? Perhaps the fall from the horse.?"

"May I remind you, Commander, that this 'child' has an exceptional mind, one of the rarest I have encountered in one so young. She speaks several languages, including Persian and Orch'tai, almost fluently. It is probable that our meeting was not by chance" Nichassor interjected.

"That is your problem, Nichassor, not mine!" Tar'gai smiled tightly.

"No, it is not!" Nichassor blazed. "I fear Corelya was sent on the explicit instruction of Queen Illir'ya herself. That she was sent to gather intelligence on the disposition of your forces in the region and report back timeously."

"That is pure conjecture, Nichassor!" Tar'gai countered. "Surely Queen Illir'ya would not entrust so dangerous a mission to a mere child! As I have said, perhaps the fall from the horse has disturbed your wits?" he smiled wryly.

"The damage is done, you fool!" Nichassor hissed dangerously. "Your failure this afternoon, of which you personally bear no blame, has the unforeseen consequence of revealing the presence of an Orch'tai cavalry contingent stationed deep in Argata territory. Further, to this, we can no longer dismiss the possibility that we were betrayed by others who were well-prepared in advance" Nichassor mused silkily.

Tar'gai furrowed his brow, for, if the man was right, there could be quite serious consequences. "You refer to those bastards from the western woods? We would pursue them, if we could, yet it is likely that they have long gone by now!"

"How else would you explain their presence, dear Tar'gai? Their arrival was most fortuitous for Corelya and her companion, you agree? Perhaps you should not have signalled your advance with trumpets?"

"We could not have foreseen such treachery!" Tar'gai

retorted hotly.

"Treachery is a watchword of the Ur'gai. They are a ruthless people, are they not?"

"You think the Ur'gai planned this?" Tar'gai seemed unconvinced.

"I think Corelya had assistance from certain quarters in Qu'ehra. The place swarms with Ur'gai agents Their sympathies with the Sauromatae cause are well known!" Nichassor ventured.

"The Scythians and the Sauromatae loathe one another" Tar'gai protested.

"But even the bitterest of enemies can be united in their hatred of a common foe?"

"And what of Persia's designs on 'the lands between the seas', Nichassor? Your intent toward the people of this region, and beyond, are questionable, to say the least?" Tar'gai hissed.

"But we are friends, are we not, dear Tar'gai?" Nichassor said soothingly. "We are, at least for the moment. So, what would you have us do?"

"I have despatched a trusted rider to Qu'ehra with instructions to keep watch for Corelya and Nirch'ii. I suggest you send word to your most proximate garrisons, perhaps your reserves stationed to the immediate west of Astrach'yi. Aggressive patrols along the northern coast of the Azovi should be encouraged, in the event our fugitives head that way."

"What of the ports?" Tar'gai smiled tightly.

"I have considered that possibility" Nichassor confided. "It is highly unlikely that they would openly seek passage to Panticapaeum or Nymphaion. Corelya would be keenly aware of where the sympathies of the political and merchant classes currently lie."

"They could seek passage to Chersonesus?" Tar'gai proposed.

"I suspect not, Tar'gai. Nor would I favour Olbia"

Nichassor smiled tightly.

"I will send word immediately to our agents in Nymphaion and Panticapaeum. I will order them to kill the whores!" Tar'gai stated brusquely.

"In the event they were successfully located in the eastern peninsula, perhaps it would be wiser to take them alive? They could be interrogated for information about the network of Ur'gai agents in Qu'ehra? Perhaps they may even enlighten us with the identities of the architects of this afternoon's treachery?" Nichassor mused grimly.

"And yet, a few short hours ago, you were adamant they should both be killed?" Tar'gai's eyes narrowed with suspicion.

"I still consider that the safer option, in the unlikely event that they be captured in Qu'ehra" Nichassor persisted.

"It would be safer for you, I presume?" the Orch'tai officer mocked.

"Yet, we are friends, are we not, Tar'gai? Surely you would defer to my judgement, in this matter alone?"

"Do not indulge yourself with such presumptions, Nichassor" Tar'gai growled warningly. "Cementing our alliance with the Argata is our priority, remember that. Without it, we cannot further our plans for a new regional alliance to counter the ambitions of the Ur'gai?"

"And such an alliance would be entirely desirable in Susa, of course. I have given my express assurances on this?" Nichassor opined.

"Then I shall defer to your judgement, on this matter alone" Tar'gai conceded with little grace or enthusiasm. "What do you need from us?"

～

The virginal cries of an infant, a healthy new-born, cleaved the tension and foreboding that had cloaked the villa in recent days like a scythe through sun-ripened wheat.

Artemis embraced her father with effervescent joy at the news of the delivery and the rude health of mother and baby, both. As was tradition, the sex of the newest member of their family had yet to be disclosed. Artemis busied herself conveying jugs of boiling water from the kitchen and fresh linen from the cupboard to the spare room where her mother had spent the last days of her confinement. Within an hour, her mother and baby sibling had been bathed, and the latter was ensconced, sleeping soundly, in a bundle of swaddling cloths.

Aeschus and his three elder children waited patiently outside the door for the invitation from the Nurse or Handmaiden.

The Nurse, Nichelle, appeared in the doorway and addressed Aeschus. "Mother and baby are safe and well. Would you like to meet your child, Aeschus?"

"We all would, wouldn't we?" he smiled warmly at the children who beamed back.

As they enter the room, Sybillya reclines on the bed, clothed in a pearl chiton, her golden hair freshly washed and carefully combed, her cheeks flushed a radiant pink. She looked exhausted, as was only to be expected, yet to Aeschus' eyes she could not have looked more beautiful. She cradled the sleeping infant close to her bosom, a perfect image of maternal joy.

"Are you well, darling wife?" Aeschus whispered softly.

"I am, darling husband" Sybillya sighed happily. "Would you like to meet your daughter? I am certain that she would dearly love to meet her Papa."

"A daughter? Our daughter?" Aeschus sighed blissfully.

"Yes, darling husband, our daughter. A baby sister for Artemis, Hermes, and not-so-little Hera." She nodded in turn to their brood. "I have not disappointed you?"

"You have not! How could you ever?" Aeschus beamed at the Handmaiden, Nae'veh, who gingerly handed him his 'baby girl' who slept peacefully, unaware of the glow of a fathers' loving gaze. "She is absolutely beautiful, Sybillya, as is her mother. Do we yet have a name for her?"

"I would name her Persephone. I think it suits her perfectly."

"It is a truly beautiful name, for a beautiful little girl" beamed Nichelle.

Aeschus turns away and strolls the short distance across the room to kneel in front of the three elder children, each of whom gaze upon their baby sister with looks of wonder and joy. "This is Persephone. She, like all of you, is most precious. You will take care of her, won't you?"

"We will father, we promise!" the children chirrup in unison.

Aeschus was not aware of the tears which, with those words, flowed freely down his wife's cheeks. They were surely tears of joy, and not sadness? Yet, with those words, a dull pain throbbed remorselessly within Sybillya's heart. For, only a brief time past, there had been another babe, also a daughter, who had been equally precious.

She had long since journeyed with the ferryman across the Styx Her name was Corelya.

～

On the eastern outskirts of the market in Qu'ehra, twelve men sit around a campfire, chatting as they sip wooden goblets of plum wodki and scalding mint tea. All are sporting weapons, as is the custom, yet on this night they are a necessity. A short distance away, safe from the threat of the fire, a wagon is shrouded by heavy cloths. In an adjacent tent, its drapes closed to the world, Minas sleeps soundly on the floor, tightly wrapped in a blanket. A little further away, Corelya and Nirch'ii are ensconced under a blanket in the land of dreams. They are safe, they are uninjured, and they have drunk heartily this night of wodki and rye beer.

Despite the best endeavours of their enemies, and by grace of sweet Tabiti, they are very much alive!

⌒

Nichassor drained a goblet of wine through gritted teeth and pours himself a refill.

His left arm ached abominably. He tainted the wine with a few drops of poppy oil from a small ceramic vial. Despite the pain, the wound had been re-examined, cleaned, and re- bandaged by the Surgeon, Mosh'ii, who had pronounced it free from infection. *For the present, to be sure, but in a few days' time?* The Surgeon had requested a further appointment with the patient, his dear Nichassor, in three days', to ascertain that the wound would heal naturally over the course of the next few weeks without undue complication. Nichassor was in a foul mood, for he had been sorely rattled by the treachery of those bastard Armenians! Was there a soul left in this world whose word could be trusted implicitly?

A fist hammered at the door. Nichassor grimaces at the prospect of an unwelcome visitor. "Enter!" he clipped icily. The door opened partially, and Siladar pops his gruff head warily around. Nichassor smiled wryly. "Ah, it is you, my old friend! You are always welcome, naturally."

"How are you feeling, Honourable Nichassor?" Siladar enquired in a concerned tone.

"I am tired and sore, my friend. Nothing a few goblets of fine Hellenic red, a light dose of poppy oil, and a good night's rest will not redress. Please, come and sit with me for a while. Come and sit, old friend, for we must toast our successes, must we not?"

"I am not sure that I follow, my Lord?" Siladar's brow furrowed with consternation.

"We are alive, are we not? Given the treachery this day, we must give praise to Zoroaster for our deliverance!"

"I would rather drink to the death of those filthy Armenian whore-sons!" Siladar hissed, grimacing with the pain of the wound to his shoulder. This too had been treated and dressed by Mosh'ii, for a price, of course!

Siladar gratefully accepted a goblet of wine, tainted with a few drops of poppy oil, and drained it in a single gulp. Nichassor smiled warmly and poured him a refill.

"The men are well, my Lord. We have sent out word on that bitch! I will personally start looking for her at first light. You have my word on that!"

Nichassor waved his right hand placatingly. "That will not be necessary, old friend. I fear Corelya and her accomplices may already be far away. It would do little good to advertise our hunt and may only serve to warn our enemies of our intentions" he cautioned.

"I am sorry, my Lord, I merely thought." Siladar shuffled uneasily in his seat.

"Put your mind at rest, at least for a few days. The Orch'tai will have notified sympathisers in both Panticapaeum and Nymphaion. They are better suited to reconnoitre the Wharf on either side of the straits."

"Do you trust them?" Siladar seemed dubious.

"On this matter alone, I do" Nichassor replied emphatically. "They have fucked up regally this day, have they not? Their Commander is young, vain, and far too readily manipulated. It is a common failing among soldiers, I confess."

"What are we going to do?" Siladar seemed unsettled.

"We both need sufficient time to recuperate, for we are neither of us in any fit state for action! We will see the Surgeon in a few days' time and make plans for a timely departure."

"Are we going to Panticapaeum?"

"No, my old friend, we are not. If I were Corelya, given the current climate, I would be inclined to seek the safety of allies. The real nest of Ur'gai sympathisers lies in Nymphaion, not Panticapaeum. And it is there that we shall set our snares for her!"

～

Later that evening, two lovers stroll hand-in-hand from the rear entrance of *The Mount Olympus* into the dying light of a fading sun. "I hope you enjoyed yourself tonight, my love. I am truly sorry for what happened the other night. They should not have treated you that way!" said Chisos beseeched the girl.

"You still refuse to tell me what it was about, don't you? Who were they? They are certainly not from Nymphaion, not judging by appearances!" Naealla said icily.

"I am sorry, my love, I truly am. I didn't want to talk about it in there. Not in front of *those* people" Chisos soothed.

"In case you hadn't noticed, we are alone now!" the girl snorted.

"I got in to trouble with a money lender, if you must know. I was going to pay the bastard the next day, I swear it! He's a foreigner, a bloody Lydian, and I misjudged him. I had no idea he had those kinds of friends, honestly I didn't."

"You *have* paid him back?" Naealla eyed him sternly.

"Of course, I have! Everything is going to be fine from now on, I promise. Nothing like that will ever happen again, I swear it!"

"You really are a prick, Chisos, do you know that! They saw *everything* of me! *Everything*! Do you think me some game slut who flashes her fanny at anyone! Do you have any idea how humiliated I was? *Do you*? I should walk away right now and never have anything to do with you again!"

"I am sorry, my love, I truly am. How many times must I say it? If I could do anything to make it better, then I would! You know how much I love you, don't you?" He turns the girl to face him and gazes longingly into her eyes.

Naealla is not so easily gulled. "I am just another of your little tarts, aren't I? My mother warned me all about you! You didn't know, did you? Half my street has been in your bed at one time or another! You think I don't know, you wanker!"

"Honey, please! It isn't like that with you, I swear it! Those other girls, well.you are right, of course." Chisos shrugged and grinned inanely. "They were just a quick shag, and that is all. They meant nothing to me, I swear it. I know it sounds awful, and, before you say anything, I am not proud of myself! But you are different, baby, can't you see that? You are special to me, Naealla, and do you know why? It's because I love you, Naealla, I truly do!"

"I have heard it all before! Like that last time, you cheated on me with that little slag from round the corner!" Naealla blazed. She didn't care who heard her!

Chisos was perplexed, for he couldn't remember who the 'little slag' was. They were *all* sluts, after all! Even this prinked-up little tart, with her girlie tits and tight little arse! She was a hot fuck, that was certain, which more than made up for her constant whinging. "Let me make it up to you, Naealla. I have a surprise for you. You are going to love it, I promise! It's the bollocks!" he simpered.

"Really?" the girl cooed with excitement. She stopped and eyed him sternly. "It will be your fucking bollocks on a platter if I don't!" she raised an eyebrow mockingly.

"Yes baby, you will" Chisos simpered. "We are going to a friend's place, if you would like that. I have a couple of flagons of fine Hellenic red, just to get us in the mood. It is good stuff, Naealla. Not the cheap swill. It's expensive! I got it especially for you."

"Oh, is that it, then? A couple of flagons of good wine and you can bend me over a table! Is that what you think of me?" the girl seethed.

"Of course not, honey! How many times do I have to say this? You are special to me, Naealla. I have already told you that!" Chisos pleaded. *She had better fuck, after this palaver, the little tart!*

"Special enough for a 'pearl necklace'?" the girl fluttered her eyelashes outrageously.

"All the pearls you can handle, my sweet pea! Just you see!"

"Well, in that case, you can take me *anywhere*, you horny devil!" she simpered.

Chisos had meticulously planned this sortie, for, whilst he assuredly did *not* love Naeella, she really was a good fuck! *A proper little vixen in her birthday suit*! He had arranged everything with Iscaertes, who had called in a small favour with one of *The Delphine's* most sought-after companions. She had a nice place, just up the road in the Residential District, and he had the key! Chisos was still quite badly bruised from the beating, but that old bastard Naeschaxes had been fine about things in the end, all things considered, hadn't he? Chisos didn't even know the other fucker in the office and, as far as he was concerned, that oily twat could fuck right off! His cock was hard, or it soon would be, his balls were full, and, with a few goblets of fine Hellenic red, tainted with poppy oil, this slut was destined for a good night's rogering! And boy would she know about it in the morning, that's for sure!

"Wow! Is this the place?" Naeella cooed, as they strolled, together, up the steps to the elevated walkway that skirted the side of the building and led to the second-floor apartment. "Does this belong to a friend of yours?" the girl asked disbelievingly.

"It certainly does! Just you wait until you see what it looks like on the inside" Chisos lied smoothly, for he had never before visited the place. "Stick with me, baby, and we shall have a place of our own like this one day?"

"Really?" Naeella cooed. She was hot for sex! She wanted his cock as often as she could get it! They were now at the front door.

"Close your eyes until we get inside" Chisos whispered in her ear.

"Are you serious?" Naealla gasped incredulously. "Just open the fucking door!"

"Just do it, honey, for me. And cover your eyes with your hands" Chisos implored. "No cheating now!" he mocked.

"I can't believe I am doing this?" Naealla sighed irritably She obediently closed her eyes and covered them with her hands. Chisos fished the key from his pocket and unlocked the door, gently pushing it open.

The Reception Room is cast in darkness. The eager Naealla, with so much life to live, is courteously ushered by her lover inside. Chisos turns, whispers to his lover to keep her eyes covered, then locks the door securely. They are alone!

Early the following morning, a coterie of ashen-faced Guards from the Civis Militia undertook the grim duty of removing the bodies, for the mortal remains of three deceased persons had been discovered by the tenant when she returned from work. All three had been decapitated, their eyes brutally gouged out! The bodies were identified by a visibly disconsolate Harrin, a teenage companion of *The Delphine* as Iscaertes, his friend Chisos, and the latter's young lover, a local girl named Naealla.

The Gods had not indulged Mestarches of Susa with levity in respect of patience, mercy, or failure!

⌒

Two days later, before the sun has reached its zenith, a single rider passed through the Polis Militia Guards at the North Gate of Nymphaion and stabled his mare in the yard of *The Merchants Chalice*, close to the Market Square. He climbed the steps and headed through the back door, along the narrow corridor, then turns right before the entrance to the public bar. He knocks on the door of the private room and enters, closing it firmly behind, without waiting for a reply. Two men and a woman sit at table leisurely sipping goblets of plum wodki. They are startled by the intrusion. "This is a private conversation, stranger!" one of the men challenged brusquely.

"A very private conversation among mutual friends, I trust. If it is not, perhaps I have come to the wrong place?" the visitor smiled wryly.

"Are you Mas'ga of Chersonesus? You are an armourer, are you not?" said the man.

"I am indeed. You would be Akhenassor, would you not?" Mas'ga smiled slyly.

"I am him. We are all mutual friends of our esteemed Apothecary, isn't that so?"

"And loyal and humble subjects of Her Royal Majesty, is that not equally so?"

"Our true allegiance is not in question" Akhenassor replied evenly. "I would be honoured to make the introductions, dear friend. This is Agur'ki and Aeschylla. They rank among my oldest and most trusted friends. I would trust them with my life, as you can."

"It is good to meet you, Agur'ki and Aeschylla" Mas'ga acknowledged the man and woman.

Agur'ki eyed him steadily. Aeschylla bats her eyelashes flirtatiously. "Would you like a drink? A small wodki, perhaps?" enquired Akhenassor.

"That would be very kind of you" Mas'ga sat down in a vacant chair across from the group. "Now, you have obviously been briefed about the forthcoming Royal visit to Chersonesus, I presume?"

"Indeed, we have. Her Majesty has many friends in Chersonesus, does she not? Also, here in Nymphaion and, of course, in Panticapaeum" Akhenassor lied smoothly.

"Her Majesty also has enemies, does she not? It is my understanding that there is a plot, however fanciful, to assassinate her. That plot might be executed during the planned visit to Chersonesus?"

"There will be a parade before the Banquet, will there not?" asked Agur'ki.

"There will be a welcoming parade. We are expecting a thronging crowd and, whilst we have considered all possible security breaches, there are serious concerns about policing such a large crowd. It is our understanding that we may expect planned protests."

"You fear these dissidents might be inclined to recruit killers from the streets of Nymphaion?" Akhenassor probed.

"We have considered all relevant lines of inquiry, as a matter of course. We think the most profitable avenue for these treacherous rogues lies here, in Nymphaion" confessed Mas'ga.

"Archers present an obvious threat, of course?" stated Akhenassor.

"We intend to post a formidable rooftop security screen. It would be impossible for a single archer to accomplish such a feat! Let us presume that we are dealing with a single, highly- skilled hunter, if such a soul exists?"

"You are not expecting an attack at close quarters?" Agur'ki interjected.

"We would be well prepared for any such affront to Her Royal Majesty's dignity! I can assure you of that. It is the lone fox, that most patient and guileful of predators, who presents the gravest threat" Mas'ga said evenly.

"A fox, you say! Never a vixen?" Akhenassor's eyes twinkled mischievously.

Mas'ga could not hide his astonishment "Why would you ask such a thing? No woman would be suited to the task, surely?"

Aeschylla eyed the man steadily and sipped her wodki. "There is a rumour that the Ur'gai possesses a new kind of weapon. A modified bow, of sorts, highly accurate and lethal, and which is capable of being fired from a standing, kneeling, and even a concealed firing position. Is this true?"

"We have such a weapon. I have been trained to use one personally. However, for obvious reasons, we would never equip our enemies with such a device."

"Yet, you are an armourer?" Akhenassor interjected slyly. "You have the knowledge and skills to manufacture any such precision weapon, especially if the life of our beloved Queen depends upon it?"

"I could accomplish such a feat! Of course, I could!" Mas'ga remonstrated.

"As with a conventional longbow, the larger the weapon, the greater is effect, in terms of distance and killing power?" Aeschylla spoke sultrily.

Agur'ki smiled and bowed his head in reverence. "I think my darling paramour alludes to something far more potent!"

Aeschylla giggles softly, as her eyes twinkle like stars. "In this particular case, I think the Lady may have misjudged her distance!"

The table convulses with laughter. Mas'ga sips his drink and returns to the matter in hand. "That is true, my Lady. Yet, these weapons are not designed for long-range killing" he confessed.

"You have the necessary skills and the knowledge to design such a device, do you not?" the woman pressed.

"It can be done, my Lady! Of that I am confident" Mas'ga replied evenly.

"We will monitor the activities of these dissidents and malcontents in Nymphaion, for a price, of course. These things cost money, do they not? Yet, to guarantee the safety of our beloved Queen, we require the ability to engage all and any threats. These may come from the streets, buildings, or the rooftops, as you have already acknowledged?" Akhenassor surmised.

"I can design and fashion such a weapon within the space of a week. We would then require a test of its accuracy and prowess, merely as a precautionary measure" said Mas'ga.

"That would give sufficient time for us to assess the situation on the ground, both here, where the real threat lies, and Chersonesus, before the planned Royal visit?" Akhenassor ventured.

"I have been assured by my friends that any such visit would not take place before the Shabbat following the next."

"We will do our duty, my friend, and you must do yours. The life of our beloved Queen, and the security of our Duchy, depends upon it" Akhenassor beseeched.

"It will be done; I assure you of that" Mas'ga smiled thinly. He fished within his robe and removed a leather purse, heavy with Persian gold. "There are eight pieces, would this suffice?"

"That would be more than sufficient, my dear friend. For we are all, every one of us, loyal subjects of Her Royal Majesty, are we not?" said Akhenassor.

PART THREE

TEN

The message was written in Hellenic script. The papyrus was of a common variety and the ink a composite of fine powdered charcoal and water, with traces of ground iron, akin to that within the ceramic jar at the corner of the desk. The papyrus was rolled into a slender scroll and inserted into a hollow silver ingot, sealed at both ends with beeswax, then squirreled within a sealed jar of dried poppy flowers. Whilst the mode of conveyance was typical, the communication was unexpected, perhaps even unwelcome, given her recent excursions. The woman adjusted herself gingerly on the chair, for she was still sore, and frowned, lips pursed with worry. By her own reckoning, the communique had been despatched with haste no later than the morning after the last Shabbat. It was a portent of doom.

> *There is much to fear, the Hawk is hunting a new prey.*
> *What tales of the passage of the gold witch?*
> *This girl-child has enemies, they will not*
> *slake until her breath has stilled.*
> *The Great Pretender beset with maudlin.*
> *No time to waste, Scythia in its throes of passion.*
> *Seek riches elsewhere but Chersonesus,*
> *the Hawk is master of the east*

The 'girl-child' in question, this *gold witch*, whoever she was, had evidently caused an unprecedented commotion, in Susa and elsewhere, much to the recipients' delight. Even the 'Great Pretender', King Darius himself, was allegedly plagued with melancholy by the apparent threat posed by a mere child, a girl at that! Sufficiently so, that he had commanded his most senior intelligence agent in the region, known as 'Hawk', to pursue her with vigour! The girl was in mortal peril, for her enemies wished her dead, and would direct their energy to this end. According to her own source, current intelligence favoured her destination, even her present location, as the southern Crimea. Yet not, according to the trusted agents of the mysterious 'Serpent', in Chersonesus itself. The allusion to the Hawk's 'hunting-ground' strongly favoured the eastern Hellenic polities of Panticapaeum or Nymphaion.

The recipient re-read the communique and was satisfied with its authenticity and significance. She would not take the risk of notifying her trusted agents in both Panticapaeum and Nymphaion, for obvious reasons of security! Rather, given their proximity, she would notify her agent in Nymphaion. With any luck, this source may have already learned of these developments and alerted their contacts in the Ur'gai Royal Court. Heeding the cautionary tone of the communique, she would not notify agents in the Royal Cities of the Nur'gat, the Orch'tai or the Argata. Whilst the Ur'gai themselves may learned something of the travails of this mysterious 'gold witch', given the urgency, she would also notify her agent in Chersonesus to deliver a secret communique to the Ur'gai Queen in person, notifying of these sinister developments. As for this 'gold witch', she must entrust her fate to Artemis, Hellenic Goddess of the hunt. The woman uncorked the stopper on the vial of ink, selected a parchment from a sheath, and began to draft her own *kryptos*.

⌒

Qu'ehra, July 493 BC

Almost a world away, ensconced in his study with explicit instructions that he was not to be disturbed, the 'Hawk' reclined lazily on a dais and yawned tiredly. It had been an eventful week and his body ached from the exertion. He closed his eyes and pondered both the *dilemma*, and its logical *solution*. That the 'gold witch' must die is of paltry consideration, nor is the manner of her death of any great concern. It must be swift, to be sure, yet a swift death would not accrue anything in the way of capital. The child's killing was a political *act* and must create its own political *maelstrom*. Known traitors in the Ur'gai Royal Court might yet prove indispensable, but only if the plot were allowed to ripen. The girl, this 'gold witch', must not be allowed to escape her covert in Nymphaion, for it was surely there that she would seek refuge, yet it might be wise to grant her the freedom to contact her mistress.

Haste was a curse, not a virtue, in such a delicate ploy! With sufficient guile, and the grace of Zoroaster, the death of a child would yet unseat a Queen, heralding a new era of global stability.

A world in which the might and glory of Persia was unrivalled and unchallenged!

Nymphaion, July 493 BC

Corelya entered the kitchen and smiled sweetly at Nirch'ii, busily preparing a sumptuous meal of fresh fruit, olives, vegetables, goat's cheese, and fresh bread. The older girl glances quickly at the child, a look of pity and distaste, and returns her gaze to the chopping board in front of her. She seems distant and troubled.

"That looks delicious, Nirchi'ii" Corelya smiles

brightly.

"How are you feeling?" Nirch'ii asked Corelya, furrowing her brow with distaste. "I do not approve of what he did to you!"

"He only did it because I asked him to! I told you this a thousand times!" Corelya sighed irritably. "He certainly didn't enjoy it. I actually feel a lot better than I look" she grinned.

"That can't be too hard, can it? You look terrible, Corelya!"

Corelya was a *monstrosity*. Both eyes were blackened and swollen, her lips puffy and bloodied. The right side of her face was a grotesque bruise. The right side of her body was equally discoloured from the merciless beating she had sustained in the rented room at *The Lion of Judah*, a hostelry on the eastern side of the straits. The golden locks that she had cultivated since early childhood, a source of such pride, had been brutally shorn with common shears! The humiliation had been administered, albeit reluctantly, by a gang of thugs hired by Minas at Corelya's behest. Nirch'ii had wept inconsolably after she found Corelya, unconscious and bloodied, on the floor in the late afternoon. Even now, she could scarcely bring herself to speak with Minas, despite the truth of the matter. As far as Corelya was concerned, all was well in the world, given the circumstances! She had availed herself of the tatty, stinking rags she had arrived in and had since bathed in hot water, a luxury after the travails of the past week. Corelya wore a lilac chiton in the Hellenic style, whereas Nirch'ii, as befitting the wife of a successful merchant, was regaled in an ensemble in accordance with her status: chic, tasteful and expensive.

Minas and Nirch'ii had sequestered a villa in the most expensive part of Nymphaion, paid for with a generous bequest from the Ur'gai Queen in gold and silver! The property belonged to a wealthy Hellenic merchant and his family, who had vacated for the summer to Athens.

According to the letting agent, the couple were truly blessed to have found such a beautiful home, available immediately, and at such reasonable rates, given the popularity of Nymphaion as a holiday destination in the summer months! A cynical Corelya had snorted derisively, for such blatant horseshit did little to dissemble a growing despair at the turpitude of humanity in general!

"Like anyone in their right mind would holiday in this dump!" the girl snorted.

Not that there was anything wrong with the villa, quite the opposite, in fact. It ranked among the most beautiful and tastefully furnished residences she had ever seen in all her life, certainly comparable with the Royal Palace of Susa! That being said, Corelya had spent a considerable time of her brief life in accommodation that would make the hairs on a Spartans scrotum stand to attention!

"I have to leave on an errand this evening. I can't tell you where I am going. I may only return in the early hours of the morning" Corelya confessed.

"You will be safe, won't you?" Nirch'ii implored.

"I will be fine, I promise" Corelya chirped. "It is you that I am concerned about. You need to make your peace with Minas! You are supposed to be a doting and dutiful wife, remember?"

"You are enjoying this aren't you? Teasing me about Minas?" Nirch'ii sighed irritably.

"I thought that you would be the one enjoying teasing Minas!" Corelya snickered.

"My opinion of him has changed entirely after what happened at *The Lion of Judah*" Nirch'ii sighed sadly.

"It should not! It was necessary! I asked him to arrange it. You do know he cried when he saw me later that evening? He came to see me in my room after you had gone to bed, if you want to know."

Nirch'ii was astonished. "No! I didn't know!" she stammered breathlessly.

"Well, now you do!" Corelya clipped icily.

⌒

Saiga Plains, Crimea, July 493 BC

Yari adds more twigs to the fire and then vigorously stirs the mint leaves in the kettle. The girl is immersed in her private thoughts, when, to her surprise and glee, she espies Korta approaching across the grass.

"I was just about to make some tea, if you would like some?" Yari motioned towards the kettle.

"That would be lovely, Yari. Thank you" said Korta.

"I still can't believe you came back. It really is lovely to see you again. We have missed you, Corelya especially, not that she would ever admit it" Yari lowered her voice to a whisper. "She was devastated over what happened. She cried for weeks afterwards."

"You are teasing me, surely?" Korta smiled slyly.

Yari adopted an expression of indignant consternation. "*I am not!* I heard her. I never mentioned it, obviously. But she cried most nights. She must have thought I was asleep."

"You surely can't be serious?" Korta chided.

"Corelya worships you, surely you know that?" Yari chided. "She can be incredibly loyal, but only to those who are loyal in return. You were always good to both of us, but especially to her. She was outraged by what happened to you. She can never admit it publicly, but she thinks the Queen was wrong to dismiss you in disgrace and that Her Majesty ought to apologise."

"How are you keeping?" Korta diplomatically steered the conversation to less treacherous ground.

"I am well. My horsemanship and skill with a sword are improving steadily. I may even survive combat" Yari grinned.

"Perhaps the peace will last? You may never need to test your battle skills?" ventured Korta.

"Corelya does not think so. She is convinced something sinister is afoot" Yari whispered.

"She intimated as much. There are certain worrying developments of late, that much is clear. To what degree the Persians are ultimately responsible is a matter of fervent speculation."

"I worry about Corelya's safety! I couldn't give a fig-leaf for the machinations of the bastard Persians!" Yari spat. She frowned and stirred the mint leaves methodically in the bubbling water.

"You didn't want her to go on this mission?" Korta probed.

"Not alone I didn't. I am glad she had company for most of the way, and it is lovely that she sought you out."

"I think she was as much interested in any news I may have imparted to her, as much as she was in seeing me again" Korta mused.

"You are meeting with the Queen and Counsel this afternoon?" Yari smiled brightly.

"I have that pleasure" Korta grimaced.

Yari grinned and poured the mint tea in to two wooden goblets. "Here you are. As good as I have ever made."

"Thank you, Yari. This is most welcome. So, has anyone 'courted' you yet?"

Yari giggled. "Of course, they have not! I am a little young, am I not? Not to mention my lowly status. Why would any older girl from a respectable family wish to take me as a lover?"

Korta smiles sweetly at the girl, whilst averting his gaze from Yari's increasingly inconspicuous buxom! "I think you do yourself a grave disservice, Yari. You are an extremely attractive girl, in every imaginable way. You are also extremely popular. Nor are you truly a child anymore, for you have since turned thirteen. Gor'ya certainly doesn't treat you like a slave, does she?"

Yari grins slyly at the old man's unease. "My boobs

have certainly gotten bigger this summer, that much true!"

"I hadn't noticed" Korta said mildly, averting his gaze from the girl.

"Liar!" Yari chided, in mock severity. "You are right about Gor'ya, though. She is different from most people. To be honest, the 'mysteries' are not something I have given much thought to."

"I spoke briefly with Corelya about what the future may hold, for both of you. You may not remain slaves forever, you know?" Korta confessed.

Yari giggled breathlessly. "You spoke with Corelya about 'the mysteries'? I can't believe you, Korta! You are truly awful sometimes! She is petrified by the idea of sex, didn't you notice? I tease her all the time about it, well, mostly about Gor'ya!"

"Perhaps you should not tease too enthusiastically, especially after what happened to her all those years ago" Korta reproved the child lightly.

"It is only gentle teasing, I promise" Yari lowers her voice to a whisper. "I do think Gor'ya fancies Corelya, though. Sirch'i is due to marry at the end of the summer and she would be free to court again."

"I suppose we could ask her, couldn't we?" Korta indicated Gor'ya's approach with a sly nod of his head.

"Hi Gor! Would you like to share some tea?" Yari waved eagerly at the approaching girl and flashed her a smile of genuine warmth.

"Normally, I would love to Yari. But I am here on business of State." Gor'ya's formal manner startled Yari and, for the first time in their acquaintanceship, friendship even, she felt uncomfortable.

"Perhaps I should excuse myself?" Yari stood up to bid her leave.

"You should gather your weapons, Yari. You too, Korta! Your presence is requested at an emergency Counsel meeting."

"Me?" Yari gasped.

"That is correct'" Gor'ya smiled thinly. Something was wrong. Yari was scared.

"Perhaps you could partake in a quick cup of tea. Yari's weapons are readily to hand. I will go and collect mine right away" Korta soothed. Taking her cue, Yari dived into the tent and stepped back out almost immediately, fitting her sword belt and crossed- shoulder strap. In short order, her sword and scabbard were suspended at her left hip.

"As soon as you can, if you please" Gor'ya clipped curtly.

"I will return shortly" Korta replied formally, proffering a freshly filled cup of mint tea to Her Majesty's most trusted messenger.

"Is something wrong?" Yari whispered. There was genuine fear in her voice. Something clearly was wrong.

"You will find out soon enough. I pray that you are as surprised as I by this latest revelation?" Gor'ya replied coldly. Yari began shuffling her feet and kept her gaze fixed firmly at the ground. Her fear now bordered on terror.

Gor'ya sipped her tea without anything further said between them. Korta returned presently, armed with his battered sword and shield and, without further ado, the trio set off in the direction of the Royal Enclosure. Something was clearly wrong, and Yari was deeply troubled. In contrast, Korta was reassured by the fact that no armed guards had been despatched to escort them. Whatever had precipitated this most unwelcome development, there was at least some comfort in the knowledge that, for the present at least, neither he nor Yari were under formal arrest.

~

Chersonesus, July 493 BC

Mathos, renowned vintner of Chersonesus, sits across the table from his visitor in the back room of his store. Two walls of the room are garlanded by barrels of fine wine, neatly arranged on trestles. The rear is decked with shelves upon which arraigned sealed ceramic flagons of wine and wodki. Mathos is one of the wealthiest merchants in all Chersonesus. *He is no friend to the Persians*!

"You would like some wine? Of course, you would! We have wine from Euboea, Sparta, Crete, and even as far west as Massalia" Mathos the Vintner smiled wryly. "Perhaps you would prefer some wodki?"

"Is the wodki good?" asked the visitor.

"Our wodki hails from 'the lands between the seas' and the plains east of the Wol'yi. We have plum, apricot, even pomegranate, all of which are excellent. We even have wodki from the finest estates in Rost'eya. Would you expect anything less from Mathos of Chersonesus?" said Mathos, spreading his arms and grinning at his guest. "Nothing but the best for you, old friend, and long may our friendship last!"

"Your friendship is most valued, Mathos, both by myself and my Master."

The visitor smiled serenely. He had dark hair and blue eyes that rarely gave anything away, especially in meetings such as this. It was true that he and Mathos were 'old friends', in the sense that Mathos had never cheated him out of a payment, had never swindled him with overpriced and inferior merchandise, nor had he ever betrayed a confidence. Mathos was a valued contact in a world beguiled by treachery and naked self-interest and, if this continued, he would be wisely considered a friend rather than a mere acquaintance.

"Your master is worried?" ventured Mathos. He stood up from the table, paced across the room, and returned with a ceramic flagon of apricot wodki and two goblets. He filled both with a generous measure and passes one to his visitor.

"Perhaps, these are troubling times, are they not?" the

visitor enquired searchingly.

"Trade has never been better! At least for myself, though I cannot say the same for some of our Orch'tai friends."

"The Orch'tai have been enchanted by a dangerous melody these few years past" the visitor ventured.

"I know of no such things. Except that the timber trade is booming" Mathos replied guardedly.

"Is it true that the Ur'gai Queen will be visiting Chersonesus in the coming weeks?"

"There is talk of such things, but nothing has yet been formally arranged. The City Guild is in constant communication with the Royal Court, for they are overly eager to court the Queen. We expect news within the next week or so. I am arranging a large consignment of Hellenic wine for despatch to the Saiga Plains" Mathos confirmed.

"If that is true, then perhaps one of your retainers might venture to confirm with Her Royal Majesty that the consignment will be delivered on time, as requested?" the visitor proposed.

"That would be diplomatic, I suppose. You would recommend such a thing, old friend?

Alas, these are things of which I know little. The customs of the Royal Court, so to speak, are a mystery to a simple trader such as me" Mathos chuckled.

"I would strongly advise it, old friend. Perhaps the man could carry some small votive, gratis, of course, as tokens of your esteem and affection."

"As I have already alluded, dear Krathac, such subtleties are quite alien to a simple man like me. You would advise haste?" Mathos smiled slyly.

"I would, dear friend. It does no mere mortal any good to incur the displeasure of a Queen."

"As it happens, I have a delivery scheduled to depart for Nymphaion early tomorrow morning" Mathos confessed. "The driver could make a detour to the Royal Camp on the Saiga Plains, for it would be a small inconvenience to his journey."

"If I may ask a small favour in return, old friend, in lieu of the courteous advice I have freely given?" Krathac stressed the harmonious relationship between them.

"It is always a pleasure to grant favours to old and valued friends, is it not? If it is in my service to give, that is?"

Krathac drew a small leather purse, closed at the top by drawstrings, from within his robes and removed the silver ingot. It was sealed at both ends with beeswax. This is slid across the table to Mathos, who secrets it away in a slip-pocket deep within his own robes. The message would be safely delivered to the Ur'gai Royal Court on the morrow, for Krathac had every faith in Mathos of Chersonesus, as did his master. The two men drained their goblets and once replenished, talked happily of all manner of things, present and past, as old friends do.

~

"Wait here, if you please. Her Majesty will summon you when she is ready" Gor'ya spoke curtly.

The teenager turned on her heels and disappeared into the Audience Chamber where the Royal Counsel was huddled with the Queen in an emergency session. Unlike Yari, who had gone a deathly pale, Korta was nonplussed by the presence of armed guards. This was, after all, the Royal Enclosure.

"Do not be afraid, sweet child. It is probably nothing" Korta soothed.

"Do you seriously think that this is nothing?" Yari yelped. "I have never been summoned to Counsel before, not like this. And I have never seen Gor'ya acting the way she was! She was very cold! Something bad has happened! I just know it!"

"I am sure that you have nothing to fear" Korta soothed.

"Could it be something to do with Corelya?" Yari quipped.

"Possibly, yet it could be something else entirely" Korta replied soothingly. "We will know soon enough, won't we?" Yari replied gloomily.

~

Gor'ya loomed in the entrance and informed them formally that Her Royal Majesty commanded their presence in the Audience Chamber. As they entered the chamber, Queen Illir'ya was seated on the High Throne, with her Counsellor's seated in a curve on either side. Her Majesty's three pages, including the identical twins with hair as golden as Corelya's, were perched on cushions at Her Majesty's feet. Yari knew them well. Their presence re-assured her, for surely things could not be that bad if they had been permitted to remain. Gor'ya obediently took her place in the vacant chair on Her Majesty's immediate left. The Queen normally smiled, for her perpetually sweet and personable nature was a fair a bellwether as the summer sun. Yet now, she eyed her visitors with a cool detachment. The atmosphere was icy in contrast with the glorious heat of the summer's day. Yari was deeply worried.

"How long have you been here, Yari?" Her Majesty enquired formally, startling the child with the unexpected question.

"Since I was four-years-old, Your Royal Highness" Yari replied. "Are you happy here?"

"I have always, and continue, to serve at Your Majesty's pleasure. I am content. Things could have been far worse, for both Corelya and I."

"You and Corelya are very close, are you not?"

"Corelya is like a sister to me. She always has been, ever since we were toddlers."

"And you discussed Corelya's forthcoming mission?"

"Only that she would be away for a brief time and

would be heading northwards across the steppe towards the Donets River and the north-eastern fringes of the Azovi." Yari confessed. "I already knew her concerns about possible Orch'tai cavalry units in the region, obviously, yet we never discussed anything that was said in Counsel"

"You are quite sure of that?" interjected Morch'ti, Kor'nai of the Royal Counsel.

"Indeed, I am, Honourable Kor'nai. Corelya would never breach a confidence of State."

"You *are* certain of this?" ventured Alazar, the most slippery of the Queen's Counsellors and the sole individual that Yari genuinely disliked.

Yari bristled with indignation at the thinly veiled allusion to her own and Corelya's disreputable, even treasonous, conduct. "I am certain, Honourable Counsellor", she replied, stressing the Honourable to emphasise her displeasure. She wrinkled her nose with distaste. Korta struggled not to laugh out loud! Yari was, after all, Sauromatae, and the *fury* of such feminine souls was legendary.

"Does the name 'Nichassor' mean anything to you?"

Yari blanched. "Nichassor? Why would you ask?"

"You are familiar with the name, Yari?" enquired Naz'mir. He smiled to reassure the girl, who was visibly reeling with shock.

"Yes, I am. Nichassor is a Persian. He travels with a large group of warrior kinsmen. It was Nichassor and his band who found Corelya and I after.what happened, all those years ago. It was Nichassor who sold us to Her Majesty as Handmaidens."

"Perhaps we should enlighten you in respect of certain information that has only just reached us from Qu'ehra?" said the Kor'nai.

"Qu'ehra?" Yari gasped. "Why would Corelya have gone to Qu'ehra?"

"So, you think it is entirely possible that Corelya may

be, or may recently have been, in Qu'ehra?" Alazar said coldly.

"I am not… I mean, I don't… I thought this might be about Corelya, that is all?" the girl stammered.

"We have received intelligence from Qu'ehra that is rather troubling, Yari" interjected Queen Illir'ya. "There is talk of a 'gold witch', a girl-child who speaks fluent Sarmati and Scythiac, and who appears to have been involved in a series of alarming incidents, including two murders. There is also report of an attack in the public market which left several people dead."

"An attack?" Yari gaped. Her eyes betrayed her bewilderment at the revelations.

"According to our sources, it would appear the attack was directed against the girl and her companions, one of whom was wounded. According to our sources, this man was a Persian. Most of the attackers were killed. Several of their number by this girl, apparently." confirmed the Kor'nai.

"Nichassor?" Yari gasped.

"Our sources confirm that the man is known by the name 'Nichassor', although it is possible that this is not the figure from your past."

"I see" said Yari.

The Kor'nai turns his head towards Queen Illir'ya to indicate that he was now addressing Her Majesty in Counsel, rather than the two attendees. "This man, Nichassor, subsequently received medical treatment from one of the finest Surgeons, whose repute is famed throughout 'the lands between the seas'. Sometime later, this girl, this 'gold witch', as some have named her, was witnessed in *The Silk Road* inn, where she made enquiries concerning the merits and demerits of the *Accord* between the Scythian Ducals. Soon afterwards she left.

"And you think this girl, this 'gold witch', is Corelya?" Yari asked evenly.

"It is worth stating that much of this tale remains unsubstantiated by our own sources at the present time. Nevertheless, several witnesses testify that the girl left *The Silk Road* and headed in the direction of the market. She appears to have been followed by two men, widely reputed to be killers for hire, both of whom were subsequently murdered. Their bodies were discovered early the following morning. One appears to have been killed in the most barbarous fashion and this has caused consternation among the authorities in Qu'ehra" the Kor'nai addressed the Counsel, rather than Yari and Korta.

"As you can see, Yari, these are deeply troubling developments" the Queen smiled tightly. "Yes, Your Majesty, they are!" Yari spoke humbly. She was visibly reeling at the revelations. "You may continue, Honourable Kor'nai," said the Queen.

"There is a further possible sighting of the same girl later that night in *The Silk Road*, although other sources suggest that this child was a young prostitute bearing only a passing resemblance to this 'gold witch'. She herself appears to have vanished without trace" surmised the Kor'nai. *Yari stifled a giggle at the thought of Corelya trading sexual favours for money!*

The Kor'nai continued. "There is talk, perhaps mere tittle-tattle, that this 'gold witch' was an assassin. The most worrying aspect of this entire sordid affair is the wild-talk circulating in Qu'ehra and the hinterlands of an alleged conspiracy to assassinate Queen Lezika of the Argata."

"Involving this girl?" Yari chirped.

"We have credible information to support this" Alazar confirmed icily.

"Is your information sufficiently credible to sustain a conclusion that this 'gold witch' must be Corelya, and none other?"

"As I have already stated, Yari, much of our intelligence is little more than unsubstantiated rumour. And yet, we have been placed in an unfortunate position where we have sufficient grounds to suspect that this 'gold witch' is Corelya. We are, quite naturally, extremely concerned that a Courtier is so deeply implicated in a rumoured plot to murder the Argata Queen and de-stabilize the regional peace." The Kor'nai confessed.

"Unless you instructed Corelya to kill Queen Lezika, she would never countenance such a course of action, regardless of any personal animosity to the Argata!" Yari stated boldly.

"Are you insinuating that we had prior knowledge of, and even condoned, Corelya's conduct?" Alazar gasped.

"I am insinuating no such thing, as you ought not to insinuate anything in respect to Corelya's loyalty" Yari bridled.

The girl turned directly towards the Queen, then, tellingly, at Gor'ya. "From what you have said, too much of this is nothing more than unsubstantiated rumour. We cannot confirm that this girl is Corelya, or that she was involved in any murders in Qu'ehra, much less a conspiracy to kill Queen Lezika! I can understand why you might be led to the conclusion that the girl in question is Corelya and, perhaps it is? Yet Corelya would never be involved in any plot to murder Lezika. That is absolutely implausible!" Yari directed her gaze to Gor'ya, as if imploring her to rise to Corelya's defence.

"For myself, if my opinion counts for anything, Your Royal Majesty, I think Yari is right. The girl in question may well be Corelya, but, if she was involved in any such killings, it would surely have been in self-defence. I simply cannot countenance she would be involved in a plot against the Argata Queen" Gor'ya interjected.

"Your opinion is valued, Gor'ya, more than you would credit" Queen Illir'ya smiled for the first time during the entire audience.

"For myself, I have grave concerns about her close

association with this Nichassor fellow"

Alazar simpered. "If we could confirm that this 'gold witch' is Corelya, I am afraid we may have grounds to reconsider her loyalty to the Crown."

Yari gasped in horror. Yet, it was Korta, who replied to the Honourable Counsellor. "You surely cannot be serious, Counsellor Alazar?" he blazed.

"With all respect, Your Majesty, I have grave concerns in light of these reports. It is my duty to commend those concerns to Counsel" Alazar clipped.

"I concur entirely with the merits of Alazar's concerns and their relevance to this Counsel, dear Sister" Sag'ra interjected, giving voice to his opinion for the first time.

"I thought *you* might" Yari snorted, a little too loudly.

Sag'ra gapes at the girl in astonishment. "I beg your pardon?" he gasped.

"Beg all you want to, sleazeball, but you can fuck right off!" Yari snarled.

"How dare you! Arrest her!" Sag'ra yelped.

"On what charge should we arrest her, young man?" Korta spoke evenly, yet his eyes twinkled with mischief.

"High Treason!" yelped Sag'ra.

"Her retort was directed against you, Sag'ra, not Her Majesty, you simpleton!" Korta sneered.

"Your own treachery has long been a subject of concern!" Sag'ra bridled.

Korta smiled thinly and drew his sword from its battered scabbard. "Would you like to repeat that charge, runt?"

The entire room is aghast by the act. The three young Handmaidens gape in dumbstruck terror at the old man, standing proudly, his blade drawn defiantly. Not surprisingly, it was Commander Zar'cha whom recovered her wits first.

"How dare you draw a blade in the presence of Her Majesty and Counsel!" Zar'cha screeched. "Guards!

Guards!"

Six armed guards enter the tent and pause, momentarily dumbfounded by the sight of the old man with his drawn sword.

"Arrest them both!" Zar'cha commanded.

Yari turns to Korta and smiles ruefully. "Please Korta. Sheath your blade. This isn't going to do either of us any good, is it?"

"Your time will come, child!" a smouldering Korta sheathed his blade and sneered at Sag'ra, who had gone a deathly pale.

In contrast, Queen Illir'ya had kept her composure throughout the entire confrontation. When she did finally speak, her voice had the authority of one born to Royalty.

"Disarm them and take them away!" Her Majesty commanded.

Panticapaeum, July 493 BC

Mas'ga laid the stock of the weapon, a little under two-and-a-half feet long, on the battered table facing upwards. He retrieves the front piece, a recurved bow slightly under two feet in length, from the table behind him. The recurved limbs on either side of the centrepiece are nine inches long and are carved from yew sourced from the forests of the coastal fringes of the eastern Black Sea. The ends have been reinforced with carved bone, in the style of all Scythian and Sauromatae longbows. The ellipsoid cross-section of each of the recurved limbs factors extreme strength with an astonishing lightness. The centrepiece is carved from oak and measures some five inches in length, an inch in width, and two inches in depth. This is bored at both ends to house the recurved limbs, secured in place with deerhorn glue.

The centrepiece has been bored in the centre and varnished with beeswax prior to assembly. It fitted snugly into a revetment on the front-piece of the stock, secured with a heavy bronze bolt, measuring three-and-a-half inches in length, passing through the depth of the centrepiece into the body of the stock. Additional support is provided by two leather straps with thin plates of bronze glued on either face at both ends. These have been perforated a short distance from their termini. When the centrepiece is secured by its retaining bolt, these could be slipped around its curved perimeter on either side of the stock and fixed to two retaining plates, also bored, fixed on either side of the front of the stock, an inch-and-a-half from its end. These were secured with bronze retaining pins.

The bowstring itself is silk. It is secured at the ends of each limb by beeswax and hemp-rope binding, as good as any military longbow, and Mas'ga was confident it would not fail! The resin must be first allowed to set. Only then could the drawstring lever he had devoted so much time to engineering, be tested. Unlike the weapons the Ur'gai had modified, designed to be used even by children, for it was a child herself who had obtained a crossbow in the first place and conceived of its modification, a drawstring lever was a pre- requisite in a weapon such as this. Only superhuman strength could have manually drawn the bowstring to its required position behind the trigger mechanism. This comprised a heavy iron bolt that passes through the centre of the stock, much like the axle of a cart, to which heavy bronze clasps could be slipped over on either side, fashioned in the form of crescents, much like the pieces of the trigger mechanism, terminating in two blunt-edged projections around which the drawstring could be hooked. These had been fixed precisely to the iron bolt on either side of the stock by smaller circular disks of bronze and deer-horn glue.

It is here that the true engineering genius of the

Mas'ga's new weapon lay! As elegant and as far-sighted as the trigger mechanism designed by the Chinese was, unlike the weapons modified by the Ur'gai, this stock comprised two distinct halves, bored along much of its length to allow passage of the cocking lever to the rear of the trigger housing, where it could be safely retreated below, once the trigger was taut and was ready to fire. The two parts fitted together to form an elegant body, strong and light, with deer-horn glue and bronze retaining pins inserted through bored holes at the front, the lower centre, rear of the stock. The resin should be allowed to set for a day at least, and so it would be the following day before his masterpiece could be test-fired in the covered yard of his workshop, free from the prying eyes of any interested observers. Mas'ga was confident that he had fashioned a long-range killing weapon with an unparalleled accuracy the like of which the world had not yet known!

The man and woman were perched on stools at a table outside a vintner's shop adjacent to the Central Square, leisurely sipping goblets of fine Gaulish red. The woman, petite and slender, with dark chocolate curls, fashioned in the current style of ringlets at the sides, wore a simple, yet stylish, emerald chiton with saffron trim. Her companion, freshly bathed and clean shaven, not his usual style, sported a two-piece silk ensemble in pale blue. "I am beginning to enjoy this lifestyle, my sweet, aren't you?" the woman purred.

The man smiled. "Nice to see how the other half lives, isn't it? Not that they do much work for their wealth, do they?"

"It is surprising, isn't it? I lived my whole life in this squalid little backwater, and I have never been to Chersonesus. I quite like the place, don't you? It is certainly far wealthier than Nymphaion."

"They do a lot of trade directly with the Greeks, don't they? Far more than we will ever get! Think they are better than us, don't they? They get the cream, and we get the dregs from the bottom of the bucket!" the man grumbled.

"Don't spoil it, honeycomb! We are having such a lovely time" the woman reached across the table with her right hand and stroked her lovers with heart-warming tenderness. "It is really nice to get away, isn't it? Just the two of us, away from everyone else and all their bullshit! Maybe you could bring me here again, after we get married, perhaps?"

"Please don't start harping on about that again, Aeschylla" the man sighed.

Aeschylla is stung. "And why should I not? I love you, Agur'ki, I truly do. I can't imagine spending my life with anyone else! All I want, more than anything in the world, is for us to have a home of our own. I wish for nothing more than a garden where our children can play."

"We would have to leave Nymphaion, wouldn't we? There is no other way that you could have a home with a garden?"

"We could move to where my sister Nevah lives, I think it would be perfect for us?"

Agur'ki sipped his wine. "Please don't start with that again, Aeschylla. How many times do I have to explain things to you? You know how I earn my living, much in the same way that you earn yours? We are not ordinary people, you, and me! Don't you get that?"

"But everything will change, won't it?" Aeschylla beseeched, lowering her voice to a whisper. "We will all have to leave Nymphaion when this is done, don't you see? And we will have the money we need to be able do it! More money than we could ever spend! We could leave Nymphaion forever! We could pack our things and leave everything, and everyone, behind us. It would be a fresh start for us, for us and our children?"

"Just leave it alone, will you? I understand far more than you credit me! I am not quite the thicko some people think I am! Like that flash twat Akhenassor with his fancy new friends. Who the fuck does he think he is nowadays?" Agur'ki hissed.

"We can deal with that bastard when this is over. I don't trust him, do you? Only the Gods know who he may have blabbed to? He could get us both hanged, with that big mouth of his, the stupid prick!" Aeschylla spat venomously.

Agur'ki smiled. "I like the way you think, my little plum, but I am afraid. For the first time in my life, I am truly afraid, and I am not in the least ashamed to admit it."

Aeschylla was deeply touched by the admission, for it meant that he did truly love her, and none other, for he would never have uttered those words to another living soul. She reached across the table and stroked his hand once more. "Why are you afraid, my sweet? Tell me, I beseech you?"

"Do you know the kind of people we have gotten mixed up with? Do you understand how this works?"

"Then tell me, my love. Together we can fix it, I promise you! I would never betray you! You know that?"

Agur'ki sighed ruefully. "These aren't a bunch of drunken sailors looking to settle scores, or the odd wealthy family who are not too sentimental as to how they acquire some of their trinkets! Nor are they a bunch of dopey young whores who need protection. These are truly dangerous people, Aeschylla? They are powerful, wealthy, and have objectives far beyond our comprehension." He leaned across the table and spoke in a whisper. "I think we might be in over our heads, my love, I truly do."

"I will take care of Akhenassor! I have told you that already, haven't I? When this is over, I will deal with him, and with that other snake Meschasses. You are right, my love, they have both gotten too big for their boots of late, haven't they?" she purred.

"I have a terrible feeling about this whole affair. This plot to kill the Ur'gai Queen could be the death of all of us!" Agur'ki mused sombrely.

⁓

"It is good to see you again, friend!" Akhenassor greeted the armourer as he closed the door of the private room at *The Merchants Chalice* behind him. All of the four conspirators were now present: Akhenassor, Agur'ki, Aeschylla, and the unwitting Mas'ga. "Please, have a seat? Now, what would you like to drink? We have wine, wodki, or rye beer?" Akhenassor indicated three jugs and assorted goblets and drinking-jars on an adjacent table.

"I will take a jar of rye beer and a small draught of wodki, if it pleases you?" Mas'ga smiled gratefully.

"Of course, friend, for it was good of you to come. You bring good news, I trust?"

"I received a communication from a trusted friend with an ear close to the Ur'gai Royal Counsel. Would you like to see it?"

"Is that necessary?" Akhenassor said guardedly.

"No. My contact assures me that the Royal visit to Chersonesus is scheduled for the day following the next Shabbat, as we expected" Mas'ga confessed. "The Banquet will take place in the Hall of the Guild of Merchant's, not at the City Father's Chambers. There will be a parade in the afternoon prior to the Banquet, and Her Majesty will be staying at the Hall of the City Father's, adjacent to the Temple of Zeus. Would this present a problem?"

"We have done our duty and have identified a group of dissidents in Nymphaion who pose a grave threat to Her Majesty" Akhenassor confirmed. "They have been closely monitored and we are ready to strike, if that is your desire?"

"Have your enquiries confirmed a specific threat to

Her Majesty's life?" Mas'ga pressed.

"Persian and Orch'tai treachery abounds in this city, especially of late" Akhenassor spoke sadly. "These dissidents are proclaimed enemies of our lawful Queen. They are enraged by the declaration of our Protectorate in the Crimea and, though it pains me so, they have the necessary resources and political connections to mount an attempt on the life of our beloved Queen."

"Then we are sworn to protect her, are we not?" Mas'ga sipped his drink.

"Our dear friends, Agur'ki and Aeschylla, have reconnoitred the lie of the ground in Chersonesus and, once again, I am at pains to report we have much to fear, especially at the hands of determined assassins!" Akhenassor sighed sadly.

"Please continue, dear friend" Mas'ga implored.

"The principal threat we identify comes not from the ground, as we discussed, but from the rooftops. We believe they will attempt to assassinate Her Majesty with a longbow! There is rumour a skilled hunter from the forests of the coastal plains has been engaged to undertake the assassination of our beloved Queen!" Akhenassor seemed bewildered by the prospect.

Mas'ga sighs sadly. He drains the remnant of his wodki in a single gulp. "Things are worse than we could ever have imagined?" he grimaced with distaste.

"Do you have the weapon?" Aeschylla spoke softly. "May I be permitted to see it?"

"Of course, my Lady, but such a weapon as this, it has not been constructed to be used by a woman."

"I simply requested to see such a wonder, nothing more" Aeschylla flashed her teeth and fluttered her eyelashes provocatively.

Mas'ga grins and retrieves the wooden case. It is some three foot long, eight inches wide, and three inches in depth. He lays it on the corner table in front of the group.

He flicks the bronze clasps on either side and removes the lid to reveal his masterpiece. Soon thereafter, the weapon is assembled and the three natives gaze at it in wonder. Also inside the case was a leather quiver of tailor-made arrows. "There is nothing like it in the known world!" Mas'ga said proudly.

"How do you load such a thing?" Aeschylla purred.

"It is quite simple, my Lady. I will demonstrate it for you."

Mas'ga cradled the weapon in both arms and nodded to the cocking-lever, which was in its forward position with the bowstrings slack. "You simply retract the lever to its rear position here, to the rear of the trigger mechanism. As you can see, the trigger itself is not taut, as the weapon is not loaded. Yet, when I pull this to the rear and the bowstring is drawn back, the trigger is now taut and ready to fire. It requires strength, of course, perhaps beyond the capacities of a woman or child, but any man could, do it?"

"Of course, I understand" Aeschylla smiled tightly.

"And then?" Akhenassor interjected.

"You simply slide an arrow into position, just like this" Mas'ga plucks an arrow from the quiver and lays it in the grooved carrier which ran the entire length of the stock to terminate in the centrepiece at the front.

"Have you tested the weapon?" Akhenassor pressed.

"I have, my friend! I can report that is both powerful and highly accurate. I have even tested in the woodland outside of Panticapaeum. It is unparalleled" he smiled with satisfaction at the deathly portent of his creation.

"Is it heavy?" Aeschylla asked interestedly.

"It could be hefted by a moderately strong man, but never a child or a woman."

"I see" said Aeschylla. "May I?"

"My Lady?" Mas'ga was astounded.

"Darling Aeschylla is no ordinary lady, I can assure of that" Akhenassor smiled thinly.

"It can be fired from a sitting or a prone position. In the interest of accuracy, you may wish to balance the front piece upon a rest of some kind."

"Can it be fired from the hip?" Aeschylla had taken hold of the weapon and was testing the wight of it in her hands. It was nowhere near as heavy as the fool claimed, and most of the weight was positioned at the front, as she had correctly deduced. "I do see what you mean, friend. In the interests of accuracy, it would be best to balance the front of the weapon with some sort of rest" The woman stepped away from the group and strolled towards the window.

"Have you killed anything with it?" Akhenassor probed.

"I will freely admit that I have not yet tested the weapon on any living thing?"

"Not an entirely satisfactory state of affairs, is it, my love?" Agur'ki spoke for the first time.

Aeschylla smiled sweetly. "You are quite correct, my love, as you so often are! We will correct this deficiency with haste, shall we not?"

"My Lady?" Mas'ga gaped at the woman, who gazed intently at the deserted yard. Suddenly, he understood everything. "No!" he screamed.

Aeschylla pivoted lithely on the balls of her feet and turned towards the group, steadying her stance, right foot in front of the left, the weapon held tight at her right hip, front piece levelled dangerously at Mas'ga's belly. She fired. The recoil was astounding, yet not perhaps as astounding as the sharp crack as the arrow passed cleanly through Mas'ga's left side and buried itself deep within the wall behind. The man did not even utter a scream. Mas'ga's face contorted in agony, his last breath hissing from his lungs, before slumping to the floor, bleeding copiously. Aeschylla shrieked with glee. "It is most satisfactory, is it not?" she addressed her comrades.

"What will we do with his body?" Agur'ki asked Akhenassor.

"We need to get rid of it. It is imperative that he is not discovered" Akhenassor said firmly.

"Take him to the woodland and let the carrion feast upon him!" Aeschylla smiled sweetly.

~

A woman passes through the Royal Guards stationed at the gate and enters the Royal Enclosure. On the far side of the central green, a man sits at a table in the shade of a canopy. Glancing up, he espies the woman and waves. He strolls across the green to greet her.

"If you have come to see Her Royal Majesty, my Lady, I fear she has not yet returned from riding" the man smiled brightly.

"A pity, to be sure. Perhaps I shall return tomorrow" the woman sighed wistfully. "Is your husband away hunting again, my Lady?"

"Yes."

"Perhaps you would care to join me for a goblet of wine? It is a hot day, is it not?"

"When it is not? Your kind offer of refreshments would be most gracious."

The man leads the woman across the green to the table in the shade. There are two chairs and two goblets. "Please be seated, my Lady."

"I came as soon as I could. I presume you have news?" said the woman.

"Indeed, I do, for I would not have requested a meeting otherwise?" said the man.

"What news of that bitch? That feral Sauromatae cunt!" the woman hissed.

"I have heard nothing of her travails, my sweet. You must be patient, for it could be weeks, perhaps even a new moon, before we learn of her fate."

"Is this about Chersonesus, then?" the woman pressed.

"I have news of your new dress, my love. A merchant will be arriving at the camp within the next few days. He will be carrying the latest creations from Corinth and Susa. Would that please you, my love?"

"It would, my sweet, and you have kept your promise to me, after all?"

"Did you ever doubt me, my sweet?" the man soothed.

"There were moments, I freely confess, for you are another woman's husband, are you not?" the woman said silkily.

"As you are another man's wife, my darling, are you not? Is your husband out whoring?"

"Do not taunt me! Of course, he is! A man has his appetites, does he not?" the woman bridled.

"You bear his shame, and his neglect, with commendable fortitude. It pains me to see you treated so shabbily, it truly does" the man said silkily. "Your hair is damp. Have you bathed recently?"

The woman smiled mischievously. "I have only just bathed, my love! And I am fresh and wanton!"

"For a woman too has her needs, does she not?" the man teased.

"You speak too freely, and with such an idle tongue. You might put that tongue to more enlightened endeavours" the woman purred.

"You shall be the belle of the ball, my darling Princess, I promise you, my love."

"And what are your promises worth to me, my sweet?" the woman sighed.

"My tongue could never lie to you, my darling rose?" the man simpered.

"Then use that idle tongue of yours to please me, all of me!" the woman whispered hungrily.

⌒

311

It was early evening in the city of Nymphaion. The moon had risen, yet it would still be light for a few hours more. On this evening, the night before the Shabbat, the Mercantile District of the Northern Quarter, just beyond the North Gate, had long since bade farewell to its shoppers and was now closing for the day. Its streets were deserted, save for the merchants and staff, who were busily packing their wares in storerooms or loading them on to carts to be ferried to the warehouses beyond the East Gate. There would be no trade on the morrow. Within the gradually dimming hum, an elegantly attired man pads solemnly through the narrow lanes between the stalls, occasionally stopping to chat briefly with a trader. The man is accompanied by two burly retainers, each sporting a heavy pine staff and aged iron sword, who had sworn a life debt to protect their master from harm. The weapons were a necessity, for their master was neither short of money nor enemies, for he was Iaestes, the shrewdest and most despised money lender in all Nymphaion!

Iaestes was making the last rounds of his collections among the merchants and, soon afterwards, he and his retainers stroll cheerfully past the Polis Militia Guards at the North Gate and head toward the Business District and, beyond it to the west, the Market Square. Iaestes made his final collections from the credit dealers and merchants, before retiring to a private room of *The Merchant's Chalice*, where he refreshed himself with a draught of the famed rye beer and a small goblet of plum wodki. An hour later, whilst the sun was fading in the sky, he threads his way across the Market Square, heading diagonally south of the Business District on the west side of Olympus Way, towards the Central Square and a carriage that would spirit him to his apartment in the Northern Quarter. Whilst Iaestes had many enemies, and it was well-know that he made his weekly collections on the eve before the Shabbat, he had never been mugged, and felt safe in the company of his minders. It never occurred to him that there were those in Nymphaion whom, for obvious reasons, had long since decided that his lucrative business should be foreclosed at the earliest opportunity.

Aeschylla lay flat on a table stationed a desired distance away from an open window of a top-floor apartment, with a perfect view of the Market Square and the adjacent buildings below. The loaded crossbow, constructed to her specifications by Mas'ga the armourer, is now trained on her unsuspecting target as he strolls leisurely toward his waiting carriage. Her finger curls lovingly around the trigger. She smiles thinly as she steadies her breathing and, holding the exhale, she fires, her lips pursing as her breath is released. Iaestes did not scream! He died instantly as the arrow, never a quarrel, punched through his ribs to sear his heart. He collapsed immediately and bled copiously. His minders were paralysed by terror, then, their wits recovered, they turned on their heels and sprinted towards the cover of the alleyways of the Business District. There was nothing they could do for poor Iaestes, for he was surely dead, murdered with a lethal insouciance by a concealed killer.

Aeschylla wraps the disassembled weapon and the quiver of tailor-made arrows in a heavy muslin cloth and leaves the apartment. This had been sourced the previous afternoon by Akhenassor from a letting agent who for a princely sum with no questions asked. A play was scheduled at the Theatre for the following evening and the apartments were in high demand. She skips gaily down the steps to the wagon where her beloved Agur'ki awaited her. "Did everything go well, my treasure?" he enquired mildly.

"Iaestes made his final collection, my sweet. You have my assurances on that."

"Did I ever doubt you, my rose? And now, how should we celebrate such good fortune?"

"I wish to fuck like an animal! Would you entreat me, my little pearl?" she simpered.

ELEVEN

The man was tall, muscular, and adorned with a terrifying collage of inking's, including on his face. He is a Briton, a scion of the infamous 'cursed isles', located off the wilds of the North Atlantic coast of Gaul. The man's name is Sorriwen. He waved through the evening throng in the public bar of *The Mermaid and Moonbeam* in Panticapaeum, heading for a large table at the far end. The table is occupied by a gang of gruff-looking foreigners. Most of the regulars give them a wide berth, for they have gained something of a reputation in Panticapaeum these past few months. Their leader, a blonde-haired colossus of a Gaul, espies the approaching Briton and scowls. He is Orbellin, eldest son and heir to a North Atlantic Chieftain.

"Where the fuck have you been?" Orbellin demanded.

"I have been to see our mutual friends, my Lord. They have an intriguing new assignment for us" Sorriwen smiled brightly.

"And what would that be?" Orbellin asked guardedly.

"They wish us to widen our nets for the elusive 'gold witch'!"

Orbellin scowled and reached for his tankard of rye beer. "Does she even exist? There have been no sightings of her here in Panticapaeum." He drained his beer and laid the tankard down on the table, glowering malevolently at the man sat at the far end of the table. "That jar won't fill itself, cunt!"

"Which is why they wish us to sally forth to pastures new" Sorriwen sighed happily. "They seem to think our elusive badger has a set in Nymphaion."

"They want us to start searching Nymphaion, is that it?"

"That, dear friend, is precisely what they desire" Sorriwen seemed enthused by the prospect of a new adventure.

"They want this bitch alive?" Orbellin growled. He was not in good humour.

"It would please King Darius, by all accounts" said Sorriwen.

"Not in the business of pleasing King Darius, are we? Nor do we take orders from his lickspittle, Nichassor!"

"They are our paymasters, my Lord! We are a long way from home. We would all do well to remember that." Sorriwen cautioned.

"She is a feisty little runt, this 'gold witch', is she not?" Orbellin grimaced.

"She is good with both blade and bow, by all accounts. She is a resourceful and dangerous enemy."

A young serving girl morphs at the side of the table, ferrying a tray of tankards filled with rye beer. Sorriwen smiles graciously and flips the girl a single bronze disk. It will cover the cost of the drinks and a generous tip. The girl smiles sweetly and disappears. Orbellin watches her leave.

"Tidy little arse on that! We have faced worse, have we not? And we have slain far worse, haven't we? That heathen swine from north of the Danube, you remember them?"

Sorriwen grinned. "They were Germanic filth! They die all too easily!"

"We have no idea where this 'gold witch' is? Do these fuckers expect us to spend a better part of the rest of our lives seeking her, as pigs on a truffle?" Orbellin scowled.

"Our enquiries in Panticapaeum have uncovered

nothing, as yet" Sorriwen confessed.

"And so, we head south to Nymphaion?" Orbellin sighed irritably.

"The Orch'tai have contacted certain friends in the City Administration. They have a billet prepared in the Upmarket District. We could be there in a little more than an hour!" Sorriwen confided.

"Very nice of them, I am sure! How many men do they wish us to take?"

"No more than six would be advised, my Lord. After all, we do not wish to draw unnecessary attention to ourselves, do we?" confirmed Sorriwen.

"Of course, we do not!" Orbellin replied testily. "Have you arranged transportation?"

"Everything is ready, my Lord. We could leave within the hour."

"Fine by me, within the hour it is! Those bastards better have stocked the place with decent wine" he smiled thinly.

"Not as good as we have at home though, eh?" Sorriwen smiled slyly.

"But you are a Briton, old friend. You people prefer beer?" Orbellin ventured airily.

"That is true, my Lord. And yet, as our Persian paymasters seem so fond of reminding us, we are a long way from home, are we not?"

"Fuck those cunts! We shall deal with those 'Gypo's when all of this is done!"

~

Nymphaion, July 493 BC

Corelya scaled the rear wall of the property with ease and nestled close to the wall, concealed within the undergrowth. She warily eyed the track that skirted the coastline for any sign of fellow travellers, before breaking cover and journeying south. She wore a tattered black cloak, its hood drawn close, and openly carried a heavy pine staff. Whilst she had left her sword back at the villa, she wore her sword-and-cross-belt around her naked hips with the twin daggers in their sheaths at her left side. She followed the track south until she had cleared the rear wall of the first villa at the junction with First Street. The paved causeway segregated the villas from the palatial townhouses of the most northerly part of the Upmarket District, principal residential area of the Northern Quarter. She turned right, crossed the road, and immediately headed left along North Lane East, which ran parallel to the east of the North Road for its entirety to the intersection with Nymphaion Way, the main west-east road that ran parallel to the North Wall of the city itself.

The child crossed the intersection with Third Street, demarcating the townhouses of the wealthiest merchant families from the salubrious apartments favoured by the political and less wealthy merchant classes. Corelya continued south along North Lane East until she finally arrived at the intersection with West Street, the main east-west thoroughfare of the Northern Quarter. To the west, at the intersection with the North Road, is the famed Vintner's District, yet if one turned east, as Corelya now did, you were heading directly towards the coast itself and, via the Avenue, the North Quay and Docklands. Corelya's destination this night was an address in the northern part of the Southern Quarter yet, in the interests of security, she had elected to arrive circuitously, without ever passing through walls of the city itself. Whilst she had taken all necessary precautions, in truth she had not expected to encounter her enemies in the Northern Quarter, for it would surely be the last place they would seek her. The fugitive was now embarking upon the most dangerous part of her journey, for the Wharf and Docklands were notorious havens of criminals and killers. Here, even the poorest beggar-child would attract attention if she were a stranger. It was imperative that she avoided the Avenue, the Docklands, and the Warehouse District, which lay immediately to the west of the sea front.

Corelya turned right and headed west along Nymphaion Way, for a course, before heading south, weaving through the lanes and alleys of the Residential District of the Eastern Quarter, warily avoiding congregations of strangers who huddled on street corners. The streets were busy, for there was much trade at this time of the year, most of it casual. Flocks of eager young prostitutes huddled at every street corner, beggars were legion, and gangs of organised pickpockets and footpads warily scanned the streets in search of easy pickings.

Few took notice of the scruffy child who wandered amongst them with her formidable pine staff. Soon enough Corelya had crossed the Athena Way, main thoroughfare of the Eastern Quarter leading directly to the East Gate and Central Square, and now travelled south along Olive Street. Not surprisingly, given the hour, Olive Street was thronging with carriages and pedestrians, for this was home to both *The Mount Olympus* tavern and *The Delphine*, the most salubrious Pleasure Garden in all Nymphaion.

At the end of Olive Street, she headed west along Poseidon Way, which ran parallel to the south wall of the city, then tacked south through the Baker's District, thence west until she reached Euboea Square, situated in the prosperous northern district of the Southern Quarter. Presently, she came to the premises of Sokos, a renowned merchant of fine ceramics to the Ur'gai Royal Court. Despite being a Theban by birth, Sokos was an agent of Corinth and a trusted ally of the Ur'gai. Corelya rapped a coded tattoo on the door: one-two-three, one-two, one-two-three, and one! Presently, she heard a noise from within, close to the door, and repeated the sequence once more.

"Who is that?" a voice enquired testily.

"My Lady sent me, my Lord! She urgently requires

ceramics, the finest you have" Corelya replied.

"Inform your Lady that we are closed for the evening. She should send you tomorrow."

"My Lady is most insistent, my Lord. She will not take no for an answer."

"Does your Lady pay in gold?" the voice mocked.

"Don't push your luck, Sokos! Your price is never higher than silver!" she chided.

The door opened fractionally and Corelya stared down the furrow of a loaded crossbow. "I think you had better come inside, child?"

Corelya stepped through the door which closed firmly behind her. She turned to face Sokos and drew back her hood.

"Sweet Hera!" Sokos gaped in awe. "How much did you pay for that?" he grinned at Corelya's battered face.

"More than enough, and that should be enough for you! It was money well spent, if you ask me" Corelya replied.

"They will do far worse to you if they catch you alive. You do know that Corelya?" Sokos mused sadly.

"Yes" Corelya replied simply.

The old man is startled and saddened by the young girl's easy acceptance of the will of the Fates. "The Persians want you alive, if possible. That is the rumour" he shrugged ruefully.

"I figured as much. Things are far worse than any of us could have imagined."

"You look like you could do with a drink?" Sokos smiled brightly.

"A small wodki, if you please? We have much to discuss" said Corelya.

～

Saiga Plains, Crimea, July 493 BC

The woman sips her wine and scowls. Her reaction to the revelations seems to amuse the man. He sits opposite, nursing a small goblet of plum wodki. "Is there something wrong with the wine, my sweet?" he smiled thinly.

"I fear that there is something wrong with your wits! The Queen will not stand for this. You do know that don't you?" said the woman.

"The Queen will never know of the matter. I have no intention of telling her, do you?" said the man.

"Of course not!" the woman snapped. "It has to be tonight?"

"Yes. We need to move fast. Things are becoming dangerous."

"Perhaps our friends will do us the favour of killing Corelya?" the woman grinned wolfishly.

"Perhaps they shall. Now there is this Nichassor fellow to contend with. I have composed a request for as much information on him as possible. It could take weeks for any intelligence to reach us."

"You think that that little whore-bitch, Yari, may be a source of useful information?"

"Any information on this Nichassor would be of considerable import" the man sighed. "There are rumours, unconfirmed as these things so often are, that the Orch'tai are extending their patrols along the north-eastern fringes of the Azovi Sea into our own territory. Why would they not seek to control its southern margins and, by extension, secure an alternate gateway to the Crimea?"

"The Argata would see that as an act of war!" the woman protested.

"Not if the Persians have persuaded them of the merits of the ploy, my sweet."

"We have much to fear, do we not?" the woman whispered.

"We have accomplished much, my sweetheart. The tides are surely moving in our favour. Yet, we have this pesky child to contend with."

"Then kill her!" the woman scowled.

"The Queen would never sanction it, not unless she is tainted as a traitor" the man soothed.

"We have at least planted a seed of doubt in her mind, have we not?"

"The Queen trusts Corelya, my flower! She is, after all, Her Majesty's Royal Retainer" the man cautioned.

"But if we could poison her mind against the other little bitch?" the woman ventured.

"Have you spoken to her?" asked the man.

"Not on the matter of Yari? I have not had chance. Her Royal Majesty returned to her Chamber and has spent the past few hours brooding."

"A good sign, surely, that Illir'ya is worried! Has word spread about what happened this afternoon?"

"I would think that everyone has learned that Yari and Korta are under arrest. Do you think that could work in our favour?" the woman seemed bemused by the affair.

"Popular resentment against Yari and Corelya might be useful leverage over the young Queen. She might be more readily persuaded to do her Royal duty" the man ventured wolfishly.

"And put them to death?" the woman purred.

"If they are widely perceived to be traitors, that would be the common consensus, you would agree?"

"Then we must persuade Her Majesty of the merits of keeping Yari under arrest?"

"Sag'ra will not be difficult to persuade, not after the way she ruffled his feathers at Counsel! But the Kor'nai and Naz'mir...?"

"You have him wrapped around your little finger, don't you?" the woman smiled slyly.

"Sag'ra is vain and shallow, yet he is also ambitious. He dreams of the Crown?"

"Then his sister must die" the woman whispered the words, almost as if she could scarcely credit that she herself had uttered them.

"If you hadn't already accustomed yourself to it, my Darling, that is precisely our objective" the man chided.

⌒

Corelya sits at a table. Sokos stands opposite, pouring two goblets of plum wodki from a ceramic flagon. He passes one to the girl, who sips it gratefully. Sokos sits down, facing the child, and appraises anew her battered face. "I am surprised you are not missing any teeth!"

"Have you made contact recently with the Royal Court?" she asked.

"I sent a coded despatch with a consignment of honey yesterday. It was safely delivered" Sokos confided. "You should be worried Corelya. Perhaps I should be, fool that I am! There is rumour that you have thrown your lot in with a Persian, a fellow called Nichassor, and that you colluded in a plot to murder the Argata Queen."

"None of it is true!" Corelya retorted. "Nichassor informed me that rumour of a plot against Lezika was circulating in Qu'ehra. If you could credit such a thing, the Ur'gai Royal Court was its instigator! My own enquiries in Qu'ehra furnished nothing to substantiate it. After what happened a few days later, I wouldn't trust a thing that slimy bastard told me! Nichassor is as full of shit as a cow has feathers!"

Sokos chuckled. "There is word you were mixed up in a fight in the market in Qu'ehra and that Nichassor was wounded. Several assailants were killed. Also, two hired killers were done for later that night, one of them quite brutally! I presume they were your handiwork?" Sokos enquired searchingly.

"All of that is true" Corelya confirmed. "I suspect they were hired by the Orch'tai?"

"Why the Orch'tai? Surely Nichassor…?" Sokos gasped in astonishment.

"I have confirmed that at least one Orch'tai detachment is stationed deep in Argata territory. They were operating just south of Qu'ehra and engaged in an action against a band of brigands. You have heard of Seart'i?"

"I have heard of him, of course? I have also heard that he is no more?" Sokos smiled slyly. "It has caused something of a stir in Qu'ehra, though I suspect that few will be sorry to see them go!"

"Something is definitely going on, Sokos. Whatever it is, it seems to be directed towards destabilising trade and, with it, the *Accord*!" Corelya sipped her drink.

"What actually did happen in the woods south of Qu'ehra? No-one really seems to know?" Sokos smiled thinly.

"Seart'i and his brethren were annihilated. Sokos! It was a trap! Nichassor must have made a pact with Seart'i to kill me, but he had already made arrangements to deal with the matter himself!" Corelya smiled grimly.

"And Seart'i and his brother?"

"I killed Seart'i and his brother! It was revenge for the slaughter of my community, and countless others! Intriguingly, whatever Nichassor offered in return, Seart'i and his ilk didn't trust him to deliver? They double crossed Nichassor and attacked us as we were leaving."

"And how did you escape? You must concede that this looks more than a little suspicious?" Sokos spoke softly.

"I should break that flagon over your fucking head!" the child seethed with righteous fury. "I was lucky to escape with my life! Even that treacherous bastard Nichassor looked done for, at least for a time!"

"You think it possible these renegades had an arrangement with the Argata?" Sokos ventured.

"It is possible, of course! They have been their paymasters for years. I don't trust anything Nichassor told me, with one obvious exception! I think that the powers that be, both Orch'tai and Argata, had decided that Seart'i's band had taken their last ride!" Corelya smiled grimly.

"How does this phantom Orch'tai detachment fit in to all of this?"

"They looked pretty real when they were slaughtering the brigands, Sokos! Not to mention coursing me like a fucking hare!"

Sokos raises a hand to silence the girl's temper. "I apologise, Corelya. Please continue."

"As I have intimated, the attack by the brigands was desperate. Then, if you could even credit it, a detachment of Orch'tai cavalry appeared, seemingly from nowhere. I recognised their Commanding Officer in Qu'ehra, I am positive of it! Moreover, he recognised me. I can't yet put a face to a name, but I believe he is one of their rising stars and has recently been promoted to the command of an Ochta."

Sokos whistled. "So, the rumours are true? There *is* a military alliance between the Orch'tai and the Argata?" Sokos whistled.

"I can now provide a definitive answer to the virtues of those rumours. The Orch'tai have been extending their patrols along the fringes of the Azovi coast and now have a sizeable disposition within striking distance of the 'labyrinth'!" Corelya confessed. "There is no true de-militarised zone. Not unless these conditions were only ever supposed to apply to ourselves?"

"We know of the existence of a large concentration of troops in the vicinity of Astrach'yi, and of a substantial detachment stationed near Tanais. Yet, we have no precise intelligence on their whereabouts. It could be in either Orch'tai or Argata territory?" Sokos confided.

"I encountered some of their ilk to north of Qu'ehra, far beyond the border with the Argata!" Corelya confirmed. "They were slaughtering a Sauromatae family. Korta reckons they may even have been operating within our own territory, just south of Rost'eya along the fringes of the Donets. They are masquerading as brigands, yet their weapons are standard Orch'tai issue. Their attire is irregular, not standard issue. I killed them, well, most of them. That is when Nichassor showed up. He saved my life, the twat!"

"The meeting with Nichassor was entirely by chance?" Sokos smiled grimly.

"It most certainly was not by prior arrangement, if that is what you think!" Corelya hissed.

"Where is Nichassor now?" Sokos asked.

"I have no idea, I honestly don't. If I do find the bastard, I will kill him!" said Corelya emphatically.

Sokos sips his drink and eyes the girl closely. She was a dangerous enemy that much was true. "You elected to accompany him and his men to Qu'ehra?"

"What was I supposed to do? I had the poor orphan girl to consider! I had to come up with a plausible cover story as to why I was there in the first place. In any event, after all I subsequently learned, I am glad I did so" Corelya confessed.

"You would like me to get a message to Queen Illir'ya?" Sokos drained his wodki.

Corelya smiled tightly. "I will be staying on in Nymphaion, Sokos. There is obviously something troubling afoot! Whatever it is, I have a distinct feeling that I have upset the apple cart. This might work to our advantage, if we can draw the conspirators and traitors out of the shadows."

"This place swarms with the agents of Persia. Not to mention, traitors and malcontents!"

Corelya grins and sips her drink. It tasted heavenly. "We have known as much for some time, old friend. Things could get very dangerous, for all of us!"

"What do you require of me?" Sokos smiled wryly.

"I have accommodation in the Southern Quarter. I won't tell you the location, for obvious reasons. I require an alternative billet, simply as a precaution. Can you help me?"

"I have a rented room here in the Southern Quarter that is currently available. It is attached to Cosimandes Saddlery, just down the street. It is basic, yet will suffice for your current needs?"

"Then it will do. I need you to inform the Royal Counsel that I am safe and that I have made contact. I will remain here to attend to other matters. The Counsel will know precisely what it is I am alluding to, if Korta made it safely to the Saiga Plains?" Corelya implored.

"You don't trust me, is that it? And, for your information, he did!" Sokos smiled wryly.

"I do trust you, Sokos. It is best that you know as little as possible, at least for the moment."

Sokos drains his goblet and rises from his chair. He strolls across the room to a chest of drawers and fishes out a key. He slides this across the table to Corelya. "I will draft a message tonight. This will be delivered to the Queen tomorrow; you have my word on that! That is for the room at Cosimandes."

"Thank you, Sokos. I am in your debt, upon my honour" Corelya drained her wodki, graciously refused a refill, and bade him goodnight.

"No more the moon, sweet child!"

"No more the moon!"

⌁

A Captain of the Royal Guard enters the tent in the company of two other guards. They approach the sleeping figure in the far corner. The child is shrouded in a blanket. The Captain of the Guard carries a sword, shield, and a heavy pine staff, which is used to prod the prisoner from their slumber. A scowling Yari gazes up at the soldier in disgust.

"Pack that in!" she hissed.

"Get up!" the senior Guard commanded. Yari stood. "Bind and blindfold her!" The blindfold was tied tightly around her head by the two other guards.

"Where are you taking me at this unholy hour?"

"Silence traitor!" the senior guard hissed.

"Fair enough! I have sod all to say to you, anyway!"

The captain slaps the girl hard across the face. "If you have a mind to, you will still that heathen tongue of yours!" he warned.

Yari grinned. "That heathen tongue of mine could make you come like a treat!"

The guard slaps the girl a second time. "Hold your hands out in front." Yari did as she was instructed, and her hands were tightly lashed at the wrists. "Lead her out!"

Yari is dragged out of the tent by the two-armed guards some distance from the entrance. She can smell the horse, though she cannot see it. "Lay her down!" With that command, Yari was picked up and placed down on her back on what felt like a wooden sled. "Bind her! Make sure that she is secure!"

A short while thereafter, Yari heard the distinctive sound of a lash striking a horse's flank and they began to canter away from the tent. Yari was not afraid. If it were fated that she should meet her end this night, then she would do so with the pride of an *Amazon*.

"Scythian slime! I am a Sauromatae daughter, you heathen fuck-pigs!" Yari hisses.

After Corelya had left, Sokos busied himself drafting a communique to be delivered with haste the following morning to the Ur'gai Royal Court on the Saiga Plains. He would entrust his eldest son, Hektor, with this duty. Hektor was heading to Chersonesus anyway, for a pre-arranged meeting with a trusted Merchant, and the Royal

Camp lay only a short distance from the Causeway. The message was drafted, rolled into a scroll, and slipped inside a hollow silver tube. This was then sealed at both ends with beeswax. It read as follows:

> *You seek the "gold witch"? – I have seen her*
> *She is alive and loyal – no treachery to fear*
> *No news of Nichassor – will keep mindful ear*
> *Troubling news from the East – alliance beware*
> *Urgent contact requested – at Saddler's lair*

The ingot is secreted within his robes. Fortified with a night-cap of wodki, Sokos retires to his room, blithely unaware of the consequences of his blind loyalty. The coded communique would ultimately seal his own, and Hektor's, fates.

The ropes which bound Yari's to the sled were cut and she was lifted respectfully to her feet by two Guards, most likely those who had bound her in the beginning, before being escorted inside a large tent. She could feel the heat from the fire-pit in the far corner. She remained blindfolded, with her hands bound at the wrists in front of her.

"Hold your arms out straight in front!" a voice commanded. It was a man's voice, but not that of the captain who had roused her from her slumber, Yari thought.

Yari did so and the rope binding her wrists were cut. "Keep your arms where they are!" a new voice rapped. Yari recognised the voice. It was Zar'cha. Strangely enough, given the circumstances, the presence of the Commander of Her Majesty's Royal Guard reassured the child. Once again, she obeyed the command. "Remove your clothes!" Zar'cha clipped.

"Excuse me!" Yari gasped.

"Naked, you little whore!" Zar'cha hissed.

"Sweet Tabiti! You must be horny? Have you tired of your Handmaiden's brother?" Yari sneered as she removed her kurta and britches.

While she had none of Corelya's brazen confidence, she was unashamed of her nakedness and burned with the same Sauromatae fire. Zar'cha slid a knife blade gingerly against Yari's cheek. The blade slipped between her hair and the blindfold, and this was swiftly severed, falling to the floor. Yari gazed around her. She was in a tent facing a single man. There was a fire to the left of her in its centre. Zar'cha stood behind her.

"I do hope that you have not been overly inconvenienced?" Alazar enquired politely.

"Not at all, Honourable Counsellor. I rather enjoy being woken up in the early hours of the morning by heavily armed guards, being trussed and blindfolded, thence dragged on a sled across the ground by a horse! Where am I, may I ask?"

"Is that important to you?" Alazar asked.

"Not if you intend to kill me. But if Zar'cha intends to ravish me then it may be of some small import, simply for posterity's sake."

"You are a confident little bitch, aren't you? Just like that other feral cunt!" Zar'cha scowled. She stepped around Yari and stood a few paces in front of her, appraising the child's virtues. "Given a few years of growth, you might make quite the bedfellow, little whore! It's probably all your fit for! Is it not, slave?" she chided. Zar'cha turned to the remaining Guard who now stood to Yari's right. "Would you like to fuck her? I can assure you that she is fresh!"

The Guard remained tight-lipped. Alazar raised an eyebrow at Zar'cha and smiled at Yari. "You stand in taint of treason, Yari. You surely understand the significance of the charge, and its consequences?"

"Who am I have alleged to have betrayed, Honourable

Counsellor? Is it you, or is it my loyal Queen? Please don't tell me I have committed treason against *that*?" Yari cocked a snook at Zar'cha.

Zar'cha raised a hand to strike the child in fury. "Don't!" Alazar commanded. Zar'cha turned away and took her place obediently on a vacant chair next to Alazar.

"Where is Corelya now?" Alazar enquired.

"I have no idea. For all I know she could be back at camp" Yari replied sweetly.

"I assure you that she is not. According to our sources, she is probably hiding in Panticapaeum or Nymphaion. Which would *you* consider to be the most likely?"

"I have never been to Nymphaion. Nor has Corelya, at least to my knowledge."

"The Persians are hunting her. I thought that might at least be of some small concern to you?" Alazar smiled thinly, for he enjoyed the girl's initial shock at the revelation.

"Why are the Persians hunting her?" Yari asked coldly.

"She has betrayed them! Just as she has betrayed her lawful Queen! I have little doubt of her involvement in this alleged conspiracy to murder the Argata Queen and undermine the *Accord*!" Alazar quipped icily.

"Those allegations are pure rumour, Honourable Counsellor! You have no evidence to establish Corelya's treachery, have you?"

"We will endeavour to uncover the truth of the matter! And, when we have done so, there will be a trial!" Zar'cha spat.

Yari smiled sweetly at the woman she now openly despised. "*You* will endeavour to uncover the truth of the matter! Corelya has less to fear than I thought! You are scarcely the sharpest blade in the armoury!"

Alazar smiled wryly at the child, for it was now clear that he had misjudged her. He raised a hand to silence Zar'cha's rage. "As you are aware, Yari, a series of unfortunate incidents have occurred in Qu'ehra this past week. I harbour few doubts that this girl-child, this 'gold witch', so heavily implicated in these events is Corelya. Nor have I any doubt of her treachery with this Nichassor. Do you?" said Alazar.

"I think it is probable that Corelya was in Qu'ehra. Yet I do not think that she is in league with Nichassor. Neither of us ever really trusted him! Why should we?"

"So, you concur that it is likely that Corelya would have betrayed Nichassor, if the opportunity ever presented itself?"

"I think it far more likely that Nichassor would have betrayed Corelya, at any given opportunity?" Yari replied icily.

"Why is that?" Alazar seemed intrigued by the response. "Nichassor is a snake! Much like others I could mention!"

Alazar retained his composure, while Zar'cha smouldered. "Who is Nichassor? Our intelligence on him is admittedly sketchy. Perhaps you would care to enlighten us?"

"He is Persian, as you already know. Nichassor always claimed to be a trader, but neither Corelya nor I really believed him. The only thing that bastard sold was the poppies he harvested from our lands after the slaughter, and Corelya and I, with innumerable other children, as slaves!" Yari responded coldly.

"Is he a wealthy man, this Nichassor?"

"He hails from a good family" Yari sighed. "I learned a little more of him when Corelya was terribly ill, for she nearly died. Nichassor saved her life. He told me that he had been banished after he committed murder. Some Medes cheated his father over a shipment of silk from the East. Nichassor allegedly killed them for the insult to his honour."

"That doesn't answer the question?" Alazar clipped.

"He and his band live off the land. Yet there was always money to buy food when they needed to. And weapons! They were all armed with good iron swords and fine recurved bows. Their armour was mostly Hellenic. Such things cost money, don't they? My father never owned such a sword?"

"Perhaps that is why he died?" Zar'cha sneered.

Yari let the insult go, no matter how she burned with hatred. "We all die someday, Commander, even you?" she smiled sweetly.

"How many men were in Nichassor's band?" Alazar asked.

"I have no idea as to the present, do I? Back then there were twenty of them, but Nichassor said that he had more men on an errand in Qu'ehra. About fifteen, I think?"

"So, we could be dealing with a 'band' of possibly thirty-to-forty heavily armed men?" Alazar continued his interrogation.

"Surely our sources in Qu'ehra would have gathered more reliable information?"

"Perhaps they have, my child?" Alazar ventured airily.

"That is all I can tell you. I have no idea where either Corelya or Nichassor are right now. I do care about Corelya's well-being, obviously, but I couldn't give a fig about Nichassor!"

"You think that they are still together?"

Yari smiled wryly. "Don't you know?"

"We do not, insolent cur!" rapped Zar'cha.

"The picture is somewhat hazy, Yari, which is why I value your insights. According to our sources, Nichassor's band was badly mauled in a melee with a group of Armenian bandits in the plains to the south of Qu'ehra. Nichassor survived and returned to Qu'ehra, where he has made considerable efforts to locate the whereabouts of this 'gold witch'." Alazar smiled mischievously, as he savoured the bewilderment registered on the naked child's face.

"At least we know Corelya survived the fight with these Armenians!" Yari mused grimly.

"Perhaps this sordid little incident was in some way

related to the plot to murder the Argata Queen? The Armenians are no friends to the Argata, is that not so?" Alazar mused.

"Is that the best our intelligence sources in 'the lands between the seas' have come up with? You would have Corelya conspiring with the Miletans soon enough!" the child sneered. "You have no real idea where she is right now, do you?"

Alazar reclined lazily and studied the naked child afresh. There were hidden deaths to this slave bitch, that much was true! "We are liaising closely with our agents in both Panticapaeum and Nymphaion, for we suspect that Corelya has made it safely across the Straits. We will soon discover her whereabouts" Alazar confirmed.

"*No, you won't!*" Yari sneered inwardly. "May I get dressed now?"

"Of course," replied Alazar politely. His response surprised the child. Yari dressed quickly.

"Am I still under detention?"

"You are!" Zar'cha clipped coldly.

"Then perhaps you might bind and blindfold me again. I am tired and I would like to go back to bed."

Alazar raised a hand to silence Zar'cha's temper. "For the moment, you may go?"

Yari held her hands out, wrists crossed, and these are tightly bound by one of the guards. Yari remained silent throughout yet, as the guard stepped to the back of her to fasten the blindfold she spoke. "You will pass on my regards to Her Majesty, won't you? When you tell her and the rest of the Counsel about our little chat?" For a moment, the briefest of moments, Alazar's mask slipped and Yari saw the fear in his eyes.

Perhaps Corelya had been right after all, she mused silently to herself.

A single wagon arrived at the Royal Camp the following morning and halted at the piquet-line. The driver gave his name as Celen and claimed to represent a well-known merchant in Chersonesus called Mathos, a retainer of Her Royal Majesty, no less! He also claimed that he had been sent with re-assurances for Her Royal Majesty that a planned shipment of fine Hellenic wine would be duly delivered the following week. The visitor had brought several flagons of wine as a gift for Her Royal Majesty. Normally, the visitor would not have been ushered through the piquet line, yet the man had been most insistent and had asked for Gor'ya herself. A brief while later, Gor'ya arrived at the piquet line and shepherded the visitor through. The pair strolled north along the avenue towards the Royal Enclosure, leaving both wagon and wine in the custody of the Guards.

"You are well, fair Celen?" Gor'ya smiled sweetly.

"Indeed, I am, my Lady. And how is Her Royal Majesty?" Celen enquired.

"She is well. And your master fares well?"

"Mathos of Chersonesus is in good health, my Lady" Celen replied happily.

"Am I to take it that you have something for Her Majesty, other than the wine?" Gor'ya spoke in a whisper.

"Indeed, I do. My master was most insistent that this be delivered in person. I have an urgent communique for Queen Illir'ya."

As they reached the Royal Enclosure, Gor'ya gave the day's password and the Guards allowed them to pass. To Celen's astonishment, Her Majesty was sat with her three young Handmaidens, including the twins, Mis'cha and Mas'cha, on the grass in the central green, enjoying the morning's sun. Queen Illir'ya and her Handmaidens stood to greet Gor'ya and the visitor as they approached.

"Your Royal Highness!" Celen greeted the Queen with a bow and flourish. "I have come with re-assurances from

Mathos of Chersonesus. Your shipment of wine will be delivered as requested in the middle of next week."

"You must be tired from the long ride" the young Queen beamed at him. "Please come and sit. Would you arrange some refreshments, Gor'ya?"

"Of course, Your Majesty." Gor'ya approached the banqueting tent and rapped out a request for wine, wodki and several goblets.

"Your Majesty is most kind" said Celen graciously. "I was instructed by my master to give this to you in person" he handed over the hollow silver tube sealed with wax at both ends. To his astonishment, Her Majesty turned and handed the silver ingot to Gor'ya, who paced towards the entrance to the Audience Chamber. She disappeared inside.

"I trust Gor'ya with my life, Celen! She can certainly be trusted with urgent matters of State" Queen Illir'ya reproved her guest mildly.

"My master believes this matter to be of the utmost urgency. It pertains to certain recent developments in the east."

"I see" the Queen smiled tightly. "Please, you must be thirsty after such a long ride. Drink!"

⌒

Inside the Audience Chamber, Gor'ya sat at a table carefully worrying away the wax seal at both ends of the hollow silver tube with the sharp point of an ornate bronze needle. Once this had been cleared, the parchment was slid carefully out and unfurled. The coded script was Hellenic, a language with which Gor'ya was familiar. Yet, while the code itself was a mystery, what little she did comprehend gave grave cause for concern. The message, undeniably a communique of some urgency from a seasoned practitioner in the dark arts of espionage, read as follows:

Have the seasons turned so soon? Petals wilt on cherished blooms
Golden maiden – no more the moon – a Nymphs glory, seek warily
Serpent's milk – Persia's curse – Eastern riches – Medusa's curls
Fruits of labour – tainted joy – seek the Nymph – frustrate a boy!

As Gor'ya re-read the communique, she felt sure this 'golden maiden' was Corelya herself and, if it was, news of what had recently transpired in Qu'ehra must have reached the ears of the chief spymaster in the region. The reference to a 'serpent' also piqued her interest. *Had not the communique discovered by Korta, squirreled deep in the clothing of a corpse in the heart of the Great Steppe, alluded to a 'serpent' and Persia?* Surely this communique was the work of the same mind and hand? The Queen and Counsel must be told of its content immediately.

Gor'ya stepped out of the entrance of the tent and coughed lightly. Queen Illir'ya turned and, seeing the worried expression on her trusted confidante's face, immediately went to speak with her.

"Is it troubling news?" the Queen asked softly.

"I fear so, Your Highness" Gor'ya confessed. "I am certain this concerns Corelya and that it hails from our new Hellenic source. There are obvious correspondences with the communique Korta discovered near Rost'eya. I freely admit there is much in this that I cannot comprehend."

"If only Corelya were here?" the young Queen sighed sadly.

"I simply don't believe that Corelya is a traitor, whatever some others may think!" Gor'ya remonstrated hotly.

"I will assemble my Counsellors," said the Queen.

"Begging your grace, Your Majesty, perhaps Korta may be able to shed some light on this?" Gor'ya ventured.

"That will not please either Sag'ra or Alazar?"

"There is only one mind equal to Corelya's in matters such as this, isn't there?"

"Have the guards fetch Korta immediately." Queen

Illir'ya turned back to Celen and flashed him a smile. "Thank you for your service, young man. Tell your master that I will not forget it."

With a bow and a flourish, Celen bade his farewell to the Ur'gai Queen. He returned presently to the piquet line, where his horses had been grazed and watered, a courtesy extended to all guests of the Ur'gai. As he climbed aboard his wagon to return to Chersonesus, a single rider trotted past towards the piquet's. The man turned in his saddle and waved in greeting. Celen instinctively waved back. Both the man and the horse looked tired, like they had ridden hard for several hours. Whilst he could not be certain, Celen was sure he had seen the man before, perhaps even quite recently?

⌁

Korta smiled brightly as he heard a Senior Guard rap an order to his subordinates stationed outside the tent. "The Queen requests the prisoner to be brought to Counsel!"

"Sir!" the junior guards bark their reply.

"On your feet, old man!" the Senior Guard commanded as he entered the tent.

Korta rose unsteadily. His muscles ached with the lack of exercise over the past day. "Am I to be tried?"

"I know nothing of such things, old man. Only that the Queen requests your presence. You are to be unbound but unarmed."

"And Yari?" Korta pressed.

"My orders only pertain to you. Nevertheless, the child is safe and well. She has not yet been tried."

"You have no evidence of her treachery, nor of mine, for that matter?"

"That may be so, old Surgeon, but I have my orders to convey you to Her Majesty and Her Majesty's Counsel."

As they stepped outside into the morning sun, Korta

espies Gor'ya striding purposely across the grass towards them. "Wait here!" she commanded.

"My Lady?" the Senior Guard furrowed his brow in puzzlement.

"A messenger has just arrived at the piquet's. I would like to speak with him quickly and return. I will accompany you back to the Royal Enclosure" Gor'ya enlightened him.

"Yes, My Lady" the Senior Guard replied obediently.

Gor'ya turned to Korta and smiled brightly. "Are you well?"

"I could do with the exercise. Is there something afoot?" Korta's eyes twinkled expectantly.

"I think so. You are not in any trouble this time, I assure you. Just remember to keep your temper with the Queen's brother!"

"That shouldn't be too much to ask of me" Korta chuckled, stretching his arms and legs to work out the kinks in his tired muscles.

When Gor'ya returned, a short while later, she was positively buzzing with excitement and could barely contain the news so recently imparted to her. "Corelya is in Nymphaion! She has contacted one of our agents there. I have a coded message for the Queen!"

"Is she well?" Korta asked. He was obviously relieved, yet equally troubled.

"She is alive, albeit it rather worse for wear, from what I gather!" Gor'ya smiled ruefully. Her relief at the news was as palpable as her joy.

"She is incognito. She knows *they* are hunting her?" Korta felt no need to specify who '*they*' were.

"She knows. Nor is she in league with Nichassor. She wants to kill him, apparently."

"More fool Nichassor!" Korta mused coldly.

The woman strolled unannounced into the man's private chambers and sat down on a vacant chair. The man eyed her icily and rapped an order to his manservant. "Leave us!" The young teenager turned and disappeared outside. The man smiled thinly and appraised the woman closely, a twinkle of mischief gleaming in his pale eyes. "Is this wise, my Lady?"

"I thought you had all this under control. Perhaps you are not as clever as you think?" the woman hissed.

"This is most unfortunate news, to be sure" the man sighed exasperatedly. "I had hoped the Persians would do us all a service and kill the little Sauromatae bitch!"

"The Queen will not hear of her treachery now, will she?" said the woman.

"Not if the word of that silly errand girl is credited! It is all too clear that we have gravely misjudged the reliability of our allies in this matter! We must now exercise our own judgment, and do what we must, to fix things."

"How so?" clipped the woman.

"I have an idea. If this works, Corelya may yet die a traitor's death!" the man smiled serenely.

"You know how much it would please me to watch her die" the woman mused gleefully.

"Yet, we have another problem, do we not?" the man sighed exasperatedly.

"You refer to that irascible old fool, Korta?"

"He is a quarrelsome as he is meddlesome!" the man seethed. "He is also as slippery and as dangerous as an asp, for there are few who can match his mind in matters of espionage. Why could he not enjoy his retirement in his cabin in the forest?"

"Might we perhaps kill two birds with the same stone?" the woman ventured.

"I think we may kill several more, my sweet, and yet convince the Queen and Counsel of Corelya's treachery" the man smiled thinly. He had spent the past few hours exercising his mind to a timely and satisfying resolution of this pressing issue and had devised an ingenious solution that was certain to reap bountiful rewards! The ploy he intended to set in play had the rare beauty of simplicity itself.

It was child's play, no less!

⌁

"What is your opinion of all of this?" Queen Illir'ya directed her question to Korta.

"Begging your grace, Your Royal Highness, I concur with much of what has already been said. Taking the coded communiques, the one I discovered, and this recent one from Chersonesus, I believe they are from the same hand."

"There is surely no means to prove such a hypothesis?" ventured Alazar silkily.

"Begging your grace, Your Royal Highness, but all codes work on a set of simple principles. The correspondences between the two communiques are striking!" Korta replied evenly.

The Queen shot Alazar a warning glance. "Then carry on, my old friend" the Honourable Counsellor nodded politely.

"This source has learned that this 'golden maiden', almost certainly Corelya, is in mortal peril and that her capture, even death, has been ordered in the name of King Darius.

And yet, no communique could have reached Susa in so short a space of time? It is likely that our confidante has received a communique from an agent in possession of recent and more dated intelligence and, as such, it is difficult to distil fact from conjecture. Corelya and I suspected that the 'serpent' referred to a Hellenic agent in Susa, and this is confirmed by the allusions in this recent communique."

"We also have the apparent treachery of the Argata and Orch'tai to consider, have we not?" the Kor'nai interjected.

"Corelya revealed her suspicions when we met. It would now appear that she has uncovered evidence of military collusion between the Orch'tai and Argata in 'the lands between the seas'. This recent despatch from our new source alludes to an imminent end to the *Accord*, on two occasions, in the first and last lines. It is further intimated that such a drastic shift in the regional balance of power would be received favourably in Susa" Korta continued.

"Perhaps we are in danger of reading too much into this?" ventured Alazar.

"We would surely concur that Corelya's loyalty to the Crown is no longer in question?" interjected Naz'mir.

"Not by me!" Alazar stated baldly. The Queen turned to him and smiled sweetly. Korta was astounded by the Counsellors volte-face.

"If Corelya is in danger from the Persians, it can only be because of what she has discovered during her recent travels in Qu'ehra?" said the Kor'nai.

"I fear she is in grave danger, and not just from Persia and her agents. There are the Orch'tai and Argata sympathisers in Nymphaion to consider" ventured Naz'mir.

"If that is so, we must make valiant effort to extricate her - "*no more the moon*! It must surely be tonight?" Alazar proposed.

"Yet, we must proceed with caution, must we not?" advised the Kor'nai.

"Given that we know where she is, we could extricate her with a minimum of fuss. There is no necessity to undermine the *Accord* on our part, surely?" replied Alazar.

"You have a suggestion, Honourable Counsellor?" the Queen beseeched.

"With your grace, Your Majesty, I do."

"You may speak freely" the young Queen commanded.

"Any armed incursion in to Nymphaion would

potentially provoke an unwelcome military response, we would agree? Yet there are subtler methods, are there not?" Alazar let the question hang in the air. "Corelya trusts you Korta, more than anyone, save perhaps Her Majesty and young Gor'ya. I would recommend the following. We could infiltrate you in to Nymphaion, secretly, tonight or by tomorrow morning at the latest. You would require a cover story, obviously, and it might be better if you were not travelling alone?"

"Would you be willing to travel to Nymphaion, Korta?" the Queen beseeched.

"Of course, Your Majesty. Perhaps Gor'ya could accompany me? That would make for two friendly faces, rather than just the one. Even Yari, perhaps?"

"I would be willing to go!" Gor'ya said eagerly.

"I think it unwise to send someone so obviously tied to the Royal Counsel, dear Gor'ya. In my considered opinion, this situation requires a more subtle resolution, despite its urgency" Alazar interjected.

"Then Yari and I?" Korta replied.

"Yari is known to this Nichassor fellow, and you are not? There is a real possibility that she might be recognised?"

"A very moot point, Honourable Counsellor" said the Kor'nai. "I could go alone?" ventured Korta.

"I have no reservations as to either your loyalty to your Queen or your personal bravery, dear Korta, but I do not think it wise you travel alone" Alazar pressed. "Our objective is to extricate Corelya without attracting undue attention. A single armed stranger, in the current climate, might attract unnecessary interest from our adversaries. We must surely accept the reality that the child is actively sought by them?" Alazar soothed.

"Then who do we send to accompany Korta?" enquired the Queen.

"Why not send the twins, with their father, of course?" Alazar nodded in the direction of Mis'cha and Mas'cha, who exchanged excited glances with one another.

"You surely can't be serious?" the Kor'nai gasped. He glanced quickly at Gor'ya.

"Why not, may I ask?" exclaimed Alazar. "They are both known to Corelya and their presence with Korta, would re-assure her."

"Begging your pardon, Your Majesty, but I must protest. I do not agree with this ploy. There is too much that is dangerous!" Gor'ya chimed. The twins were momentarily crestfallen and gazed icily at Gor'ya, much to the older girl's discomfiture. They were obviously piqued at her brutal injunction of what seemed, to their innocent minds, a most welcome adventure.

"There are none in Nymphaion would harm them? We are, after all, a civilised people, are we not?" Alazar said silkily.

"Would you be willing to go to Nymphaion?" the Queen addressed the twins, barely six- years-old.

"Oh yes, Your Majesty!" they cooed expectantly.

"Then we shall leave early tomorrow morning. As soon as it is light" said Korta.

⌐

Alazar pours two large goblets of wodki and passes one across the table to his visitor. Commander Mos'chi, of Her Majesty's Royal Guard, sits in contemplative silence.

Alazar smiled thinly and raps his dismissal to the two-armed guards, stationed on either side of the entrance to his private chambers.

"You may leave us!"

The two guards leave the room. Alazar smiles brightly at the sullen thug perched uncomfortably in the elegant chair. "It is good of you to see me at such a late hour, Commander Mos'chi!" the Honourable Counsellor Alazar greeted the visitor in his private chambers. "Would you care for a small draught of wodki? I take it you are off duty?"

"A small draught of wodki would be most welcome, Honourable Counsellor, and thank you" Mos'chi replied respectfully, through gritted teeth. He was a professional soldier with a keen distrust of all politicians, no more so than this creature!

"Concerning this forthcoming mission to Nymphaion on the morrow, I have it on good authority that you will lead the scouting party in advance."

Mos'chi looked startled. "I have only just received the order myself, Honourable Counsellor! Yes, I do have that honour."

"You are taking a detail of good men with you, I presume? All trusted servants of Her Royal Majesty, loyal and faithful, no less?"

"Are we not all loyal and faithful servants of Her Royal Majesty?" Mos'chi replied woodenly.

"Of course, we are! Yet, there is more than a whiff of treachery in these most recent developments? Surely you have heard the whispers, for I doubt such rumours could have escaped the attention of Her Majesty's Royal Guard?"

Mos'chi smiled thinly, for, he despised the naked mendacity of the man sat opposite. "I have heard a little, of course. There is word of an apparent plot to murder the Argata Queen and destabilise the *Accord*. There is also rumour of a plot by dissident conspirators against the life of our own Queen?"

"This is a dangerous time, both for the Queen, and our people! We are surrounded by enemies, foreign and domestic, and these treacherous elements seek to destabilise the Duchy, provoke conflict with our neighbours, and even imperil the life of our beloved Queen!" Alazar opined.

"Begging your pardon, Honourable Counsellor, but I do not see how such factors impinge directly on our mission tomorrow morning?"

"Do I have your confidence, Commander?" Alazar

asked evenly.

"Of course, Honourable Counsellor, I am Her Royal Majesty's loyal servant."

"It might surprise you to learn that your name has been brought to my attention as a man I might implicitly trust in such a delicate matter as this. Your loyalty to the Crown, and to the Duchy, is not in question."

Mos'chi smiled tightly. "I see, Honourable Counsellor." For now, he did see.

"Let me enlighten you further." Alazar continued silkily. "It has been brought to the attention of Commander Zar'cha and I that a group of traitors and malcontents in Nymphaion plot to murder Queen Illir'ya at the Royal Banquet in Chersonesus, the day after the next Shabbat. Do I have your confidence and discretion in this grave matter of State?"

Mos'chi is visibly outraged by the revelation. His entire face suffuses purple. "You have my silence on this matter, Honourable Counsellor."

"We are liaising with our agents and sympathisers in Nymphaion to thwart such an outrage, yet these treacherous elements are cunning, resourceful, and surprisingly well-financed" Alazar confessed. "We have reason to suspect, and you will forgive me if I do not disclose names, that these dissidents have the allegiance of several leading lights on the Council of the City Father's and the Guild of Merchants. There is rumour of an assassin, a skilled hunter from the coastal fringe. We have yet to verify this last and most insidious claim. That is, that this hunter will be furnished with a weapon of unparalleled malice, do you understand?"

"You are talking about a 'lone wolf', are you not, Sir?" Mos'chi ventured uneasily.

"Would you credit such a ploy as plausible?" Alazar clipped.

"It is entirely plausible, my Lord, of course it is! Who

could fashion such a weapon?"

"You remember Commander Mas'ga, the Royal Armourer? Of course, you do?"

"You must surely be mistaken, Honourable Counsellor!" Mos'chi was aghast at the charge. "Commander Mas'ga involved in a plot to kill Queen Illir'ya! I simply cannot countenance such a thing! He retired to Panticapaeum, did he not?"

"Where he scratches a living mending battered farming implements, from what I gather. For a man with such a proud legacy, and a young family to clothe and feed, you can easily see how old loyalties might be corroded, can you not?"

"I can't believe what I'm hearing, Honourable Counsellor! This is outrageous!" Mos'chi gasped.

"It came as a profound shock to all of us, dear fellow! You may rest assured of that. Mas'ga has subsequently disappeared, at least according to our devoted agents in Panticapaeum. His young wife is fraught with worry?"

"You think Mas'ga is our 'lone wolf', Honourable Counsellor?"

"For myself, Commander Mos'chi, I put little faith in this theory of a 'lone wolf', stalking Her Royal Majesty from the rooftops, with a weapon that may not even exist! Do I malign you?" Alazar said silkily.

"Of course not, for a man in your position would be privy to secrets that a man such as I, a mere soldier, could never hope to comprehend" said Mos'chi.

"And so, it would be my solemn duty, as a loyal servant of Her Majesty, to enlighten you, dear fellow" Alazar smiled thinly and poured his guest a refill. "I do not credit the theory of a 'lone wolf'. However, I do fear Mas'ga became unwittingly involved in something he did not fully comprehend. In short, I believe a new weapon has been commissioned and, moreover, that poor Mas'ga was murdered, presumably at the behest of these treacherous dissidents in Nymphaion."

"I see, Sir, but if such a weapon exists...?"

"It is a ruse, nothing more" Alazar sighed. "Of course, we must take all necessary precautions, but I have received new intelligence! I will now share this with you, Commander Mos'chi. It directly pertains to tomorrow's mission, and it is truly chilling, in both its treachery and malice."

"Go on, Sir?" Mos'chi sipped his drink.

"These dissidents aim to decapitate the entire political hegemony of our Duchy, and of the City of Chersonesus, in one foul swoop. And I must emphasise the foul, my dear fellow, for is not poison amongst the vilest of methods?" Alazar sighed sadly.

"I would heartily agree, Sir, for it is known that poison is the purview of the woman."

Alazar smiled thinly. "Or a child, Commander, consider that, if you will! Now, if such a thing were to be conceived, it would surely involve an agent whose loyalty is beyond question? One endowed with the complete confidence of Her Royal Majesty?"

"Like one of Her Majesty's Handmaidens, perhaps?" Mos'chi ventured. "But surely, Sir, the little twins.?"

"Their loyalty is not in question, I assure you! Yet, the Sauromatae are renowned for their treachery, and with the assistance of a skilled Surgeon, one with unparalleled insights of toxins and their effects upon the human form.? Are you beginning to comprehend the scale of the terror we now face?"

"Indeed, I do, Sir!" Mos'chi was outraged by the revelation of such a sinister ploy.

"Corelya must be eliminated, do we understand one another?" Alazar looked steadily at the Commander.

"I do, Sir! Indeed, I do!"

"We know that she is presently in Nymphaion and that she has contacted at least one of our agents, possibly two. Regrettably, the loyalty of both is now in question and it is highly probable that they have thrown their lot in with these malignant dissidents, and their harpy of deliverance, that treacherous Sauromatae whore!"

"We could always pay them a little visit, my Lord. Carrying a token of Her Majesty's affection for their loyal service to the Crown, of course?" Mos'chi said

Alazar smiled brightly at the fool, for this was just his kind of brute! "I appreciate your enthusiasm, my good fellow, but that will not be necessary. I do, however, require your assistance. There is no other that I would trust!"

"You may only ask, my Lord, and it will be done!" Mos'chi clipped dutifully.

"We have loyal servants in the city of Nymphaion, which include the Guard of the Civis Militia, and these men are poised and ready to strike!" the Honourable Counsellor confided.

"I understand, Sir!"

"Corelya is a wily foe, Commander Mos'chi, and she is not to be underestimated. The twins are young and naive, yet their childish innocence could well be the key to unlock this vile conspiracy. Neither they, nor their father, and most certainly not that wicked serpent, to whom treachery comes as easily as breathing, must contact these treasonous elements! Do we understand one another, Commander?"

"I understand, Sir! I give you my word that it will be done" Mos'chi said coldly.

"Your advance party of scouts will be fated to meet one of the Commanders of the Civis Militia, a loyal soul named Mur'ga. He is Orch'tai, yet entirely dependable. He is also utterly devoted to King Tagar and the regional peace these traitors seek so insidiously to undermine."

"I will do my duty, Honourable Counsellor, no more, no less!" Mos'chi rapped.

"See that you do, Commander, for the entire future of our people depends upon it!"

TWELVE

Corelya waited until the early evening to venture out and appraise her new billet at Cosimandes' Saddlery. It was still light, yet the day's trading had long ceased in the Market Square and in the Merchant's Districts of the Northern and Southern Quarter. Minas and Nirch'ii had received an impromptu invite to the Annual Grand Dinner of the City Fathers and Guild of Merchants yet were in two minds whether to accept. Corelya had counselled them on the necessity of their attendance. It would be an act of supreme gracelessness not to. Nirch'ii had been plagued with doubt that she could ever convincingly carry off the part of a dutiful wife of a wealthy Hellenic merchant, not in front of an audience such as this, yet Corelya had fortified her with the following advice: "Smile rarely, feign detachment, and be appallingly rude to the serving staff! We may yet make a Queen of you!" Not that such naked bigotry could ever apply to Queen Illir'ya, a model of cultured deportment if ever there was, having been schooled in Athens. And yet, so too had her brother Sag'ra, at least for a time, and in Corelya's opinion, he was both uncultured brute and arsehole!

The Merchant's District was quiet when she arrived in the Southern Quarter. The few people she passed in the streets paid little heed to the child in a tatty black cloak armed with a heavy pine staff. In contrast, Corelya paid attention to everyone, particularly their accents, when she seldom heard them. Nymphaion's citizens were mostly of Hellenic descent but, as the colony had prospered and grown, immigrants from throughout the region had flocked there, including a few Persian families. For better or worse, the Persians tended to keep to themselves, yet it was likely that all would attend the Annual Grand Dinner. None of the accents of passing strangers alarmed her until, reaching Vintner's Row, a small cluster of properties on Grove Street to the far west of the docklands, she happened upon a shop that was apparently still trading. Therein, an animated discussion was being conducted in a bewildering cacophony of dialects. An empty wagon stood stationed outside the gate, ready to move, yet there was no sign of the driver. Corelya slipped stealthily into a small passage between the yard and an adjacent Vintner's premises to eavesdrop on the disputation.

"This is daylight robbery! What do you take us for?" growled a disgruntled customer in broken Hellenic.

"You have requested only the finest Gaulish wine, Sir?" the Vintner beseeched. "This has come all the way from Massalia. You have been to Massalia?"

"Frequently, as it happens, and we have never paid prices such as this before?" the first man snorted.

"But such 'luxuries' are expensive here" the Vintner said silkily.

"What the fuck is he on about, *luxuries*?" another voice growled in an alien tongue. "This is the cheapest shit they ply in Massalia! That is why we asked for it. I care little for that poncy shit they drink in the Bordeaux!"

"I cannot understand your friend, he does not speak Hellenic?" the Vintner stated icily.

"He wonders why you don't speak Hellenic?" the first man turned to the second.

"Because I am not from there, am I?" the man growled. "Never been to fucking Greece, have I? I don't fucking want to either. Pack of fucking tunic-lifters, the poncy bastards!"

"My friend is from just north of Massalia. He is a Gaul.

He cannot understand why we must pay such prices?"

"Well, there is the *tax*, for starters. Then there are the import duties, of course" the Vintner smiled.

That information was relayed by an alien tongue to the second man by his companion. It did not have the soothing effect the Vintner had hoped. "Does this tit think I'm touched, or something? We know this! Why are his prices higher than the Vintner's in Panticapaeum?" the second man fumed.

"Your prices are much higher than in Panticapaeum, where we have recently been?" said the first man. Corelya's ears pricked at the revelation.

"But the quality of wine is quite different. This is superior quality" oozed the Vintner.

"He says his wine is superior" the first man shrugged.

"It is the same fucking swill, isn't it? The same as what we brought with us from Massalia! Is this prick taking the piss?"

"My friend thinks you are not honourable. That you are trying to swindle us?"

The Vintner bristled with indignity and hisses an insult in Greek. Corelya, who spoke fluent Greek, had never heard the phrase before, yet knew enough to know that it was scarcely flattering, to either the man, or his mother! By strange coincidence, the second man, who by his own admission spoke not a word of Greek, also had some inkling of its aetiology. Orbellin glowers at the merchant and spits on the ground in disgust.

"I have had enough of this prick!" he snarled. The beginnings of a scuffle were soon followed by the bittersweet melody of fists impacting repeatedly upon another soul's head! Sorriwen watches the initial beating of the rogue trader with some bemusement, yet even he is soon appalled by the enthusiasm of the Gaul.

"God's teeth Orbellin! Don't kill him!"

"Just teaching the little fucker some manners, that is all" he snarled. "Right! Let's get these barrels loaded and get the fuck out of here. Leave him enough money, just enough, get it? The only tip I'll give this snarky little prick is, don't piss me off!"

"It is a good thing that we are only here for a short while?" his comrade sighed resignedly.

"The sooner we locate that little blonde slag and hand her to that bastard Nichassor, the better. I can't wait to get back to Panticapaeum. This place is full of wankers!"

Corelya waited in the shadows until they had left. She went to see if the Vintner was still alive. He was breathing, albeit it laboriously, lying unconscious in a pool of blood. The poor man had been beaten insensible! It was probably wiser not to hang around, Corelya thought, not wishing to draw unwelcome interest from the authorities to either she, or the strangers! "Bastard Celts!" Corelya swore feelingly. The language the two men had spoken, whilst alien, was not unbeknown to her. That little Gaulish tart Mau'rae had spoken a similar tongue all those years ago. Corelya left the yard and continues south along Grove Street.

Was there anyone in this world that cunt Nichassor was not in league with?

⌇

The Causeway, Southern Crimea, July 493 BC

Early the next morning, whilst the air was still cool, a wagon led by two doughty ponies' trundles along the Causeway in the direction of Nymphaion. It was driven by Sir'zar, the twins doting father, who is perched in the cabin next to Korta. Mis'cha and Mas'cha, who had, in the eyes of their disapproving mother, been roused from their precious slumber at a scandalous hour, lay asleep under a mountain of blankets in the back of the covered wagon. "Nice to be that age again?" Korta said breezily. He was in considerable fettle that morning.

"Their mother would not agree with you! She did not want them to come" Sir'zar sighed tiredly. He had evidently had both a tiring and trying evening. "They do, though!" he chuckled.

"The world is one big adventure when you are that age, is it not?" Korta observed. "Queen Illir'ya would never have commanded them to come if she feared for their safety" he soothed.

"Counsellor Alazar has despatched a forward scouting party to check for any raiders?"

"I saw them leave myself, about an hour before us. Perhaps we may even see them on their return?" Korta confirmed.

"There is word that bands of marauding brigands are roaming the plains. I heard such tales in Chersonesus?" Sir'zar confessed.

Korta chuckles wryly. "Corelya mentioned it. Apparently, there may be more to it than meets the eye" Korta mused.

"How so?" Sir'zar raised an eyebrow.

"A disputation between a group of wealthy merchants and a band of Orch'tai lies at the heart of it, apparently. There is no truth in the rumour about roaming bands of murderous brigands, I can assure you. Perhaps these hired mercenaries merely wished to cause trouble for their paymasters and make a tidy profit in the bargain?"

"It never changes does it, this world of ours?" Sir'zar chuckled. "No matter who governs, the same vices always seem to prosper."

"That is true, my friend. Perhaps too true" Korta concurred sadly.

~

The Ur'gai scouting party were enjoying a ration of mint tea graciously served by a small detachment of Civis Militia, the guardians of law and order in the Nymphaion, hired by the City Fathers. The men carried the obligatory bronze disks that verified both their status, and their right to bear arms, and had been happy to accommodate their unexpected guests.

"I never thought to see a group of heavily-armed Ur'gai scouts so far to the east?" said Mur'ga, nominal Commander of the Civis Militia, to the Senior Officer of the Ur'gai Royal Guard. "Not expecting any trouble, are we?"

"My comrades and I simply fancied a ride, my friend, nothing more. There is nothing to fear, for we are not a portent of doom!" Mos'chi sipped the tea gratefully.

"Ah, the delights of the Royal duties, how well I remember them. We used to say it was the most luxurious jail a man could wish to be confined in" mused Mur'ga.

"You served King Tagar?" Mos'chi asked interestedly.

"For a time. Until I fell from a horse and broke my arm quite badly. No bloody use to them then, was I?"

"A soldiers' oath is a single-edged blade, is it not? It always has been, and always will be" Mos'chi sighed.

"The work here pays well enough! The City Fathers pride themselves on paying well, and regular, unlike some I could mention" Mur'ga spat.

"We have all heard the rumours of the "Swindlers Guild" of Chersonesus!" Mos'chi chuckled.

"You are never sure how long the contract will last, though, are you? Then again, there is talk about increasing the strength of the contingent over the next few weeks. It seems like certain people are getting worried, perhaps with good reason!"

"It is the nature of the rich to worry about their lucre! Never seem to go short though, do they? Always seem to have enough to keep Merchants like Sokos rolling in it?" Mos'chi grumbled.

"I have never heard of him. Not unless he is a pimp?" Mur'ga snorted. The men laughed raucously.

"Sokos is a retailer of fine ceramics. By all accounts,

there is none finer in all Nymphaion. He supplies Queen Illir'ya herself, or so it is rumoured?"

"Fine ceramics, eh? No trade for an honest man!" Mur'ga nodded at the Ur'gai horses. "Nice saddles you have there?"

"Not sure where we get them from. I do hear that a fellow in Nymphaion does good saddles. A local man, born and raised, goes by the name of Cosimandes?"

"I have heard of him! He has premises in the Southern Quarter. A Greek fellow, isn't he?"

"I believe so. His saddles are extremely durable and practical."

"They would be expensive though, I would wager?" ventured Mur'ga.

"Definitely worth the price though, you can trust me on that. I would pay the man a visit, I think you will be most impressed by his crafts!" said Mos'chi.

"I am not sure I trust Greeks; they have something of an unsavoury repute, do they not?" Mur'ga grimaced.

"This fellow comes highly recommended. He is certainly no friend to the Persians, or so it is rumoured."

"Then he sounds like a capital fellow! I never trust those oily swindlers! Thanks for the recommendation. Maybe I can buy you a drink when you're next in town?" said Mur'ga.

"Is *The Dancing Bear* still a good watering hole?" asked Mos'chi.

"It does a roaring trade, no complaints on that front. A bit of a rough house on some nights, though! It isn't the kind of place you would take the missus or the kids!" Mur'ga whistled.

"Safe enough though, if you are careful, that is?" Mos'chi pressed.

"Where isn't? Still, it always pays a man to be careful, does it not? You never know who is about these days, do you?"

"Has there been trouble of late?" Mos'chi raised an

eyebrow.

"A wine merchant in the Southern Quarter got himself beaten to a pulp last night. He is in a bad way. From what they could get out of him, he reckons it was a bunch of strangers! Not like that gives us much to go on in a town like Nymphaion, does it?" the Militia Commandant chuckled.

"Bloody Greeks!" Mos'chi spat. "They are always causing trouble!"

"But this fellow *is* Greek. And he reckons they weren't. There is rumour that a bunch of Celts have been hanging around Panticapaeum for a few moons, apparently. They always seem to have plenty of money for drink, and 'the right sort of girl', if you take my meaning?"

"No such thing as the wrong 'sort of girl' is there?" Mos'chi mused. The men roared with laughter.

"They are funny buggers the Celts, at least the few I have met were. They seem to have a thing for younger flesh, just as long as she is pretty and pliant!" Mur'ga chortled. The men laughed again.

"I have heard rumour they have a thing for red-heads?" Mos'chi ventured.

"They love red-heads and golden-haired girls too, from what I have heard said. Now, there is word of a rare young beauty who was working quite recently in *The Pharaoh's Crown* in Qu'ehra. Quite a doll, by all accounts, or at least so it is told! Have you ever been to Qu'ehra?" Mur'ga asked searchingly.

"I have never been. Nor do I have any bloody intention of ever going!" spat Mos'chi. "Not that it matters, for surely a girl like that could ply her trade anywhere, could she not? Even here?"

"I suppose she could, if she is a rare a beauty as they say she is" mused Mur'ga. "Now, the owner of *The Delphine* is always on the look out for pretty girls. He is a friend of mine, if you take my meaning. This 'Rose of Qu'ehra', as some have named her, is unusually tall, extremely comely, and has gorgeous blue eyes. She is reputed to be richer than Croesus, at least judging by the way she dresses. She must have some pretty good patrons!"

"Perhaps she has a Royal patron?" Mos'chi ventured airily.

⌐

Corelya looked anything but beautiful on this fair summer's morning! The darkened rings around her eyes and disfiguring bruise on her cheek had mottled and jaundiced over the past few days. She had woken early, just after sunrise, and had spent a few hours preparing a knapsack of food and drink, enough to last the next few days. She was sure that emissaries from the Ur'gai Royal Court would contact her at some point, given the urgency of the situation.

"It is a good thing we take you to supper last night, isn't it?" Nirch'ii chided when she saw her.

"I will be fine in a few days, trust me. Did you have a good time last night?"

"Yes. It wasn't at all what I imagined. The food and wine were excellent, naturally, and the City Fathers were eager to make us feel at home here" Nirch'ii sighed happily.

"They think you have lots of money!" Corelya snickered.

"We have been invited to supper this evening by young couple who live just down the street. They are Persian, if you would credit it? Her Father supplies medicines and such like to the Hellenics. They are extremely wealthy" Nirch'ii cooed.

"Her father is a drug dealer?" Corelya raised an eyebrow mockingly.

"It's an honest trade, isn't it? Buying and selling poppy oil?"

"It is a living for the farmers, Nirch'ii, and that is all. You do not want anything to do with the mercantile side of things, trust me. It attracts all kinds of souls, normally the bad ones!" Corelya cautioned.

"You are quite the cynic sometimes, Corelya!" Nirch'ii sighed despondently.

"And you are fast becoming quite the Madam!" Corelya mocked. "Have you and Minas 'done it' yet?"

"Corelya!" Nirch'ii shrilled. "I can't believe you sometimes. And, in answer to your question, no, we have not!"

"He hasn't even made a pass at you?" Corelya was astounded.

"We are quite civil to one another, if you must know! Ever since that little misunderstanding at *The Lion of Judah* was clarified to everyone's satisfaction. He really is quite easy to talk to."

"Where is Minas now?" Corelya quipped.

"He has gone to the Market to buy fresh flowers. Apparently, it is the done thing nowadays to take fresh flowers when you are being entertained."

"I normally make do with a razor-sharp dagger! Two of them, given the company I am often minded to keep!" Corelya snorted.

"You can be quite the brute sometimes, can't you?" Nirch'ii scolded.

"Let us both pray I haven't mellowed this past week!" Corelya mused snidely..

⌐

"They are ours! I am certain of it!" Korta attested. The riders, some nine in all, were not far away now.

"Should we slow down?" asked Sir'zar.

"I could do with a cup of mint tea. So, could they, I imagine."

"It might be best to stop for a while. I should wake those two sleepy heads!"

"A good idea" Korta concurred.

Mos'chi and his group reached them presently and dismounted. To Korta's surprise, they accepted only two cups of tea between them, but all downed a draught of wodki graciously proffered by Sir'zar. "Anything to report, Commander Mos'chi?"

"We had tea with the Civis Militia? Hired mercenaries!" Mos'chi confirmed.

"Really?" Korta asked interestedly.

"Their leader was an amiable fellow, was he not, lads?" The men nodded eagerly. "He is an Orch'tai soldier that once served King Tagar, if you would credit it? Until he had an accident, that is."

"Is there any news?" Korta probed.

"I played it cagey, just like the Honourable Counsellor commended me to" replied Mos'chi.

"And?"

"They have all heard of Corelya, although he didn't mention her by name. He made sure I knew about the 'golden-haired' girl in Qu'ehra, the one everyone thought was a whore!" The men grinned inanely.

"Is there anything else?" Korta grimaced with distaste.

"Nothing to report, Sir, except that the City Fathers are giving serious consideration to strengthening the Militia contingent, if that might be of interest?"

"It sounds like they are expecting trouble! Nymphaion *is* still safe, Commander?" Korta pressed.

"Some wine merchant was badly beaten-up last night in the Southern Quarter, but he probably tried to swindle someone! That is the usual story, isn't it?" Mos'chi mused cynically.

"I suppose so. So Nymphaion *is* quite safe?" Korta stressed.

"I would say so, Sir. Corelya is likely having a grand time, the lucky beggar?"

"There are men trying to kill her, Commander!" Korta

said icily.

"Nobody in Nymphaion seems to know anything. Not according to this chap."

"Good work, Commander. I will note your service to the Queen" Korta sighed.

"Thank you, Sir! I am sure things will be fine. The two little girls should do quite well all by themselves, shouldn't they?"

"I don't follow you?" Korta stammered. He glanced quickly at Sir'zar.

"I was led to believe by the Honourable Counsellor that the one of the twins would go to ceramics trader, Sokos, whilst her sister would go to Cosimandes the Saddler."

"Are you quite sure?" Korta was bewildered by the revelation.

"I am quite certain of it, Sir." Mos'chi replied evenly. "The Counsellor wanted this to be low key. It wouldn't attract any unnecessary attention, would it? They would just be two little girls out on an errand for their dad?"

Korta grimaced. Whilst the suggestion did have the merits of logic, he was disturbed that Alazar had intimated nothing to him. "You are quite right, Commander."

"I even asked about a decent watering hole for you and Sir'zar, Sir? A place you could go to while the two little girls are on their errand. *The Dancing Bear* came highly recommended."

"Did it indeed? Not a rough house, is it?" Korta seemed dubious.

"There is never any trouble at *The Dancing Bear*. It is a family establishment. Good food and drink, and good company, by all accounts. People take their kids there all the time, at least according to this Militia chap."

"It was recommended by this mercenary, was it?" Korta asked searchingly.

"I asked him to confirm it, Sir. It was suggested by the Honourable Counsellor himself, if you would credit it?"

"I see, Commander. This Militiaman didn't mention anything about Celts, did he?"

"Celts, Sir?" Mos'chi furrowed his brow. "He never mentioned them at all, Sir?"

⌒

Corelya had taken the precaution of securing lodgings in the Southern Quarter, situated on Maple Street, as close to Cosimandes' Saddlery as possible, and had paid a month's rent and a deposit of one half-month with silver. The girl claimed the lodgings were requested by her Lady for a string of servants who would be arriving in Nymphaion late the next day. Her cover story raised few concerns with the agent, who had been visibly overjoyed to secure the lease on such generous terms. Upon entering the property, the visibly crestfallen child immediately saw why, for the place had likely never seen better days! The plaster peeled on almost every wall and a leaky roof stained the ceiling upper storey ceiling in several places! The main balcony afforded no direct view of Grove Street and Saddler's Row yet did provide a good view of the side street and a cursory appraisal of the layout confirmed it was perfect for defence. Any attempt to storm the upstairs rooms would be repelled before the attackers even reached the middle steps! The lodgings also gave access to the flat roof, which was entirely satisfactory.

Having safely corralled her sword, crossbows, longbow, heavy axe, and quivers of quarrels and arrows, carefully wrapped in leather covers in the far corner of the living room, Corelya stepped out into the side street and headed north into the warren of backstreets. She intended to purchase fresh bread, sufficient for the next few days, and had elected to head to Baker's Row in the far northeast of the Southern Quarter. The nearest bakeries lay south of her billet in the vicinity of Vine Street, a notorious haven of villainy and the beating heart of poorest sector of the city. Even the Civis Militia feared to tread these streets after the setting of the sun! In deference to the precariousness of her current position, it would have been a grave error of judgment to enter this part of Nymphaion. No matter their lowly status, any stranger to this part of the city would attract unwarranted attention, irrespective of the hour of the day. Instead, Corelya headed north to the opulent part of the Southern Quarter, just beyond the South Gate and perimeter wall, where the Spice Merchants, Ceramics Traders, Bakers, and even Jewellers, had their premises and private residences.

Corelya's immediate foray through the backstreets was uneventful, for it was still quite early in the day, as she weaved through warren of narrow, stinking alleys dressed in the obligatory tatty black cloak, hood drawn tightly, armed with the formidable pine staff and twinned daggers at her belt. As she reached Quay Street, the main west-east thoroughfare of the Southern Quarter, she crossed and dived into the tangle of alleys in the residential section adjacent to the Butcher's Market. By now the market was beginning to bustle, with a thronging cascade of city-folk, including shoppers from the more affluent parts of the Northern Quarter. In devotion to her assumed calling, she took brief respite in the vicinity of *The Naiad of Troy*, known to everyone as 'The Nymph', and was blessed with sufficient charity in copper coins to buy a hearty draught of wodki before she vanished into the tangle once more and headed north to Baker's Row. Here the trade was also bustling, not surprising given that most of their business came early in the day. Having bought sufficient bread to last three days, and honey cakes as a treat, she weaved through the side streets towards the Fishmonger's Market, due northwest of the Butcher's Market, to buy fresh sardines for an early evening supper.

The Fishmonger's Market stank worse than the Butcher's, but she harboured no reservations as to the quality of the produce. Corelya bought three sardines, which could be cooked in a single pan, saving one for breakfast the next morning. After she had completed her purchase, Corelya made to head south towards the Butcher's Market and Quay Street when she espied a group of seedy youths who appeared to be taking undue interest in her. She instinctively touches the twinned daggers at her left hip. Comforted by their presence, she turns back and scurries through the stalls to the safety of Tyre Lane, keeping a wary eye for her pursuers. Corelya then headed due west, towards the intersection with Grove Street.

At this hour, pedestrian traffic on Grove Street had swollen with morning shoppers and Corelya drifted anonymously through the throng, keeping to the left, her back to any oncoming vehicles. And so, against her better judgement, she elected to continue straight along Grove Street and approach Cosimandes' Saddlery directly from the north, rather than taking the circuitous route through the side streets, for it seemed safe enough to do so. Soon after she made her fateful decision, the girl heard the rumbling of cartwheels fast approaching from the direction of Poseidon Way and the South Gate to the north.

$\backsim$

The general layout of Nymphaion is akin to any other major Hellenic polis, whether it is Athens, Sparta, Chersonesus, or Olbia. There is a Central Square, serving as the economic and spiritual focus of the community, dominated by the impressive Temple of Aphrodite, the Hellenic Goddess of Love, to the south. Flanking the west and east sides, respectively, were the marginally less impressive Council Hall of the City Father's and Hall of the Guild of Merchant's. The northern side of the Central Square is open and joins the Olympus Way, the main avenue which leads to the North Gate. Flanking the west and east sides of the Olympus Way on the north side of the Central Square, we see two large

Civic Buildings, home to the Courts of Restitution and the Militia Station and City Dungeons, respectively. The West Gate, now the main gateway to the city, is reached via Zeus Way, whereas the East Gate and Wharf, site of the North and South Quays, are linked by Athena Way. The four gates were guarded by a detachment of Polis Militia, mercenaries hired from the four Scythian ducal states, nominally under the control of the Guild of Merchants.

To reach the Central Square from the South Gate, one must first venture along South Street and join Aphrodite Way, parallel to the rear of the Temple, then turn right into Peloponnese Street to reach Zeus Way. Within the perimeter wall, the city of Nymphaion is divided in to four sectors: northwest, northeast, southwest and southeast, each with their own civic landmarks. The Mercantile District lay in the northwest, home to the Market Square, *The Merchant's Chalice* hostelry, Credit Unions, and other commercial sectors. The northeast was home to the Guild of Apothecaries, Guild of Surgeons, the City Infirmary and Mortuary, as well as the City Armoury and Grain silos. The southeast sector is dominated by Thessaly Square, flanked by its elegant townhouses and *The Dancing Bear* hostelry, and the southwest sector is home to the City Theatre, with its majestic outdoor stage and palatial gardens, flanked on the north and south sides by equally bespoke townhouses.

As the economic prosperity of the polis and its populace had grown, the mercantile sector expanded its reach beyond the ancient city walls in the north and south. In addition to the ubiquitous fruit and vegetable sellers, the Merchant's District in the northeast sector of the city was home to tailors and garment retailers, jewellers, precious metal and spice dealers, apothecaries and, of course, innumerable purveyors of poppy oil. The 'Golden Gate', the most prestigious shopping district in all Nymphaion, lay immediately beyond the North Gate, on either side of the North Road. In contrast, the Fishmongers, Butchers and Saddlers all had their outlets in the sprawl that now extended beyond the southern wall of the city, far from the wealthier residents. Surprisingly, few families lived within the walls of the city, and those who did were generally wealthy families who had emigrated to Nymphaion in search of their fortunes. The wealthiest of all lived in the Northern Quarter of the city, mostly in spacious apartment buildings with generous allotments of land. As for the most prosperous of all, they had built and furnished their palatial villas on the far northern outskirts of the city. The less wealthy lived in the south and, the further one travelled along Grove Street, the main artery of the Southern Quarter, the poorer people were. Immediately beyond the East Gate, lay the metalworkers and builders, with their stores and furnaces, a prosperous residential district, including many small hostelries for visiting sailors, and the Warehouse District. The Avenue, the main promenade of the Wharf, is home to the North and South Quays.

Sir'zar and Korta passed through the West Gate and headed east along Zeus Way towards the Central Square. When they reach the junction with Peloponnese Street, just before the Central Square, they turn south and drive along its course towards the Theatre. At the junction with Aphrodite Way, they turn left, journeying east towards Thessaly Square.

They had been informed by the Polis Militia Guards at the West Gate that they could park their wagon in a lot adjacent to *The Dancing Bear*, for a reasonable fee, of course. Mis'cha and Mas'cha, sit in the back of the wagon, chatting animatedly, delighting in all that they saw.

The little girls were enthralled by the antics of the performing animals in Thessaly Square, including monkeys and even a chained bear. Their father was equally smitten with the sights, sounds, and smells, of the city, yet Korta appeared indifferent and surveyed all before him with a wary eye. If Ur'gai sources were to be believed, killers were actively stalking the 'gold witch' in these very streets, and it would pay to be wary. They park the wagon in the vacant lot at the side of the hostelry, pay the fee of a single copper coin, and stroll towards the front entrance of *The Dancing Bear*, bathed in the glorious morning sun. Korta scanned their surroundings with the eye of an expert hunter! And yet, even he could never have seen the two men skulking in the shadows of an upstairs room of a nearby townhouse, furnished with a balcony which afforded a commanding view of the square.

"I recognise the old man. His name is Korta. Once upon a time, he was the Chief Surgeon to the Ur'gai Royal Court" said Simmachor, the chief Persian agent in the city.

"No Surgeon can save him this day!" Nichassor said chillingly.

⁓

Corelya stepped close to the wall of a fine food merchant. The merchant sold exotic dried fish, cured meats and cheeses, from across the region and beyond, and the smells emanating from inside enchanted her nostrils. Whilst the wagon was covered, the rear doors were wide open. As it passed by, Corelya espied a group of men sat in the back, and several perched on the right side took obvious note of her. She bowed her head and increased her pace. She had not recognised any of them and felt sure that none had recognised her, yet, in the interests of security, it might be wiser to walk on the opposite side of the street, facing the oncoming traffic as it approached from the south. The girl stopped, checked left and right for oncoming traffic, and skipped across the street, heading south. As she passed the last of food merchants and entered the Vintners section, she noticed a group of men, all of whom were heavily armed, loitering at the entrance to the yard of the Vintner who had been beaten to a bloody pulp by the two Celts the previous night. All sported weapons and were attired in the garb of the Civis Militia. Corelya was eager to avoid any unwanted attention. She glanced quickly to the north and the south, and crossed back over the street, a little further north of the junction with Quay Street.

As Corelya reached the junction of Grove Street and Quay Street, the olfactory delights of the fine food merchants were cruelly dispelled by an almost unbearable odour wafting from the Butcher's Market to the east. She crossed over Quay Street and, as soon as she had, she took a welcome gulp of fresh air. To the east, lay the Residential District of the Southern Quarter, a little to the north of her rented apartment. Across the street were the shops of the leather merchants, retailing a bewildering array of fashion and workwear, including aprons, tunics, pantaloons, and such like. Further along lay the Saddler's district. Corelya glanced to her left to check for oncoming traffic along Cypress Lane, and, seeing this was clear, she was about to cross when, suddenly, she froze. The girl shuffled quickly into the cover of a gateway to yard of a purveyor of olive oil.

The wagon that had passed by earlier was parked a short distance further along on the opposite side of the street from Cosimandes' Saddlery. The wagon had discharged its passengers, numbering some seven men, all of whom were armed. Whilst she had not recognised any faces in the back of the wagon that brief time earlier, now she certainly did! A tall, heavy-set brute armed with a heavy pine-staff, iron sword and woodsman's axe, stood in three-quarter pose, engaged in lively discussion with the others. *It was Siladar!*

"You treacherous cunt!" Corelya hissed. For posterity's sake, it is worth noting that, as she uttered the curse, it could have been aimed at any number of persons. At Siladar himself, perhaps even Nichassor, for the two were never estranged and, if Siladar was in Nymphaion, Nichassor was sure to be. It may even have pertained to Sokos himself, who may have betrayed Corelya for a princely sum in gold, rather than his usual terms in silver.

It was to Sokos that she would now go, blazing the fury of an Amazon!

⁓

The interior of *The Dancing Bear* is spacious and well-lit by natural light from the windows on the west side. The ceiling was low and the bar, which lay at the north end, spanned almost the entire breadth of the room. The stairs leading to the upstairs lodgings could be reached via a narrow corridor at the end of the south wall, which leads to the rear entrance and the stables at the back. The group weave through the throng and approach the bar.

"What can I get for you?" said the Hosteller, an extremely pale and thin man named Sar'ghit. Despite his languid appearance, he was renowned for both his generosity and congeniality.

"Four large wodki's and two draughts of rye beer" replied Korta.

"And what would the two little ladies like?" Sar'ghit nodded at the twins.

"This is for them!" Korta guffawed, causing raucous laughter to ripple among the drinkers at nearby tables. The twins grinned.

"Scythians?"

"Of course, they are!" Korta grinned. There was further laughter from the tables. The twins are mesmerised by the attention.

They sequester a vacant table, far away from the bar, close to the passageway leading to the rear entrance, and directly facing the main entrance on the west side. The twins sipped their wodki, a rare treat, whilst Korta and Sir'zar busied themselves with their rye beer. They were not sat long before a stranger approached the table and introduced himself. Whilst he was unarmed, he was attired in the garb of the Civis Militia. He smiled genially at the twins and addresses the two men.

"My name is Mur'ga. I am with the Civis Militia. Are you in town for a couple of days?"

"We are only in town for the day. We came to pick up some medical supplies and assorted bits and bobs" said Korta.

"You should be spoilt for choice, with the Spice Merchants in this town?"

"The prices here are lower than in Chersonesus. That is why we came."

"If you require assistance, or advice, if you take my meaning, we would be only too happy to help" Mur'ga said.

"And pass some much-needed business on to your friends?" Korta smiled to soften the reproof.

"Certainly not!" the man protested with a grin. "That being said it would be remiss of me not to caution that there are some in this town who would be perfectly happy to take you for a ride."

"We will bear that in mind, Commander, and thank-you" said Korta.

"As I said, Sir, we are here to help."

"Is the Merchant's District of the Southern Quarter still safe to travel?" Korta asked mildly.

"There are always pickpockets and the like, Sir, aren't there? It is no less safe than anywhere else. Certainly not for these two little treasures" he smiled at the twins who beamed back.

"Is Cosimandes the Saddler still doing a good trade?" Korta raised an eyebrow.

"I believe so, Sir. He is a Greek fellow, isn't he? By a strange coincidence, I was chatting about him with one of Queen Illir'ya's scouts earlier this morning" Mur'ga confessed.

"These two little ones are due to be getting the first horse later in the summer. They have been especially good this year and I hear that Cosimandes would be the man to talk with about getting them saddles. Good quality and made to last" said Sir'zar.

"Then Cosimandes is your man. If you would like, Sir, me and the lads are due to be relieved anytime now. After chatting with your man this morning, I wouldn't mind having a look at Cosimandes' wares. Perhaps I could accompany the two young ladies. They will be safe as houses with me."

"That is very kind of you, Sir" said Sir'zar.

"I will leave you to your drinks then. We are over in the corner, when you need us"

Mur'ga left the table and strolled back across the room to where a group of Militia were drinking steadily at west corner of the bar. Korta and Sir'zar noted wryly that most of the other drinkers tended to give the group a wide berth.

"I didn't know that Militia were allowed to drink on duty?" Sir'zar whispered.

"They are not really supposed to. What do you think, should we trust them?" Korta raised an eyebrow mockingly.

"I wouldn't trust those buggers as far as I could spit! It doesn't look like anyone else in this place does, does it? We cannot allow them to discover Corelya's whereabouts, can we?" Sir'zar whispered conspiratorially.

"Maybe the young ladies might make their own way there. We could always apologise once Corelya was safe and well" Korta suggested.

"Are you both ready, my honeycombs?" Sir'zar gazed lovingly at his daughters. The twins nodded eagerly. "Mas'cha, go and wait by the wagon. Mis'cha, go to the bar and order another round of wodki's. That way, people will think you are both still here."

The twins rise and nod silently. As Mis'cha grabs the empty wodki goblets and weaves her way through the throng, Mas'cha flits down the corridor to the left, quickly disappearing round the corner. No-one has noted her departure. Mis'cha approaches the bar and raps an impatient tattoo on the heavy oak bar with the base of one of the battered wooden goblets.

"Two more rye beers and two wodki's, kind Sir!"

The nearby tables erupt with raucous laughter. Sar'ghit eyes the child wryly. "Keep your kurta on, little Miss! I shall bring them across shortly!"

"As shortly as you please, Mister!" the child quipped.

The room convulses with hysterical laughter. Mis'cha smiles slyly as she makes her way back to the table. Shortly thereafter, she too has vanished from *The Dancing Bear* to join her sister in the yard. Their departure had gone completely unnoticed by Mur'ga and his comrades, hogging the corner of the bar, but not Sorriwen, who slipped out of the front entrance after Mis'cha. He glances quickly around Thessaly Square, yet the twins appear to have vanished. Suddenly, he espies them, weaving through the fruit sellers at the north side of the square. He follows the two girls, a safe distance behind, as they head west along Aphrodite Way towards the Theatre.

Sorriwen carries a razor-sharp knife at his hip He has no reservations about using it on a child!

⤙

Having weaved through the backstreets of the residential areas to the south and north of Quay Street, thence through the narrow lanes of the Fishmonger's Market now bustling with shoppers, Corelya finally reached the premises of the ceramics dealer, Sokos, on the west flank of Euboea Square. Strangely, the shop was closed. The square was thronging with shoppers, some of whom were exquisitely dressed, and it was puzzling that Sokos had not yet opened for trading. The girl glanced left and right, ensuring the coast was clear, then slipped into the covered alleyway and strolled towards the door to Sokos' private residence at the rear. She raps her tattoo impatiently and, when no sound came from within, she repeats the code. When no-one answered, she tried the handle. The door was unlocked, and it opened. The sight which greeted Corelya almost made her scream in terror. The place was like an abattoir, for blood was literally everywhere. There were three bodies, all cruelly despatched to the next life with a singular brutality that could only have emanated from a wicked mind.

All three victims had been decapitated, their heads arranged in a grisly votive on the table, faces orientated toward the door. Poor Sokos and his son, Hektor, had their eyes completely gouged, presumably before they had been killed. Yet, it was the sight of the third victim that sickened Corelya to her soul. The child whimpered and instinctively retched, her vomit splattering the floor as she gasped for breath, tears streaming down her cheeks in torrents. "Who the fuck did this?" she screamed, no longer caring who heard her torment. There had been treachery, of that she was certain, and it may yet be too late to save the others! Corelya steps into the alleyway, almost in a daze, and closes the door firmly behind her. She darted to the edge of the alleyway and hurried along the perimeter of the square, before crossing the street and racing in the sanctuary of the backstreets to the north of Tyre Lane. Corelya would now go back to Cosimandes' Saddlery, to where Siladar and his cut- throats awaited her. Firstly, she would return to her billet to retrieve her weaponry.

Her blood was spitting! Someone would pay dearly for this!

~

Mis'cha and Mas'cha reached the end of Aphrodite Way and gaped in wonder at the splendour of the outdoor stage and ornate gardens of the Theatre, oblivious to the skulking presence of the hooded figure who had tailed them from *The Dancing Bear*. Yet, there were many souls in Nymphaion of a sweet and generous disposition, and the sight of the two angelic little girls, seemingly without an adult chaperone, caught the attention of a woman who lived in the more prosperous residential district of the Southern Quarter. She approaches the two girls and enquired, in a friendly and courteous tone, if they were lost. The twins, who spoke not a word of Hellenic, were quite bewildered, yet the woman, whose lineage on her mother's side was Nur'gat, addressed the startled youngsters in the Nur'gat dialect, which she spoke fluently. The twins grinned and happily informed her that they were heading south to the Merchant's District on an errand for their father, whilst taking care not to reveal their exact destinations.

"We can catch a carriage to the Merchant's District, if you would like to accompany me?" the woman had smiled at them kindly.

The little twins' glance at one another quickly and decide it might be wiser to indulge the kindly woman, who seemed pleasant and could surely not pose any threat to themselves or Corelya. The girls skipped gaily away, hand-in-hand, on either side of the friendly stranger towards the carriage stand to the south of the Theatre, where a small throng waited to board the recently arrived shuttle. Sorriwen seethed at the woman's unwelcome intervention, not that he felt in the least concerned at the prospect of killing her, in the event of necessity!

"Why couldn't you keep your fucking nose out, interfering old biddy!" he seethed.

He follows the trio, a safe distance behind, towards the carriage stand and the congregation of waiting passengers. To Sorriwen's alarm, a trio of love-struck couples, aged in their early teens, emerge from the gaggle of fruit-stalls and flock to the carriage stand to take the remaining seats on the back of the charter. Sorriwen burns with a wholly unjustifiable rage, for he must not lose the little whores, even though he had a good idea of their ultimate destination.

He sullenly stands at the back of the queue as the first passengers are permitted to board, each proffering a single copper coin to the driver. The twins boarded and sat on either side of the friendly woman, chatting animatedly in an alien tongue. Finally, the lovestruck couples gaily pay their dues and climb aboard, securing the last seats in the back of the charter. Sorriwen is visibly crestfallen yet, to his eternal gratitude, the driver smiled warmly and beckoned him to take the additional seat in the front cabin, if her were willing?

"It would be nice to have some company!" the driver smiled grinned.

Sorriwen thanked the man for his grace in Hellenic and boarded the cabin. Moments later, the driver whips the mares to a trot, and the charter sets of, circling back towards South Street, to turn right, heading towards the Polis Militia Guards stationed at the South Gate.

The carriage turned right at the junction with Poseidon Way, the main west-to-east thoroughfare just south of the perimeter wall and ditch, and then left into Grove Street heading south. From his travels the previous evening, Sorriwen had taken due note of Euboea Square, by now bustling with shoppers. He was greatly relieved when the driver announced the first stop, and the kindly old woman bade her goodbyes to the little twins.

She gingerly scaled the ladder at the back of the carriage, graciously assisted by two of the young males, who were only too eager to impress their girlfriends by their chivalry. Sorriwen glanced at the seated twins, who were oblivious to his interest in them, then at the back of the departing woman. He smiled wolfishly! The next port of call would be the residential district, a little to the north of the Fishmonger's and Butcher's Markets, yet the twins remained seated, as several other passengers disembarked.

A cursory glance to his rear saw the twins in conversation with one of the older girls, who was now preparing to depart. It was all too clear to Sorriwen that these guileless little waifs would ride the carriage all the way to the Saddlery, and he exchanged a few remarks with the driver about his day thus far. The twins were safely ensconced in their seats, among the few remaining passengers for the onward journey south. As the driver whips the horses to a trot, Sorriwen took note of the Civis Militia Guards outside the Vintner he had visited the previous night, and instinctively turned his face away, the reflex reaction of a career criminal! As the ponies trot past the Militia Guards, Sorriwen turns and glances at the passengers seated behind. To his horror, the little whores are nowhere in sight!

Sorriwen curses inwardly and turns to the driver. "I forgot something. I need to get off!"

"No problem at all, Sir!" said the driver.

The driver cajoles the ponies to a halt at the side of the road and Sorriwen leapt down from the cabin and skulked north, searching in vain for the twins. They appeared to have vanished! "Shit!" he cursed audibly, drawing fearful looks from a group of pedestrians stood waiting to cross the road. He walked swiftly up to Quay Street and, glancing along, he espies one of the girls turning left into the warren of backstreets heading due northwest towards the Fishmonger's Market. Her sibling must surely now be weaving her way through the backstreets south of Quay Street to approach the Saddlery from the west. Sorriwen is incandescent at the treachery of these innocents!

"For fuck's sake! Duplicitous little cunts!" he hissed furiously.

Sorriwen was not in good humour, for, if he failed to kill one of the girls, he would lose the bounty Nichassor had placed on their heads! Sorriwen quickly made his decision. He would not follow the little bitch heading north, for there was no hope of catching her now and it was obvious that she was headed to Euboea Square and the premises of that rat bastard Sokos. There she would meet her fate, for a select band of Nichassor's thugs eagerly awaited her arrival!

Sorriwen strolled further along Quay Street and, first glancing left and then right, he disappears into the rabbit warren of the residential area to the south, seeking in vain for his quarry. Soon thereafter, a grinning Mas'cha materialised at the end of a narrow alley directly across the street. She strolls east along Quay Street towards the Butcher's Market, before crossing over and diving into the alleyways of the metal workers yards, heading towards Wharf Lane. When Mas'cha reaches the end of the alley, she moves tight against the wall and peers around the corner. She freezes, and shuffles back into the shadows, glancing quickly behind her. A hooded figure, clothed in a tatty black cloak, wielding a heavy pine staff, looms out of the end of an alley in the residential district to the east, heading north towards Quay Street. Mas'cha waited for the danger to pass, and then morphed out of the alley to quickly cross the street.

⁓

Tanais, July 493 BC

Three riders arrived at *The Grey Goose* tavern and stabled their horses in the yard at the rear. Whilst all three are attired in civilian garb, to any trained eye accustomed to viewing the most cursory minutiae with detached eye, the clothes could never cloak the identity of the strangers. *They were soldiers!* The tavern was not especially busy at this hour, and the newcomers had little problem securing a table in the far corner of the room. They were soon joined by a fourth man, dressed in the uniform of an Orch'tai Cavalry Officer, a General no less, nominally in command of a division of four Ochti, some twelve hundred men and additional Staff Officers. He approaches the table and sits down, scowling at the young sub- altern sat directly opposite.

"I read your despatch with some interest, little brother! You have fucked up royally on this one, haven't you?" he sighed exasperatedly.

"The King is not best pleased, is he?" Tar'gai stated simply, blushing hotly.

"The King doesn't know, not yet at least! He is scarcely going to be best pleased, is he? How the fuck could you let this happen?"

"We were betrayed, Os'gu! There is no other explanation?" Tar'gai protested.

"Nobody knew of your plans, apart from this Persian emigre and his band of savages?" Os'gu pressed.

"Of course not! We encountered no opposition on our approach to the objective. Apart from the debacle on the plain, the operation was an overwhelming success?"

"You were ambushed by Sauromatae renegades?" Os'gu grimaced with distaste.

"That seems the most like explanation, does it not?" Tar'gai muttered darkly.

"So, I am expected to tell the King that we lost eighteen good men? And all because you were outwitted by some feral Sauromatae whore and her ill-bred kinfolk! Is that what you would have me do?" Os'gu hissed.

"I have no idea where these renegades came from? It never occurred to us that this child had any such contacts in the region" Tar'gai sighed miserably.

"But Nichassor seems to have harboured suspicions about the significance of this girl? You never thought to question him more closely? Did it never occur to you to engage your mind! We received reports confirming that Queen Illir'ya had appointed a new intelligence officer to the Royal Counsel last summer. Intriguingly, this officer was a girl!" Os'gu bridled.

"We hired assassins to deal with her. They were not up

to the job" Tar'gai spoke defensively.

"According to your report, you made two unsuccessful attempts on her life before the debacle with the renegades, did you not? And on both occasions, she eluded you!"

"That is true, I'm sorry."

"Well, it may be of some comfort to *you* to learn that she has not eluded *us*. We have confirmed this feral bitch is currently residing in Nymphaion. The Celts are searching for her as we speak. That prick Nichassor is also there, if it interests you?" Os'gu confessed.

"You would like us to eliminate them?" Tar'gai ventured, without hesitation.

"Those are the King's orders, little brother. No more, no less. Kill them all!"

⟶

Mis'cha heads south along Wharf Street. To her immediate left, the majestic Warehouses tower above her, and yet, their impressive size is strangely comforting. In the event of necessity, these offered the surest hope of flight to safety, for every building had some permanent armed security detail to protect its wares. Mas'cha had learned from the friendly old woman that if she turned right at the next junction, heading west along Maple Lane, she would arrive at Grove Street just to the south of Cosimandes' Saddlery. She could have had no idea that her course would take her past the apartment block with Corelya's rented billet! The girl eventually reaches the junction with Grove Street where she turns right, heading back toward the city. Soon enough, sweet little Mas'cha, the eldest by a mere few minutes, arrives at the gates of Cosimandes' Saddlery.

A wagon was parked further along on the opposite side of Grove Street, facing south, yet no-one sat in its cabin. This puzzled her. The gates to Cosimandes' Saddlery were firmly closed, and this was equally surprising, for surely they ought to be trading at this hour? Mas'cha tries the gates. They were firmly bolted from inside. Something was clearly wrong, for Corelya must surely anticipate an emissary from the Ur'gai Royal Court to contact her?

Seemingly from nowhere, two men appear at the side of the wagon stationed further along Grove Street to the north. Mas'cha turns to face them. A tall man, armed with a long iron sword which is drawn from its scabbard, hails her in broken Scythiac.

"Little girl! Do not be afraid! We are friends of Cosimandes! We have been expecting you! Come here little one!"

Mas'cha glances quickly right and espies another three thugs, all sporting long iron swords and other weaponry, stealthily approaching from the south. She knew instinctively this was a trap! The terrified girl sprinted across the street and dived into an alley, running for her life toward the safety of the Butcher's Market to the north of the residential district. If she could reach the Market, she would surely be safe among the throng of shoppers? She dived into an alley to her left and takes shelter in the doorway of an apartment. Mas'cha can hear the footfalls of her pursuers to the south, but their fleet would surely be encumbered by their swords. A scuff of feet at the end of the alley startles her. She shuffles tight into the cover of the portico as the three thug's race past. Mas'cha was a mere child, yet she was a Scythian child, and her only fear was for the safety of her 'baby sister'!

Mas'cha skips across the alley to the opposite side and heads north until she reaches the corner. She peers slyly around. Some twenty yards along to the east, the three thugs now stand in the middle of the lane. The girl waits until their backs are turned and races across the lane to dive into the cover of the alley directly opposite. She dives into the cover of the portico on the left side of the alley, cloaked in the shadows. Her mind is racing. The thugs are clearing each of the alleys in turn, from east to west, concentrating on the northern side of the lane. Surely, they must hope to catch her as she breaks cover. Perhaps the two thugs from the cart are waiting to cut her off as she heads for safety to the Butcher's Market on Quay Street? *And yet, they would be sorely disappointed if instead she headed south and made her way east along Maple Lane towards the Warehouses?*

Mas'cha glances quickly to her rear, confirming the coast is clear, before moving swiftly to the opposite side of the alley, edging south to the corner with the lane. This was the dangerous time! The girl hugs the wall tightly, her heart racing, as she peeks slyly around the corner for signs of her pursuers. The coast is clear! She darts across the lane and races into the cover of the portico in the shadows where she had previously hidden. In the next lane along to the north, the three thugs troop despondently out of an alley and make their way quickly west, disappearing into the next alley to the north. As they do so, a lone figure in a heavy brown cloak, looms out of the alley directly north of Mas'cha's hiding place. It is Sorriwen! He smiles grimly as he espies the little blonde child, skulking in the shadows of the portico on the right side.

"Well! Well! We are a fly little vixen, aren't we?" he spoke in barely a whisper.

A shout from the lane to the south, possibly from one of the two thugs from the cart, startles the little girl and distracts her attention from the threat to her rear. Mas'cha slows her breathing as the sound of her heartbeats thrum in her ears. She does not hear the lithe footfalls of the hunter who now stalks her from behind. She could have had no conception that he too was a stranger to the City, or, that whilst he had hunted her for much of the past hour, he had lost her, then happened upon her again purely by chance. Her only recognition of his presence came when his hand clamped like a vice around her mouth. In her final struggle, she saw the wicked gleam of a razor-sharp blade that severs her throat almost to the bone in a horrific fountain of blood. Little Mas'cha died quickly, in much the same manner as her 'baby sister' had done so only a brief while earlier.

～

That brief while earlier, having stopped briefly at a Potters shop a little further along, chiefly to determine that she had lost her tail, Mis'cha strolled south and arrived at Sokos' store. To her astonishment, the shop was closed, and she hammered repeatedly on the door, but to no avail. Presently, a smiling stranger approaches the frowning child and informs her that the store had been open a short while earlier when he had passed on his way to the Vegetable Market. Perhaps she might knock on the door at the end of the covered alleyway and ask Sokos to open for her, for he was always extremely obliging to his clientele. Mis'cha strolled along the alley until she reached door. She rapped the tattoo that she had memorised. At first no answer came but, shortly after she had repeated the code in its entirety, a gruff voice challenged her from within. "Who is it?"

"Are you Sokos?" Mis'cha asked.

"I am Sokos. Who are you?" the voice enquired politely.

"I am Mis'cha. I am one of Queen Illir'ya's Handmaidens. I have an urgent message from Her Majesty."

The door unlocked and opened slightly. A bearded man with hazel eyes peered warily round the door at angelic child. "Please, come inside, young Lady" he insisted. "Things are most desperate, and we have little time to waste."

"I understand. My mistress sent me as a matter of urgency."

"Then let us talk. Please, come inside and I will close the door behind you?"

The man shepherded Mis'cha inside and closed the door. Mis'cha was surprised to see a heavy iron sword lying on the table in front of her. Beside the sword were two wicker baskets covered with heavy muslin cloth. The bearded man smiles reassuringly at the startled child. "Please, young Lady. Do not be afraid, for you are most welcome at the home of Sokos. The weapon is merely a precautionary measure against any unwelcome guests. As I have already said, things are most desperate, and we have no time to waste."

"Have you seen Corelya?" asked Mis'cha

"Not in the past few days. Did Queen Illir'ya receive my message?" the man turned away and busied himself with something in the basket on the table. He had his back to Mis'cha, who obediently stands a few paces away.

"She did, my Lord, and sends her gratitude for your service. You will be rewarded for all your efforts. Is Corelya safe and well?"

"Your Queen is most generous, sweet child. But, if I could have a moment of your time, there is something urgent that we must attend to. It is most pressing."

"My Lady has instructed me to inform you that I am at your service" said Mis'cha.

"Step closer to the table child. I need to show you something."

"What is it?" Mis'cha asked excitedly, her childish inquisitiveness aroused.

The man picks up the sword and laid it down the table at the far side of the second basket. The first basket is placed directly in front of Mis'cha, who now stands to his left. The muslin cloth is whipped away. Mis'cha squeals in terror! Inside the basket is a freshly severed head. Both eyes have been brutally gouged out.

"This is Sokos" the man said simply.

Mis'cha turned to flee. As she did, the man deftly retrieved the sword and swung the blade in a vicious arc aiming for the nape of her neck. The momentum of the blade carried true though its arc and severed the child's head cleanly from her body with a terrifying grace! Mis'cha's head spins in the air and lands heavily on the tiled floor. Her tiny body, venting so much blood from the ruined arteries of her neck, fell lightly to the floor a short distance away. Siladar grimaces as he cleans the blood from his blade and face with the muslin cloth.

"You may walk with your sister, little whore!"

Without giving the murdered girl a further glance, Siladar turns and pads across the room toward the door. In the next room, a much-earned draught of wodki and his villainous accomplices await. He had killed children before, but never one so young or innocent!

Time is of the essence, yet there is much work still to be done!

⌒

Sometime after leaving Sokos' premises and its horror, Corelya became attuned to a strange panic that had gripped the populace of the Southern Quarter. Everyone seemed to be streaming north towards the South Gate and the city, many in a visibly anxious state.

When Corelya arrived at the Butcher's Market, the place was eerily deserted of shoppers. Most of the Butcher's appeared sullen and edgy. Surely, they could not have learned of Sokos' fate so soon, the girl thought. She approached one of the Butcher's, who was busily skinning a rabbit.

"What has happened?" Corelya asked the Butcher.

"There is talk of a killing. The word is that something terrible has happened at *The Dancing Bear*. Most likely drunkard's disputing a woman or an outstanding debt, I don't doubt. I despair of this place some days, with what it has become" the Butcher sighed despondently.

"Are there many dead?" Corelya asked.

"There is talk of two of them. Slain by the Civis Militia, or so is the rumour. It doesn't pay to get on the wrong side of the Civis Militia, sweet child" the Butcher cautioned.

"The Civis Militia is supposed to protect the citizens, are they not?"

"This new crowd are a different breed. They have a reputation for turning a blind eye to certain other elements that are plaguing the city of late. People are scared. A wine trader was savagely beaten just last night."

"I heard that it was Celts?" Corelya ventured. She was eager to draw the Butcher in to her confidence.

"There are a group of Celts recently arrived. Some say they have come from Panticapaeum. They have a deserved repute for causing trouble wherever they go. Not that I am looking for any trouble, you understand?" the Butcher added quickly.

"How many of them are there?" Corelya probed.

"There are six of them, or so it rumoured. They are staying at a villa in the upmarket part of the Northern Quarter, if you could credit it? Not everyone is happy, their neighbours especially, I don't doubt. Rumour is they have the blessing of the City Fathers."

Corelya whistled at the revelation. "What in Hades name would Nymphaion's City Fathers want with a bunch of belligerent Celts?"

"Now that's the question to which a lot of people would like an answer. There have been some strange goings on of late, some even stranger rumours. Everyone is on edge! That is why they have all flocked to Thessaly Square to find out the truth of the matter" the Butcher confided.

"What about the Civis Militia? Have they not followed up on the rumour that these Celts may have something to do with the beating of the wine merchant?"

The Butcher scoffed. "I very much doubt it. Not when they were witnessed drinking together in *The Dancing Bear* until the early hours. They are extremely easy with their money, these Celts, or someone else's, I don't doubt? They were far less generous patrons at *The Merchant's Chalice*, from what I hear?"

"Has there been trouble?" Corelya raised an eyebrow.

"They trashed the place and scared away most of the decent custom. Then they moved on to 'the *Bear*'. That is why it has raised such an eyebrow, them drinking so tightly with the Civis Militia. It just doesn't seem right? Like I say, I am an honest trader who has learned not to ask too many questions about things anymore."

"I had better be going. It was nice to have met you" Corelya smiled.

"I would take care, if I were you, Miss. This used to be a safe city, but not anymore."

It would be extremely dangerous for some, when Corelya finally caught up with them

THIRTEEN

Having left the Butcher, Corelya stalked warily through the backstreets of the Residential District south of Quay Street, threading her way towards her billet on Maple Lane. The streets were eerily deserted, for it seemed like everyone had flocked to Thessaly Square for news of the deathly happenings. The girl kept a wary eye for ambushers as she weaved the interconnecting alleyways and side streets. At the end of the last alley, far to the east of her dwelling, she paused briefly, her body hugging the wall, as she peeked slyly around the corner to confirm the lane to the immediate rear of her apartment block is deserted. Corelya walks swiftly round the corner and crosses to the opposite side, slowing her pace at the corner of each narrow passage between the buildings to the north and south, staggered on either side, her trusty staff at the ready. She was almost home when, glancing along the narrow passage that ran between the apartments to the north, she espies, further along in its gloom, what looked suspiciously like the body of a child. The body had been laid close to the wall in an area of shadow.

She raced towards the prone form and stopped dead in her tracks, a few feet away, tears springing instantly. There was so much blood! Corelya turned Mas'cha's body over and gasps with horror at the ugly, disfiguring wound inflicted upon her throat. At least it had been quick, as it must have been equally so for her twin. The girl slumped next to Mas'cha's corpse and wept hysterically. After a time, she picked up the body of the sweet little girl and carried her solemnly back to her lodgings.

The hour of retribution was nigh! An Amazon's vengeance!

⌒

The bodies of Korta and Sir'zar were removed from *The Dancing Bear* with the appropriate solemn reverence to be conveyed on the back of a covered wagon to the underground cold room at the City Mortuary. They had been first knifed, and then beaten to bloody ruin by a gang of assailants, before being repeatedly stabbed. All the witnesses, many of whom were terrified for the safety of their families, unequivocally attested that the old man had provoked the ire of a group of newly arrived drinkers in the bar, Celts, by all accounts, and that the off-duty Civis Militia had been powerless to intervene. The old man had drawn a blade and attacked the group without provocation. This was plainly a distortion of the facts. It was true that Korta had drawn his blade and attacked the Celts, but only after one of them had slid a knife between Sir'zar ribs as he had innocently stepped past with a tray of drinks. The Civis Militia had witnessed everything and done nothing! In fact, they had watched with interest as the two strangers, both of whom had been expertly subdued by mortal wounds early in the encounter, were dragged to the rear of the bar and kicked almost to death by the Celts. Further wounds were inflicted solely for amusement. The terrified onlookers, including the Hosteller and his staff, could have done nothing to stop the killings, for, they would surely have been subject to the same uncompromising brutality had they tried to intervene!

In the stable yard at the rear of the hostelry, Commander

Mur'ga watched on dispassionately as the two bodies were loaded on to the back of the wagon. The doors are closed and bolted. Mur'ga turned to his subordinate, Mus'char. "Inform those useless twats at the city mortuary to put these two in a separate room. We don't want to offend the Ur'gai Queen, do we?"

"I understand, Sir. Will you be staying on here?" Mus'char asked nervously.

"I shall!" Mur'ga growled.

"What about the Celts, Sir? Should we not detain them as a matter of course?"

"There will be no charges, do you understand?"

"That would surely depend upon the witness statements, surely?" Mus'char ventured uneasily.

"I shall be taking the witness statements!" Mur'ga replied curtly. "The entire incident was witnessed a coterie of your brothers; in case it had slipped your mind!"

"I understand, Sir!"

"Of course, you do, sunshine!" Mur'ga smiled grimly.

A visibly worried Mus'char watched as his superior skulked back towards the rear entrance of *The Dancing Bear*. He would almost certainly be drunk by the time he started his night shift! Quietly, among themselves, the witnesses would later lament that something truly terrible had taken place this day, and that their beloved city was fast becoming a place no more suited to raising children than a hyaena's den. Something had to be done! Things had been bad for a while, but not like this. Never like this!

They could never have known that this day would bring a terror hitherto unimaginable!

⌒

Corelya carried Mas'cha's lifeless body to the bathroom, stripped her naked, and cleaned her up as best she could. She had washed and combed the child's hair, wrapped her in a bed-cloth, then laid her reverentially on the spare bed. Corelya fitted her sword-belt across a fresh, dark blue kurta, the twinned daggers at her hip, and grabs the crossbows and wicker basket in which to store them and the quiver of quarrels. She lithely mounts the stairs to the roof, and, once there, she lies flat on her tummy and shuffles across almost to the edge of the ornate parapet which skirted the four sides of the building. The girl peered over the parapet and down on to Maple Lane. Comfortingly, this was eerily deserted. Corelya crawled like an infant, orientating her body north, and shuffled across to the far parapet to confirm the narrow lane at the rear of the property is equally deserted. Whatever tragedy had unfolded at *The Dancing Bear* that morning, it had whipped the populace to a state of mass panic! Such hysteria was entirely conducive to the furtherance of brazen public murder!

Corelya slithered back to the entrance to the stairwell and retrieves a sturdy ladder, purchased the previous day at a Tiler's Merchant in the Eastern Quarter. This is carried this to the rear side of the roof where she could not be seen from Maple Lane. Having first confirmed that the coast in the lane below was clear, the ladder is laid flat across the gap, and, drawing a deep breath, Corelya steps lithely across to the roof of the adjacent building at the corner of Maple Lane and Grove Street. She dragged the ladder across, lays it flat against the ornate parapet, and immediately went to ground. She slithered to the far end of the building with a commanding view of Grove Street and Saddler's Row. Further along to the north, the wagon was now parked on the opposite side of the street. At some point since she had left, it had been driven away and thence returned, possibly from Sokos' place.

Corelya had no proof of the identity of the perpetrators the atrocity in Euboea Square, yet every sinew screamed that Siladar must have had a hand in the slaughter of the twins. Two of his henchmen were at the side of the wagon, chatting idly, and not another soul in sight. Corelya slithered back across the roof and, after first confirming the narrow lane below was deserted, she laid the ladder across and returned her own building to collect her weapons. It was time to unchain the fury!

Corelya retrieved the basket of weaponry and descended the stairs to the front door of the apartment, situated on the left side of narrow passage connecting Maple Street and the backstreet to the north. The alley was deserted. She closed the door firmly behind her, locked it with a key, and strolled quickly to the corner with the backstreet. There was not a soul in sight! The dwellings at the rear were equally humble, arraigned in neat rows, as was her own. Corelya turned the corner, crossed the street, and padded stealthily down the alley intersecting the first and second buildings. Eventually, she reached the narrow lane which separated the semi-detached apartments from a foreboding terrace structure, housing multiple smaller dwellings that spanned the entire length of the street. This was home, such as it was, to some of the poorest families in all Nymphaion. Corelya pauses briefly at the corner, her body tight against the wall, and appraises the lay of the land. Mercifully, if not for those she now stalked for death, the lane was deserted. She turned left and walked swiftly to the end of the lane and the junction with the backstreet at the immediate rear of the apartment buildings that face on to Grove Street and Saddler's Row.

As Corelya reached the junction, she crossed and turned north, hugging the west wall of the tenement, before crossing and diving into the nearest alley which led directly to Grove Street. Her pulse raced, yet her mouth felt strangely cold and moist as she closed, ever closer, with her prey. A sly peek around the corner confirmed that the two hired thugs remain stationed at the wagon, apparently oblivious to the mortal peril of their predicament. Grove Street was deserted, except for a few stray cats and Siladar's

The Hawk and the Handmaiden

hirelings and, as everyone knows, neither cats nor dead men relay their tales! Corelya strolls brazenly around the corner, hood drawn close, and closes stealthily with her quarry. If the two men had been expecting her arrival, it was clear that this was to be from the south, rather than the north.

Corelya clears the cover of the wagon, laid the basket gently on the ground, and took aim at the nearest man with a loaded crossbow. The thug stands in three-quarter pose, his back to the girl. Corelya fired!

The quarrel took the first man cleanly through the nape of his neck and, as it punched through his skull and ripped effortlessly through his brain, his head snaps violently back, a torrent of blood erupting from his mouth to shower his horrified companion. The second man is momentarily paralysed with terror. Corelya dropped to one knee, laid the weapon down, and deftly plucked the second from her basket with an effortless grace. She took aim at the man's left groin and squeezes the trigger. The man screamed as the quarrel tore into his leg, missing the vital artery, severing the vein, and he slumped agonisingly against the front wheel of the wagon. The wound was mortal, yet he would live far longer than if the artery had been severed! Corelya quickly reloaded her weapons and, nonchalantly disregarding any witnesses to her barbarity, she strolled over to the prone man. She plucked the fallen sword and laid this on the ground, kneeling before her stricken victim, her blue eyes locking with his own.

"Filthy Sauromatae cunt! I'll fuck your eyes out of your skull!" the man hissed.

"I doubt you shall fuck anything ever again! Not with that wound. It looks painful, by the way?"

"Fuck you, you filthy whore!"

"Where is Siladar?" she asked evenly.

"Why don't you go fuck your mother!"

Corelya drew a dagger and stabbed the man viciously

in the left groin, just below the protruding shaft of the quarrel. The man screamed as she twisted the blade free. Corelya knew her business, for the artery had been severed. As the blade was drawn free, her hood and face were showered by an arterial spray. "You will talk, I assure you of that! Is he inside?"

The man grimaces with pain. "Only one man is inside. Not Siladar. He went north to the Potter's shop to wait for the little girl."

"Did Siladar murder the child? Answer me!" she hissed, moving the point of her blade towards the man's left eye.

"No!" the man screamed. "Please, I am begging you?"

"Then talk to me. You have little time left. Was it Siladar who killed the little girl?"

"Yes" the man sighed. "No-one else would do it. Not to one so young. Apart from that twisted bastard Sorriwen. He was stalking her sister here."

"Who the fuck is Sorriwen?" Corelya demanded icily.

"He is a Celt! A Briton, I think! He came south from Panticapaeum a few days ago to look for you. That is all I know. He tailed the twins were from *The Dancing Bear.*"

Corelya felt the blood freeze in her veins. "How did this Sorriwen fuck-pig know where to find the little girls?"

"The Civis Militia told us; I swear it."

"I don't believe you!" Corelya said icily. She knew in her heart the man was telling the truth.

And yet, it was a mere fraction of the whole.

The man sighed sadly. He was dying and was resigned to this fate. "Why should I lie to you? The Militia found out about their visit only this morning. They passed the word on as soon as they returned to the city."

Corelya moved the tip of the dagger close to the man's left tear duct. "Who tipped them off? Didn't Siladar trust you, is that it?"

The man's eyes widen with terror. "Don't! I'm begging you! The Militia met a group of scouts from the Ur'gai

Royal Army early this morning. Out in the plains, fuck knows where! They passed on the information to the Militia; *The Dancing Bear*, Cosimandes, Sokos, the little twins, all of it!"

The man said no more. He was in no fit state to, not after both eyes had been brutally gouged. So too, for posterity's sake, were those of his fallen comrade. The third thug, assigned to watch duties inside the home of the recently deceased Cosimandes, was mercilessly shot in the stomach by Corelya as she sauntered breezily through the rear door. The door was firmly closed and bolted. When the girl left, a while later, she had washed the blood from her face and cloak. Her mind was racing, for she had learned much from the troubled soul! Much to her evident distress, she had learned of the brutal slayings of her former tutor and the twins' father in *The Dancing Bear*. She had also learned of Nichassor's spectre in Nymphaion, currently residing at an elegant townhouse on the north side of Thessaly Square, with a perfect view of *The Dancing Bear* and the adjacent lot. The townhouse belonged to a merchant named Simmachor, notorious child-defiler, and chief Persian agent in the Crimea.

Corelya was now in receipt of crucial information pertaining to a group of Celts, currently quartered along from Nirch'ii and Minas, with the lemon trees beside the front gate. It had been they who had perpetrated a sickening murder in *The Dancing Bear*, in front of scores of witnesses, including a contingent of Civis Militia. The latter had lifted not a finger to intervene. A promised glory in gold or silver is sufficient to turn a man's eyes and conscience, not that Commandant Mur'ga had been gifted with much in the way of a conscience. He would be dealt with last, for Corelya had learned that he was due on duty shortly after the rising of the moon. The flame of this illumination would burn no more, for his soul no longer haunted the land of the living, having succumbed to the fabled death of a thousand cuts.

He did not, of course, go to his maker with his eyes intact!

~

Nichassor was incandescent. He had been outraged by the public murder of the old man and his companion in *The Dancing Bear* in front of so many witnesses, any of whom might speak the truth, if persuaded to do so. It was now late afternoon. He paced furiously along the length of the elegant rug which furnished the upstairs room of Simmachor's house. Moreover, despite the slaying of the little twins and the silencing of the Ur'gai's most trusted agents in Nymphaion, there was yet no sign of Corelya herself!

"Things are getting out of hand! My instructions were quite specific, were they not? If people were to be killed, it must not attract any undue attention" Nichassor seethed. "The witnesses will not talk; I assure you of that. They are rightly terrified by what has happened" Siladar soothed.

"Once these Celts have left Nymphaion, will they still be terrified?" Nichassor demanded.

"The Civis Militia will not take any sworn testimony to the contrary. The old man started the fight, and now he is dead. And besides, these Celts may not even leave Nymphaion alive?" Siladar said woodenly.

Nichassor smiled grimly, for the brute had his uses! "There is that, of course! Yet, you have seen the reaction of the citizens this afternoon. They are outraged by these recent events.

How many more murders will they stomach? More to the point, where in Hades name is Corelya?" Nichassor demanded.

"She has not yet been located" Siladar shifted his feet uneasily.

"Is she still even in Nymphaion?" demanded Nichassor.

"According to our sources, it is unlikely she has fled. The gates to the city have been closely monitored since this morning. I think that she will remain, comforted by the futile expectation that her friends in the Royal Court will yet save her!" interjected Simmachor.

"We must lie low, at least for a day or so. Can you trust these hirelings of yours, Siladar?"

"They are loyal enough and have been paid enough. The Orch'tai have know ledge of the whereabouts of their families, immediate and extended! They will do as they are instructed."

"Where are they now?" Nichassor sighed.

"There are three of them downstairs, stationed outside the gate. The other three we left at Cosimandes' place, just in case that bitch turns up."

"Do you think that a reasonable expectation? What with talk of a gruesome murder in a public tavern? Perhaps Corelya has already learned of the death of Sokos and, if so, she will not venture anywhere near Cosimandes' place?" Nichassor addressed the question to no-one. If he wished for a considered reply, he was fated to be sorely disappointed. At that moment, Simmachor's Secretary, an elegantly dressed teen named Marrakor, loomed in the open doorway, his face creased with anxiety. At his side, stood Commandant Mur'ga of the Civis Militia, a wolfish smirk playing upon his lips.

"Your men at the Saddlery are dead. The 'gold witch' has slain them" Mur'ga announced with a chilling certainty.

～

The Celts are something of a mystery to Classical observers. They were famed throughout the world for their belligerence, a breath-taking capacity for causal brutality, and an inordinate penchant for drunkenness.

By the late afternoon, quite regardless of any concern for their own safety considering their earlier escapades at *The Dancing Bear*, Orbellin and his gang, almost to a man, were gloriously inebriant. Only Sorriwen, who had missed the party so to speak, and was now charged with the duty of driving the wagon back to their luxury villa, was marginally sober. The rest of the gang were ensconced in the back of the open wagon, enjoying the last of the day's sunlight, as it trundled north along the North Road past the Golden Gate shopping district. At this point, it is worth recalling a final peculiar characteristic of the Celts, if such an entity even existed as a natural race. That is their cold certainty that at some point, perhaps today, maybe tomorrow, or at any given hour, the sky itself will come crashing down upon their heads. Alas, it was not the heavens that descended upon their skulls this day with righteous fury, but paving slabs!

News of the barbarity at *The Dancing Bear* had horrified the townsfolk. As talk spread openly of a series of other grisly slayings, including a young child, where the victims had been defiled by eye-gouging, righteous indignity of the populace had reached fever pitch. It was the discovery of a second child, recognised as the identical twin of the decapitated girl, in a narrow lane behind the City Fathers' Hall, her throat horrifically disfigured by knife- wound, which had decided matters. The Celts were no longer welcome in Nymphaion!

Indeed, they were no longer welcome in this world! Corelya had sobbed uncontrollably over the murders of the twins into the comforting arms of Simonisthes the Butcher, whom she had spoken to earlier in the day. He had who found the girl distraught and mildly drunk in an alley near to his stall; "How could anyone be so beastly? Surely no believer in the grace of sweet Tabiti could commit such wickedness?" The Celts, who were no believers in Tabiti, were adjudged to be guilty as charged. By strange vein of justice, all six corpses had their eyes gouged by a vengeful mob.

Corelya did not witness the incident, for she had other pressing matters to attend to

～

Nichassor was no fool. Whilst he had requested a spacious private suite at Simmachor's house, he had also taken the liberty of securing an elegantly furnished apartment, immediately adjacent to the Merchant's Guild on the eastern side of the Central Square, a necessary precaution in an increasingly lawless world. Everything had been arranged through a third party, a trusted agent of the Argata who was beholden to Queen Lezika herself. Not even Simmachor had been told of his plans. After a leisurely bathe and a small repast of bread, cheese, and olives, he had been working on an urgent despatch to King Darius when Siladar brought news of the fate of the Celts.

"The Celts are dead, master" Siladar spoke evenly.

"Of course, they are! Did these ill-bred halfwits think they could behave in such a barbarous fashion without consequence?"

"It would appear so, my Lord! I would not have hired these animals! They are barely human!" Siladar spat.

"It is likely as not for the best, you would agree?" he challenged coldly.

"It saves us the trouble of killing them. That was always the plan, was it not" Siladar responded with equally chilling indifference.

"I fear you often misconstrue an objective, that is, the desired outcome, with strategy, which is the means by which we attain it, my dear friend! That may have been my ultimate intention, yet these brutes had a prominent role in our plans over the course of the next few moons!" Nichassor smiled tightly.

"I have neither your intellect, nor guile, for such grandiose ploys! I forget myself, my Lord!"

"You are readily forgiven, old friend! Is there any news of Corelya?" Nichassor sighed tiredly.

"That feral bitch has probably long gone, what with everything that has happened."

"The Civis Militia will have to inform the Ur'gai Royal Court, merely as a matter of courtesy, you understand?" Nichassor opined.

"We will be leaving tomorrow then?" Siladar sighed. If he had not been so before, he was now visibly nervous.

"I think that would be the wisest course of action, don't you?" Nichassor raised an eyebrow.

"What about the men we hired? I can vouch for their loyalty, my Lord. They could be useful to us in the weeks to come?"

"King Darius is scarcely tolerant of failure, my friend? Even less so where matters of security are concerned, do you understand?" Nichassor sighed tiredly.

Siladar did understand. The hirelings may be loyal, unswervingly so, but they were tainted with failure, at least in the eyes of the powers that be. They also knew of Simmachor, and so must be silenced. "I shall take care of it tonight, my Lord!" he stated simply.

"Quietly, I beseech you?" cautioned Nichassor.

～

Later that evening, with a new moon visible in a glorious sky, Commandant Mur'ga stands on the steps of the Militia Station, his heavily armed juniors, arraigned in two neat rows before him. The Militia Station was quartered on the northern side of the Central Square, east of the Olympus Way. Considering the day's events, the place was deserted. The men are muttering darkly among themselves. "Silence!" bawled Mur'ga.

A few muted conversations continue unabated. Mur'ga is not impressed. He fixes his gaze, and his ire, on Hir'jik. "Silence! You impertinent cunts! If one more word passes your lips, Hir'jik, I will personally feed your balls to the pigeons!"

"I never said a word, Sir!" Hir'jik said woodenly.

"You wish to test my mettle? Is that it, you impudent little fucker?"

"No, Sir!"

"In light of the day's events, the City Fathers have requested that we undertake vigilant patrols in both the Merchants District of the Southern Quarter and the Northern Quarter, including the residential districts. People are terrified! Perhaps with good reason!" he bellowed.

The men groaned. For once they would be required to earn their pay. "How many men per patrol, that is if you don't mind us asking, Sir?" Jar'tin challenged.

"Six in all" Mur'ga confirmed. There were twenty-six guards on duty, including Mur'ga and the Station Clerk, Mus'char, a fellow Orch'tai.

"So that means all of us, basically!" Jar'tin spat.

"Yes, that means fucking all of you!" Mur'ga replied testily.

"Will that be one patrol for the rich bastards and two for the Southern Quarter?" Hir'jik enquired mischievously, to raucous laughter from the assembled ranks. The richest families in the city had likely as not demanded double protection for the night!

"When do we leave?" asked Jar'tin.

"Right fucking now! Do you understand me? Get to it!"

The men assembled into their respective patrols and departed immediately, twelve men in all to the south, six to the north, and six to the east. Mur'ga watched them go with a burning sense of pride. Mur'ga turns to his subaltern, Mus'char, who stands silently on the steps beside him.

"There will be no further trouble this day! By the Gods, there will not!"

"Of course, there won't be, Sir. Salt of the earth, our lads! No-one will think about messing with them!" said Mus'char dutifully.

As Mur'ga's gaze follows the patrols trooping solemnly west towards the North and South Gates, he espies a figure, enrobed in a shoddy black cloak, perched upon the steps of the City Fathers' Hall on the west of the Central Square. The figure appeared to be eating something, the remnants of which were carelessly tossed down the steps to the ground. "What the fuck is that?" he growled, pointing in the direction of the shabby figure.

"It is probably just another beggar, Sir, likely as not? There are a lot of them about!" replied Mus'char.

"Get rid of it!" he bellowed, loud enough for the beggar to hear. The beggar stood and appeared to stoop to retrieve something, possibly a basket, before skulking diagonally down the steps and slipping into the shadows of an alleyway. "That will teach that fucker a lesson. I simply cannot abide beggars! Idle, mangy, flea-riddled bastards! The lot of them!" he hollered after the figure.

He was certain that his warning had been heeded, and so paid the departing spectre no further consideration. *He wouldn't be seeing that again tonight, would he*? It never occurred to Mur'ga to consider that even the wealthiest beggar would never be so foolish as to carry a basket as they plied their trade.

～

Simmachor had spent the entire late afternoon labouring under a state of increasing alarm. The shocking catalogue of events had left him reeling. If he were being honest, a virtue prized by some above all others, yet scarcely of value in the dynamics of *his* world, the imminent departure of Nichassor and his ill-cultured brute would be a blessing. He had dismissed his own Secretary, Marrakor, and dispensed with those remaining hired embarrassments, for they were of little utility now, and he trusted their fate to Nichassor's prerogative. "Are we not all accountable to King Darius himself?" he mused silently. And yet, there was at least some small compensation for the day's misadventures.

The rise of a new moon is an enchanting sight. Simmachor steps out on to the balcony and gazes at its wonder, its outline clear in the glare of a dying sun. The Gods themselves had surely blessed King Darius' endeavours. The day had been eventful and yet, despite its high drama, there was much with which to be satisfied. With a single stroke, the pernicious tentacles of the Ur'gai Royal Court had been severed. If anyone had failed, it was Nichassor. Yet, to Simmachor's mind, his catalogue of failings had been entirely predictable. The Orch'tai were useful allies, yet had proven dangerously unreliable, whereas these Celts were simply indescribable! Nichassor had been wrong, it was all so clear to him now. *Our entire efforts wasted on the fate of a bastard child* The King would learn the truth of it, he would see to that personally. And so, he padded back into the room a far happier soul than he had left, blissfully unaware of the cloaked figure nestled in the shadows of the abutting balcony.

Armed with her crossbow, Corelya slips over the balcony and enters the room. As she did so, Simmachor caught sight of the hooded figure in a mirror and turned to face her, his hand moving instinctively to the sword at his left side. The figure took aim and discharged the quarrel in to Simmachor's right eye. His head rocketed backwards, and his body fell heavily to the ground. Corelya reloaded and fired a second quarrel through the left eye. A message must be delivered, yet there had surely been enough eye-gouging for one day! She slipped back across the balcony to the adjacent house where a ladder, stolen a few hours earlier from a Tiler's yard, lay perched against its far end in the shadows. She would ensure it was returned in good order.

⌇

"What happens now, Boss?" said Mear'chi, the nominal leader of the three remaining hirlings as Siladar entered the room with two flagons of Hellenic red wine, the best he could afford.

"We will leave tomorrow morning to catch the early ferry across the Straits. After that, we will arrange transportation to Qu'ehra. Is that acceptable?" he confided.

The men glanced at one another nervously and nodded. "If you say so, Boss" Mear'chi shrugged.

"In the meantime, you must drink! You have not failed me; I assure you of that. Those bastard Celts should never have been involved in this! The Argata are to blame for arranging their visit" Siladar brooded.

"What about the girl?" Mear'chi asked.

"That bitch is of no concern to us! I will have fresh instructions for you once we reach the other side of the Straits."

The men smiled. Siladar was a man of his word and they trusted him. They accepted the goblets of wine gratefully. "We are happy to remain in your service, Boss."

"Then drink and be merry! There are two flagons of fine red wine, the best I could afford. I don't want to see a drop left in either of those fuckers!"

The men grinned. "As you are, Boss!" they chimed. Siladar left the room and closed the door behind him.

None of the men thought it strange that Siladar had not touched a drop of the wine himself

⌇

Commandant Mur'ga's thoughts had also turned to drink. He had been on duty for several hours, or it seemed, and *The Dancing Bear* would like as not be doing good trade, despite this morning's incident. "I need a drink!" Mur'ga announced. He resented the interference of the City Fathers in the business of policing the streets, yet not nearly as much as the curtailment of his habitual sojourns to *The Dancing Bear*.

"Would you like me to bring back a couple of jars from *The Bear*?" Mus'char well knew his Superior Officer's fondness for the local rye beer.

"Bring back a flagon of wodki as well, if you would be so kind, for I have a thirst? Tell that slimy bastard Sar'ghit that it will be on the house, if he knows what's good for him!"

"I am pretty sure he will be gracious, for he knows all too well what is good for him, doesn't he?" Mus'char grinned. He would have a quick jar himself, whilst he was there. Just the one, of course, for Mur'ga wouldn't mind, would he?"

As Mus'char pads down the steps of the Militia Station, he espied the same beggar, perched once more upon the steps of the City Fathers Hall, seemingly eating something. "You are a plucky bastard, I shall give you that!" he muses silently and headed south in the direction of *The Dancing Bear*, paying no more thought to the cloaked figure who, unbeknown to him, watched his departure with considerable interest.

～

Some time later, Siladar returns to the downstairs room adjacent to the kitchen and peers inside. The three men had finished both flagons, as instructed, and were, at least to a casual observer, sleeping soundly. They were not, for the wine had been tainted and the poison had done its work. Siladar grimaced with distaste at the thought of the gruesome task ahead. He strolls into the kitchen and uncorks the stopper on a flagon of plum wodki, pouring a generous measure, which he drains immediately. He poured a second and downed it in a single gulp. "That should do the trick!" he mused silently. He assembled up a selection of knives and a razor-sharp butcher's cleaver on the table, and then paced towards the back door which led to the courtyard. The veranda is covered, well-lit by oil lamps, and none of the neighbours could bear witness to the night's work. He went back into the kitchen and slips inside the door of the adjacent room.

Mear'chi was the first to be taken away and dealt with. Siladar cut the man's throat with little effort and let him bleed out. As it takes some time to bleed a man, and time was of the essence, he fetched the other two corpses and prepared them with the same tasteless grace. Soon enough, Mear'chi was ready to be dismembered. Siladar took a butcher's knife and effortlessly sawed through his neck. The head came away and was placed to one side.

The arms were taken off with a butcher's cleaver, a palms width below the shoulder, and subsequently cut in two below the elbow. The hands are left attached. Mear'chi's feet are hacked off above the ankle with a hatchet. The leg is cleaved a few inches below the knee and thigh a little higher than the mid-point, both accomplished with the hatchet. Including the head, Mear'chi's body now comprises twelve portions. It was thirsty work, and by the time Siladar had finished the third body he had drained the flagon of wodki entirely. It had taken him the best part of an hour to dismember the corpses. *Now, what to do with them?*

⌒

The cloaked figure discarded the apple core, plucked the basket from the step beside them, and padded stealthily across the square towards the Militia Station. As they approach the steps, they pause, quickly glancing left and right, and then behind, to ensure no-one was either present in the square or was approaching from a converging thoroughfare. The figure walked to the side of the Militia Station and peers around the corner. The coast was clear. The basket is laid at the side of the steps, minus one of its loaded crossbows, and Corelya skips up the steps and saunters breezily through the open door.

Commandant Mur'ga gaped in bewilderment at the apparition. "What the fuck do you want?" he snarled.

Corelya drew back her hood and smiled serenely at the Militia Commandant. "I came for your life, Mur'ga! Treacherous, murderous cunt that you are!" she hissed.

Mur'ga opened his mouth, presumably to upbraid such bare-arsed temerity from a child; a flea-bitten, stinking, bastard of a child at that, and a girl to wit, when Corelya fired. The quarrel flew cleanly between his teeth and tore through the soft tissue at the back of the mouth, punching through the skull and tearing almost half-way into his brain. A fountain of blood explodes from his open mouth as his head snaps back. Mur'ga toppled from the chair and slumped against the wall, bleeding profusely on to the floor. Corelya adjusts her hood and slips out of the Station. As she retrieved the basket, she was startled by a sound and, glancing quickly left, she espies a large man, labouring towards her rolling what looked suspiciously like an empty beer barrel. It was too dark to make out his features and, paying heed to the murder she had just committed with a brazen insouciance, she crept silently into the shadows and went quickly on her way. It would be several hours before Mus'char returned from *The Dancing Bear* and discovered the Commandant's body.

By the time he returned with the second empty barrel, appropriated unlawfully from the yard of *The Merchant's Chalice*, Siladar was thirsty and decided he had earned a large goblet of berry wine. Having drained that with haste, there was yet time for another. The horses were then fetched from the stables and coupled to the cart. The corpses, numbering thirty-six pieces in all, were dumped ungraciously into the barrels, and the lids are fixed by heavy iron nails. Siladar grunts with the effort as he lifts and then rolls the barrels to the front of the cart. The barrels are secured in place by a series of hemp-rope ties. Siladar lashed the horses and headed off east in the direction of the Wharf. When he arrived, in the early hours of the morning, a team of Stevedores were busy loading cargo on to a ship due to depart in the next hour.

"Do you have room for this?" he demanded brusquely.

"Do you know where we are going?" the Chief Stevedore replied mildly.

"I couldn't care less where you are going, could I?" Siladar retorted gruffly.

"Surely you have a specific destination in mind, Sir?" the man seemed astonished.

Siladar flips a single gold coin, newly minted in Susa, to the ground in front of the astonished man. "Just dump the bastards in the soup, you understand?"

"Right you are, Sir. I will see to it personally."

"You had better do so! Or I shall fucking see to you personally!" Siladar growled.

He glowers at the men to emphasise his intent. A few minutes later, he climbs back into the cabin, lashes the horses, and trundles back to town. It was now some hours after daylight and Siladar needed a drink!

～

Corelya pads solemnly up the steps to the second floor

of her rented billet. A flagon of wodki and two battered wooden goblets sit on a small table in what presumably passed for the siting room. She pours herself a large measure and swallows this in a single gulp. It tasted heavenly. She pours a refill and carries this through to the bedroom, placing it down on the small bedside table, before removing her stinking, gore-drenched cloak, and kurta. She pads into the bathroom, fills the tub with fresh, cold water and climbs in, scrubbing her naked body vigorously with soap. Her hair was cleaned, as it best she could with cold water, removing all traces of gore. She then quickly washes her cloak and kurta.

Both would have to be burned, yet she could scarcely stroll through the residential district of the Northern Quarter the next morning in her birthday suit, could she?

It was now early morning, for the sun had now started to rise. It was still cool, and Corelya shivered lightly as she drained her wodki and climbed under the blanket in the bed across from where she had laid sweet Mas'cha those few hours earlier. Those few hours now seemed like an eternity ago. Corelya curled into the foetal position and wept inconsolably.

With one exception, this had surely been the worse day of her life, and yet, as she slipped into the land of dreams, she was consumed with dread that things might only get worse from now on! Far worse than she could ever imagine, before they got anywhere near better, if they ever did!

~

Eastern Straits, August 493 BC

Nichassor and Siladar stand on the Wharf beside a passenger charter as their stallions are led down the gangplank by two Stevedores. Neither man is in high spirits, Nichassor especially, yet they are at least relieved to be on the opposite side of the Straits.

"Corelya has been a busy little bee!" Nichassor spat indignantly. In all truth, the news of Simmachor's killing had rattled him far less than Mur'ga.

"There is no way we can prevent her from re-joining the Royal Court, can we?"

Nichassor glowers at the brute. "That is stating the bloody obvious, is it not?" he hissed. "My concern is how she obtained her information about Simmachor. What else has she learned?"

"You think Corelya is responsible for all those killings yesterday, excepting the Celts, of course?" Siladar seemed dubious.

"It wouldn't surprise me in the slightest if she had a hand in that!" Nichassor sighed irritably. "And yes, I do think Corelya was personally responsible for five of those slayings! All executed with a brazen disregard for the rule of law! The girl is a mere savage! As immodest as she is brutish! I shudder to think of the impression she left upon the Persian Court in Susa!"

"We should have killed the whore when we had the chance" Siladar said brutally.

"That child knows enough to start a war, if they will believe her" Nichassor mused gloomily.

"The Orch'tai and the Argata will move against them, surely?" Siladar insisted.

"Not if the Ur'gai were to strike first. Corelya's methods are unconventional, to say the least. I fear she will have to be dealt with, once and for all?" Nichassor sighed resignedly.

"We have some of the finest assassins in the known world?" Siladar mused. Corelya's death was fast becoming an obsession with him.

"I think that this might be best left to insiders. Perhaps we can assist in establishing grounds for Corelya's treachery?" Nichassor said breezily.

"You really believe that she poses such a threat, to King

Darius and the Empire?"

"I believe that she would murder the King, if the opportunity ever presented itself."

Nichassor mounted his horse and kicked his heels in to its flank. There was at least some small comfort to their current situation. They were on the opposite side of the Straits and would be soon far out of reach of Corelya's *fury*!

Nirch'ii and Minas had been up since the early hours and were finishing a light breakfast of bread and cheese when Corelya arrived back at the villa. The girl strolled into the kitchen and issued a mild rebuke to the startled pair, who gape with astonishment at the bedraggled waif. "You two wouldn't last five minutes in the Southern Quarter! Leaving your front door ajar is an open invitation to thieves and scumbags!"

"I doubt we have anything to fear from thieves and scumbags in this part of Nymphaion, Corelya" Nirch'ii quipped.

Corelya laid her basket, covered with a heavy muslin cloth, down on the table. "I bought fresh bread, fish, and salad vegetables. Perhaps we could have an early lunch?"

It was Nirch'ii, who correctly sensed that all was not right with the girl. She turned quickly to Minas, and the pair exchanged a meaningful glance. Corelya grins at the two lovebirds! "You seem very familiar, all of a sudden?"

Minas smiled wryly ay the blonde girl and rose from his chair. "It is a beautiful day, perhaps we should eat outside? I shall go and prepare the coals for the hearth."

Nirch'ii gazed adoringly at him. "That would be lovely, Minas! Wouldn't it be lovely, Corelya?"

"That would be lovely! Thank you!" Corelya smiled brightly, convincing no-one.

Minas smiled politely and left via the rear door which

led to the patio at the rear. Nirch'ii eyed the younger girl steadily. "You look like you could do with a bath. Would you like some hot water?" Nirch'ii asked

"Please. I really need one." Corelya said tiredly.

"I will get you a fresh kurta. Those clothes will have to be burned, won't they?"

"I will be glad to be shot of them. It has been a terrible few day's" Corelya sighed miserably.

"We heard something of it last night. We had a contingent of the Civis Militia in the area. They were patrolling the streets! Minas and I served them with wine." the older girl seemed madly entertained.

"I do hope that you pissed in it first?" Corelya said snidely.

"Corelya!" Nirch'ii scolded. "They are the Civis Militia!"

"A pack of those bastards stood idly by in *The Dancing Bear* whilst two of my friends, including my former tutor, were brutally murdered!" Corelya bridled.

"I am sorry, forgive me, please" Nirch'ii insisted. "You knew the girls as well, the little twins?"

"They were called Mis'cha and Mas'cha. They were barely six years old!" Corelya sobbed, tears began to stream down her cheeks.

"There was talk of an angry mob. A group of foreigners were attacked and killed?"

"Bastard Celts!" Corelya seethed. "They deserved it!"

Nirch'ii studied the child closely. "But you are not an angry mob, are you?" she said softly.

"You want to know how many people I killed.. *murdered*, yesterday Nirch'ii?" Corelya said angrily.

"I am not sure that I want to know, Corelya. If they had anything to do with the killing of the little girls, then I suppose they did deserve to die."

"Nichassor and that bastard Siladar got away!"

Nirch'ii blanched. She gaped at Corelya in wide-eyed terror. "Nichassor and Siladar are here in Nymphaion?"

"They have probably long gone by now. As far away from me as they can!"

"So, we are safe? All of us?" Nirch'ii pleaded despairingly.

"I have to leave. I need to return to the Royal Court. I will leave soon after we eat. I should be there by mid-afternoon."

Corelya saw the panic in the older girl's eyes. "Are we going to have to leave, Minas and I?"

"You have paid the rent in advance, so I don't see why you shouldn't stay on. I could leave you some funds if you would like?"

"That is exceedingly kind of you, Corelya, it really is. Minas has money, more than enough for both of us."

Corelya stepped back and raised an eyebrow mockingly. "You have 'done it'? Haven't you?" she squealed with delight.

Nirch'ii flushed, partly with embarrassment, mostly with pride. "Yes, we have! In fact, Minas has asked me to be his wife."

"Wow! You must be good in the sack?" Corelya chided.

Nirch'ii giggled shrilly. "You are quite unbelievable sometimes, you really are!"

"You will be safe here, I promise. You have nothing to fear from either Nichassor or Siladar."

"You are going to kill them, aren't you?" Nirch'ii sighed sadly. Not that she cared very much for the fate of Nichassor or Siladar.

"I am going to murder them, Nirch'ii, both of them!" Corelya stated icily.

"Come on! Let's fill that bathtub and give you a good scrub! You will feel like a whole new person by the time we are done!"

Tanais, August 493 BC

Some twenty miles south of Tanais, several miles inland from the coast of the Azovi Sea and the Straits, stands an ancient fortress. This had been constructed by the Hellenics, more than a century earlier, to defend the coast and surrounding plains from marauding Sauromatae migrants. The Sauromatae crossed the Wol'yi in great numbers and dispersed south, across the plains toward the Caucasus Mountains. The fortress had been neglected for several decades and was crumbling in places, yet the walls and the main gate were still in good order. These had been re-furnished by its current occupants, a large contingent of Orch'tai cavalry. A despatch rider had ridden hard from the Wharf at Tanais, having crossed the Azovi by ferry from Panticapaeum early that morning, arriving just before midday. The rider conveyed news of a disturbing series of events that had plagued the city of Nymphaion the previous day, including the murder of a Senior Officer of the Civis Militia and a wealthy Persian named Simmachor, confirmed by Orch'tai sympathisers in Panticapaeum as King Darius' principal agent of in the Crimean Peninsula.

"That oily bastard Nichassor appears to have escaped with his life?" General Os'gu had mused brutally, upon receiving the news. "Perhaps our Sauromatae harpy isn't quite as skilled as we thought? Tell my little brother that I request his presence, immediately!" The rider had at least delivered some good news, for the slaughter of the Celts had amused General Os'gu considerably.

Tar'gai, still visibly chastened by the taint of failure on the southern plains, was shown in soon afterwards. He was astounded by the revelations. "Does this sound like the work of that little *Amazon* whore-bitch?" Os'gu had asked.

"She is a ruthless enemy, my Lord. It is her nature, is it not?" Tar'gai ventured.

"Then perhaps you might do us all a favour and

impregnate the bitch. Her children could prove worthy allies, might they not?" Os'gu replied tartly.

"If you wish for my considered opinion, then I would have cautioned against the involvement of the Celts. They are brutish and ill-disciplined rabble, is that not so?"

"I am more interested in your opinions on how the Ur'gai will respond to these events. You do have more experience than I with their ways, do you not?"

"We are certain that the little twins were Queen Illir'ya's Handmaidens?" Tar'gai grimaced at the brutal slaying of children, mere babies at that, by all accounts.

"According to our allies in the Ur'gai Royal Court, that is the case. Their father was brutally murdered, together with the old Surgeon Korta, in a public tavern, no less. If my memory serves me, he was known to you, was he not?"

"I met him several years ago, when Queen Illir'ya and the Royal Court came to Mamy'eva to begin negotiations for the concord. He was the young Queen's personal physician at the time, and she was, at that time, some months pregnant. The rest, as they say, is history."

"What can you tell me about him?" Os'gu pressed.

Tar'gai was surprised. "He was both a good man and a fine surgeon. A few of the Princesses' Handmaidens were sickly, as were their children, it was the fever season. The old man helped cure them. I found him to be extremely knowledgeable and personable?"

"Do you remember if he had an assistant, a young helper, perhaps?" Os'gu probed.

"I cannot remember, to be honest" Tar'gai frowned. "I do seem to recall that he was friendly with two of the young Queen's Handmaidens, one especially so. She seemed to spend a lot of time in his company, or so it seemed. You know what the Ur'gai are like, don't you? They have strange sexual tastes, do they not?"

"Whilst that may be the case, for myself I have never considered them naturally disposed to the de-flowering of little girls, wouldn't you agree?" Os'gu said coldly.

"I am not sure that I know what you mean?" Tar'gai was chastened.

"What I mean, little brother, is this?" Os'gu slammed the table in fury. "This child the old Surgeon was friendly with, one of Her Majesty's Handmaidens no less, is possibly the assassin who killed most of these people in Nymphaion yesterday! Not to mention eighteen of our own brothers! More to the point, this little whore-bitch, who has almost certainly fled Nymphaion for the safety of the Ur'gai Royal Camp, has knowledge of the existence of a large contingent of Orch'tai cavalry to the south of Qu'ehra! How could you be so blind? You were a fool to trust that mendacious Persian so guilelessly! He has played us all for tits!"

Tar'gai had never seen his brother so angry. The withering rebuke stung more keenly because he knew that it was true. "I saw the girl in Qu'ehra myself, my Lord. I am certain she recognised me, as I recognised her. I am sorry, my Lord, it did not occur to me that the girl could be so resourceful."

"So, what can you tell me of her? Think man!" General Os'gu rapped.

"We know her name is Corelya. She is a Sauromatae orphan. Her entire family was slaughtered by Seart'i and his band of pigs! She was then sold to Queen Illir'ya by Nichassor soon afterwards."

"And she repaid that blood-debt, did she not?" Os'gu asked searchingly.

"That is true. She walked into the cabin alone and left shortly thereafter."

"Leaving three corpses behind, if I recall?" the General probed.

"Yes, my Lord, it is true" Tar'gai sighed.

"What else can you tell me about this whelpling?"

"If she is the girl I remember, then she has remarkable and unusually precocial mind. Unlike any child you could meet. In her head, she is no child, she is a woman. She has been for several years."

"An extremely dangerous woman, is she not?" Os'gu stated bluntly.

"It would appear so, my General. She is true to her bloodline."

"I have orders for you, little brother. I am going to give you a chance at redemption. Perhaps more than you deserve, given the circumstances, you understand?"

"What do you want me to do?" Tar'gai asked simply.

"I want you to go to Panticapaeum and take over operational command of the current initiative, is that clear. You will not fail us, is that equally clear?"

~

Saiga Plains, Crimea, August 493 BC

In the mid-afternoon, the piquet's were intrigued by the sight of a single rider, a girl with short, tatty blonde locks, who raced down the hillside toward them. As she splashed through the stream, there were audible gasps of astonishment for, if the rider was scarcely recognisable anymore, her mare was! Over the course of the past few weeks, Corelya had tanned almost to the colour of a hazelnut. *What in Hades name had she done to her hair?*

Her Majesty's trusted messenger, Gor'ya, was duly fetched and could scarcely credit her eyes when she first saw Corelya. The bruises on her face had almost vanished yet, despite the shortness of her hair, it was her eyes that were the most troubling. There was now a flinty hardness to her gaze, almost as if she had witnessed horrors that no child of her tender years should ever have seen. Despite being accompanied by a contingent of Royal Guards, Gor'ya was visibly worried and approached her erstwhile friend with trepidation.

"It is good to see you again, Gor?" Corelya smiled warmly.

Gor'ya simply nodded. "You are under arrest, Corelya! Simply a matter of protocol, you do understand?"

"Where is Yari?" Corelya demanded icily.

"Yari is waiting for you in the stockade. Please, don't make a fuss. The guards are ready to kill you if you do. They have explicit instructions from Her Majesty."

The blonde girl vaults from the saddle and surrenders her weapon's to the Guards. Sybillya is entrusted to the piquet's. An angry and bewildered Corelya is taken into detention and is marched north along the central avenue. There are no friendly faces to greet her return. All eyes seem to fix their hatred upon her. A group of young children, perhaps a dozen or so, race across camp to hiss insults at the girl. Corelya knew all of them, for they were close friends of Mis'cha and Mas'cha.

"Murderer! Traitor! Murderer! Traitor! Murderer! Traitor! Murderer! Traitor!" the children hiss.

Corelya blinks back the tears. She has never felt so alone! As they pass the next row of tents, a morose Corelya glances east. Standing aloof, is a blonde girl, a year or so older than herself. The girl, above average in height, slim and pretty, eyes the younger girl with a naked malevolence. Corelya quickly averts her gaze.

"You have nowhere to run, you filthy Sauromatae whore-bitch! I will slay you, Corelya, I swear it! I will slake my thirst with your blood!" hissed the mysterious blonde girl.

Corelya plodded on, heading north towards the stockade in the far northeast of the Royal Camp. She sighs sadly. Even Yari might not be best pleased to see her again!

After all that she had risked her life for, this was some homecoming!

THE END OF THE FIRST BOOK

Lightning Source UK Ltd.
Milton Keynes UK
UKHW010738060223
416537UK00003B/1049